Red is the New Gray

Maggie Sloan Thriller, Book 2

Judith A. Barrett

Wobbly Creek, LLC

Also by Judith A. Barrett

RED IS THE NEW GRAY

MAGGIE SLOAN THRILLER, BOOK 2

Published in the United States of America by Wobbly Creek, LLC

2020 Georgia

wobblycreek.com

Cover by Wobbly Creek, LLC

ISBN 978-1-733-12413-3 Paperback

ISBN 978-1-733-12412-6 eBook

DEDICATION

Red is the New Gray is dedicated to the colors red and gray and to those with the rare talent to interpret the world to us literals.

PREVIOUSLY...

My name is Maggie Sloan, and I always wanted to be a spy. However, sometimes life has its twists; I couldn't turn down a full scholarship, and a librarian would be an excellent cover for a spy, right? I never knew it was dangerous to be a librarian until the explosion, which, according to my doctor, left me "a mess" of broken bones.

I was in the hospital for what seemed like ages, but luckily, my imaginary men, Palace Guard and Spike helped me with physical therapy. I didn't expect them to stick around, but they did.

You might have noticed I mentioned imaginary men. After I was finally released from the hospital, Palace Guard ran with me to build up my strength and taught me how to throw a knife; Spike toughened me up and taught me how to cheat.

My dreamy boyfriend, Detective Parker Coyle, introduced me to his sister Kate, an FBI agent and my new best friend. After a heart-wrenching murder, Kate and my imaginary men pushed me to think and act like predators, not prey, and taught me some pretty cool shooting and fighting skills.

Did I mention all the murders? Evidently, a librarian with the soul of a spy is a murder magnet. I named my police officer protector Larry because Kate didn't tell me his name; he's a great guy with curly hair and a dang good partner, especially when it comes to taking down bad guys.

I can't imagine being without Larry, Palace Guard, and Spike.

CHAPTER ONE

I raced past the horse farm, and the horses galloped along the fence and whinnied at me and my pursuer. I couldn't hear his footsteps but knew he was behind me. My heart pounded, and the sweat stung as it poured into my eyes.

When I reached the gate to my driveway, I whirled around in the dusty dirt road to face him. I threw my hand high into the air, and my imaginary Palace Guard smacked a high-five. Palace Guard had short, brown hair and clear, blue eyes and was a trained soldier in the Queen's Army. At six-foot-four inches, he was a good fourteen inches taller than me.

"Good run." I pulled my shirt at the neck and wiped my face. The heat and humidity in southern Georgia were relentless, even in the morning, and the clear sky promised no relief as the bright sun rose higher in the sky.

"Tomorrow, I'll chase you." As we headed to the house, a pale blue cottage with gray trim, I quickened my steps to keep up with his long stride. "Sad our run is the highlight of our boring life. We need some excitement around here."

Lucy, my old brown dog with her soft gray face, and my other imaginary man, Spike, waited on the porch. Spike was a retired police detective and a legend when I was a kid. The big kids said Spike was so tough that bad guys would turn themselves in. Spike was five-eight and almost as broad as he was tall, but his mass was all muscle. He had thick brown hair, a broken nose, bushy eyebrows, and a leathery face from years of sandlot ball games with kids. His biceps were bigger than most kids' heads. His smile was like a shark's or a panda's, depending on his mood. Kids worked hard for his panda smile.

Spike pointed to the cell phone I'd left on the step. I dashed to answer the phone. *Kate.*

"Maggie, are you packed for our vacation? My leave's approved, and I'll pick you up in two hours. Dad's on his way to take Lucy to his house."

She hung up. Palace Guard and Spike had crowded next to me to listen.

"Either of you know what she's talking about?"

Palace Guard narrowed his eyes, and Spike shook his head.

"When the FBI calls, I better hustle." I hurried to my bedroom and pulled out my largest piece of luggage.

When I opened the suitcase, I sneezed at the musty odor. *Been a while since we've traveled.*

I rolled my clothes and organized them into neat rows in the open gray suitcase. After I added the shirts and pants from the closet, I topped off with a warm coat and a lightweight jacket and had room left over. Spike pointed to the coats and raised his eyebrows.

"Not everywhere is as hot as Harperville, Georgia," I said. "Maybe our destination is Iceland."

Palace Guard shook his head.

"You don't know." I grabbed my phone and checked the weather. "It's thirty-one degrees there today."

I lugged my suitcase into the living room. Lucy's yip announced Glenn's arrival as I added my camping gear and go-bag to my luggage. When I opened the door, Lucy dashed outside to greet Glenn. Kate's father was a retired police detective. He was tall and lean, and his short hair was curly and gray. His sad blue eyes revealed the senseless tragedies he had witnessed over the years, and the grief from losing his only son a year ago etched his face. Lucy danced on the porch while he climbed out of his car. She rushed to his side, and he stooped and rubbed her face.

He rose and smiled. "Before you ask, Maggie, I don't know what Kate has planned." He took two steps and smashed me in a Glenn hug. His arms surrounded me with his familiar citrus and sandalwood scent.

"You and Kate be safe," he mumbled, then released me. "If you have an open bag of dog food, I'll take it.

Jennifer sent you a jar of strawberry jam and asked for Lucy's blanket. Otherwise, we're set."

I cuddled Lucy, and then Spike and Palace Guard rubbed her belly. She bounded to the car and waited for Glenn with an expectant grin.

Glenn opened the back door for Lucy and stopped at his car door. "Are the imaginary men still with you?"

I nodded.

"Good," he said. "Jennifer will ask. She won't worry as much about you."

After Glenn pulled out of the driveway, the three of us headed into the house. "I need to stow my extra ammo, gear, and toiletries in a separate suitcase in case we fly."

Palace Guard pointed to the refrigerator.

"You're right; I need to eat. I'll pack, take a shower, and fix a sandwich."

Tires crunched in the driveway before I took my last bite, and Kate burst in the door. She had twisted her long brown hair into a knot at the back of her neck. Kate was ten inches taller than me, and her western boots added another two inches to her height.

She grinned at Spike. "Hey. Glad to see you. Palace Guard still here, too?"

Spike nodded and danced his jig.

Kate laughed and glided with the grace of a ballerina to my refrigerator. She peered inside, pulled out the pitcher, and sniffed. "What's this?"

"Half and half. Lemonade and tea."

She downed a glass. "Let's load up. We'll be in Galveston before midnight. Sergeant Arrington's telling your mother you'll be on vacation with a friend."

She grabbed my large suitcase and surveyed the rest. "Camping gear. Your emergency go-bag and your computer bag. What's in the travel case?"

"Ammo, guns, knives, toiletries, and strawberry jam from your mother."

"I like how you think, Crazy Lady."

We rode in silence for an hour. Kate was FBI. She'd trained me to fight, shoot, and wait for instructions. I was a librarian; I waited in silence.

"Officially, I'm on vacation. Unofficially, you and I will find a missing spy," Kate said.

"Ours or theirs?" I asked.

"Ours. Gary," she said.

I cleared my throat. "Gary, as in Gary Sloan?"

When I was a kid, I thought my father was dead. Gary, except I thought of him as Ernie, was the homeless guy who lingered at my library like other homeless men, but he was too healthy, too aware, and too clean to fit the role.

After the library explosion almost killed me, I learned he was my father. Even though he claimed he stayed away from Mother and me for our own safety, the nagging thought he'd abandoned his family for his career created a wall between us. I shook off the memories and the hurt.

Kate glanced at me. "Yes. You okay?"

I shrugged. "What do you two think?"

Spike wiggled two thumbs up, and Palace Guard pursed his lips but nodded.

"Spike's excited," Kate said. "What about Palace Guard?"

"Has reservations. So do I. Are you sure he's missing and not just hiding?"

"Yes and no." Kate tapped her fingers on the steering wheel. "He disappeared two weeks ago and missed his check-in two days later and again last week. He's never missed check-in. But if he's gone underground, it's for a good reason."

"We'll search for him even though he's hiding for a good reason?"

"That's why it's unofficial. Just you, me, and a small, trusted team. No one outside the team knows I've brought you in."

"What's the plan?"

"You do plans. I just set things up," Kate said. "I got you a job in a diner. You'll be a cook."

"That's awesome, Kate." I held up my hand, and Kate, Spike, and Palace Guard smacked my high-five.

"Fuel's low. You ready for a break?" Kate pulled into a truck stop west of Mobile, Alabama.

When Kate opened her door, the breeze from the south brought the distinctive aroma of salty ocean water and Gulf fish mixed with a nearby light but pungent chemical odor. After she filled up, Kate parked near the café.

When we approached the diner, Kate froze. "Do you smell that?"

"It's real frying grease," I said with awe. "We found an authentic diner. Can I work here?"

"Maybe I can get us an assignment in Mobile." Kate wiggled her eyebrows, and we giggled.

The customers filled the diner even though it was late afternoon. We grabbed the last two empty stools at the counter. An overweight woman, whose hairnet contained her short blue-black hair, flopped menus on the counter in front of us. "What kin I get y'all?"

"What do you suggest?" Kate asked.

"Fish," the server said without hesitation. "Striped bass, fresh-caught this morning."

"Fish sandwich, fries, and tea," Kate said.

"Same for me."

The server jotted on her notebook as she waddled to the order window. "And buttermilk pie."

"Yes, ma'am," Kate said.

While we sipped our drinks, I said, "I'll bet your mom would know how to make a buttermilk pie." I sprinkled salt on the napkin under my glass to stop the damp napkin from sticking to it. "Where will we stay? A fancy resort with a pool?"

"A friend of a friend has a two-bedroom apartment near the Gulf and close to the diner. You'll stay there. I'll be on the road most of the time, but I'll stay with you when I'm in town. Gary will find you. He'll trust you. I have a gut feeling he's hiding from a rogue in the organization."

After I ate half my sandwich, I pulled out the remaining fish and scarfed it down. "Finger food." I saluted Kate with my last bite.

"This pie is awesome," Kate said. "The diner where you'll work is a lunch-only place surrounded by distribution warehouses. The owner, Diane, went to visit her daughter in Minneapolis. Her mother used to run the restaurant before she retired. I told her mother I'd find the right person to fill in for Diane."

I set my fork on my empty plate. "Can Diane's mother share her recipes with me?"

"Sure can. The diner has a jewel of a baker who also waits tables, and Diane's mom, Irene, pops in to visit with her customers. The diner is open Monday through Saturday. It's within walking distance from the apartment but a rough neighborhood. We'll find you a car."

"I'll be fine. What could happen in the middle of the day?"

Kate snorted. "When you're involved, anything."

It was after one in the morning when Kate pulled up in front of the well-lit apartment complex. Three buildings made a U with the parking lot in the middle. The two-story structures were adobe; each apartment opened to a covered breezeway.

"I expected the cleaning crew today. Let's see how good they are. Your apartment is on the second floor. It's furnished and has a well-supplied kitchen, but I brought sheets and towels. I'll stay here tonight."

As we carried in our bags, I caught a whiff of lemon. Kate checked the kitchen, and I checked the living area and bathroom. We grabbed our flashlights and checked for bedbugs.

"Clean enough," Kate said. "Here are your sheets."

I woke at six and stumbled into the kitchen. Kate measured coffee into the coffeemaker basket and glanced up. "Fifteen minutes."

"I'll dress and unpack."

We carried our coffee out to the eight-by-eight-foot balcony. Our view was dumpsters, a parking lot, and the rear of one-story apartment buildings with faded and chipped paint. The wind whipped around the corner from the south, but two sturdy rocking chairs, a rusty wrought iron patio table, and a planter with a blooming cactus invited us to spend time outdoors.

"Not the greatest view," I said. "But I'll bet the sunset is beautiful."

"I'd forgotten how windy it can be so close to the water." Kate held her hair away from her face. "Let's go inside."

Kate refilled our cups and took her coffee to her room. "Won't be long."

"Is it just me, or is it lonesome here without Lucy?" I asked.

The sadness on my imaginary men's faces mirrored my misery.

"Kate, we quit. We miss Lucy," I said.

"Two weeks," Kate called out from her bedroom. "Just give me two weeks of the Gray Lady. Nobody sees patterns in random incidents like you do. Just discover some unrelated critical details, but don't get entangled."

"I don't get entangled. Will we dye my hair gray?"

"Only if you want to."

I frowned. "How else could I be the Gray Lady?"

"Perfectly logical. Let me make a quick call."

"I need cowgirl boots, too." I inspected my white running shoes.

"Easy. We're in Texas."

After her call, Kate said, "We're set for eight thirty. After your hair's done, we'll pick up a car for you and then go to the diner to meet everyone."

Kate slowed to pull into a taqueria's rutted parking lot. We bumped across the packed sand and the gravel-covered holes as we eased toward the line of five cars at the drive-up window. The faded sign and discolored adobe building hinted at the longevity of the business. "Adds to the ambiance, doesn't it?" Kate asked.

I inhaled the aroma of roasted peppers mixed with the fragrant corn masa, and my stomach growled.

"Good answer," Kate chuckled. "Breakfast burrito and coffee?"

"Yes." I swiped at my mouth. "I think I drooled. There's a picnic table." I pointed to a park across the street. "Let's eat there."

Kate pulled in at the park, and we tore the sack open to serve as a plate for both of us.

Kate took a bite. "It's spicy. We'll have time to pick up your car, and then you can follow me to the beauty shop and cafe."

"Makes sense." I licked the dripping salsa off my fingers. "I love this burrito. If we ever open another breakfast place, we may have found a new specialty menu item."

After we wolfed down our fiery meal, we picked up the rental, and I followed Kate to the hair salon. Kate focused on her phone while the hairdresser dyed and styled my hair. In less than an hour, my hair was back to my beloved gray. Kate glanced up. "Hello, Gray Lady. Let's go."

I flipped my hair as I climbed into my car. "Lead on, FBI."

I followed Kate for a short distance to the diner. The old railcar style reminded me of Reggie's Diner, where Kate taught me to cook.

After we parked, Kate pointed to the red and white striped barber pole next to the *Diane's Diner* sign. "That's different for a food establishment. Can't wait to hear the story."

When Kate opened the door, the aroma of hot grease, fried onions, and fresh apple pie welcomed us. The interior lights were old-style fluorescents with a droning buzz. The spinning stools with red vinyl seats repaired with black tape at the counter and the spacious wooden booths with burn-marked tables and black vinyl seats reminded me of Reggie's.

"Our kind of place." Kate ran her fingertips across the back of the nearest booth and smiled. "Protected with a light covering of years of cooking oil."

I glanced at the tall, slender server in blue jeans as she passed me. She had twisted her dark brown hair into a bun on top of her head and tied a red bandana around her neck with the knot to the side. Her shirt strained across her ample chest. The lines of a tattoo on her neck appeared above the scarf on the left. I frowned. *PJ? She's lost weight, but the lines match the top of her three-heart tattoo.*

PJ's blue eyes narrowed, and I sensed a warning as she turned to the order window with a quick shake of her head.

"Come on in and meet Irene and Rosa." Kate led the way to the kitchen. "Rosa, this is my friend, Maggie. She's the Gray Lady."

Rosa peered at the plates at the order window and waved without turning.

My eyes welled up when we strolled into the spotless, well-organized kitchen. *Just like Reggie's Diner.* A wizened woman with wisps of gray hair that escaped from her red Alabama Crimson Tide ball cap pulled a basket of chicken livers out of the freestanding deep-fat fryer and tossed them onto a screen to drain. She sidestepped to the sturdy six-burner cast-iron stove with double ovens and stirred the mustard greens.

"Irene," Kate said, "This is my friend, the Gray Lady."

Irene wiped her hands on her white utility apron and rushed to hug me with her wiry arms. She was shorter than me, and I breathed in the heady cloud of sizzled grease and grilled onions that swirled around her. She turned back to her fryers. "Nice to meetcha. You're not as old as I expected." Irene glanced over her shoulder and raised an eyebrow.

"I get that a lot."

"I bet you do. Reckon you could be here tomorrow morning at eight? Thursdays are busy, but then Fridays are our lightest days because most of our customers start their weekends early. Saturdays are unpredictable. Diane says it depends on the phase of the moon. Rosa bakes the pies, and Diane and now me cook the daily specials."

She pointed at a poster on the wall. "Each day has a different special. Our customers aren't very adventuresome. Makes it easy, but sometimes we get bored. Diane tried a new Wednesday special one time, and I never saw such a bunch of crybabies carry on." Irene cackled. "Recipes are simple to follow. I made you a recipe book. It's out by the cash register along with your keys to the front and back doors." She narrowed her eyes. "You ever cook on a gas stove?"

"Eight's great, and thanks for the recipe book." I stepped closer to the stove. "The gas stove I learned on was newer, but not by much." I opened the cold oven. "Manual pilot light?"

"Good catch. Yes, it's manual. It's cantankerous, so we leave it on."

I peered behind the oven. "The gas stove I'm familiar with had an automatic shutoff if the pilot light went off, but I don't see one."

Irene snorted. "You cooked on a newfangled stove. No automatic anything on this old gal, but she's indestructible. Sure am glad to have you here, Gray Lady. Diane's visiting my granddaughter. She's a college girl and in her third year at the University of Minnesota. Diane will help her move into a new apartment." Irene waved her wooden spoon at Kate. "Thanks for the Gray Lady, Kate."

"You're welcome." Kate perched on a kitchen stool. "Irene, tell us about the barber pole."

Irene chuckled. "My daddy was a barber. He always told me he was sorry I couldn't take over his barber shop. When I was young, girls could work in a beauty shop, not barbershops. Seems strange now, doesn't it? After Diane was born and my husband died, Daddy bought me this diner. I named it after my baby girl and put up the barber pole as a joke between me and Daddy."

"I love family traditions," Kate said. "Thanks for the story."

I headed to the register to pick up my recipe book and keys. PJ-Rosa stopped me on my way past the counter with a light touch on my arm. She spoke in a voice so soft I had to strain to hear her. "I work for Kate."

She cleared her throat and spoke in a normal tone. "Thanks for coming, Gray Lady. Nice to meet you." She held out her hand, and we shook hands. She smiled, and dimples circled her mouth.

"Nice to meet you too, Rosa. See you in the morning. I'll be here to help until Diane gets back."

"Good. Diane worries about her mother even though Irene can work rings around anyone half her age. Glad you're here."

When we were outside, Kate handed me a sheet of paper. "Addresses for a grocery store you'll like and a great boot store. Tell me when you have a plan."

I headed to my car. Spike leaned against the driver's door, and Palace Guard stood at attention. Spike narrowed his eyes.

"I met PJ, who is now Rosa when I was job hunting after college. She was in a bad personal situation, and I helped her to break away. You didn't know her because that was before the library explosion. Her father is Tony at the church, and he and Mother are old friends. Mother said PJ went to Nevada to finish her college work. She must have graduated if she works for Kate. I guess our Rosa is undercover. Now you know everything I know."

Spike shaded his eyes with his hand and scanned the area, and Palace Guard raised an eyebrow.

"No, we will not get involved. I'm the cook at the diner. That's enough excitement for me."

Spike grinned. I climbed into my car and slammed the door. It didn't sound angry enough, so I opened the door and slammed it again. "There. That's better."

Palace Guard was in the passenger's seat. He turned his head away. Spike leaned over the seat to the front and golf-clapped.

When I stepped inside the boot store, I breathed in the heady aroma of leather. *I need a saddle and a horse.*

My eyes widened at the rows and rows of women's western boots. Spike pointed to pair after pair, and I shook my head as we wandered through the aisles. I stared at a pair of boots on a bottom shelf. *Those are beautiful.* Spike held his nose and waved his other hand in front of his face.

"No, they don't. They'd be great. Red boots accompany Rosa's red bandana, Irene's barber pole, and the Alabama cap." I put my hands on my hips. "I'd blend in. Red and cowgirl boots. I can't think of anything better."

Spike tugged on Palace Guard's sleeve. Palace Guard pointed to a pair of blue boots.

"I know you like blue, but I need the red ones." I found my size, tried them on, and then flounced down the aisle and back.

Palace Guard scrunched his mouth and wrinkled his nose.

"Quit that. Red's the new gray." I posed in front of the ankle-high mirror and inspected my boots from all angles.

"Yes, ma'am." A young clerk who had stooped to restock boots popped up in the next aisle.

My face heated, and the two imaginary men bent over with laughter.

I cleared my throat. "These fit."

My men followed me to the front, and the cashier smiled as she slid the box closer to her cash register. "Boot socks are on the rack behind you, ma'am, if you're interested."

I picked out gray socks with horses and red socks with dogs. After I paid, I pulled on my new gray socks and red boots and dropped my shoes into the box.

Before I climbed into the car, I admired my reflection in the store display window.

Awesome. Love these boots.

I strutted through the grocery store and filled my cart with snacks, drinks, and staples for the week.

After we returned to the apartment, I carried in my groceries and then put them away. I poured a glass of sweet tea, and Palace Guard and Spike rushed to the window and peered out. Spike put the back of his hand on his forehead and swayed in an exaggerated swoon.

I stared at Spike. "Officer Heather's here?" Palace Guard grinned, and my two imaginary men fist-bumped.

We hurried to the door, and I threw it open. "Heather!" My voice rose and cracked in a squeal.

"You have good radar, Maggie." Officer Heather stepped out of the passenger side of a silver sedan and waved. She wore tight blue jeans, Western boots, and a form-fitting red plaid shirt. Her black hair was in a single braid that trailed to the middle of her back.

"We're here on unofficial police business. I brought tacos." She waved the large sack in her hand as she closed the car door.

I squinted at the man who eased out of the driver's seat and smiled as Larry strode to the stairway behind Heather. He was slim and as tall as Palace Guard. He wore blue jeans and a plain black T-shirt. His brown curly hair covered the tops of his ears and was longer than I'd ever seen it.

"I bet Spike told you Officer Heather was here. I brought beer. The kind we like. Cold." Larry chuckled and winked as he put the beer in the refrigerator.

"I picked up a cherry pie and ice cream at the grocery store," I said. "Jennifer Coyle says you never know when you might need pie. I'll warm it up for dessert."

Heather pulled out plates and napkins while I put the pie in the oven. "Who's Spike?" she asked.

Larry opened three beers. "Tell you later. Right, Maggie?"

"What business?" I set a bright orange bowl on the table and joined Heather and Larry.

"Eat first." Larry stuffed a big bite of taco into his mouth.

After Heather dumped a sack of tortilla chips into the bowl, she pulled a jar of hot salsa out of her backpack and doused her taco. "Besides, our business isn't with you, Maggie. It's with the Gray Lady."

Larry nodded and gulped his beer.

"Well, I refuse to eat until you tell me what's going on." I scooted back my chair and crossed my arms.

"Suit yourself, cuz." Larry grabbed another taco out of the sack and reached for the hot salsa.

"I'm just being sociable." I wrinkled my nose at Larry, took a long sip of beer, and put a taco on my plate. When Larry rose for a glass of water, I bit into my taco while he stood at the sink. The seasoned ground beef, grated cheese, homestyle taco sauce with diced tomatoes and spicy peppers, and crunchy corn tortilla melted my resolve to boycott lunch.

After we polished off the tacos and chips, I pulled the warm pie out of the oven. "No ice cream on your pie unless you talk."

"We need to talk to the Gray Lady," Larry said.

I set the pie on the table, marched to my bedroom, and slammed the door behind me. When I returned to the kitchen, Larry had opened three more beers, and Heather had dished up our dessert.

I sashayed to the table and spun to show off my gray T-shirt and yoga pants before I sat down. "Gray Lady reporting for duty."

Heather handed me a fork and pointed with hers. "We didn't mean literally, but no matter. Does the literal Gray Lady wear red boots?"

"Red is the new gray." *Sounded better the first time.*

"I learn something new every day." Heather crossed her arms. "So, back to my original question. Who's Spike?"

"Spike and Palace Guard are my imaginary men," I said. "They were with me in the hospital after the library explosion and helped me recover. When Kate accepted her new FBI assignment, Spike and Palace Guard took over my defensive and offensive training."

"Imaginary men. Do you see these imaginary men who trained you? And is Palace Guard like Buckingham Palace?" Heather asked.

"Yes, Buckingham Palace," Larry said.

When I raised my eyebrows, he shrugged. "Glenn told me."

"Glenn Coyle sees the imaginary men?" Heather's eyes widened.

"No, he doesn't. But Lucy does, and Glenn says he trusts Lucy."

"Why didn't I know about this?" Heather asked as she rubbed her forehead. "And who is Spike?"

Spike stood next to Heather with his arms crossed.

"Taking sides?" I raised my eyebrows, and Spike grinned. "I don't know. Never came up. Spike was a mentor for all of us kids when I was little. He's tough and a cheater. He taught me to fight dirty."

Heather stirred her ice cream and scooped up a large mound of soft slush. She clutched her forehead when she put the sweet coldness into her mouth. "Brain freeze, not to mention the concept of real, imaginary men, bedazzles me."

"I never thought of them as real imaginary men, but you're right. Good description," I said. "Put your tongue on the roof of your mouth. It'll ease the pain."

Larry stared at me.

"What?" I asked. "I'm a librarian. I read and know things. And cooks are smart. So, what's the plan?"

"Thanks, that worked," Heather said. "We think Gary's disappearance was deliberate. There's no record of what he worked on. You could check that, right?"

"Sure. When do you want it done?"

"You could hack into...don't do it." Larry's eyes widened.

I shrugged. "It's how I would check the records. You have a different idea?"

"We'll take care of that. Don't hack the federal employee system." Heather shook her finger at me. "I thought I cracked a joke."

"Not only is my cuz literal, Heather, she's also the Crazy Lady. You'll adjust." Larry grinned.

"I'll try to remember. Maggie, the last time anyone saw Gary was at Diane's Diner, and the last person to see him, as far as we know, was Irene. That's why we arranged for Diane to visit her daughter. You're our eyes and ears. Kevin will be your contact."

"Who's Kevin?" I asked.

"My cover name," Larry said.

Spike frowned at Larry, and Palace Guard narrowed his eyes. I snickered.

"Did I miss something?" Heather asked.

Larry put his hand on Heather's shoulder. "Glenn told me sometimes it's best to ignore them. Her."

Heather shook her head. "While I'm adjusting, why does Kev, I mean Larry, call you *cuz*?"

"When we were trying to catch Parker's killer, Kate assigned Larry to guard me, and I said he was my cousin. Simple."

"Drove her crazy when you called her Aunt Katherine," he said.

"Not as much as when you called her Mom." I snickered.

"Adapting is my superpower," Heather mumbled as she rinsed her bowl and spoon. "I brought something for you to test for me."

Heather pulled a bracelet out of her bag. A silver dolphin and horse dangled from the delicate chain. "Despite how fragile it looks, it's sturdy. We track the horse by satellite, and it disconnects from the bracelet if you tug its tail. In theory, you'd never be alone, but it hasn't been field-tested. Officer Ewing..."

When I cocked my head and furrowed my brow, Heather sighed. "...Larry is our contact if we lose your signal. Anything else?"

"Where's Lucy, Mags?" Larry asked.

"With Glenn. She loves the Coyles. She was Kate's dog before she came to live with me in the country."

"Diane's Diner is in a rough area. Are you sure you'll be okay?" Larry asked.

"I'll be fine. What could..."

"Don't say it." Heather inclined her head and glanced in Larry's direction. "Just until Diane returns. Temporary, right?"

Larry crossed his arms and growled. "Still don't think it's safe."

"Only two weeks. Temporary," I said.

After Heather and Larry left, I turned on my computer. Palace Guard and Spike leaned over my shoulder. "Give me some room, guys. I won't hack into any personnel records. I want to check my database for anybody who might have ties with Galveston."

Two hours later, I rose and stretched. "Let's check the balcony." I poured a glass of tea.

When we stepped outside, low clouds dominated the sky. "I can't see any stars."

The light breeze from the Gulf kept the evening temperature and humidity that were as high as daytime in Georgia tolerable.

"Wonder why Rosa's at the diner? Kate must have needed somebody on a more permanent basis. Wonder why she is going by *Rosa*?"

The parking lot lights bounced off the hovering clouds and bathed everything around me with an eerie orange glow. I rocked, drank my cold drink, and gazed at my other-world surroundings until the buzz of mosquitos chased me inside. "Good break. I'll review the recipes before returning to the deep dive analysis on my database."

A little after midnight, I woke up. I had leaned back in my computer chair. My mouth was dry, and my neck was stiff. I turned off my computer and desk light and stumbled through the dark to the kitchen. I poured a glass of water, plodded to the back door, and cracked it open. The heat and humidity slammed me with the force of a damp gym towel. *How can it still be this hot?*

Two men stood in the shadows near the alley light. The first man was of average build and wore glasses. His hair was thin, but his mustache was thick. The second man was clean-shaven, tall, and overweight. His back's C-curve emphasized his hunchback stance. His dark, curly hair sprung away from his head when he removed his ball cap.

The older man handed an envelope to the curly-haired man. His whisper was clear in the night stillness. "This month's bonus plus instructions."

The overweight man lumbered across the alley to the apartment complex. He unlocked the back door of an apartment and slipped inside. The older man scanned my apartment complex balconies, and I stepped back. *Precautionary?* My heartbeat quickened. *Did the alley light catch my shadow?* When I dared to peek again, he wasn't there.

I locked the door and changed into pajamas before I flopped onto my bed. *It's too hot for covers.*

Chapter Two

Early the next morning, I sipped my coffee on the back porch while the sky underwent an imperceptible fade from black to tones of gray to soft blue.

"Time for work." I stretched. "I like the sound of that."

After I dressed in my gray clothes, red boots, and a gray ball cap, I finished my coffee and headed to the parking lot.

I opened the car door, and Spike was in the passenger's seat. "You can stay."

Spike waved his hand toward the road.

"Suit yourself. Just don't get into any trouble."

Spike smacked his hands to his face and raised his eyebrows.

"Yes, you." I giggled.

Two muscular men who wore dark green T-shirts that strained across their chests, jeans, and brown work boots lingered on the street corner nearest to the diner. "Anything for me to worry about?"

Spike flexed his arms with his fists tight.

"Thanks. Backup is always good."

After I parked in the employee spots across the street from the diner, Spike pointed to my boots. "Yep, my knife is in my boot, and my pistol is in my waistband." I patted my waist.

Spike held both thumbs up, and we sauntered to the door. Garbage pickup was on Fridays, and the dumpster emanated the sour odor of decayed food scraps. I unlocked the back door, and the enticing aroma of herbs and roasting chicken swirled a welcome that canceled the parking lot stench.

"Good. Your key works." Irene had vegetables lined up on her chopping table. She wore her Alabama ball cap with the brim turned to the back. She brushed a stray lock of her wispy gray hair off her forehead with the back of her wrist. "Did you look at the recipes? Thursday is chicken pot pie. Simple. I've got the chickens in the ovens. Did you smell it when you came in? I stuffed the chicken cavities with onion and celery leaves. I don't know if I listed that."

Rosa perched on a stool at the table. She wore jeans and her red bandana around her neck. "Good morning, Gray Lady." She peeled and sliced apples. "Apple pie today. I've wondered. Tell me about the origin of the Gray Lady."

"I always wanted to be a spy. Spies wear black. Every four-year-old knows that, right?"

Rosa grinned and nodded.

"I wore black until college when I read about the gray man." I raised my eyebrows.

Irene guffawed. "And the Gray Lady was born."

"Best story of the day," Rosa chuckled.

I threw on a white apron that had a machine-embroidered barber pole on the bib. After I wrapped the sash around my waist, I tied a square knot in front. "Where do you want me, Ms. Irene?" I asked.

"We need potatoes and carrots peeled and cut up. After we get them in a pot, we can go over the accounting system. It's all simple." Irene raised an eyebrow and inspected me. "You're a little more like the Gray Lady."

Irene and I raced as we chopped and dropped potatoes and carrots into the commercial-sized pots, and Rosa snickered. "You two are entertaining. I never knew vegetable prep was a competitive sport."

"No way will any youngster outdo me," Irene grumbled. Spike stood next to Irene with his arms crossed and his mouth pursed.

I tried to control myself, but Rosa snorted, and I laughed.

"See there? I got the best of you, Gray Lady." Irene smirked.

Rosa shook her head as she rolled out pie dough. "Y'all aren't right in the head."

After we popped the pans of pot pie into the ovens, Irene said, "Let's go over the accounting system, Gray Lady. Pour us some coffee."

I poured two cups and followed her into the office.

"Monday through Thursday our customers show up in groups between eleven-thirty and one. It depends on what time their assigned lunch break begins," Irene said. She sat at her desk and pointed to a chair.

"They're on a tight schedule. We feed 'em, never let their tea or coffee run dry, take their money, and send them on their way for the next wave of workers to claim their seats. The good news is just about everybody wants the special. Rosa takes care of the tables by herself. I keep the coffee pots full and dish up the plates when she calls out the orders."

After Irene explained her accounting system, she closed the journal and returned it to her file cabinet. "On Fridays and Saturdays our customers include retired folks who enjoy the camaraderie of lunch with former coworkers. Most groups show up around the same time for their weekly get-togethers."

Irene cocked her head. "Reggie was an old friend of mine. It was a blessing when Kate stepped in to help him. You two drive from Georgia? That's a long drive. Did you stop in Louisiana by chance?"

"We stopped in Mobile then pushed on."

"Just wondering. I have an old friend in Louisiana, Chef Daryl. He's the best Cajun cook I've ever known and a good-hearted man." Irene gazed at the ceiling then shook her head. "Ignore the ramblings of an old woman."

The timer for the ovens dinged, and Irene hurried to the kitchen with me on her heels. When the customers burst into the diner, I hung out in the kitchen near the order window and listened to the good-natured kidding and trash talk.

Irene said, "Let's dish up today's special." She grabbed a stack of white plates. "We've been together since we were all teens. That's why they come here. We're all young again."

After I scooped up pot pie onto the plates, Irene carried the three orders to the window. "I hope everything goes well for Diane up north. I miss her when she's away. It's hard here alone. Some people aren't what they seem, but when you find someone you can trust, that's gold." She waved her hand. "Don't listen to me."

We cleaned the diner and prepped for the next day before two o'clock.

"You do good work, Gray Lady. See you in the morning. No need to be here until nine. Friday's an easy day." Irene locked the door behind me, and Spike and I headed home.

"Irene said she misses Diane, but who are the other people she mentioned? Didn't sound like a casual comment to me."

Spike shrugged.

When we got home, Palace Guard waited on the stairs. He wore his running shorts and shoes and his royal blue Chelsea Football Club shirt. I hurried inside, changed into my running shoes and gray shorts and shirt, and bounded down the stairs. Palace Guard darted to the road before I reached him. We faced traffic and ran on the paved street near the curb as we raced east toward the diner. When the occasional car appeared, we hopped out of the street until they passed. The heat and humidity soaked me and slowed my pace. Palace Guard grinned and sped ahead of me. I pushed my pace and caught up with him. He U-turned, and we raced west past the apartments. A truck sped toward us, and I diverted to the nearby parking lot. Palace Guard ran backward in front of me.

"Show off." I wheeled around to return to the apartment and pushed hard to stay in front of him. We touched the bottom stair at the same time. Sweat drenched my shirt, and I fell against the railing to catch my breath. "Good run. I needed that."

Spike waited near the front door. When I trudged past Spike, he held his nose and waved his hand in front of his face.

"Not funny. For your information, I already planned to take a shower." I pushed the hair strands off my damp neck and marched into the apartment.

Later in the afternoon, I turned away from my desk and stretched. "Let's go outside. I need fresh air to clear my brain."

Spike settled on the sofa. I grabbed a glass of iced tea, and he yawned and sank back on the soft pillows. When I opened the back door, Palace Guard joined me on the balcony. White clouds gathered and darkened as they billowed, and the cicadas buzzed a song of impending rain. After I drained my glass, I went inside to my computer. I selected five large US metropolitan regions and searched for news, hospital admissions, and police reports for the last twelve months. My goal was to find a sudden jump in activity of any kind.

At five o'clock, thunder rumbled, and the sky darkened. I rose to watch the storm roll in then returned to my computer when the showers turned to a deluge.

Two hours later, the storm had passed, and I leaned back in my chair. "It would be easier if I knew what I was doing. I need a sandwich."

I slathered butter onto two thick pieces of sourdough bread, topped the unbuttered sides with cheddar cheese slices, and opened a can of diced New Mexico green chile. While my cast iron skillet warmed up, I read the ingredients on the potato chip bag. *I'll skip them and have ice cream instead.* After I pan-fried my sandwich, I cut it into four equal triangles and poured myself a large glass of tea.

I ate and scrolled through the screen. My eyes widened, and I texted Larry: "Call?" I saved the files to the cloud that Mother and I shared.

Tires screeched in front of my apartment, and Palace Guard rushed to the front door. He peered out and wiggled his fingers over his head.

"Larry?" I asked.

Palace Guard nodded.

I opened the door, and Larry dashed inside. He wore running shorts and a Texas Tech ball cap. His white 5-K logo shirt was damp at the neck.

"You okay, cuz?" he asked with a growl.

"I'm fine. Why didn't you call?"

He stared at the floor. "I was close."

"Right. I have something to show you. Pull up a chair." I scrolled through the summary.

Larry scooted a chair over and frowned at my screen. "Increasing trend in overdoses. Big jump in cases of Hepatitis B. Scroll down."

Larry leaned closer while I scrolled past a few screens. "That's interesting. The distribution of overdoses across income is flat. Hep B, however, shows a spike with higher income." Larry rubbed his chin. "Is that what you saw? Isn't a steady uptick of overdoses what we'd expect? Hepatitis isn't seasonal, is it? Why is it in direct correlation to income? Where does Gary Sloan fit in?"

"Good questions. Now look at this." I replaced the income search with age.

"Overdoses are younger. No surprise. But why is the average age associated with hepatitis twenty-five years older? What does that mean? And it's across the board not just one region. I need to call Heather."

Larry pulled out his phone. Palace Guard held his hand up, palm facing outward.

"Wait a minute," I said.

Spike rose and made a fierce, growly face.

"Palace Guard and Spike say contact Kate."

Larry scanned the room. "I don't see anybody."

"I know," I said.

"But the men I can't see because they are imaginary say call Kate."

"Yes."

"Who should call Kate? You or me?"

Palace Guard pointed at me. Spike strode to Larry and patted him on the back. Larry reached for his back. "Thought I felt something," he mumbled.

"I should call," I said. "Spike patted your back. It's his way of saying *great question*."

I texted Kate: "Got something. Call when u r available."

Larry frowned. "What if you change your search criteria to less populated regions?"

Palace Guard raised an eyebrow and stared at Larry. I attacked the keyboard. "Palace Guard's impressed. What made you think of that?"

"I'm a number-cruncher at heart. I majored in Math and Statistics."

"Interesting. Similar trend in overdoses, just lower numbers, but almost no reports of hepatitis."

"Proves nothing." Larry leaned back. "Wonder if there are any research studies of a sudden rise of hepatitis in older people who live in urban areas? Maybe it's environmental."

"We missed a variable, or maybe we found a rabbit hole to distract us from Ernie."

"I can't keep up." Larry scowled and rubbed his forehead. "Who's Ernie?"

"Sorry. Long story. I meant to say Gary. My father, the spy."

Larry rested his arm across the back of my chair. Spike swatted Larry's elbow, and Larry frowned as he jerked his arm away. I bit my lower lip to stifle a giggle.

Larry crossed his arms and rubbed his elbow. "Do the imaginary men talk to you? Do you hear what they say?"

"Nope. They're masters at charades. Spike does a terrific Kate face: it's ferocious."

"Oh, really." Larry narrowed his eyes. "What about..."

My cell rang. *Thank you, Kate.*

"Whatcha got?" Kate asked.

"Not sure. I found a spike in reported cases of hepatitis in the higher income, over-forty set who live in urban areas."

"I don't get it. Cook breakfast. I miss our diner food." Kate hung up.

"What did she say?" Larry asked.

"Cook breakfast."

Larry rose. "I'll be here early."

Palace Guard grinned and applauded. Spike waved goodbye.

After Larry left, I poured a glass of tea, and we headed to the patio for a break. "You know, my cousin's sharp."

It wasn't long until I swatted a second mosquito, and we went inside. I mixed a batch of brownies and threw them into the oven. After I swept the floor in the guest bedroom and dusted the windowsills and blinds, the timer sounded, and I pulled out the brownies. When they cooled, I cut the chocolate nut goodness into twenty-four equal servings and wrapped each one.

"All ready for tomorrow. Back to the computer."

I changed the regions to midsize cities and ran another report. The results matched the urban locales. I rose and stretched. "Time to take Larry's advice and find recent hepatitis studies."

At eleven o'clock, I saved my data and wandered to the patio. The moon hid behind passing clouds, and a low hanging mist covered the parking lot behind mine. The warm, humid night air was sticky, and my shirt clung to me before I had finished my tea.

I stumbled into the kitchen before dawn and made coffee. Low growls of thunder hinted at early morning showers. While my cinnamon rolls rose, my fingers flew over the keys as I searched for hepatitis studies. When a crunch of tires in the parking lot broke the silence between the rumbles, Palace Guard peeked out and wiggled his fingers over his head.

"Do you have another sign for Larry? Something I could tell him?"

Palace Guard grinned and held up his index finger in front of his mouth and blew.

"Smoking gun? Much better."

I opened the door as Larry bounded up the stairs. The beginnings of a scruffy beard with light auburn streaks, jeans, and western boots gave him a local look. He strode inside, poured himself a cup of coffee, and peered at my computer. "Whatcha got?"

"Not much. Hepatitis is blood-borne, and I've found a plethora of research papers but nothing that explains what I found." I handed him several sheets of notes and references to read.

Larry frowned. "Are the titles of these papers obscure for a reason?" He flipped to the next page and continued reading. "Wait. Here's a paper about hepatitis and income." He turned the page. "Never mind. It focuses on diseases common in poverty conditions."

I glanced at Spike. *Fierce face.*

"Kate's here." I rushed to the door.

Kate climbed out of her car. "Truce."

I stepped back and crashed into Larry who had slipped up behind me.

"Why did Kate say *truce*?" Larry whispered.

"So I wouldn't ambush her." I rushed to the refrigerator and pulled out a carton of eggs. "We'll eat first. Then talk. It's a Coyle rule."

When Kate came into the apartment, she waved. "Hey, Spike."

"Kate sees Spike?" Larry whispered. I nodded, and he shook his head.

Forty-five minutes later, I refilled our cups with the remaining coffee and started another pot. While the coffee perked, I gave Kate a quick summary of what I'd found.

"Change in plans." Kate brought the coffeepot to the table and refilled our cups. "No way are you to pursue the hepatitis angle, Maggie."

"Fired before I even started," I said. "Do I still cook at the diner?"

"Maybe. Tell."

"I don't see how any of it relates to Gary Sloan."

"Right," Kate said. "So, you can drop it and cook. I'll have Detective Ross make a few inquiries to see if anybody's interested in what you found, though."

"Who?" I asked.

Larry bit his lip. "Moe."

"Right, Moe," Kate said. "Are the guys helping at the diner? Never mind. They are. I have people to check on. I'll return to crash here for a power nap then head out later this afternoon. Larry's your contact." She waved to the guys and left.

"I'll see you later." Larry cleared his throat and waved to the sofa as he left.

I snorted, and my imaginary men, who stood near the kitchen table, bent over double in laughter.

I wiped my eyes. "He's trying."

I sang under my breath while I took a quick shower and dressed. When I stepped into the living room, Spike covered his ears with his hands.

"Hilarious. Time for me to go to work. You can stay home if you have no appreciation for fine music."

When I opened the driver's side door, Spike was in the passenger's seat. He wore a pair of camo-colored hearing protection earmuffs.

"Comedian." I tightened my lips to hold back a smile then sang a song about happy fish jumping into the fryer on our way to the diner.

After I unlocked the back door, Rosa glanced up as she carried lemons and eggs to her pie station. "Hello, Gray Lady. Fried fish day. Lemon meringue is always a hit. Irene was here when I arrived. She said she had an errand to run."

I peeled carrots and threw cabbage into the food processor to shred. While I mixed the coleslaw dressing and tossed in the cabbage and carrots, Rosa answered the knock at the back door. A white-haired, muscular man with leathery, tanned arms pulled in a dolly loaded with crates. He wore a once-white apron over a red T-shirt and overalls. The briny smell of fresh fish drifted into the kitchen.

"Thanks, Rosa. Hiya, Gray Lady. I'm Gus. Got yer fish here. Ms. Irene told me you were the new cook. Ms. Diane always had me put my deliveries straight into the walk-in."

"Please do. Nice to meet you, Gus," I said.

Rosa opened the cooler door while Gus rolled in two large crates of fish with *Pesckey's Fish Market* printed on the wooden crates.

"Now, you call me if you run low. Ms. Diane gives me a holler once or even twice a month sometimes. My number's on my crates. I can be here in ten minutes if you need more fish. First Ms. Irene and now Ms. Diane's my best customer and has been for twenty-five years. If you see Ms. Irene, tell her I said I appreciate her business." He stacked the empty crates from the cooler onto his dolly and left.

"I didn't expect the fish to be fresh," I said, "but I don't know why I assumed frozen. All the other ingredients are fresh."

"Diane's Diner is old school. We cook everything from scratch." Rosa stirred the lemon custard for her pies.

I washed and cut up potatoes to soak. "I didn't know I needed to fry French fries twice until I read my recipe book." After I drained them, I fried the potatoes at the prescribed lower temperature as the first step.

I was a whirlwind as I cut up and marinated the fish in buttermilk, mixed the batter for the fish and hush puppies, and set up an assembly line at my fryers that would have been Kate-approved for the process of deep-frying fish, hush puppies, and French fries.

After Rosa pulled her last pie out of the oven, our first customers filed into the diner.

"It's like there's a secret signal that tells them lunch is ready." Rosa chuckled and rushed to fill coffee cups and take orders.

"Friday special," a familiar male voice said.

I snorted. *Larry.*

"Everything okay here?" Irene came in the back door.

"Everything's ready. What about you?"

Irene scanned the room. "A little something came up this morning. Had to take care of it. Nobody here except you and Rosa, right?" She gazed at the order window.

I frowned. *Why won't she look at me?* "We have customers, but just Rosa and me. Did you expect someone?"

"No. Gus delivered the fish?" She perched on a stool and drummed her fingers on the chopping table. She grabbed her fingers in a squeeze with her other hand and forced her hands into her lap.

"He did. Is something wrong?"

"No. Everything's great. He didn't have any messages for me, did he? He better not have. Just stopped by to tell you to take tomorrow off to get settled, and we'll see you on Monday."

"Thanks, Irene. Will you call if you need me?" I dropped fish into the fryer. "Gus said to tell you he appreciates your business."

Irene scowled. "He did, did he? Gotta go." She scurried out.

"Was that Irene I heard?" Rosa peered in from the order window.

"Yes, but she was in a hurry." I plated up a special and handed it to Rosa.

"Speaking of which…" Rosa glided away with the plate.

Twenty minutes later my phone buzzed with a text. "Food's great. C U this afternoon. L"

Rosa carried in dishes to the sink. "Police officer was here. Ewing. He may be new to the area. Cute guy and nice too." She rushed out with the coffeepot.

Larry's cute?

On my way to the apartment, my phone dinged. After I went inside, I read Kate's text: "Sent u email with link. Send your data."

"Yes!" I pumped my arm, and Spike performed his wacky dance. Palace Guard raised his eyebrows.

"Kate wants my data. I'm off the hook. Moe found somebody to investigate the hepatitis surge."

Palace Guard pointed to the computer.

"On it, spoilsport," I grumbled.

My fingers flew over the keys. I uploaded what I had and sauntered to the back patio to stretch. The front door squeaked, and Larry came into the apartment.

"I'm out back," I called.

"You left your front door unlocked. Anybody could have come in. Well, except I'm sure Palace Guard and Spike are standing next to me. Am I right?"

"Almost. Palace Guard's close to you. Spike's behind..."

Spike shoved Larry's shoulder, and Larry stumbled as he stepped onto the patio.

"Dang it, Spike. Don't push." Larry growled.

Palace Guard and I stared at Larry, and Spike danced his jig.

"Just for that, I will concentrate on seeing Palace Guard first," Larry grumbled as he sat on a rocker.

I snickered. "You're getting there. Want some ice tea?"

"Sounds good. What do you mean?"

I handed him a glass wrapped with a paper towel to catch the condensation drips. "Immature. You're getting there."

"Thanks. I think." He gulped down his tea. "This tea is excellent. You make it fresh, don't you? So, what's our plan?"

"I will read white papers on hepatitis. Just in case Moe's team needs a little help."

"Well, that'll make Moe happy." Larry snorted, but then he stopped rocking and raised his hand. "That was sarcasm."

"Thanks. Sarcasm confuses me. Back to the medical research: we need more information."

"Thousand-piece puzzle, and we have three pieces," Larry said.

"Exactly."

Palace Guard and Spike high-fived. I held up my hand, and they smacked my palm. Larry held up his hand, and Palace Guard smacked it.

Larry stared at his hand. "Palace Guard, right?" he asked with reverence.

I glanced at Palace Guard, and his eyes were wide. Spike elbowed Palace Guard, and I chuckled.

"What?" Larry asked.

"You're right: it was Palace Guard."

Larry narrowed his eyes. "What else?"

"You surprised him."

Larry frowned. "I don't believe you. There's more. Fine. Don't tell me."

I flounced to the door with our empty glasses. "You know, sometimes I tell the truth."

"Ha."

I was up before dawn the next morning. I frowned at my computer screen as I sipped my coffee. "My brain's fried. Let's pick up a breakfast taco and go to the beach and run."

Palace Guard and I sailed through the drive-through like pros. I parked near the beach and feasted on my morning coffee and taco in the car. I found a packet with a moist hand wipe in my sack. *Maybe I can cook for a taco place when Diane returns. Lucy might like Galveston.*

The wind whipped my hair into my face when I stepped out of the car. I jammed my cap on to hold my hair, but when the wind lifted it off my head, I caught it and put it on backwards.

"This wind is fierce. Let's run."

Palace Guard grinned and jogged to the beach. I dashed past him, and the race was on. After two miles, I bent over and put my hands on my knees. "Go back." I wheezed.

Palace Guard faced away from the Gulf and crossed his arms.

I closed my eyes and focused on catching my breath. *Good to have a guard.*

When my breathing and heart rates slowed, I headed back, and Palace Guard jogged at my pace. When I shifted to a run, he stayed by my side. We were within a half-mile of my car when Palace Guard whirled to face the opposite direction and stopped. I copied him.

My eyes widened; two men followed us. I mimicked Palace Guard's stance as he shifted to an offensive position. I kept my hand near my pistol in the holster under my sweatshirt. The two men slowed. They wore jeans, work boots, heavy coats, and the black knit caps Mother called toboggans. *Not typical beach clothing: stalkers.*

The shorter one was overweight and appeared winded from his brisk trot on the beach. The younger man was thin and wore an ankle-length trench coat. His gait was stiff. He picked at his face and jerked his head to examine first the road then the beach behind them.

"What's your story?" I flipped my sweatshirt aside and rested my hand on the butt of my gun as I prepared to pull and shoot.

The two men froze.

"Wh-what?" the younger man asked.

I glared at the younger man and shifted my gaze to the other man with my best killer-Kate look. "Just asking."

"Excuse us. Nice talkin' to ya." The older man strode over to the road at such a quick pace his companion broke into a stiff-legged run to catch up.

Palace Guard and I shifted to face their retreat.

"What was that all about?" I asked.

Palace Guard's eyes narrowed, and he stepped closer to me.

The two men crossed the road. When they approached the curb, the younger man turned toward the water and tore off his coat. He reached over his shoulder, lifted a long gun over his head, and handed it to the shorter man.

Palace Guard spun around and sped away in a zig-zag pattern, and I stayed at his side. When we reached the closest dune, Palace Guard and I dove over it and landed face down into the sand. *Zing, zing, zing, thunk.*

The seagulls screamed, and I grunted at a sting on my right arm. The birds took flight, and screeching tires peeled away. I raised my head enough to brush grit off my face with my left hand. I sputtered and spit wet sand.

Palace Guard pointed to my right arm. My arm burned. Under my ripped sleeve was a two-inch gash that dripped blood onto the sand.

"Ouch. My arm hurts."

Blood soaked into my shirt, and I slapped my left hand over the wound to slow the bleeding. I struggled to get to my feet but dug myself deeper into the sand.

"Dang. Now what?"

Palace Guard raised his index finger and blew.

"Call Larry? Can't you help me up?"

Palace Guard glared, and I eased my weight to free my right arm while I maintained pressure on the bleeding wound. I pulled my phone out of my bra. "I'll text. Maybe it won't sound pitiful."

I dropped the phone on my lap and typed: "GPS test."

Larry: "On my way."

I moaned as I shifted. "On top of everything else, I got sand in my shorts. It's okay if I whine, isn't it?"

Palace Guard knelt next to me and placed his hand on my back. The sound of a soft, comforting melody swirled through my head. *Imaginary music. Thank you.*

"Mags, Maggie!" Larry shouted from the road.

"Here."

Larry leaped over the dune and showered me with sand.

"Who did this? Are you okay?" He moved my left hand and gripped my right arm tight with his hand.

I spit out more sand. "Two men dressed in cold-weather clothing followed me. One was tall, thin, and fidgety. He carried the hidden rifle. The other was short and overweight. He held the rifle in a shooting position. Palace Guard and I ran in a zigzag and dived behind the dune. There were four shots. The fourth one hit me then they drove away. My arm hurts. The crosswinds and Palace Guard's reflexes saved me."

Larry's radio crackled, and he said, "Gunshot. Upper arm. Flesh wound."

A siren wailed in the distance.

"Help me sit up."

Palace Guard smirked.

"I know I sounded whiny. I meant to sound fierce."

Palace Guard rolled his eyes.

Larry helped me to a sitting position. "Where's your weapon?"

"Holster. Right side. And I have an ankle holster with a knife in my left sock."

Larry unbuckled my belt and slid off my holster. He unfastened the knife holder and stuck it in his pocket.

"What about the Heather bracelet?" I asked.

"Keep it. I'll keep these for you. I don't want anyone else to confiscate them." He stuck the gun inside his waistband, wrapped my belt around the holster and knife and holder, and tucked the pack under his arm.

The wail of the siren became closer until it cut off in the middle of the high tone. The low rumble of the ambulance's diesel engine broke the sudden silence.

"What's your theory, Mags?"

"The attack was because of my association with Ernie or the diner. The common denominator is Irene saw Ernie last. I have no answer."

"What do you want me to do?"

"I have a question for Kate. Ask her if it's okay for me to text her."

Larry's eyes narrowed. "Do we have an inside problem?"

The ambulance crew carried a backboard across the beach.

"I don't know, but it's easier to be cautious up front than to plug the holes later. No pun intended."

Larry snorted. The young paramedic wrapped my arm with a dressing, and the driver with a gray mustache and a tic in his right eye positioned the backboard next to me.

"I can walk." I growled. "Just help me up."

Larry waved off the crew and lifted me to my feet. I leaned on him, and when we reached the ambulance, he eased me onto the cot. The paramedic snugged my seat belt, and the driver clicked the gurney onto a latch and rolled me into the back of the vehicle. Palace Guard jumped into the ambulance after the crew loaded me inside, and Larry saluted the back of the ambulance before the driver closed the rear doors.

When we reached the hospital, Palace Guard remained by my side while the medical team cleansed and assessed the wound. My eyes watered from the powerful odor of hospital disinfectant and its underlying tone of unwashed bodies, and I shuddered.

"Are you okay?" The elderly tech asked after he wheeled me back from x-ray.

"I think I'm allergic to hospitals."

He nodded as he left. "Not unusual. It gets worse as you get older."

A nurse in dark green scrubs stuck his head inside my curtain. "Your cousin's here if you'd like to have someone with you."

Palace Guard grinned, and I said, "That would be great. Thank you."

Larry stepped inside my cubicle and glanced around. "You doing okay, Maggie? Palace Guard here?"

"We're waiting to hear about stitches. You gonna bust me outta here?"

"Just give the word."

A short doctor whose tangled blond curls offset her crisp demeanor entered my cubicle followed by the nurse. "Ms. Sloan, your x-rays showed no fragments. We'll put in the stitches then you can leave." She removed the bandage and inspected the wound. "We'll fit you with a sling to give that muscle support until it heals."

The nurse set up a suture tray next to the stretcher.

My whiny voice returned. "I don't think I can cook in a sling."

"You're right," the doctor said as she tied off the final suture. "You can go out to eat."

"My cousin is a cook at a restaurant," Larry said.

"Oh." The doctor straightened up and faced me as she removed her gloves. "Sorry, Ms. Sloan. Didn't mean to be insensitive. Keep the sling on for at least three weeks then you'll need physical therapy to build back your strength. Return in ten days, and we'll take out your stitches. Or see your own doctor. Do you need written documentation for your employer?"

"Might be a good idea. Could you give my cousin a suture removal kit? He's a paramedic."

"Sure." The doctor smiled at Larry. "An apology for my gaffe."

Larry returned her smile and nodded. Palace Guard wrinkled his nose.

The nurse removed the sling from its package and sized it to fit. "Looks good. Remember to keep your fingers higher than your elbow. Keep your stitches dry when you shower. You can buy a protective sleeve, but some people use plastic wrap."

"Bubble wrap," Larry mumbled and held out his fist. Palace Guard grinned and tapped a fist bump. I glared at Larry and Palace Guard.

After I signed all the paperwork with a left-handed signature that resembled a first-grader's forgery, Larry took my good arm by the elbow to escort me while Palace Guard hovered.

"Good grief. I don't walk with my arm. Give me some space."

"Humor me. Us." Larry loosened his grip but stayed close, and Palace Guard shadowed us to the car.

"Paramedic, huh? Fast thinking." Larry opened the passenger's door for me.

"X-rays confirmed I have an allergy to hospitals."

"I don't get it." Larry shrugged.

When we reached the apartment, I asked, "Does Kate know?"

"Yep," Larry said. "She'll call you later. Let's pack and leave."

Palace Guard shook his head.

"Palace Guard disagrees."

"What do you mean?" Larry said to the back seat. "She can't stay here."

"You're arguing with an imaginary man that you can't see." I snorted. "I agree with Palace Guard. Two against one. We win."

"You can't win. Kate agrees with me."

"Spike." I waggled my eyebrows.

"Cheater." Larry jerked open his car door and slammed it after he got out. He stomped around the front of the car and glared at me as he opened the door.

"You're going," he growled.

I climbed out and jutted out my chin. "Make me."

His face reddened, and he slammed the passenger's door and returned my glare.

Spike appeared at the top of the stairs and did his wacky dance, and I laughed.

"What's so funny?" Larry asked.

I exhaled. "Spike..."

Spike scowled a fierce face then winked, and I couldn't continue. I burst into raucous laughter, and Larry chuckled.

"Wacky dance, right?"

"You're right." I swiped at my damp cheeks and slipped my left arm around Larry's. When we reached the top of the stairs, I handed Larry my key, and he unlocked the door. When I stepped back, he frowned and entered the apartment.

"Well, it's about time." Kate rose from the sofa and set her empty glass on the table. She had piled her dark hair on the top of her head and held it in place by clips or magic; she wore jeans, a faded blue T-shirt, and scuffed up western boots.

"What's our plan, Spy Girl?"

Chapter Three

Larry narrowed his eyes at me and crossed his arms. "Spike told you, didn't he? I'm not speaking to any of you. Except Palace Guard. He wouldn't have tricked me."

Kate chuckled and poured three glasses of tea.

I sat at the table and gulped down half my tea. "Thanks, I was dry. I assume you don't know why I was a target. I have a question for you. Rosa at the diner says she works for you. Is that true?"

Kate stiffened. "How do you know Rosa?"

"She was the receptionist at the art studio when I interviewed for the job there. She's the daughter of one of Mother's friends. You assigned us to the same diner?"

"Her assignment differs from yours, but she's your backup if you need her. I have no hard data, but I do have a few indications that Diane's Diner is a focal point for something."

Larry refilled tea glasses.

Kate tapped her index finger on the table. "Back to my question. What's the plan?"

"The bad guys tipped their hand. No reason for me to leave the diner. If Irene was the last person to see Gary, I need details. I'll work that. We need to know if the hepatitis outbreak is relevant. I triggered the assault by something I saw or did. But what?"

"What do I do?" Larry asked.

"You disappear. You're known at Diane's Diner as a cop," I said.

Larry's brow furrowed, and the corners of his mouth drooped. Palace Guard stepped close to Larry, and Spike frowned and shook his head.

Kate's eyes widened. "Spike disagrees. Palace Guard too?"

Spike popped up a thumb and grinned at Kate.

"The imaginary men say Larry stays. I suppose it's up to me to come up with a reason." Kate pursed her lips. "Maybe Galveston has a cold case they'd like to have investigated. I'll see if I can extend Larry's temporary duty."

"Sounds great." Larry jumped up and pumped his arms as he danced a jig. All of us chuckled, and Larry shrugged. "Best I can do until Spike teaches me the wacky dance."

"You need to rest today and tomorrow, Maggie." Kate carried her empty glass to the sink. "I'll make you a pizza you can heat and pull together a shopping list. Larry, you want to grocery shop or do the laundry?"

"Shop."

Kate scribbled her list, and Larry left.

"Kate, can you waterproof my arm so I can take a shower?"

After my shower, I fluffed the pillows on my bed to support my arm and put my feet up to relax with a book. When I woke, the apartment was quiet and dark except for the kitchen light.

I found a note from Kate on the table: "Pizza ready for reheating & cinnamon rolls in fridge. Ready to bake in the am. Call if you need me."

I set a glass of tea on my desk and positioned a slice of pizza in the center of a paper towel.

Spike pointed at his open mouth and made a gagging face.

"What's wrong with you? Cold pizza's good." I plopped into my chair and turned on my computer.

Three hours later, I rolled my shoulders. "I fell into internet rabbit holes. Consequences of haphazard searches."

Spike made hopping motions with two bunny ear fingers, and I grinned.

"Exactly. I found a few interesting things, but I've reached my limit. Time for bed."

My throbbing arm woke me, and I peered at the clock. *Four o'clock. Too early.* I punched my pillow and listened for Lucy's click. *Galveston. No Lucy.* I plodded to the kitchen and started a pot of coffee.

"I would enjoy a stroll on the beach without being shot at. Suppose that's possible?"

Palace Guard glared.

"You're right. But I need a breakfast taco to go with Kate's cinnamon rolls."

We raced down the stairs to my car. When I reached for the handle to open the car door, Palace Guard held up his hand.

"Right again. Let's check." I ran my hand along the underside of my back bumper and peered underneath the car. "Wonder if that's the only one."

I sent a text to Kate: "Found gps on car. Pls advise."

"Leave it 4 now."

Palace Guard peered at my phone, and I shuddered. "We must have multiple devices attached. Creepy to ride around knowing they are there, though. Let's go back inside."

I carried a cup of coffee to the balcony, propped up my feet, and pointed to the south. "Can you read the weather here? Those vertical, billowing clouds are beautiful against the clear blue, but back home in Georgia, a sky like that would mean a storm later in the day."

Spike pointed at the gulls invading the dumpster contents behind us and covered his ears.

"Their boisterous squawks drown out everything else, don't they? I'm homesick for more musical birdcalls. Let's rustle up breakfast."

Kate left the cinnamon rolls in the refrigerator. "She's the best."

I popped the pan into the oven and set the timer. The aroma of the baking yeast, sugar, butter, and cinnamon swirled around me and chased away my homesick blues. Palace Guard and Spike took seats at the table. Spike tucked a napkin into the neck of his shirt.

"You two are silly, but I don't blame you one bit."

I pulled the rolls out of the oven to cool. I reached for plates but a knock at the door interrupted me. Palace Guard strode to the window and peered out. He held up his index finger and blew. *Larry.*

When I swung open the door, Larry frowned. "You shouldn't...the guys told you, didn't they? You made cinnamon rolls?" Larry took off his aviator-style sunglasses, hooked them onto the neck of his new Texas Tech T-shirt, and strode inside.

"Kate did. Have a seat. What brings you here?" I poured coffee for both of us and dished up four cinnamon rolls.

"Four plates?" Larry asked.

"We're pretending." I sat at my place and took a bite of my cinnamon roll.

Larry bit into his roll and licked the frosting off his upper lip. "Let me get this straight. You and the imaginary men are pretending?" Larry snorted and choked on his roll.

"Serves you right." I took another bite. I held up my hand, and Palace Guard and Spike smacked it.

Larry stared at my hand. "Once again, I'm not speaking to any of you. Can I have another one? Wait. Bad timing. I suppose I have to get my own."

I snickered as I rose and brought the pan to the table. "Help yourself."

At the sound of another knock, Spike pulled his fierce face.

"Kate." I rushed to the door and opened it.

Kate had pushed up her hair under a Bulldogs ball cap. She wore her Bulldogs T-shirt, jeans, and new Western boots. "Whatcha got, Spy Girl?"

"Coffee and the best cinnamon rolls in the world," Larry said.

"He's trying to make up for being wrong," I said.

"You two are not pulling me into another family squabble. Hey, Spike." Kate strode to the coffeepot and poured a cup while I served up a pastry for her. She stared at the four plates on the table. "Where do I sit?"

Larry jumped up. "Here, Kate. Sit here." He held the chair for her.

"Wow. You are in trouble." Kate took a bite of cinnamon roll. "Tell."

"I found a GPS tracker on the back bumper of my car. I didn't see any others, but I didn't do a thorough search."

"Why didn't you tell me that?" Larry asked.

"Because you didn't give me a chance. You were too busy..."

"Redeem yourself," Kate said. "Go check."

"On my way." Larry rushed out the door.

"What else you got?" Kate rose, refilled our cups, and started another pot.

"On one of my random internet searches, I discovered a news article about the murder of Irene's younger brother two years ago at a Galveston truck stop. The reporter said it was a random killing with no real leads."

"That's interesting. I'll suggest it for Larry's assignment. What else?"

I pouted. "We miss Lucy."

"She's doing great. She goes to work with Mom and Dad. He tells their clients Lucy's a retired K-9. Mom fussed at him, but he said she's retired and a canine." Kate chuckled. "He admitted he might have told a few stories about Lucy's heroic past and her many awards. He said he doesn't worry about leaving Mom alone with Lucy in the office. Lucy adores Mom. If Lucy's napping and Mom goes into another room, Lucy wakes up and pads along behind her."

"Thanks. I'm glad she's doing so well and has Jennifer to look after."

Larry rushed inside. "I found four. Now what?"

"Pull them and give them to me," Kate said. "I'll hand them off to the Galveston police. Maybe they'll put them on a patrol car for a few days before they give them to their tech lab."

I cleared my throat. "We should leave them and turn in the car."

Kate strolled to the back door with her coffee. After she drained her cup, she returned to the stove, refilled her cup, and sipped. "I like your idea. They won't know whether you found the trackers. I need to head back to Georgia." She stared at the door. "Is that door secure enough? Rent your replacement car through a different company. Just in case. You'll handle the logistics, right Larry?" Kate set down her cup, strode to the front door, and left.

Larry raised his eyebrows.

"That's Kate's in-person version of hanging up when she's done talking," I said.

"You ready to go?" Larry asked. "Shall I follow you?"

"Sure, but when we get to the rental place, drive past it and park a half-block away. We'll walk to your car after I finish all the paperwork. Just in case."

Spike waited outside the office while Palace Guard and I went inside. When I opened the door, the office smelled stale. The overweight clerk glanced up from his cell phone, yawned, and resumed scrolling on his phone.

"I'm returning a car." I placed the key and the paperwork on the counter.

He squinted at his phone. "I need the keys, contract, and mileage."

"Right here on the counter. What was your name again?" I stood on my tiptoes and leaned on the counter to see his nametag.

"Albert." He didn't look up.

"Nice to meet you, Albert. I'm Margaret. They call me Peggy. I need a receipt. Have you worked here very long? Do you like it?" I craned to see his cell phone screen. "What game is that? Are you any good?"

"Yeah, I guess." He pushed himself to his feet and shuffled to the counter. He squinted at the paperwork. "Everything here?"

"Sure is. I filled the tank and marked it on the sheet."

"Right." He typed on the computer keyboard at the counter and ambled to the printer. He brought me the receipt, and I read it with care.

"Everything's here. Appreciate your help. You need anything else from me?"

"Nope. Uh. No, ma'am."

When I reached the door, I glanced back. Albert had returned to his seat and his game. Only one other car was in the parking lot besides the one I just returned. "That your car? It's nice."

"Naw. It's my mom's. She lets me drive it to work sometimes."

"Good luck with your game."

As the three of us walked down the street, I said, "Did you notice the security cameras? I'm glad Larry didn't park in their lot."

"How'd it go?" Larry asked as I climbed into his car.

"Turned in. Security cameras, but the only car was the clerk's."

"Kate arranged for another rental in Texas City. It's about forty-five minutes away."

On our way to the new rental, I gazed at the passing scenery. "Flat land and sand. Lucy would love it here. She hates grass. Must tickle her feet."

Larry snorted. "Max used to snack on fescue grass. Only fescue. My dad said Max was a vegetarian at heart."

"I didn't know you had a dog."

"Max died two years ago. You'd have loved him. He was a black German shepherd and was at the top of his class in K-9 school before he was mine, but he washed out. Max focused on his work unless a child was nearby then he'd break concentration and run to greet a kid. Kids were never afraid of him because he was so gentle in his approach."

"Lucy scrunches down when she sees little kids." I smiled. "Glenn says she thinks she's the same size they are."

"I've seen her do that." Larry exited the interstate and pointed to the right. "If we'd gone the other way, we'd have gone to the Port of Galveston Cruise Terminal. Excellent restaurants, I hear."

"Shouldn't be too hard, but first I'd have to learn to cook seafood."

"No, another chef would cook. I meant we might want to eat there later," Larry said. "Anyway, my dad was Max's trainer. He said it was funny to watch him rip into an aggressor then trot to the fence when an elementary class showed up for a field trip. Dad encouraged me to adopt what he called the soft-hearted dropout. He said Max was the right dog to keep me out of trouble."

Larry pointed to two pelicans as they soared overhead then swooped low on the water.

"Graceful birds. Max went to class with me when I was in college and sometimes to work with me, unofficially, after I was out of rookie school. Parker was a great boss. He'd always look the other way."

My eyes filled. *Parker should be here.* Palace Guard patted my arm, and I relaxed.

Larry stared at me. "Why can't I see Spike or Palace Guard?"

"You aren't immature enough. At least, that's the theory Kate and I came up with." I smiled. "One time she threatened to leave me on the side of the road because I told her she wasn't immature enough to see Spike."

Larry threw back his head and laughed. "I can see Kate doing that. The two of you are intensely competitive. At least now I have a goal: be as immature as you and Kate."

Spike and Palace Guard high-fived.

"What do the guys say?" he asked.

"They approve."

Spike waved his arms in the back seat as a seated version of his wacky dance. I snorted.

"What?"

"Spike offered to teach you his wacky dance."

"Dang, I miss out on everything." Larry pulled into the rental lot in front of the office. "Wait here. Kate said I'm supposed to rent the car, and you take mine."

I moved to the driver's seat. When Larry entered the office, a young woman with bright yellow curly hair had her back to the door. When she turned her head, her bored expression transformed to a toothy smile. Spike was in the passenger's seat, and he narrowed his eyes as he peered at the office.

The clerk reached the counter at the same time as Larry. She fluttered her eyelashes and brushed her hair behind her ear.

"She's acting strange. Do you suppose she has a tic?"

Spike stared at me and shook his head.

After Larry signed the forms she placed on the counter, the clerk grabbed keys off the board behind her and handed them to Larry. She didn't release the keys, and when Larry tugged, she threw her head back in a hearty laugh before she pulled back her hand.

As Larry left, she continued talking to him. He shook his head and strode to a blue SUV. He pulled out the vehicle and waved for me, and I followed him to the highway.

"Do you suppose she thought she knew him?" I asked.

Spike shook his head.

When we reached the apartment, I parked next to Larry's new vehicle.

"Want to try a restaurant near the Galveston Port?" he asked.

"No, I have to update the customers on my diner database and do more research."

Larry opened my car door and offered me a hand. I frowned and climbed out. *What's wrong with him?*

Larry crossed his arms. "It's important to eat."

I lifted an eyebrow. "I will. Thanks."

"Who's with you? Palace Guard? Spike?"

"Spike. Why?"

"Spike, talk to her." Larry stomped to his car and drove away.

"Can you talk to me?" I unlocked the apartment door.

Spike rolled his eyes.

"I know, right? Larry's acting strange."

Spike raised his eyebrows and shook his head.

After two hours on the computer, I was ready to take Larry's advice and grilled my cheese sandwich to perfection then cut it into four equal portions. After I sat at the table, I pulled away the crust of one section and popped it into my mouth. Spike's eyes widened.

"Mother said I used to call the crusts *sandwich bones*. She claimed only a spy would call crusts bones. It always surprised me when she understood my spy-ness."

I sipped my beer. "This is Larry's favorite beer. It's cold. Larry's funny sometimes." Spike lifted an imaginary bottle, and we toasted Larry.I carried my plate to my computer to finish my sandwich. "One more search." At midnight, I rubbed my eyes and turned off my computer.

Spike and I arrived at the diner on Monday morning fifteen minutes before eight. When I went inside, Irene sat at the chopping table with her hands in her lap. Her eyes widened. "I had planned to let you do all the work today. What happened to you?"

"Little mishap on my beach run Saturday. My sling is my arm warmer for at least three weeks."

Irene shook her head. "That's too bad. I can do the work if you'll ask questions. You're in charge."

Rosa strode into the kitchen. "What was that, old woman? You want to say that again? I'm not sure I heard you right."

Irene shook her finger. "You're lucky I'm not in charge, Pie Girl. I would fire you on the spot."

Rosa grinned and rolled out her dough. "Sorry about your arm, Maggie. You sure you feel up to working today?"

"Thanks, Rosa. I'll be fine."

"Tell me, Gray Lady, what's our plan for today?" Irene asked.

"Today is chicken fried steak with gravy, mashed potatoes, and green beans. Steak prep then potatoes. Let me know if I miss anything."

"My best skill. Being a bossy busybody." Irene's eyes twinkled.

A little after twelve, Rosa rushed into the kitchen. "Need you out front, Ms. Irene. Mona lost her job, and she's inconsolable."

"What? She's worked there over fifteen years. They gave her the Employee of the Year award last month. What's wrong with those yahoos?" Irene stormed out of the kitchen.

After a half hour, Irene returned. "Might have been a misunderstanding. Somebody from payroll told Mona she wasn't on the payroll after this month. She plans to talk to her supervisor this afternoon. When I offered to go along with her to smooth things over, the entire place laughed. Buncha clowns. Mona will text me later."

After the last group of customers left, I helped clean, and Rosa and Irene prepped for the next day. "Good work, you two," Irene said. "See you tomorrow."

"Irene, do you have a few minutes?"

"See you." Rosa waved as she left.

"So what's up, Gray Lady?"

"I'd be okay if you want to bring in someone else to fill in for Diane to free you up."

Irene flopped onto a stool. "Should have thought of it myself. Suppose you could manage the kitchen? One of my brother's former coworkers has a son who is a bang-up cook, and Chip has helped me before. Tell him the day's special, and he'll take it from there. People underestimate his talents because he's different." She rubbed her forehead. "I've got too much going on."

I nodded, and Irene stared at the floor then turned her gaze to me.

"My baby brother died two years ago. The cops gave up on finding his murderer, but I haven't. He was a porter for a cruise ship. Nothing fancy or important enough for anyone to kill him. He was a good-looking guy and a hard worker despite what my dad thought about him, but all he did was load and unload luggage for the passengers and supplies to run the ship."

She rose and left the kitchen. When she returned, she said, "Checked the front door. Rosa locked up. She's smart too, but sometimes I feel like she's hiding something or hiding from somebody."

Not much gets past Irene.

Irene narrowed her eyes. "I always wondered why anyone would kill a porter, and I got a lead last month. Good hard evidence but no sense in taking it to the cops. They quit working his case six months after he died. Somebody got paid off."

When I arrived at the diner at seven the next morning, the kitchen was dark, but the front was bright. I flipped on the lights, and Rosa appeared in the doorway to the dining area. "You need me to do anything?"

"Today's special is meatloaf, mashed potatoes, and green beans. Basic. I can handle mixing the meatloaf since you and Irene cut up onions and celery yesterday."

Rosa washed her hands and nodded. "Diane's Diner is a time machine where our customers enjoy the home-cooked meals just like mama made when they were growing up. Or how they remember mama's cooking."

Irene opened the back door. A man in his mid-thirties followed her. A maverick cowlick stood straight up at his crown and accented his straight brown hair. His round face, flat forehead, and almond-shaped eyes suggested Down Syndrome. He wore a red and black Bulldogs T-shirt, khaki pants, and white tennis shoes.

"Chip, this is the Gray Lady, and you remember Ms. Rosa?"

"Hello, Ms. Rosa." He waved. "Nice to meetcha, Ms. Gray Lady." He held out his hand, and we shook.

"Nice to meet you too, Chip. Ms. Irene said I should tell you today's special. It's meatloaf, mashed potatoes, and green beans."

"Thank you, Ms. Gray Lady." Chip washed his hands, put on an apron, and laid out knives and utensils in a neat row before he gathered the meatloaf ingredients.

"Come into the office," Irene said, and I followed her. She pointed to a card pinned to the bulletin board. "That's Walt's number. He's Chip's father. Chip walks back and forth to work, but Chip will ask you to call Walt if it's raining hard."

"Thanks, Irene. Anything else I can help you with?"

Irene pursed her lips and stared at the floor. "Can you help with some research? The computer stuff befuddles me."

"I'm free this afternoon."

"If I can pull my notes together, I'll bring them by later."

Before we finished cleaning the diner at the end of our day, Irene came in the front door. "Heard nothing from y'all all day. Needed to check whether you'd burned my place down."

When Chip's face blanched, Rosa said, "Ms. Irene made a joke. I'll tease her back. Is that okay?"

"Yes." Chip grinned.

Rosa crossed her arms and scowled. "If that's what you want done, you need to put it on the Gray Lady's list. I just do pies, and Chip's too busy."

Irene slapped her thigh and guffawed. "I can count on you, Rosa, to make me laugh."

Chip laughed. "That was funny, Ms. Rosa." He hung up his apron. "We're done, right, Ms. Gray Lady? I can go home now?"

"Yes, we're done. Thank you, Chip. You're an amazing cook."

After Chip left, Irene sat on the stool at the prepping table. "Mona and I will see a lawyer tomorrow. Some unknown so-and-so accused her of embezzlement. It's a mess. Glad I've got you two here so I can straighten out the rest of the world."

Irene stormed out, and Rosa shook her head. "Never a dull moment. See you tomorrow."

The next morning, Irene was in the office when I arrived. I unloaded the dishwasher, and the back door slammed when Chip and Rosa came in five minutes later. Irene rushed out of the office. "What was that?"

"Sorry. Wind caught the door," Rosa said. "Thought you planned to take today off, Irene.".

"I got a call from Mona's sister last night. Mona's missing." Irene slumped against the door. "The whole family is frantic. Thought I'd kind of hang out today to see if anyone says anything at lunchtime."

"I'm sorry to hear about Mona, Irene," I said. "Chip, today's special is chicken livers with grilled onions, mashed potatoes, and greens."

"Thank you, Ms. Gray Lady." Chip hurried to put on his apron.

"I'll make cornbread," Rosa said. "What kind of pie do you want today, Chip?"

"Chocolate," he answered.

Irene elbowed me. "Anytime you want Rosa to make chocolate pie, ask Chip to decide. That man loves his chocolate pie. Don't you, Chip?"

"Yes, ma'am." Chip laid out his knives, opened the cooler, and pulled out chicken livers and milk.

"Nothing better than chicken livers. Let's get cracking." Irene clapped her hands.

"Milk? And eggs too? Like a batter?" I asked.

Irene laughed. "Chip soaks the livers in milk. Forgot you were literal. *Get cracking* means *get busy*."

I frowned. *Then why not say get busy?*

"Sometimes people spice up their language. Can you imagine gravy without that bit of cayenne pepper you like to add?" Rosa said.

"*Get cracking*. Got it," I said.

"The milk helps mellow the flavor. He'll peel and cut up potatoes while the livers soak," Irene said.

A little after one, a shrill voice from the diner interrupted the routine buzz of activity in the kitchen. "That embezzler ran off because she got caught."

I peered out the order window in time to witness the scuffle. Irene swung at a woman at least six inches taller and thirty years younger than she was. Rosa grabbed Irene's arm inches from the woman's nose. Rosa glanced at me and raised her eyebrows. When she shrugged her shoulders, I covered my mouth to stifle my giggle.

"Better skedaddle out of here, Veronica, before I get arrested for smashing your ugly face." Irene growled and tugged to get away from Rosa.

Veronica shouted, "You wish!" and stomped out of the diner.

"Didn't see a thing." The man slid onto a stool at the counter and winked at me. He was one of our regulars, but the only customer who drove a red truck. The rest of the customers nodded in agreement.

"What? Are you all blind fools? I would have rearranged her mug, except for this interfering Pie Girl." Irene stomped to the kitchen. The back door slammed with a bang, and everyone applauded.

Rosa and I strolled to the kitchen. "Nice drama," she said.

"I thought so."

At the end of our shift, Chip left, and Rosa said, "See you tomorrow, Gray Lady."

At three-thirty, Larry showed up at my apartment and set a white sack on the kitchen table. He took a brown shopping bag to the guest bedroom. "Thought you might like an afternoon snack and a break from your computer. You haven't moved since you got home, have you? I picked up scones."

I stretched my back and rolled my shoulders. "You have great timing. I need a break. Maybe the beach?"

After we ate our scones, I put our plates in the dishwasher. "Did you start your new assignment?"

"Let's go for a jog on the beach, and I'll tell you about it." Larry grinned and held up his backpack. "I brought running clothes."

"Don't have to ask me twice."

Larry rushed to the bathroom to change. I threw on my running shoes, shirt, and shorts, and when I came out of my bedroom, Palace Guard wore his usual running gear. Spike sported a sleeveless muscle shirt and a Hawaiian-print pair of shorts.

"All set. Where are the guys?"

Palace Guard and Spike had stepped next to Larry. Spike grinned and shook his head. Palace Guard glared.

"On the sofa. They're hanging back." I bit my lip and headed to the door.

"Ha!" Larry said. "You're lying."

"Am not." I growled.

"Oh yes, you are." Larry swaggered to the door and waved to the refrigerator. "Bye, guys."

"You're still wrong," I said.

"Am not." Larry grinned and stepped out on the porch. "Are you coming?"

Palace Guard held up his finger and blew on it. I stomped to the curb and jogged with slow, cautious steps to avoid jostling my arm in the sling.

"You doing okay? Should we walk?" Larry jogged alongside me.

"I'm holding my arm tight against me to splint it. Seems to work." I increased my pace. Larry passed me, and Palace Guard jogged behind me. I glanced back, and

Spike waved from the front door. I sped up to catch Larry.

On the way to the beach, Larry slowed and ran next to me. "You said Kate sees Spike. Why doesn't she see Palace Guard?"

"We don't know. Sometimes people feel it when Palace Guard or Spike touches them, but I can't explain that either." I asked over my shoulder. "Any theories?"

Palace Guard shook his head.

Larry glanced down. "You've got red running shoes."

I stared at my feet. "Seemed like the thing to do."

When I neared the first dune at the beach, I sprinted ahead of Larry. Palace Guard raced to my right and pushed me with both hands to the left.

CHAPTER FOUR

I stumbled, threw my left foot forward, and caught my balance before I hit the ground. "What is wrong with you?"

"Are you okay?" Larry called out.

I turned to scold Palace Guard and froze. Palace Guard pointed to the rattlesnake as it slid away.

"Palace Guard just kept me from stepping on a diamondback. I'm a little rattled." My voice cracked, and I was close to hyperventilating. When Palace Guard held out his hands with palms down and lowered his hands, I inhaled and snorted an exhale. "I just realized what I said."

Palace Guard jogged down the beach.

"Palace Guard's on the move. Break's over."

"Wait up," Larry said.

When I got close to Palace Guard, he took off.

"We're racing. Palace Guard started it. Gotta catch up."

After two miles, we circled back, and Larry came into view. I slowed to a jog, and Palace Guard swerved over the dunes to the street.

"Where's Palace Guard going?" Larry asked.

My eyes widened. "You see him?"

"You stared at the street." Larry grinned and jogged along with me.

I shrugged and picked up the pace. After a few yards, I realized why Palace Guard went to the road. "Dang. Palace Guard is racing me. See you at the apartment." I bolted down the beach and left Larry behind.

When I was a half block from the apartment, I slowed my pace and focused on a silent run. I circled around to the parking lot's back entry. Spike stood at the base of the stairs, and Palace Guard faced the entrance. His back was to me, and I lowered my head and ran at him with every ounce of speed I had. As I crashed into his back and knocked him down, Larry jogged down the street. I couldn't slow my momentum and slammed Larry to the ground then landed on top of him. Spike danced. Palace Guard and I rolled to a sitting position on the ground, and I laughed with tears streaking down my cheeks.

Larry rose and dusted himself off. "I will take my miniscule amount of remaining dignity and wait for you at the stairs while you compose yourself."

I strolled to the steps with my head down.

Larry cleared his throat. "The only reason you are hanging your head is to keep from laughing. You'd think I'd learn not to ask, but what happened?"

"I sneaked around to the other side of the parking lot and ambushed Palace Guard. It was awesome. Couldn't stop. Sorry."

"You sure can run fast. You know that, right?" We all headed to the apartment.

On the way, my phone rang. *Mother.*

"Margaret, you're famous. You were on last night's late news. I didn't see it, but my friends did and called me. Everyone is so excited the Gray Lady is back. Is that the big secret Big D. wouldn't tell me? Wait until I tell Mister Smarty Pants Sergeant Duane Arrington I figured it out. Francine said the TV reran the on-scene stories from your library disaster and talked about how the Gray Lady survived the explosion. The big news is the Gray Lady is the new cook at Diane's Diner in Galveston. I need to find you some gray chef clothes, don't I?"

Mother hung up. I rubbed my forehead. *Who's Francine?*

"Mother said the Gray Lady was in the local news last night in Georgia. She said nothing about Ernie. If Mother doesn't know, then nobody knows."

After we reached the door, Larry's phone rang. He frowned and stayed outside while we went inside. When Larry came in, I poured two glasses of iced tea, and we sat at the table.

"That was Detective Ross. Moe," he said. "The newspaper published an article about the local celebrity, Gray Lady, who was a librarian and is now a world-renowned chef. The media jumped all over it. Moe says this was not part of the plan. The Gray Lady's assignment was to blend in and listen, not become a star. He's got a call in to Kate."

"Kate will tell him to handle it. You want a sandwich?"

"Yes, I'd like a sandwich. Then I think I'll go update my resume."

I pulled out the fixings for ham and swiss sandwiches. "Will you apply for a promotion? Maybe you could take over for Moe."

"I forgot how literal you are." Larry refilled our tea glasses. "It was a joke. Someone pretends the boss fired them, and they need a new job."

I frowned. "How is that funny?"

"It's sarcasm. If you think it's funny, it is. If you don't, it isn't. Sarcasm isn't funny to people who are literal. But I like your idea of applying for a promotion. Not a joke."

"Good." I set our plates on the table. I had cut both sandwiches into equal triangle halves.

Larry examined his sandwich. "Nice triangles. Not sarcasm."

I took a bite of my sandwich. "Maybe tell me when something is sarcasm then I'll know there's a joke."

Spike shook his head and patted Larry on the shoulder.

I frowned at Spike, and he grinned.

"Thanks, Spike," Larry mumbled. Palace Guard and I stared at Larry.

After we ate, Larry snatched up my plate and placed our dishes in the dishwasher. "Thanks for supper. I have a meeting tomorrow morning."

When I walked into the diner, Rosa rolled out pie dough while Irene peeled potatoes. Chip checked his roasting chickens in the ovens, and aromatic herbs swirled throughout the kitchen.

"What's up? I'm not late, am I?"

"Diane's thinking about coming home early. I couldn't wait to tell you, Chip, and Rosa, but when I got here, I had to do something. Hope that's okay, boss." Irene grinned.

"That's great news. Will you celebrate with a new recipe? Did I just do sarcasm?" I raised my eyebrows and crossed my fingers.

Rosa and Irene laughed. "It was a great joke," Rosa said.

"Y'all have the chicken pot pie situation under control." Irene put her hands on her hips. "I haven't heard from Diane since yesterday. I need to check on her. She shows up unannounced as a surprise sometimes."

At noon, Rosa dropped off four tickets. She had left her cell on the ledge of the order window, and it buzzed and danced to the edge. She caught her phone with the grace of a major league outfielder before it hit the floor.

"Diane? Irene left before eleven. She said she'd call you." Rosa craned to peek out front. "Her car's gone. Maybe she had errands to run."

Rosa frowned. "Diane hasn't heard from Irene."

I called Irene's phone, and when it rang around to voicemail, I left a message. "Checking up on you. Call us."

Rosa stood in the kitchen doorway, put two fingers in her mouth, and whistled a piercing trill. I peered through the order window, and the customers' shocked faces turned to Rosa.

"Anybody see Irene leave?" Rosa asked in a commanding voice.

A man in the booth next to the door frowned and cleared his throat. "When I opened the door, Irene almost knocked me down. She was on her phone, and I don't think she saw me. She tore out of here like she'd robbed the place."

The diner buzz of conversations resumed with speculation about where Irene had gone in such a hurry.

"Sounds like something came up. What do you think, Gray Lady?" Rosa asked when she returned to the kitchen.

"I don't disagree, but I could call the hospital to see if Irene's in the emergency department."

While I was on hold, Rosa's phone rang again. After Rosa answered, she frowned then hung up. "Diane said Irene called and claimed something unexpected came up; she had to see a friend."

I set my phone on the counter. "Maybe Irene will explain later. Will we tell the customers?"

"Yep. Won't take long if we double-team them. Grab a coffee pot and start with the counter."

I chattered as I poured coffee down the line of customers at the counter. "Diane heard from Irene. Irene-type business must have slowed her down. You know Irene."

I met Rosa in the middle of the diner. Both of our coffee pots were empty, and we hurried back to the kitchen.

Rosa leaned against the chopping table and smiled. "Well done. We're a good team."

"We'll interrogate Ms. Irene tomorrow, right?" I asked.

"Oh yes." Rosa dumped grounds to make more coffee.

After I got home, I updated my diner customer database with the day's four new customers and searched for more information on Irene's brother. The deepening shadows of the ending day had crept up on me. I poured a glass of sweet tea and stepped out on my balcony to enjoy the orange sky as it faded to the deeper tones of dusk.

Palace Guard held up a finger and blew, and the three of us trooped to the front door as Larry pulled into the parking lot.

Larry bounded up the stairs. "I sure can't sneak up on you." He peered over my head at the kitchen and sniffed. "Good. Nothing cooking. I've got a restaurant recommendation for us to try. It's near the port, and a cruise ship departs this evening."

"I can't..."

Palace Guard scowled, and Spike shook his fist.

I cleared my throat. "Think of anything better. Let's go."

Larry beamed and turned toward the door, and I stuck out my tongue at the two imaginary men.

On our way to the restaurant, I said, "I suppose you can't talk about your assigned case."

"It's not a big secret. The local papers plan to highlight the reopened case. What do you know about Irene's brother?"

"Irene told me he was a porter on cruise ships, a hard worker, and good-looking. She's convinced the police quit too soon in the search to find his murderer."

Larry pulled into the full parking lot. He cruised past the rows of cars to an empty spot in front of the restaurant.

My eyes widened. "How did you do that?"

"You see imaginary men. I see vacant parking spaces."

I bit my lip. "We both see nothing."

Larry chuckled. "That was funny. Where do your ideas for your snappy comebacks come from?"

I raised an eyebrow and my chin. Larry stared at me. *My mysterious look needs work.*

The lobby was full. The hostess brushed past me and grinned at Larry. "Do you have a dinner reservation, handsome?"

He frowned. "No."

"Well, doesn't matter." She giggled and fluttered her eyelashes. "Because you don't need one."

A few of the seated folks chuckled, and she nodded and smiled at her audience. "What's your phone number? I mean, your name?"

A woman with short white hair and wire-rimmed glasses stepped up behind us and cleared her throat. I glanced at her as she elbowed the man next to her. She was older than Mother and overweight and had swollen ankles.

Larry moved closer to me and put his arm around my shoulders.

"Our name is Bond," he said.

"First name?"

I narrowed my eyes and growled. "Em."

"Oh." The hostess bustled off, and the woman leaned forward. "Way to go, girl."

"Might not be a table for us, but it was worth it, Em." Larry chuckled.

"Care to join us?" Our new friend asked. "We have reservations, don't we, dear?"

Larry turned to me, and I shrugged.

He said, "That's very kind..."

"Don't say no," the man said. "After thirty-seven years, I've learned I'll never hear the end." His brown eyes twinkled behind his tortoise shell-framed bifocals. His gray hair was thinning, but his brown and gray mustache was thick.

"We'd love to," I added.

When the hostess returned, the man spoke to her and lifted the leather flap on the ID he had pulled out of his jacket's top inside pocket. After the four of us sat at a table next to a window overlooking the water, our server brought us menus.

Our new friend smiled. "I'm Ellen, and this is Jay. What's your other name, Em?"

"Maggie," I smiled, "and this is Larry."

"Em suits you, Mags." Larry chuckled.

Ellen and I ordered.

"What force are you with, Larry?" Jay asked.

"Harperville, Georgia, sir, but I'm on loan to Galveston."

"You got assigned the cold case?"

Ellen elbowed Jay and tapped his menu. "I'll get the usual." He folded his menu and handed it to the server.

Larry folded his menu. "Same for me. Yes, sir. Are you active or retired?"

"Retired, but still active. You let me know if you need any help."

"Maggie, they are never off duty, are they? What about you?" Ellen asked.

"I take care of the books and ordering at Diane's Diner and cook when I'm not injured."

"Small world," Ellen said. "Irene's an old friend of mine. It's nice you can help her out with Diane out of town. Is Chip cooking? He's a great chef, but he's particular and won't work with just anybody."

"Chip's there. He's amazing."

When the server brought our food, my eyes widened at the amount of fried shrimp piled on my plate.

"Looks delicious, but I'll never eat all this," I said.

Ellen chuckled. "I always say I won't eat as many hush puppies so I can eat all my fish, but I never do."

Larry and Jay talked shop between bites.

"It's what they do. Don't pay them any mind." Ellen flipped her hand toward the two men. "I hear Irene's got something going on. Nobody knows what, except it has something to do with her brother. I think an old friend of hers is helping her."

When the server brought us more hush puppies, I groaned. "I can't pass them up. I see what you mean, Ellen."

"They are scrumptious, aren't they?" She passed the basket to Jay and winked. "The basket may be empty when it's returned to us. It's my technique for cutting back. Do you know about Irene's brother? Everybody thought Paul was wonderful, but I never cared for him. Too slick for me. Jay said I have the nose of a cop. Don't look it, do I?" She narrowed her eyes. "Neither do you."

"We'd be good at undercover, wouldn't we?"

Ellen smiled, and her eyes twinkled. "The best. Emmy and Ellen Undercover Agency. Except I need a more exotic name. Em and Elise or Emelise Undercover Agency. Has a nice ring, don't you think?" She patted my hand, and we giggled. "In all seriousness, Maggie, you call or text me if you need anything." She reached into her purse and pulled out a card. She drew an "X" across the printed information on the front and scribbled on the back. "All my friends have business cards. I recycle. Here's my number. You never know when you might need an undercover friend."

After we said our goodbyes, Larry and I strolled to the port observation point. "Thanks for going to dinner with me, Maggie. Jay didn't work on the Reynolds case, but he knew the lead detective and had some insights."

"I needed the break and didn't know it. Thank you."

I stopped and stared at the glistening lights that bounced off the water and listened to the soft sound of the lapping waves. "Did Jay's voice sound familiar to you?"

"Not really. Kind of average. What about you?"

I shrugged. "You're right. Average. I wish I could think of a way to ask Irene about Gary."

"One technique is the direct approach," Larry said. "Something like, *Irene, do you know my father, Gary Sloan?*"

"You just gave me a great idea. Thanks, Larry."

"You're welcome. What did I say?"

I squinted at the rows of brilliant dots on the ocean liner. "The ship is much larger than I imagined, and I didn't expect so many lights. It's beautiful." The vessel eased its way to the open water.

"When I was a kid, my science teacher said ballast keeps ships afloat, and I envisioned big balloons tied to the sides of the ships," Larry said.

"What type of data goes into calculating the ballast and stability requirements for a ship?"

"I smell a new Maggie research project," Larry said.

I stared at the ship's rolling wake. *What about pirate ships?*

Larry touched my elbow. "Ready to head back?"

As we strolled back to the car, I said, "I'd go on a cruise if Lucy could go."

"No grass for her to roll in." Larry said. "I don't think she'd like it."

"You're right."

"Finally." Larry opened the passenger door for me.

I rolled my window part way down for the fresh air. "Anybody talk about Irene's brother?"

"Good guy. Everybody loved him. Sounded like a saint," Larry said.

"Ellen said he was too slick, and she didn't care for him. I guess she was in the minority. Except Irene hinted there might have been a problem between her dad and her brother."

"That's interesting." Larry parked and turned off the engine. "I don't suppose Ellen or Irene said anything specific."

"No, but Ellen said I could call her if I ever needed anything. Maybe she had something in mind." Larry matched my steps to the stairs, and I paused. "I have work to do."

"After you are inside with your door locked, I'll leave."

After I secured the door, I searched *ballast, ships, buoyancy,* and *pirates* which led to *smugglers* before I lumbered to bed at one in the morning. *Fascinating reading.*

The blaze of lights from the nearby refineries and chemical plants lit up the dark, early morning sky on my way to work. The diner lights gleamed their welcoming beacon; I parked next to Rosa's old car in the employee lot. When I stepped into the kitchen, Chip was feeding cabbage into the food processor, and Rosa was rolling out pie dough.

"Ms. Irene called early this morning and said she might not be in." Rosa brushed a stray lock of hair off her forehead with the back of her wrist.

Chip turned off the food processor and dumped the chopped cabbage into a bowl. "Ms. Irene's sick."

"That's what Chip and I think." Rosa draped the pie crust over the top of the apples and trimmed the excess.

Chip added more cabbage to the processor, and the din filled the kitchen. I made coffee and unloaded the dishwasher.

Gus opened the back door. "Got yer fish here. Hey, Chip. Congratulations on your promotion to head chef." Gus rolled the crates of fish into the walk-in and loaded last week's empty crates onto his dolly. "You call me if you need more fish. Hope Irene feels better."

Rosa narrowed her eyes after Gus left. "Why did he think Irene's sick?"

"Ms. Irene's car isn't here," Chip said.

"I suppose," Rosa said.

Rosa is as suspicious as I am.

After Chip rinsed and patted the fish dry, he slit a fish's belly and skinned and deboned the fish with the deft, fluid strokes of an artist. My concentration broke when Rosa cleared her throat.

"Hate to interrupt your fish infatuation, Gray Lady, but Irene just called. She's on her way in. Guess I was wrong. You can gloat now, if you like." Rosa wiggled her eyebrows, and I snorted.

"When I cut up a fish, it's butchered. When Chip cuts up a fish, it's a masterpiece. No gloats from me."

Rosa nodded. "Now you know why I stick to pies."

"I'm doubting my coffee skills." I squinted at the coffeepot. "Wonder if it's too weak? Or too strong?"

"Our customers would tell you." Rosa waved her pastry knife toward the front. "They love to gloat."

Irene bustled into the kitchen. "I've got good news. Diane will be home Sunday. And more news for you, Chip. Diane would like you to stay on. She's letting me and Gray Lady off the hook, and she'll take over the books and ordering."

"I like to cook," Chip stirred hot sauce into a bowl of buttermilk and dropped the eight-ounce portions into the mixture.

"You never told me about the hot sauce, Irene," I said.

Irene stared at the bowl. "I didn't know about it. That's genius, Chip."

"Yes, ma'am." Chip slid the last piece of fish into the bowl and cleaned his workstation.

The back door swung open, and Kate strolled in. "Heard about your little mishap, Gray Lady. Diane says tomorrow's your last day here. Want to celebrate this evening? Potato salad and steak? I'll make the potato salad, and you can grill the steak. The apartment complex has two community charcoal grills. Thought we could have a little party." Kate glanced at Rosa.

"Sounds great. Rosa, Irene, Chip, would y'all like to celebrate with us?" I asked.

"Can't," Irene said. "I've got things to do. Need to get ready for Diane's homecoming."

"I don't walk after dark," Chip said. "I like potato salad."

"You can ride with me," Rosa said. "I like potato salad too."

"We're set then. Six o'clock at Gray Lady's apartment." Kate scribbled on her notepad and tore off the sheet. "Here ya go, Rosa. This is the address."

Kate paused before she left. "I already invited Larry."

After Kate left, Irene said, "If nobody needs my help, I'm leaving too. Lots to do."

Rosa rolled out another pie crust, and I picked up a packet of napkins. Before I left the kitchen, Chip said, "Ms. Irene has a boyfriend."

I halted, and Rosa asked, "What makes you say that?"

"I saw Ms. Irene with a man I don't know yesterday. They were in her car at the grocery store. Ms. Irene looked angry. People argue with their boyfriends when they're angry on TV."

"You're very observant, Chip," Rosa said.

"Yes, ma'am."

When I reached the apartment after work, Kate had parked her car in the shade. I parked next to her car and rushed up the stairs. Kate opened the door and held out a glass of iced tea with a napkin wrapped around it.

"Spike told you I was here." I gulped down half of my tea. "How did he do that?"

"Like this." Kate circled her hands like they were around someone's throat and squeezed. Palace Guard held his index fingers and thumbs pointed up. *Pow. Pow.*

"Ha. You're busted, Kate."

She put her hands on her hips. "Maybe Spike and Palace Guard do different ways."

Palace Guard stared at Kate, and I smirked. "I'll check out the community grill. I might want to clean it."

"Sit. We need to talk." She perched on the arm of the recliner.

I changed my direction at the seriousness of Kate's tone and sat on the sofa.

"Your hepatitis find was brilliant. The team is digging deeper. But something I can't tell you is a doctor treated Gary Sloan for an exposure to hepatitis B."

"Whoa. Not a scenario I'd considered." I shuddered.

"I know. Off the wall, but a department techie claimed she channeled her inner Maggie, and I believe her. Gary used the name *Ernie Parker* and saw a doctor in Houston not associated with his employer. And paid cash."

"Do we know the source of his exposure?"

"Gary claimed he got into a drunken fight in a bar that resulted in a dirty needle stick."

"Sounds lame." I narrowed my eyes.

"True, except it's the least suspicious way for a civilian exposure to hepatitis B."

"Do we have a copy of the medical records? There's something more."

"I can't approve that. However, my techie Maggie might have saved a copy in your mother's cloud for safekeeping. How do you enjoy being profiled?" Kate grinned as she rose. "I need to get back to my potato salad. Go check your grill."

Palace Guard accompanied me on my quest to find the grills. They were behind the apartment complex farthest from the road. One grill leaned against a dumpster, and a tenant had propped the other eight inches off the ground on cinder blocks.

I glanced at the disgusted look on Palace Guard's face. "This is awful. I can't cook here."

When we returned to the apartment, Kate was on her phone in the bathroom. She closed the door.

"Do you think Kate's been acting different?"

Spike fluttered his hands, and Palace Guard raised an eyebrow.

"I agree."

Kate frowned as she came out of the bathroom. "Did you find the grills? Were they okay?"

"The grills are nasty. We need to change our menu."

"My head's stuck on grilling: steaks, hot dogs, hamburgers, ribs. I can't think of anything else."

"What about baked ham and beans? And cobbler."

"That sounds good as long as Mom never knows we ate canned beans. My potato salad's mingling its flavors in the refrigerator. Shall we shop?"

After we parked, the four of us trooped into the store. "Spike and I will pick out berries for the cobbler and ice cream. You and Palace Guard can get the ham and beans." Kate strode away.

We met at the ten-items-or-less checkout aisle.

"You got blackberries." My mouth watered at the thought of Kate's famous blackberry cobbler.

"They aren't wild," Kate said, "but they're sweet."

"They're beautiful. Excellent idea, Kate."

On our way home, Kate said, "I need for you to find out how Irene knows Gary and if she knows anything else. Take advantage of who you are. You're the Gray Lady. You survived an explosion. You see imaginary men. Bad guys shot at you, and you shot back. You've put attackers out of commission. What else?"

"I can run fast; I like to cook; I'm an excellent librarian; I love our dog, and I'm not wired like everyone else."

"You're getting it. Making sense?"

"Yes. I've got an idea."

CHAPTER FIVE

"Knew you would. You always do." Kate parked the car at the apartment. "Let's go cook."

At five o'clock, a knock at the door interrupted our cooking concentration. Spike blew on his finger.

Kate frowned. "I'm guessing, is it Larry?" Spike held his thumbs up.

"Ha. Nailed it."

I opened the door, and Larry waved at the sofa as he carried a large grocery bag to the refrigerator. "Hi, guys."

Kate stared at Larry. "Spike's over by the stove."

"I knew that." Larry opened the refrigerator and put the beer he'd brought on a shelf.

"It's our favorite beer, cuz." He pursed his lips.

"Yep. Cold." I snickered, and Larry beamed.

"What is that? A family joke? I don't get it." Kate brushed her hair off her forehead.

"So, you admit you aren't immature?" I asked.

Kate lunged, and I sidestepped. "I'm playing my injured card."

"It was a ruse to get you to show your hand." Kate sniffed. "How do I get a beer?"

I pulled out three beers. "Say please?"

"May I please have a beer?" Larry asked. "And one for my friend here?"

"Well done, Larry." Kate snatched a beer out of my hand and saluted Larry with the bottle. "You have a future in hostage negotiations, and I'm not kidding. You're a natural."

"Sounds boring," Larry mumbled. Spike feinted a left then followed with a right. He stopped inches from Larry's jaw.

I snickered and handed Larry a beer. "You're not boring."

"Spike did something, didn't he?" Larry took a swig of his beer.

"Spike think's you're a fighter," Kate said.

"Thanks, Spike."

"Can we change the subject?" Kate flopped onto the sofa. "Maggie, your impromptu get-together is a perfect cover. I need to talk to Rosa and Larry. No one can link Rosa to me. Not to sound dramatic, but it would be fatal for her."

"That sounded dramatic, Kate." I sipped my beer. "My favorite, cuz."

"Sure. I know. Cold," Kate said.

When Rosa and Chip arrived, I introduced Chip to Larry. Rosa wiggled her eyebrows and winked at me.

I turned my back to Larry and Chip and stuck out my tongue at Rosa. She giggled.

After we crowded around my small dining table, Chip said, "Ms. Irene should have canceled her meeting to come here. She says there's always time to eat."

Larry passed the platter of ham to Chip. "You're right."

After we finished the potato salad and everyone refused another serving of ham, Chip and I cleared the table. "Y'all can leave the dishes to us," I said. "We don't need anybody in our way. Right, Chip?"

"Yes, Ms. Gray Lady."

"In that case, I'll put the cobbler in the oven on low and go for a walk," Kate said.

Rosa linked her arm through Larry's. "We'll go with you."

"Ready to walk to Houston to make room for cobbler?" Kate asked as they left.

"That was funny," Chip said. "Ms. Kate told a joke."

"Yes, she did."

Chip rinsed the dishes, and I loaded them into the dishwasher while he scrubbed the pans.

I sat at the table. "How do you know Ms. Irene went to a meeting?"

"She got into that man's car. That man she was angry with before."

"What did he look like?"

"He was old. Not old like Ms. Irene, but he had some gray hair. Here." Chip brushed his temple. "He had blue eyes. The first time I saw him, he smiled at me when he saw I was watching him. He smiled with his eyes. That's how come I know what color they are. And he saw me. Most people stare, but they don't see me. He did."

"Did he say anything to Ms. Irene about seeing you?"

"It was just between me and him, and I smiled back." Chip dried the pans. "Where do these go?"

"Left of the stove. Lower shelf. That sounds nice."

"It was."

"Let me show you a picture." When I found it, I gave Chip my phone. He peered at my mother's wedding photo from twenty-seven years ago. "Is this the man?" I asked.

"No. This is a young guy. The man is old."

"You're right. When the young man is old, will he look like the man?"

Chip squinted. "He might if he had more wrinkles, and his hair was gray."

A maybe.

Chip hung the dishtowel over the oven handle. "Let me look again."

I handed him my phone, and he strode to the window. "His eyes smile. He holds his head like the old man."

He set the phone on the table and placed a napkin at each place setting.

"Thanks Chip. You have amazing observation skills. I wanted to tell you again."

"Am I on your team now, Ms. Gray Lady?"

I met his intense gaze. "I trust you. Yes, you're on my team."

I dropped my phone into my pocket. "When you saw the man, did Ms. Irene notice you?"

"If she'd seen me, she'd have climbed out of the car and told me to go home. She says sometimes I forget how to get home."

"Do you? Forget the way home?"

"I did one time when I was six. Dad said Ms. Irene worries about me."

"That's nice, isn't it? People who worry about you care about you."

"Yes, ma'am."

I glanced at Spike, and he put his hand over his heart. *I miss Parker. He shouldn't have died.* Palace Guard patted my shoulder.

"Your dad worries about you."

"And the paramedic, Mr. Larry. He worries about you."

"How can you tell? I didn't know that."

"Dad says I'm very observant." Chip grinned, and I laughed. He held up his hand, and I gave it a good smack as the front door opened.

Rosa was first to come in. "We got trouble here, folks. Chip and the Gray Lady are high-fiving."

Chip stared at the ceiling, and I smirked.

"Tell us later?" Rosa asked. "How about some blackberry cobbler? I'm starved. These two walked my legs off."

"You set the pace, Rosa," Kate said. "We couldn't keep up."

"A slower pace burns more calories," Larry said. "You weren't faster than me; I was pre-burning cobbler calories."

Larry pulled out bowls and the ice cream, and Kate dished up blackberry cobbler. "You sounded like a regular Maggie there, Larry."

"Thank you," he said.

Rosa plopped large servings of ice cream on top of the cobbler, and Chip set the bowls of dessert with spoons on the table.

"Y'all are a regular dessert-serving machine." I scooped up hot cobbler and cold ice cream on my spoon, burned my tongue, and froze the roof of my mouth.

"Put your blistered tongue on the roof of your mouth. Did I get it right, Mags?" Larry asked.

"Yes, paramedic. You did."

"Another Maggie comment I don't understand," Kate said. "What is it my dad always says?"

"Just ignore them," Larry said.

"My turn to do dishes." Kate gathered up the empty bowls and spoons and placed them into the dishwasher.

"I have homework," Rosa said. "Okay if we leave now, Chip?"

"Yes, Ms. Rosa. Thank you for the ride."

After Rosa and Chip left, Larry shuffled his feet. "Guess I should..."

"Hold up," Kate said. "I need to talk to you and Crazy Lady. Rosa will disappear, Maggie. Her ex learned where she is and intended to pull her back into the relationship through coercion. We're worried he'll discover her assignment. He's close." Kate rubbed her forehead. "Let's sit. There's more."

Kate and I sat on the sofa, and Larry pulled a dining chair closer and straddled it.

"Larry's assigned to the cold case full time. The problem is we're shorthanded."

"Just like old times."

"You got that right. Just like old times, I'm being pulled away to another case. I want you to go home. You can't do this by yourself."

I narrowed my eyes. "I'm not by myself."

Kate rose and put her hands on her hips. Spike sat next to me and elbowed me when she glowered. I snickered.

"What's wrong with you two?" Kate growled. "Maggie's in danger. She needs to go home."

Spike mirrored her fierce face, and I snort-laughed.

"Kate." Larry had stepped close to the sofa. "Your face is fierce."

"Cut it out, Spike," Kate said. "You too, Larry. Y'all are ganging up on me."

She stormed to the door, sighed, and flopped back onto the sofa.

"Do I look like that?"

Spike nodded.

You think Maggie will be okay?"

Spike shook his head, and Kate laughed. "Fine. Maggie, Spike and I have reservations, but you can stay if you like. Just keep in touch."

"Yes," Larry said. "Keep in touch."

"One more thing before you go, Larry. Stay away from Maggie. You're law enforcement. There are rumblings someone's undercover. So far, Maggie's name hasn't come up. We need to keep it that way."

Larry's face reddened, and his eyes narrowed. "How do I keep her safe?"

"Simple." Kate strolled to the door and opened it. "Stay away."

Larry headed to the door, stopped, and faced the sofa. "Keep Maggie safe, guys."

Palace Guard saluted, and Spike nodded.

"See ya, Mags," Larry said.

After he left, Kate shook her head. "He took that harder than I expected. I'm staying tonight. I leave tomorrow afternoon. Ready for shooting after work?"

"That would be awesome. I need the practice."

The popping of sizzling bacon and the aroma of honeyed applewood woke me. *Smells like the cabin.* The melancholy hit me. *No Parker.*

As I dressed, Kate called from the kitchen. "You sleeping in? I can't eat all these cinnamon rolls by myself."

When I staggered into the kitchen, Kate handed me a cup of coffee. "About time. I thought I would have to make lunch instead of breakfast."

I plopped into my chair at the table, and Kate set my plate in front of me. I stared at my plate.

"Drink your coffee. It's hard to pick a fight with you before you're awake." Kate sat across from me.

After I drained my first cup of coffee, we dug in, and I asked, "Where do we meet after I get off work?"

"I'll meet you here."

"Breakfast was amazing." I set my fork on my half-finished plate, and it clinked.

"You're such a lightweight." Kate chuckled.

The gray low-hanging clouds bore a dreary message of impending rain. A tropical smell mingled with the stronger than usual fishy odor in the wind that blew off the water. White caps dotted the Gulf, and big groups of seagulls flew in tight circles high overhead as they rode the thermals while other seagulls soared low over the water and headed inland.

When I arrived at the diner, Irene glanced up from her pie dough. "Fried chicken today, Gray Lady. Chip is an expert at cutting up a chicken."

A slender woman who was a tall, young version of Irene came out of the office. Her curly brown hair peeked out from the small red paisley scarf tied on her head biker-style. "I feel like I already know you, Gray Lady. I'm Diane. I can't thank you enough for everything you've done." Diane hugged my left side. "You didn't need to come in today, but I appreciate that you're here."

"Where's Rosa?" I asked.

"She had a family emergency and had to leave town. Unexpected, but I told her we could manage. Thank goodness Mama's here to make the pies. Otherwise, we'd have a revolt on our hands. Rosa's pies are as good as Mama's."

Irene glanced up and shook her rolling pin. "Better, but none of them yahoos better tell me that."

I stared as Chip transformed each chicken into ten pieces with a rhythmic pace that appeared to be one smooth motion. Diane rinsed the backbones and necks and patted them with a paper towel.

""I liked your fried chicken recipe, Irene, but I didn't realize we started with whole chickens. You make it look easy, Chip."

"I'll show you in slow motion." Diane removed the legs and wings and separated the breast from the back. She handed me the breast and a cleaver. "Now quarter it."

I split and quartered the chicken. "It's hard with my left hand, but I love this cleaver," I said.

Irene cackled. "Only a natural-born cook or a serial killer would appreciate a fine cleaver."

At ten-thirty, Chip mixed the final bowl of potato salad, and Irene handed me a spoonful for a taste.

"This is awesome, Chip," I said.

Chip beamed as he carried the bowl to the walk-in cooler.

"Let's go into the office and plan our day." Diane refilled her cup of coffee on her way, and I grabbed a cup too.

The top of the office desk was clear except for the planner opened to the calendar for the month and a ballpoint nestled in the planner's crease. A large "X" marked all the days before today, and there were no other notations. Pinned and taped business cards and scribbled notes papered the walls. File folders and stacks of paper occupied the visitor's chair.

"Drop them on the floor next to the chair with the rest of the papers. I'll organize them sometime soon, but not today."

Diane removed the stack of papers from her office chair and added them to a stack of papers on the floor near the door. After we sat, she said, "Chip's got the preparation and cooking covered. He doesn't need any help. Mama can make pies and cover the cash register, but she can't wait on tables too. I thought if I waited on our customers, you could take care of the drink refills and making coffee and tea."

"That will work, and if you drop off the dishes by the sink, I can load and run the dishwasher."

"We can do this. Let's get busy."

While I made tea, Diane explained her plan to Irene and Chip then loaded the salt and pepper shakers onto a utility cart.

"Chip, do I put sugar into the hot tea, or do you make a simple syrup?" I asked.

"Sugar goes in hot tea."

Irene pointed to the wall above the tea machine. "Instructions right up there."

I stood on my tiptoes. "I don't see them. The machine blocks my view."

Irene chuckled. "Know what you mean. Diane has this whole kitchen set up for her tall self. She has no pity for her short mama. You can borrow my stepstool. It's by the back door."

"It's easier to do something when you can read the instructions."

"Very philosophical." Diane came into the kitchen. "What are y'all talking about?"

"Inconsiderate children," Irene said.

The edges of Chip's mouth drooped, and he side-glanced at Irene.

"She's joking," I said. "Sometimes people say teasing things to make someone they love laugh."

Diane smiled. "That's right. My mama's a big tease."

Irene waggled her head and mouthed with a sneer, "My mama's a big tease."

Chip stared at me, and I smiled. He grinned and put his head down to focus on his cooking.

A few customers drifted into the diner at eleven-thirty, but by noon, Diane hustled to drop off tickets, and I scrambled to refill coffee and deliver orders while the food was still hot.

By one, the rush was over, and Chip scrubbed pots and pans. Diane charged into the kitchen. "I need to do some table-hopping to check in with my regulars. Can you monitor refills?"

"Sure can." I filled a pitcher with iced tea. Before I reached the doorway, Irene rushed into the kitchen. An overweight woman who was the same age and height as Irene followed her. Her dyed brown hair brushed the top of her shoulders. She wore a blue-and-white striped tunic, navy leggings, and brown suede oxfords with thick rubber soles.

"Gray Lady, this is Mona. We need to talk in private. Will you run the cash register?"

"Sure." *Mona, as in missing Mona?*

I carried the pitcher to the dining area and refilled two glasses. A middle-aged man rose from a table of four men, and I reached the register right before he did.

Diane glanced at me. "Mama okay?"

I nodded, took the man's money, and gave him the change. Diane moved to another table and had her back to me. When I stepped into the kitchen to refill my tea pitcher, Irene wasn't around.

"Ms. Irene and her friend went out back to talk," Chip said. "But I can hear them."

Diane stuck her head into the kitchen. "Need coffee too." Chip took her a pot, and I followed her to the dining room.

Diane greeted each person at every table, poured coffee, and kept moving. I copied her *speak, pour, and move on* motions except she glided on ice, and I stumbled over ruts.

"Not as easy as it looks, is it?" The man at the counter occupied his usual stool at the end closest to the kitchen. His wispy hair was a halo of silver, and his gray curly beard brushed the bib on his overalls.

I refilled his iced tea. "Sure isn't. She's awesome. I'll just schlepp on to the next table and hope I don't steep anyone with this tea."

He chuckled. "Spoken like a true librarian."

How'd he know?

As I returned to the kitchen to refill my pitcher, a loud crack followed a flash of light. Irene ran in through the back door. "Dang lightning and thunder scared the bejabbers out of me. That was close."

"Where's Mona?" I asked.

"She had to leave; oh, never mind." Irene rushed out of the kitchen.

Chip loaded plates into the dishwasher from back to front. "Ms. Mona said somebody wanted her to fix some records. She's scared."

I filled another pitcher with tea. "What records were those?"

"It made no sense because she said it was keys for a man, and they were ex-keys, or ex-Scots, or something. I didn't understand why she changed the records from *ex* to *stuff*."

"Sure sounds strange," I said.

Chip nodded. "Ms. Irene said those man's keys were nothing but trouble then it thundered."

"Maybe Ms. Irene will explain later."

When I scooted past the counter with my pitcher, Irene whispered to the slight man with a full gray beard who sat at the end; he rose from his stool. When he reached the small group at the doorway, he peered outside and lingered with the rest.

"Y'all want coffee while you wait for the storm to pass?" Irene carried a pot with her on the way to the front, but the men shook their heads.

On my return past the cash register with my empty pitcher, I sneezed into the crook of my elbow. I dribbled the few remaining drops of tea down my back, and Irene chuckled. "Bless you, Gray Lady. You got allergies to this salt air?"

"Something's tickling my nose. I sneezed like crazy first thing this morning."

"No telling what pollens blow in with a Gulf storm." Irene handed change to the customer at the register. "Ever been to Galveston before?"

"My dad's parents lived near Galveston. We visited them one time when I was three, I remember the water, but not much else."

"What's your dad's name?"

"Gary."

Irene's eyes widened. "Gary Sloan's your father?"

I beamed. "You know him? He's a great guy, isn't he?"

"Heard of him. Don't think I've ever met him." She turned to the waiting customer. "That's eight dollars and thirty-two cents. How was everything?"

The slender, gray-haired man narrowed his eyes at Irene.

Big fibber, and her friend agrees with me. Why would she lie about knowing Gary?

The rain slowed to a light shower, and the men streamed out of the diner.

When the last customer left, Irene charged into the kitchen as Chip and I emptied the dishwasher. "Why did you announce to the entire diner Gary Sloan is your father? Don't you know who he is? What he does?"

"Sure. He travels. He's a representative for a chemical company."

Irene stared. "Maybe your father's not the Gary Sloan I know. I got work to do." She hurried into the office and slammed the door.

"Your dad doesn't work for a chemical company," Chip said. "Your dad was in the picture. Ms. Irene argued with him, didn't she?"

"Yes. I don't know why."

"But you're smart." Chip hung up his apron. "Everything's put away. See you on Monday."

"Chip, did you see the man who sat at the counter stool right outside the kitchen?"

"You mean Mr. Gus's brother, Mr. Maynard?"

"Yes, that's it, thanks. Have a good weekend."

Irene came out of her office. "Chip gone? I've got a list of what I need for you to research. Mona told me she and my brother planned to get married right before Paul died." She handed me a sheet of notepaper with notes in her neat handwriting. "She said Houston, so I assume

Harris County. I wrote their full names and birthdates. She also told me Paul was a cop, but I don't see how that could be possible without me knowing. We got into a big fight when I called her a liar. She's ten years older than he was. What would he see in her? I don't know if it helps, but I listed his social security number."

I read over the sheet of paper. "What about Gary Sloan? What's this at the bottom? It's hard to read. Son of—"

Irene snatched the paper away from me. "I already told you. Forget I said anything. I don't need your help."

Irene stormed out the back door. I pulled my phone out of my pocket and noted Paul and Mona's full names and birthdates and Paul's social security number.

After my grocery stop, I pulled into the parking lot where Spike and Palace Guard waited for me at my favorite spot. "Something going on?" I opened the back door and lifted the grocery sacks.

My phone buzzed a text. I set the sacks on the hood and checked. *Heather.* "Your date delayed. More later."

Spike peered over my shoulder. He smoothed his hair away from his face and sashayed to the stairs.

I snorted. "No. Heather's not coming here. Just like Kate to stand me up. I looked forward to the range, but I'm glad to have more computer time."

After I carried in and put away the food, I typed "Gary Sloan" on the computer and over a hundred profiles and images popped up. Palace Guard pointed to my phone.

"Good idea. Sergeant Duane Arrington always says I need to call my mother."

Mother picked up on the second ring. "Are you okay, Margaret? Do you need a lawyer? Big D is at work, but we could drive to wherever you are, and I can pay your bail. How much should I bring? Big D said you went on vacation with a friend. Did your friend leave you stranded? I can get a flight..."

"Mother, I'm fine, and I don't need money, but I would like to have my birdwatching kit. Could you give it to the Coyles? Kate will bring it to me, and I wanted to ask a question. I chatted with someone here, and she said she knew a Sloan whose folks were from Texas. Where did Gary Sloan's parents live?"

"Your father's parents lived in Tennessee their whole lives, and so did their parents. I don't think you're related to anyone from Texas. Have you met any nice young men? Franklin misses you."

Larry's nice. I opened my mouth, but Mother had hung up.

Palace Guard narrowed his eyes, and I chuckled. "All of Mother's phone calls were one-sided before she got her hearing aids. She hasn't adjusted to listening. She said that her cat misses me, and Gary Sloan's family is from Tennessee, not Texas."

Next, I searched the public records for a marriage license in Harris County for Paul and Mona. I pointed to the screen. "Mona signed an application for a marriage license two days before Paul died." Palace Guard leaned over my shoulder. "Three-day waiting period in Texas, but wouldn't a groom sign too? So why did Mona tell Irene she married Paul? Is that related to Paul's death? No answers. Just more questions."

I leaned back in my chair. "I need Kate to check the law enforcement claim."

I updated my diner database and linked Maynard to his brother Gus. I searched for *Pesckey's Fish Market.*

"This is interesting." Spike and Palace Guard crowded me, and I elbowed them. "Give me some space. The owner is Giosuè Ulysses Stornelli. G. U. S.?"

Spike put his palms together and moved them apart in slow motion.

"Sure, it's a stretch." I frowned at the dull sound of a thud or distant rumble. "More rain? Harder question: here did the name Pesckey come from? His mother's maiden name or something? I can check that."

Palace Guard tapped his open mouth with his fingertips.

"Okay. I'll try saying it aloud. PES-kee. Pes-KEE. PEE- suh. Pee-SKAY." I scratched my head. "Sounds like I'm trying to say fish in Italian. PEH-seh. Pesce."

Spike made a fierce face and whirled his hands in a faux karate move.

"I agree. We need Kate here to argue with me and maybe toss me across the room. I'll update the database and classify it on the stretch list." I remembered my realtor in Harperville who put every house we looked at on a different list and chuckled. *Harriet would approve.*

"I miss home. But most of all, I miss Lucy." Tears slid down my cheeks. "And Parker." I put my head down on my desk and sobbed. When my tears were no more, I rose and washed my face. "It just hits me hard sometimes. Parker's gone."

Palace Guard put his index finger over his lips. I froze when the light scratches at the front door sent shivers through me.

Palace Guard blew on his index finger.

"Larry?" I mouthed. Palace Guard pointed at the overhead light, and I switched the light off. I closed my laptop, eased to the front door, and cracked open the door. The cicadas buzzed their greeting. *No one here.* Before I closed the door, I glanced down. Larry lay near the door's threshold. I pulled my arm out of the sling, grabbed an arm with two hands, and dragged him inside with Palace Guard's help. Spike closed the door in silence, and I locked and bolted it. I bent near Larry's mouth and listened. "Thank goodness. Breathing."

Larry whispered. "Thanks. Crashed. Maybe bruised ribs."

"Anything else?"

"Airbag broke my nose and knocked the wind out of me." He moaned. "Car ran me off the road. My ankle twisted between the pedals. Had trouble getting out of the car. I rolled away, and they set my car on fire. I crawled here."

Sirens broke the night silence. They stopped about a block away then more sirens announced the impending arrival of additional units.

"How can I get you to the bathroom so I can check you?"

"Let me rest."

Palace Guard grabbed Larry under the arms, and the two of us slid Larry to the bathroom.

"Or I'll just float," Larry said.

I placed a folded towel under his head and shoulders and closed the door. When I turned on the light, I frowned. "That airbag did a number on you."

"Am I still good-looking?" Larry's mouth quivered in a weak smile.

"Pretty as ever." I ran warm water into the sink and dunked a washcloth to clean the debris and blood off his face. "I need to get ice. I'll turn on the desk lamp by my computer. Palace Guard had me turn off the lights before we pulled you inside. Makes sense now."

I returned with a makeshift ice bag wrapped in a paper towel. "Can you hold this on your nose? You're right. It looks broken to me. Can you sit up?"

"Yeah." Larry pushed up on his elbow and groaned. "Give me a minute."

I jerked at the abrupt pounding on my door. "Stay quiet." I closed the bathroom door behind me.

"Yes?" I asked through the door.

"We're doing a door-to-door check, ma'am. Looking for a guy who robbed a convenience store and crashed his car."

"I haven't seen anybody all night."

"Can we come in and check?" asked a second male.

"I assure you there's no one here." I channeled my huffy Kate voice. "You pulled me out of the shower, and I'm cold. If you want to wait fifteen minutes while I rinse this shampoo out of my hair, dry off, and get dressed, you can come in and check for yourselves."

"I'm sure he was still in the car. Nobody here saw anything. Told you." The man hissed in a stage whisper.

"Thank you, ma'am," the second man said. "Keep your door closed."

I held my breath while the pounding footsteps of the two men echoed down the stairs.

I shook my head. "Did he say *keep your door closed?*"

Palace Guard raised his eyebrows and nodded. When I opened the bathroom door, Larry was sitting up. He took a big breath and exhaled. "No bruised ribs."

"Good. Were you on your way here?"

"Kind of." Larry stared at the floor.

"Were you just in the neighborhood?" I snickered, and Spike smirked.

"Oh, leave me alone." Larry growled. "I need a beer. And a shower."

"Let me see what Kate has. Your clothes are filthy, and you bled all over your shirt."

I found a Georgia Tech T-shirt and sweatpants in Kate's room. When I handed them to Larry, he frowned. "My only choice? No Texas Tech?"

"Your other choice is to hide in the bathroom until your clothes come out of the dryer."

"I'll toss my clothes out before I get into the shower."

"Stand up. I want to see you on your feet without wobbling."

Larry pulled himself up and braced against the sink for balance. "Happy?"

"Don't fall." After I closed the bathroom door, the lock clicked.

I leaned against the door. "I'll pick the lock if we hear any crashes."

Three minutes later, the bathroom door cracked open, and a T-shirt, jeans, and socks flew out and hit the floor.

Palace Guard raised his eyebrows.

"A man's entitled to a little personal privacy." As I tossed Larry's clothes into the washer, my phone buzzed a text. *Heather.*

"Have u seen ur cuz?"

I shouted at the bathroom door. "Heather wants to know if I've seen you."

"Tell her *no*. We need to talk first."

I nodded. *Maybe we can use this.*

Chapter Six

Larry padded out of the bathroom. Kate's sweatpants were above his ankles, and the bottom of her T-shirt grazed the waistband of the pants. "You got anything to eat? And any beer?"

"Beer's in the fridge. I've got chips and salsa. Would that hold you until I make chicken tacos?"

"That's great." Larry pulled two beers out of the refrigerator and set one next to the stove.

"Let me look at your nose." I pointed to the table, and Larry sat. "Breathe in and out with your mouth closed."

His chest rose and fell with ease. "The airbag didn't break your nose, but we'll ice that swelling." I set the bag of tortilla chips and a jar of salsa on the table. Larry grabbed two bowls and poured in the salsa while I shook ice into a plastic bag and wrapped it with a clean dishcloth.

"Bad guys make me hungry." Larry grabbed a handful of chips and dug into his salsa.

I handed him the improvised ice pack. "The fire marshal won't find a body, so the investigators, TV stations, and everyone else will know you survived. If the thugs used any accelerant, the fire marshal will find it."

After I tossed the chicken breasts with a mixture of onion, garlic, and chili powders, I popped them into the oven. "You were working the cold case, right? You must have gotten close to something."

"Maybe so. I don't have any evidence to speak of, but what if Irene's brother, Paul, double-crossed somebody? Maybe he was a smuggler and skimmed off the top. Maybe the big boss ordered his murder as a warning."

"Whatever it was, it must still be an active operation."

Larry drained his beer. "Got any iced tea? The salty chips are great, but they made me thirsty."

"Won't take much to make some." I put a pot of water on the stove to boil and joined Larry at the table. "This is what we know so far: It's an established long-time active smuggling operation but not drugs. The smugglers transport the product by ship, maybe cruise ships. The business is lucrative enough to result in murder including attempted murder of a police officer. That's all I can think of."

I scooped salsa onto a chip. "Back to your feeling about Paul, I'm convinced hepatitis fits in somewhere as a key."

"Gary Sloan's a key."

"You're right. I forgot about Gary, but none of us would be here if he hadn't disappeared."

"Blind spot," Larry said between munches.

I turned off the burner under the boiling water, dropped in two family sized tea bags, and set the timer. After I pulled out the chicken breasts, I sliced them, and dusted the pieces with the red chili mixture, and returned them to the warm oven.

"If you give me a knife and a cutting board, I can chop onions and tomatoes," Larry said.

"You sure?"

"Might be a little slow."

While he chopped, I mixed the dough for tortillas. When the timer dinged, I removed the tea bags and stirred in sugar then warmed pinto beans on low heat.

While Larry hobbled to fill glasses with ice and pour our tea, I cut the dough into smaller pieces. When I rolled them into circles, they shrank before I could toss them into the pan. "I've never made tortillas before. We may have open-face tacos. Is there such a thing?"

"My favorite." After Larry set the table, he slumped into his chair. "Wore me out."

I removed the chicken from the oven and slid the slices onto a plate. I placed the chicken, beans, tortillas, and grated cheese on the table. "We need an avocado next time so I can make guacamole."

After we ate, I rose to clear the table. "Care for a brownie?"

"Sure I can't help with the dishes?" Larry asked.

"You can get them next time. You want tea or beer with your brownie?"

"Tea. Beer would knock me out."

I packaged leftovers, cleared the table, and loaded the dishwasher. Larry flopped on the sofa, and I joined him with our dessert.

"How did you conduct your investigation?"

Larry narrowed his eyes. "That's a strange question. I met with potential persons of interest and others who might have any knowledge of Paul Reynolds. Standard procedure."

"Standard procedure: you read all the previous investigators' notes, prepared your questions, and took notes. Did you also record the interviews? Did you meet them at their home? Place of work? Galveston police station?"

"The police station, and I recorded the interviews. What are you getting at?"

"What progress did you make on your case?"

"It's early. I'm just getting started. What's with the big inquisition?" Larry growled.

I took another bite of brownie.

Larry frowned while he finished his dessert. "I've got an answer. If I'm right, can I have another brownie?"

"Sure. If you're wrong, you get me a beer." I wiggled my eyebrows.

"Standard procedure was the wrong approach."

"You're right. Why would the approach everyone else used with no results work for you?"

"You've got a plan, haven't you?"

I rose to fetch Larry's brownie. "Did you ever work narcotics?"

"Not relevant, but yes."

I grabbed a beer for myself and carried Larry's dessert and my bottle to the sofa. "How did you dress? What did you look like?"

"You saw me. My hair was longer, and I dressed in jeans."

"How did you walk?"

Larry gaped. "Wow. I walked like a cop."

Spike stuck out his chest, straightened his back, and swaggered to the back door. I snickered.

"I don't want to know. It was Spike, wasn't it? I lasted one day, and the trainer said I was a good cop. Nothing else. So, what's your plan?"

"I need your standard procedure notes. You hit a nerve with an interview. And we need Officer Ewing to return to Georgia for recuperation from his injuries. Can Heather swing that?"

"I'm sure she can."

"We've got the perfect opportunity for you to go undercover. We could shave your head or dye your hair."

"Dye my hair. I don't want to fiddle with shaving my head all the time."

"I can teach you how to lose your cop-walk with Spike's help. You need local clothes. I'll ask Diane if you can have a job at the diner. You ever wait tables? Cashier?"

"In college. I waited tables and was a clerk at a grocery store. What about Chip? Doesn't he know Larry the cop?"

"He's on my team, and I introduced him to Larry, the paramedic."

"Bad guys tried to kill you then they tried to kill me. Why aren't we leaving town? What do the guys say?"

Palace Guard frowned, and Spike did his wacky dance and pointed at me.

"They're open to the idea."

Larry glared. "No, they aren't."

"Fine. Then you leave town. My assignment is to find Gary."

Larry crossed his arms and grimaced. "My assignment is to keep you safe."

"It is not."

"Is so." Spike sat with Larry on the sofa and copied Larry's glower and crossed arms.

Palace Guard covered his mouth, and I giggled. "I'm surprised you can't see Palace Guard and Spike. You're the most immature cop I've ever met. If you don't have a better idea, I'll contact Diane."

I tossed my hair and sent Diane a text to call me. While I waited, I worked on a shopping list: shirts, pants, socks, shoes, toiletries, and hair dye.

"Do you have your phone?" I asked.

"No. Didn't even think about it when I bailed out."

I added *phone* to my list.

"One more thing." I narrowed my eyes. "Where did Officer Ewing stay?"

Larry stared at the floor and bit his lip. "Hotel."

"Is that so? Which one?"

"One in Galveston." He glanced to his right, stared at the ceiling, and glanced to the left.

That's a shifty look, if I've ever seen one.

Palace Guard nodded his head, and Spike glared at Larry.

I raised an eyebrow. "When did you check out?"

Larry raised his head and met my gaze. "After the first night. I slept in my car so I could be close."

"Then it's settled. My cousin Larry will stay with me until he can get on his feet."

Larry's neck turned red. "Okay, but you can't say I was in rehab or jail."

My phone rang. *Diane.*

"Got your text. You okay?"

"Just need a favor. My mother sent my cousin to stay with me. He's taken college courses and waited tables while he was in school. I thought you could use some relief, and I promised my mother I'd ask you if he could work at the diner."

"I could use the help," Diane said. "Mama is busy, and I can't count on her after she gets the pies made."

"I'm sure he'll do a great job. I'll bring him along to work on Monday, and you can meet him. He's a hard worker. He'll be ready to go."

After I hung up, Larry asked, "What do we do next?"

"Check with Heather and go shopping. I'll do that. You get some rest." I handed my list to Larry. "I need your sizes and any preferences for each one."

Larry added his notes to my list and handed it to me. "You plan to ignore my preferences, don't you?"

"Sure will. Just gives me an insight into how a cop thinks."

"For your database."

I shrugged. "You want a pillow?"

"No." Larry pouted as he stretched out on the sofa. "Yes."

"You can sleep in Kate's room. You'll sleep better on a bed."

"I'm fine." Larry closed his eyes.

I returned with a pillow and fluffed it. He took it from me and mumbled, "Thanks. I'll just rest my eyes."

I texted Heather: "Cuz dropped by."

Heather: "Nice."

Palace Guard scanned our surroundings while I sorted through the stack of men's jeans. "Why is it no matter what size I look for, that's the size they're out of?"

"Isn't that the truth?" A middle-aged woman pushed her cart to the opposite side of the table. "I think it's a conspiracy." Her eyes crinkled with her wide smile.

Joke? Palace Guard nodded, and I smiled. "I'm sure you're right."

She chuckled as she rolled her cart away.

"Thanks." I moved to the next stack. "Ah-ha! Two pairs here. Next, shirts."

I snorted when I read the list: *Texas Tech T-shirts.*

"His signature shirt."

Palace Guard pointed to the video game and movie-themed T-shirts. "Good idea."

We picked out four T-shirts and a zippered hoodie with the logo of a long-defunct band across the chest. I selected a pack of white socks, and Palace Guard dropped two packs of three pairs of underwear each into the cart. After we completed the list for the personal items, I wheeled to phones. While I stared at the selections, Heather sidled up next to me. She wore gray yoga pants and a plain gray workout shirt with gray slip-on shoes. She had a gray backpack slung over one shoulder.

"Hey, Sis. Mom sent you a new backpack with your birdwatching gear. Here ya go. So which phone for Cuz?"

"This one." I pointed to a random phone.

"Here's a better one." Palace Guard and I followed Heather to the corner where the discounted phones were.

"What does he need?" she asked.

"Officer Ewing..."

"Detective."

"Whatever. Needs care at a Georgia hospital for his severe injuries."

Heather picked up a phone. "I can see that. What about my favorite cousin?"

I frowned. "Not that phone. How about this one?" I stooped to the lowest shelf, and Heather bent down with me. "He'll work at the diner."

Heather stared at me. "Really? This one?"

"Yep." I rose. "Same one for both of us."

"Kind of like the red boots."

"Exactly. Glad you understand."

"Lost as usual, Sis. Text me later." Heather hugged me and left.

"Guess I get a new phone too."

When Palace Guard and I returned to the apartment, Spike sat on the sofa at the sleeping Larry's feet. I pulled tags and stickers and tossed the clothes into the washer.

"Larry." I tapped Larry's shoulder.

He drawled in a sleepy voice and opened his eyes. "I was just resting."

"Time for bed." I helped him up, and he trudged to Kate's bedroom. "I turned down the covers. Good night."

"Good night, Maggie."

I turned on my computer, and Palace Guard sat in the chair next to me. "I need to research the uncommon sources of hepatitis, but first, Gary's medical records."

Palace Guard and I read together. "Sounds like the doc treated him for the exposure right away." I leaned back. "We still don't know the source."

After two hours, I'd found a goldmine of hepatology research but kept nodding off in the middle of reading. I marked the websites and stretched. After I moved the clothes to the dryer, I padded off to bed.

The sound of *click, click, click* woke me. *Lucy!* I jumped out of bed and stared at my window where a tiny wren tapped on the glass. *Click, click.* "Good morning, bird. I knew I didn't dream that sound, but I thought you were Lucy."

After I dressed and made coffee, I took my cup out the front and down the stairs. Palace Guard joined me as I walked around the building and back. "I need to see Lucy. I've got an idea. Why don't I go back to Georgia with Officer Ewing to help get him settled in the hospital?"

Palace Guard froze and stared at me.

"What? It's a..." I smacked my forehead with my palm. "I sure am glad I didn't tell Larry about my brilliant idea."

Palace Guard and I strolled back to the apartment. "I think of Larry as my fantastic friend who pretends to be my cousin and not as Officer Ewing who was the police officer at the library after I found the murdered auditor. Officer Ewing was nice. Just like Larry."

I unlocked the door. "I miss Lucy." Palace Guard patted my shoulder, and I refilled my coffee and put the cinnamon rolls in the oven to warm while I fried bacon.

Larry stumbled out of the bedroom. "Got coffee?" He stared at his clothes. "Do I have something besides Kate's stuff to wear?"

I poured him a cup. "Your clothes are in the dryer. How about breakfast first?"

Larry moaned as he eased onto the dining chair seat.

"Maybe take two acetaminophen tablets with your coffee." I pointed to the bottle I had put on the table. While the bacon drained, I cracked two eggs into the pan. "Fried? Over easy?"

Larry nodded and sipped his coffee. "What's the plan for today?" he asked.

"My plan is to hover and make sure you rest. You go to work tomorrow. I'll dye your hair after breakfast."

"Where's your sling?" Larry frowned.

"It's in the laundry. I took it off because it cramped my style. It's been over a week now. Could you take out my stitches today?"

"I thought the doctor said three weeks for the sling, then aren't you supposed to go to physical therapy?"

"Nope. Palace Guard and Spike helped with my physical therapy after the explosion. I don't need another therapist."

After I fried my over-medium egg, I refilled our coffee, and served Larry a second cinnamon roll. While we ate, Larry asked, "Did you have any luck with your internet research last night? What did you look for?"

I answered in between bites. "Earlier I'd found the four common exposures to hepatitis, so I searched for uncommon ways. I found treatment studies but not much on unusual sources. I've got a few more studies to read."

When I rose to clear the table, Larry said, "I'll empty the dryer."

"There's a basket by the washer."

Larry returned with the clothes in the basket. "Maggie, I can't wear these."

"Why not?"

"They're too not professional."

Palace Guard wiggled his eyebrows, and we fist-bumped.

Larry dropped the basket on the floor and glowered. "Did you just fist-bump Palace Guard?"

"Sure did. Not-professional was our goal."

"I'll pick out the least offensive ones," Larry grumbled as he carried the basket to his room.

"Wear Kate's old shirt until after we dye your hair."

I found a plastic glass in the cupboard and dragged a kitchen chair into the bathroom. After I positioned the chair next to the sink, I stacked three towels close to the chair. I mixed the chemicals and trimmed off the end of the applicator with my knife.

I pulled on the gloves. "All set."

"I forgot to ask, what color did you get?" Larry asked as he sat in the chair.

"The box said it's supposed to be the right color for your gray eyes. I need to wrap a towel around your shoulders then I'll apply the color to your hair and roots. It stays on for twenty minutes. After we rinse out the mixture, we'll shampoo, apply a little conditioner then rinse and dry."

While I squirted the cream on his head and rubbed it into his hair, Larry closed his eyes. "I've been thinking, *why Galveston?* Gary disappeared. A perp shot you. Another perp or the same one ran me off the road and set my car on fire. Galveston is a popular port for pleasure cruises. And random attacks on you and me." Larry opened one eye and peeked at me.

Joke? Palace Guard winked, and I smiled.

"From everything I've read, space is a premium on cruise ships. Doesn't seem like there's any excess room available to store smuggled items, but we're overlooking something. Maybe I'm off track with this smuggling thing too." I poked at Larry's hair. "Your hair's well-covered. I'll set a timer on my phone. Back in a second. Want anything to drink?"

"Sure. I'll rest here."

I slipped into Larry's room and folded his new clothes before I poured two glasses of sweet tea. "Brought you a drink," I said as I returned. I'd left my phone on the floor next to the towels. It buzzed a text from *Unknown number*: "Don't believe what you hear. Tell G&J. Auntie."

I handed the phone to Larry to read. "What do you think?"

Larry frowned. "Kate?"

"I bought new phones last night for us. As soon as we finish your hair, I'll activate them and give Glenn a call."

"After you rinse my hair, I can shampoo in the shower. I need clean clothes to change into. Ask Spike to pick out a shirt for me."

"How did you know Spike didn't like our choices?"

Larry raised his eyebrows. "I know our imaginary men."

The timer dinged, and Larry leaned backward over the sink. Using running warm water, I filled the plastic cup and rinsed. After the runoff was clear, I towel-dried his hair and stood back to admire my work. "There. You're done. I'll bring you a change of clothes." I hurried to his bedroom.

"How is my hair?"

"Awesome. It's the look I hoped for."

"It's red!" Larry shouted.

"Which shirt?" I asked.

Spike pointed at a shirt with a vintage car.

"That one? We picked it up by mistake."

"Maggie, did you hear me? It's red. It stands out. I expected to see gray." Larry stood in the bedroom doorway.

"It's perfect. It changes your look. Even your skin tone looks different. Your freckles hid with the light brown. Now they pop. And your gray eyes are closer to light blue."

"Not convinced. Give me my clothes." Larry snatched his clothes off the bed and stormed to the bathroom. I jumped at the sound when he slammed the door.

"He'll get over it, right?"

Spike shrugged.

After his shower, Larry came into the kitchen. His slight cowlick and the shadows of darker red in his short, soft curls added depth and personality to his new look.

"Don't stare." He growled.

"I'm not staring. I'm admiring."

"Am I still good-looking?" Larry limped to the sofa.

"Pretty as ever. Red is the..."

"Not convinced." Larry swung his bare feet up onto the sofa. "Wore me out."

While Larry dozed, I activated our phones then tiptoed to my bedroom and sent Glenn a text: "New phone. GL"

Glenn texted: "Big D's title?"

"Sgt."

My cell rang.

"Are you okay?" Glenn asked.

I sat on my bed. "I'm fine. It's great to hear your voice. I miss Lucy."

"She's doing great. She's asleep on the sofa next to Jennifer who is reading. I stepped outside so I wouldn't disturb them. What's up?"

"I got a text last night from an unknown number. It said *Don't believe what you hear. Tell G&J. Auntie.* I'm sure it was Kate. When Larry was my cousin, I called Kate *Aunt Katherine*."

"She wants us to prepare for shocking news then. What do you think?"

I strolled to the window and peeked out. A mist hung low, and the windshields were damp on the cars in the parking lot. "Must be bad if she wanted to warn us. No one has this number, except for you. I'll still use my old phone, at least for a while."

After we hung up, I lingered at the window. A family came out of a ground level apartment. The man carried a toddler, and the woman carried an oversized diaper bag with owls on it. As the man strapped the child into its seat, another man crossed the parking lot, and the two men nodded in greeting. A car parked at the farther end of the lot, and a man trudged to the stairs. *Normal life.* I stepped away from the window. *Not sure I could handle it though.* I shook off my twinge of nostalgia for a different life that would never be mine and headed to my computer.

After an hour, Larry woke from his nap. "Now what, Gray Lady?"

"I need my stitches out, and you need to lose your cop-walk. What would you like to do first?"

"Now you give me a choice." Larry growled. "Not sarcasm. A complaint. Let's walk."

Spike swaggered from the front door to the back door, and I swaggered along with him.

"Cop swagger, right?" Larry asked.

"Yes."

Spike slumped his shoulders and shifted his back to a C-curve. I copied him as he bent his neck and dropped his chin closer to his chest. He ambled across the floor and glanced around the room with less of a scan but with a more rapid, furtive eye movement. Spike raised his eyebrows.

I nodded. "I think I've got it."

He returned at his casual pace, and we ambled from the back to the front. We paused then ambled to the kitchen.

"Big shift in posture and walking style," Larry said. "Even the room scan was different. Let me try."

Larry and I ambled across the room together. Spike waved his hand. *Again.*

"Ready to do this a few times?" I asked. "Take a break when you get tired."

We ambled and sauntered. When Larry stumbled, Spike called for a break.

"Ready to take out my stitches?" I asked.

Larry ambled to the sofa. "Sure am."

I handed Larry the suture removal kit and sat next to him.

"Brave of you to dye my hair red then hand me a sharp instrument. That's a joke," Larry said as he opened the kit.

I held up my sleeve, and Larry snipped and removed stitches. "All done," he said. "Your wound looks good. You have redness at the sutures but no bleeding. After Spike's satisfied with my walk, can we go to a store? I'd like to try it around people."

Larry and I practiced the walk together then Larry sauntered alone while I explained Spike's feedback, which was mostly *again*. I interpreted when Spike pointed to the sofa and slumped.

"Spike says you need to rest before you drop."

"He's smart." Larry stretched out and fell asleep.

I sat at my computer. "I need a blueprint of a cruise ship."

Larry woke two hours later.

"Good timing," I said. "I was ready to take a break. Ready for lunch?"

While I made our grilled cheese and green chile sandwiches, Larry practiced his walk and stance under Spike's tutelage.

"Was that better?" Larry asked.

Spike nodded and motioned, *again*.

"Yes, better. Again," I said.

After we ate lunch, Larry practiced his slouch-stance, and Spike pointed to Larry's phone.

"Spike wants you to go to the next level. Use your phone."

Larry cocked his head as he squinted at the refrigerator. "Appear immersed in my phone?"

Spike touched his nose.

"You got it," I said.

As Larry sauntered to the back door, he held up his phone to scroll and read. When he reached the door, he slouched against the wall while he stared at his phone and swiped. He rubbed an eye and peered at the room with a casual glance. Spike broke into his wacky dance.

"Awesome, Larry. You earned a wacky dance."

"Dang. Wish I could swagger." Larry winked, and Spike and I laughed.

"Ready to go? I'll get my sling."

When we stepped outside, Larry asked, "Want me to drive?"

"That would be great. I need to give my arm a rest."

As we walked into the super store, I said, "I have a short list that includes groceries."

"I'll look at shirts."

"Really?" I raised my eyebrows.

He snorted. "Don't worry. I'll channel my inner Spike."

I practiced Larry's surveillance techniques while I picked out apples in the produce section. On my way to the frozen food case, I wandered to the cleaning aisle and lingered. I found an old favorite in a spray bottle that delivered the clean sparkle I loved along with the sweet fragrance of lavender. I read the labels for products to clean leather furniture. I scooted a few feet to my right and gazed at furniture polish.

Larry appeared next to me and dropped shirts into the basket. "You don't have ice cream."

"Let's pick something out." I turned away with reluctance. "Mother and I cleaned together every Saturday when I was growing up. I've been nostalgic the past few days; even cleaning products make me weepy."

Larry rested his hand on my shoulder, and I met his gaze. He was a good foot taller than I was, and the sight of his reddish-brown chin stubble warmed my heart. *I knew red was right for him.*

"I am so sorry. You know that, don't you?" he asked.

"Thank you. It helps that you understand."

Larry pushed the basket, and I led the way to the ice cream.

"What about ice cream bars?" I asked when we reached our destination.

"Perfect." Larry reached inside the case and selected a box.

"Let's go," I said, and we rushed to the front to the self-checkout.

"Do I flip on the lights and siren?" Larry asked as he started the car.

I laughed. "I wish that wasn't a joke. I don't want our ice cream to melt either."

As he drove to the apartment, Larry said, "A security person followed me around the store until I met up with you. At first, I considered setting him straight then I realized Spike would be proud of me."

"Love your goal to make an imaginary man proud of you. You may sink to immaturity."

Larry chuckled. "Thank you. I'll earn that wacky dance lesson yet."

While I put away the groceries, Larry told the sofa about the store security guy. Spike rushed past him and flopped onto the sofa. When Larry finished, Spike grinned.

"Spike is proud of you," I said.

"Awesome." Larry beamed.

We took our ice cream bars to the back patio. I bit mine and held it in my mouth for the sweet goodness to melt. "I want to watch the ships."

"Let's go." Larry rose.

"And we can do some bird watching. Give me a minute. I can't eat ice cream as fast as you can."

Larry dropped back into his chair. "You aren't a bird-watcher."

"Do you have binoculars?" I licked the last of the ice cream off the stick.

"No."

"I have the highest-rated birding field glasses available." I glared.

"I should have known," he said. "Spy tools, right?"

We went inside, and I put on my khaki safari hat and sunglasses and my new gray backpack. "I'm ready."

"I feel underdressed. Give me a minute." When Larry returned from his bedroom, he wore a dark brown felt cowboy hat. "What do you think? I bought it on Wednesday before I got the scones. Thought I'd surprise you."

"It suits you."

"Thank ya, ma'am." He tapped the brim cowboy-style with two fingers.

As Larry drove to the port, I stretched out my legs and admired my boots. "Do we look like tourists or locals?"

"If anybody at the port tries to sell us anything, we're tourists. If we're ignored, we're locals."

I picked up my phone. "I'm calling Ellen."

When she answered, I said, "Hi, it's Maggie. I'd like to take a tour of a cruise ship. Do you have any ideas?"

"Maggie, it's great to hear from you. I'm glad you didn't lose my number. I might have an idea. Okay if I go with you?"

"I'd enjoy it."

"I'll check with my friends. Might be a day or so. You stay safe."

After we hung up, Larry asked, "Do cruise lines even allow tours? What did Ellen say?"

"She said maybe." I scanned the parking lot with my binoculars when we parked. "There's a food truck and a line. Tourists or locals?"

"No backpacks. I think locals. Let's eat."

We stepped into line behind three other people, and a middle-aged man with large biceps stepped in behind us. He reminded me of an overweight Spike except his nose was straight. "How far did y'all drive?"

"From Humble," Larry said. "You?"

"I got you there. North of Spring. When they text, I head out."

"Us too," Larry said. The two of them chuckled.

"So, what's your favorite?" The Spike man asked.

"I always get the chicken gyro," I said.

"Traditional for me," Larry said.

"Me too. They have the best lamb in the state."

We all nodded. The man cleared his throat. "The little lady's in the car with her dog. We don't go anywhere without that spoiled pooch. Mind if I cut in front of you? My huntin' dog died last spring. Miss him."

"Know whatcha mean," Larry said. "Go right ahead. We're in no hurry."

Larry's new friend stepped in front of us and glanced at the cruise ship. "Takes them four hours to get all them passengers off then they unload the cargo. I hear the pay's good."

"Really? I'm looking for work," Larry said.

"My cousin said they're interviewing here tomorrow morning first thing."

"I'll check that out. Thanks," Larry said.

The man ordered. After he paid for his order and hurried across the parking lot with his sack, Larry ordered.

"Thanks for jumping in with a favorite," Larry said. "I hadn't figured out what kind of truck it was yet."

"I read the menu when we parked." I tapped my field glasses that hung around my neck. "You were quick with Humble. Will you apply for a job tomorrow?"

"I saw a highway sign a few days ago, and the name stuck. I'm supposed to go with you to the diner tomorrow. Maybe I'll apply next week."

"Let's think about that." I paid for our order, and we strolled to a bench near the water.

I took a bite of my gyro. "This is great. I sure am glad you got the text. Was that sarcasm?"

Larry swallowed his latest bite and gulped his tea. "No. More like a great joke."

When Larry finished his gyro, I still had half of mine left.

"I'll see if I can sign up for the food truck text." He ambled to the food truck, and I grinned.

I trained my glasses on the docked cruise ship. Passengers filed off the ship and gathered in an area enclosed by thick red ropes. Most of the passengers were women in their mid-sixties and older. Their flowered shirts, pastel capris and pants, pastel straw hats, and sunglasses didn't match their drooping heads and overall slumping postures. When the women located their luggage, they bustled to the exit, and the waiting area emptied.

After the food truck drove away, Larry returned. "I'm on the food truck alert. It's...what are you staring at? There's nothing there. All the passengers left."

"Wait. Cargo."

CHAPTER SEVEN

After fifteen minutes of silence, Larry said, "How much longer? Do all ships carry cargo?"

"We need a better view."

"I'll cruise closer to the dock to see what our options are."

Larry sauntered away with his newfound local gait, and I snickered. When Larry drove away, his new friend stepped out of his car six or seven aisles away and headed toward me. *No wife; no dog.* He scanned the area, and his steps quickened.

When he reached me, the man grabbed my good elbow. "Where's your boyfriend going? Not enough man for a pretty thing like you?"

I pulled out of his grasp. "What was your name again?"

"You can call me Stud. What's your name?"

I cocked my head and frowned. "Did your mother or your father name you Stud? Is it a nickname for Stuart?"

"What? Do I look like a Stuart?" His face reddened, and he stepped back.

"I don't know. I've known some nice men named Stuart. Did you have something you wanted to tell my husband? He won't be long."

Stuart snorted. "He ain't payin' no attention to you. Let's go somewhere private and have a little chat about these men you've known." He grabbed my sling and yanked me toward him.

I kicked his crotch with my red boot, and as he doubled over, he pulled me downward by my sling. I twisted loose from his hold and slammed his chin upward with my knee. When he hit the ground, I kicked his left kidney.

He grunted. "Why, you sorry..." He grabbed my ankle and flipped me to the ground. I rolled and rose to one knee.

Larry roared from across the parking lot. "Get away from her!"

Stuart shifted his attention from me to Larry and pushed up to a sitting position. He pulled a nine-millimeter out of his waistband and pointed it at Larry. I reached into my boot for my knife as he took aim with his finger curled over the trigger. I threw my knife with the accuracy engrained in the muscle memory from hours of rigorous training with my imaginary men. The knife embedded in his wrist, and Stuart dropped his gun. Larry sprinted across the parking lot in a cop-run.

Stuart screamed and reached for the knife. "I'm bleeding!"

In my best commanding voice, I growled, "Leave the knife where it is."

Stuart pulled out the knife, and his opened wound gushed blood. I snatched the knife out of his hand.

"Told you to leave it." I shrugged, tossed the knife, and kicked the gun away from him. I wrapped the wound with my sling.

When Larry reached me, he hugged me, and I leaned into him.

"Are you okay?" he asked.

"I'm fine." I straightened my back. "Stuart here cut himself on my knife. Didn't you, Stuart?"

When Larry released me, I retrieved my knife and wiped it on Stuart's shirt then returned it to its scabbard in my boot.

"Emmy, Where's his car?"

I pointed. "He lied about a wife and her dog in his car. It isn't nice to lie about dogs, Stuart."

Larry glared at Stuart. "I'm taking my wife to our car. If you move, you'll bleed to death, and if you don't die, I'll shoot you."

When we reached the car, Larry opened the passenger's door. "I'll turn on the engine to get the air conditioner going. I need to make a quick call."

After a few minutes, Larry slid into the driver's seat. "Okay with you if we wait for company? I called the locals."

"He's not going anywhere. He kind of dropped these." I held up a ring of keys and jingled them.

"Oh lordy. I'll take those." Larry shook his head. "How did you get his keys?"

"They fell out of his pocket when I kicked him. While the two of you chatted, I scooped them up. Didn't I tell you about my magician phase when I was a kid?"

"I thought you were always a spy."

"Spies have many talents." I tossed my hair. "I have a question. Is *wife* an upgrade or downgrade from *cousin*?"

Larry snorted. "Hope it was okay when I said I would walk my wife to the car."

"You backed me up. I asked him if he had something to tell my husband."

Larry grinned. "Upgrade. It's real handy for me to call you Emmy."

"Yep. Too bad you don't have a nickname."

Larry chuckled.

I squinted at him. "Joke? I don't get it."

Larry guffawed and wiped his eyes.

After we arrived at the apartment, Larry pulled two beers out of the refrigerator. "We are off duty."

I took my beer to the sofa and pulled off my boots. Palace Guard and Spike sat on either side of me while Larry straddled a kitchen chair backwards. We gave the two imaginary men a rundown on our encounter with Stuart.

Larry took a swig of beer. "Do you suppose I could sit with Maggie sometime too?"

Palace Guard shook his head, and Spike crossed his arms and frowned.

"No need to interpret, Maggie; I feel the *No Way* vibes. Not that I blame them," Larry said.

Spike scooted closer to me and patted the two-inch space on his other side.

"Spike offered you a seat next to him," I said.

"Is that why you look so scrunched?" Larry cocked his head and squinted.

"On duty for one minute. When Kate and I were at the cabin in the woods and tried to make sense of what we knew, we put what we knew on sticky notes."

"How did that work?"

"Didn't do a bit of good." I finished my beer and sanitized my knife.

"Do we have any ice cream?" I checked the freezer. "Want an ice cream bar?"

When I handed Larry his sweet treat, we tapped our bars. "Cheers."

After I polished off my ice cream and scraped the stick with my teeth, I said, "Time for you to get some rest."

"You too." He rose and stretched. "It's been a busy day. Good night, Maggie. Good night, guys."

Larry ambled to his room; when he reached the door, he turned and raised his eyebrows. Spike applauded.

"Spike approves." Larry closed his door.

"He's gotten better at guessing, hasn't he? Good night." I checked the door and window locks and went to bed.

The gurgle of the coffee pot woke me at five-thirty the next morning. *Kate. No, it's Larry.* I smiled. *Almost as good.*

I dressed and ambled into the kitchen. *This non-cop walk is harder than it looks.*

Larry held a cup of coffee and stared out the back window. When he turned, his serious expression startled me.

"What?" I asked.

"Coffee first." He poured a cup and handed it to me. "Let's sit on the balcony."

I sipped my coffee. "Tell."

"Remember what Kate said?"

"Sure. *Don't believe what you hear.*"

"Heather texted me early this morning. A private plane crashed in the mountains of Tennessee near Chattanooga last night. They've located the crash site from the air, but there's no sign of Kate or the pilot."

"Uninhabited area, right? We need the coordinates. I'll bet I can find her drop zone in ten minutes."

Larry cleared his throat. "I believe you, but no. Kate doesn't want you to locate her drop zone. That's why she warned you, I'm sure."

"She didn't say don't come find her." I pouted and crossed my arms, and so did Spike.

"No, she didn't. That's my job. She's somewhere having fun in the mountains, and I'm the bad guy."

Palace Guard stood next to Larry and glared at Spike and me.

Spike raised his eyebrows at me and slid away.

"You're changing sides, aren't you?" I asked.

Spike stepped next to Palace Guard and hung his head.

"Three against one is not fair. I demand a recount," I said.

"Yes!" Larry knocked over his chair as he jumped up. He held out his hand, and Palace Guard and Spike smacked it.

"Whatever." I stomped inside and grabbed the coffeepot. I refilled my cup and glared at the three of them while I slurped my coffee.

My phone rang. *Diane.*

"Maggie, I'm in a bit of a pickle. Mama called me late last night. Mona quit her job on Friday, and Mama told her she could wait tables at the diner. Now I will have too many people. I forgot to tell Mama your cousin would help, and she forgot to check with me before she promised Mona she could work at the diner."

"Don't worry about it. Larry's versatile. He might apply at the port."

"What a great idea. I can be his reference. He's related to you, so he must be a hard worker. Interviews start at nine. Tell him to arrive no later than seven-thirty. Everyone else will show up around eight, and it's a first come-first served operation."

"Thank you for the offer. A local reference will help. Any other tips?"

"Your location is a big plus. They prefer flexible applicants available on short notice. Does he have a car?"

"We're sharing, but I can walk to the diner."

"I'll pick you up. It's the least I can do. Oh. One more thing. I'll text the address of the warehouse where they conduct the interviews. It's not at the main office. See you later."

I filled Larry in.

"What do I wear?" he asked.

"Jeans, any of your shirts will be fine. Not your cowboy hat. Too dressy."

"Can I wear my Texas Tech hat?"

"No. it's Officer Ewing's."

"I need a hat."

"Stop at the gas station. They have ball caps."

My phone dinged. "Diane texted me the address." I scribbled it on a pad. "Here's the address and her contact information for a personal reference. It's six-fifteen. I'll make you a quick breakfast then you can head out. This is a fabulous break."

"Worries me to leave you alone," Larry said.

"I won't be alone." While I made more coffee and cooked eggs and bacon, Larry took a quick shower and put on his interview clothes.

Larry strolled into the kitchen and refilled our coffee cups. He wore jeans and a shirt with a local feed store logo.

"You look great. Have a seat," I said. "Not enough time for cinnamon rolls, so we're having toast with Jennifer's strawberry jam."

"My loss is my win. Is that a saying?" he asked.

"Is now." I dished up our eggs and bacon and set a plate of toast on the table.

"This is awesome. I don't get a home-cooked breakfast. I have cereal and fruit." Larry dipped his toast into the egg yolk. We ate in silence. I had a bite of bacon, a bite of egg, and a bite of toast and jam. Larry gobbled down his breakfast before I'd eaten half of mine.

"It's a hazard of the job." He pointed to his empty plate. "Eat fast before the next call comes in. No telling when your next chance to eat will be."

"Makes sense. Makes sense for a paramedic too."

"Paramedic. I need a previous job. Do you suppose Glenn would cover for me?"

"Good thought." I set down my fork and called Glenn. "It's me."

"What's wrong? You okay?"

"Nothing's wrong. I heard, and I'm fine. Y'all okay?"

"Jennifer said you'd go with her to the mountains. You'd know where Kate is."

"Larry said I can't do that. He's being bossy."

"No, he's afraid of Kate." Glenn chuckled.

"Hadn't thought of that," I said. "Larry is applying for a job as a porter for cruise ships and needs a reference for his previous position as a paramedic. Could you handle that?"

"Sure 'nuff can. When's he applying?"

"This morning at 7:30."

"Give me his cell number, and I'll text him the information he'll need."

"I'll send it to you."

"I'm on it. We love you."

Glenn hung up.

"I'll send Glenn your phone number, and he'll text you the information about your previous paramedic position."

"Okay if I leave now? I'll pick up a hat."

"Go ahead. You had the keys last."

My two imaginary men sat with me while I finished my breakfast. "This is better than lurking with my binoculars except I wish I could be the porter. I need a list of details for Larry to investigate."

I pulled up the blueprints and technical specs for cruise ships on my computer and jotted down notes. At nine-fifteen, Larry texted me: "Got the job. Train today. Work tomorrow."

Before I powered down my computer, the headline on my newsfeed caught my eye: *Cold Case Detective Critically Injured*. Palace Guard leaned over my shoulder while I scrolled.

I stopped at a section and reread it. "This is interesting. It's re-hashing the investigation except I don't know what's true or journalistic embellishments."

I pointed to the subtitle of a section. *Ongoing investigation.* "This paragraph implies someone was working on the case the entire time. Undercover? Wonder if that's local gossip? Might explain my attack."

I read a few more paragraphs then pushed away from the table. "Wonder what time Diane plans to pick me up? Better get ready for work."

After my shower, I dressed.

"Gray shirt, gray jeans, red boots." I whirled when I reached the kitchen. "It's easy to be the Gray Lady."

Palace Guard raised his eyebrows, and I thought I heard Spike snort.

"I meant for clothing selection. You knew what I meant. Don't be silly."

Palace Guard rolled his eyes, and Spike broke into his wacky dance.

"Oops. Unfortunate choice of words." I poured the last of the cold coffee into my cup. Spike made a gagging face. "What? I don't mind coldish coffee."

Palace Guard wrinkled his nose.

"It's the same temperature as the beer you drink. Room temperature." I leaned back in my chair. "So why is my coffee called *cold*, and your beer called *warm*?"

Palace Guard frowned and stroked his chin. I turned back to my computer and raised my eyebrows. "Here's something for me: *Dead Weight Tonnage.*"

As I read the formula for calculating gross tonnage, Palace Guard put his hand in front of my computer screen and pointed to a text from Diane: "Here."

"Thanks. I better get moving." I turned off my computer and checked the backdoor locks and all the windows. Spike blew a kiss, and I smiled. "See you later."

I bounded down the stairs. Diane had leaned back in her seat and closed her eyes. I tapped on the window, and she jumped and unlocked the doors.

"Sorry. Didn't mean to startle you." I said as I climbed in. When I pulled my seat belt across my chest, Palace Guard sat behind Diane with his back straight. *The original cop.* Palace Guard winked.

On our way to the diner, I said, "I wonder how long Mona will last at the diner before she and Irene have a big blow-up?"

Diane shook her head. "Those two have been best friends since Mama was five years old. They lived next door to each other. Mama said they'd stand on their porches and throw rocks at each other. She's never forgiven Mona for telling on her when she nailed Mona with a headshot. They still act like they're five years old sometimes, don't they?"

After she parked, Diane asked, "Did your cousin get the job at the port? I got a call this morning and gave him an enthusiastic recommendation."

"He did and thank you."

"I expect both Mama and Mona will fizzle by the end of the week. Chip's coming along, though. I think he'll run the entire operation before long. And you're healing."

"People seem to make Chip nervous."

"True, but we're working on that. He just needs a little time. No sense in pushing."

When we arrived at the diner, Irene waved and stirred up a cloud of flour. Chip peeled potatoes.

"Where's Mona?" Diane asked.

"Wiping down tables," Irene said.

"Chicken fried steak, mashed potatoes, green beans on Monday," Chip said.

Diane beamed.

Mona burst into the kitchen. "Where are the napkins?"

"This way, Mona." She followed me to the storeroom. While we were in the storeroom, Mona scanned the shelves.

"Logical organization," she said. "Makes sense." She wiped her hands on her jeans. "I'm jittery. Never thought waiting tables would make me nervous. I thought it would be an easy job, but I know I'll stumble over my own feet. What if I spill something on somebody?"

"Apologize and clean it up," I said.

"You're right. I need to go back to work. You know, my real job. I didn't quit. I told Irene I did when she told me I couldn't cut it at a diner. She said my job was a sissy job, and it took a strong person to work in a diner. I just took a few days off. Irene always thinks she's so superior. You're so easy to talk to, Gray Lady. Thanks."

She flipped through a stack of papers then picked up a packet of napkins before she hurried out.

I narrowed my eyes. "I don't understand Mona and can't keep up with the Irene and Mona mess, but maybe Mona can help me find Gary."

Palace Guard frowned.

"What? It's a brilliant idea."

I collected all the salt and pepper shakers on a tray and lined them up on the lunch counter. As I refilled them, I set them on the tray in pairs.

"You're so fast," Mona said. "I'll never be as smooth as you are."

Was *that sarcasm?*

Palace Guard shook his head.

Is Mona a phony?

Palace Guard opened his mouth and pointed to mimic Spike's gagging face.

"That works," I said.

"What works?" Mona asked.

Oops. "Lining up the salts together and the peppers together."

Palace Guard grinned.

I filled a small bucket with hot water and vinegar to wipe down the menus. Mona grabbed a clean cloth and copied me.

"I understand I have a distant relative around here," I said. "Name is Sloan. You know anybody?"

"Oh, do I. Irene claims she and Gary Sloan had a business arrangement. I think it was something shady."

She covered her mouth with her hand. "Oh wait. You said he was a relative."

"My father's second cousin or something. I never met him."

"Well, she claimed he cheated her. I'll bet it's the other way around. He was here last week, or maybe it was two weeks ago, and she threatened him. I heard her myself. They were in his car, and she said she had friends who could take care of him. He laughed and said she had what they'd agreed on. She was mad and said he owed her more. He told her people were sick because of her. I didn't understand that part."

"Did they yell?"

"Irene did. You know how loud she can be. I was sitting in my car next to them."

"Didn't they see you?"

"Oh no. I ducked down when they pulled in and rolled down the passenger's window so I could hear." Mona grinned and puffed out her chest.

Palace Guard did his gagging sign.

"Quick thinking," I said.

Mona smirked and marched to the kitchen to empty the bucket of vinegar and water.

Partial truth? Hard to pick through the tangle.

Palace Guard nodded.

At eleven, Diane unlocked the front door. Two customers drifted in at eleven fifteen. By eleven-thirty, the first wave of regulars sat at their usual tables. Their rowdy jostling and chatter reminded me of a schoolyard at recess.

Smitty, the man who drove the red truck, walked in and joined a group of three at a booth. "Did you hear about Butch?" he asked. "Somebody jumped him at the port. I heard it was a gang. Like six thugs. He was lucky to survive. Bad break for him, though; he had an outstanding warrant. He went from the hospital to jail."

Mona paled.

"You okay? What's wrong?" I asked.

"Nothing's wrong. Mind your own business." She rushed to the booth to take Smitty's order.

"Special? Coffee?" She set his cup on the table, and I followed up with the coffeepot. Mona rushed to the order window and dropped off his ticket. I cruised from table to table with the coffeepot while Mona took orders as more customers arrived.

Another man picked up the conversation. "Do you think the attack resulted from the warrant?"

"He always got into fights when he was a kid," Smitty said.

"He hasn't changed. Cruise company gave him two weeks off without pay after he roughed up a porter. He's lucky he's a valued engineer. The company has fired others for less."

"It would take at least eight guys to take Butch down. He's a tough guy," the third man at the booth said.

A man at a nearby booth snorted. "He's a jerk. I got in his face when he tried to mess with my sister. He backed off. My sister told me that her friends avoid him."

"I've heard he was bad news." Gus's brother, Maynard, piped in from his usual spot at the counter.

Another man at the counter said, "He grabbed my niece at a party, and I told him I'd break his neck if he touched her again. He said he was just kidding, but he never bothered her after that."

"Don't know what his warrant is for, but sounds like he will have a hard time finding any character references," Maynard said. All the men in the diner chuckled.

Palace Guard stood at attention at the front door. He held up eight fingers and winked. I snorted.

As Mona and I bussed tables at the end of the shift, she cleared her throat. "Sorry I snapped at you earlier."

"I'm sure you have a lot on your mind."

She picked up the tray of dirty dishes. "Thanks, I do. If you're interested in finding Gary Sloan, I heard he's at that new motel between here and the Galveston city limits."

"I'll tell my dad. He might be interested." I sanitized the table Mona had cleared and wiped down the menus.

I moved to the next table. "How do you know where Gary is? Did you talk to him?"

"My friend works at the motel. She knows Irene and saw her and Gary Sloan go to lunch together last week."

"Do I know her? What's her name?"

"You don't know her. This is a strange place. Why have menus when nobody orders anything but the special?"

Clumsy transition, Mona. "Tradition." I wiped down the seats and moved to the next booth.

"Maybe, but Irene makes good money from the ads. She's all about the bottom line and letting everybody know she's better than them. That's why I get so mad at her." Mona carried the tray of dishes to the kitchen.

As I scrubbed the last booth, my phone buzzed a text. I smiled. *Larry.*

Larry: "Need a ride home?"

Me: "Yes."

Larry: "Here."

I emptied the sudsy water and rinsed the bucket. After I dropped my cleaning supplies into the bucket, I set it under the counter and hurried to the kitchen. Chip had left, and Irene and Mona weren't in sight, but the office door was closed. I tapped on the door.

"Yes?" Irene asked.

"If there's nothing else, I'll head out," I said.

"See you tomorrow."

When I stepped outside, Larry bounded out of the car and beat me to the passenger's side. He opened the door and helped me in. I leaned back in the seat and relaxed.

As we drove away, he said, "I'm in charge of supper tonight."

My eyes widened. "You cook?"

"Don't sound so surprised. I can cook." He jutted out his chin.

I peeked at the back seat, and Palace Guard's eyes were wide. I pinched my lips together to keep from smirking.

When he drove past the apartment, Larry said, "Although, this evening I chose not to cook. I've ordered tacos from our favorite takeout."

"I knew that."

"How? How did you know?"

I pointed to the note on the console and smirked. "Taco stand name and phone number."

"Funny, ha ha. You saw that when you got in the car, didn't you? I thought you were too literal to pull a prank."

"Guess not." I grinned, and Larry chuckled.

He pulled into the parking lot. "No shoptalk until after we eat?"

"Sounds good to me." I closed my eyes.

I must have dozed off because my head jerked when Larry said, "We're home."

On our way up the stairs, he said, "It's a little early for supper. Do you eat lunch at work? We can reheat our tacos later, if you like."

"I don't eat until I get home. I'm hungry."

While we ate, I said, "I could eat tacos every meal."

Larry set his glass on the table and chuckled. "We're getting our daily dose of tacos, aren't we?"

I dipped a piece of tortilla into my salsa bowl. "Kate said two weeks, and today is day fourteen. It's supposed to be time to go home. I'm tired of the daily drama at Diane's Diner; I'd say it wears me out, but dreadful daily drama at Diane's Diner does me in."

Larry choked on his tea. "Tell me when you're about to tell a joke next time. You are hilarious."

Our eyes met, and Larry put a hand over mine. "When you're ready to go home, just give me the word, and we'll leave."

"We'd go if Kate weren't missing."

"I know." Larry patted my hand and rose. He reached into the refrigerator for the pitcher of tea and refilled our glasses, then set the pitcher on the table and drifted to the back door. "So, how was your dreadful day?"

"Mona is a mess of contradictions."

Larry returned to the table while I told him about Mona's supposed friend at a motel, the conversation between Gary and Irene that Mona said she overheard, and Gary and Irene going to lunch.

"Diane said Irene and Mona have been best friends since they were five, but Mona lied to Irene. Mona didn't quit her job; instead, she took a few days off because she was mad at Irene. Mona said she wanted to show Irene she could work at a diner."

"So she told you where Gary is?"

"Yes. Except it seemed too easy."

He frowned. "Yeah. Suspicious."

"Did you know six, maybe eight, thugs attacked Stuart? And he has a history of fighting and overstepping boundaries with women."

"I knew about the fighting, and there are several protection orders on record against him. Six thugs?" Larry, Palace Guard, and Spike laughed.

"I'm not sure I've ever been a thug before," I said.

"Admit it; it fits." Larry grinned.

I threw my open paper napkin at him, and it floated onto his plate. The three men laughed again.

"What's funny about that?" I asked.

"Knife-throwing, napkin-tossing thug." Larry snorted.

I rose from my chair and marched to the back patio with my nose in the air. When I tripped over the threshold and clutched at the doorjamb to keep from falling, the stumble marred my regal demeanor. I whirled to dare them to laugh, but all three of them stared at the ceiling. Spike peeked at me and winked.

"I want to go to Tennessee. Do we pick up Jennifer?"

Larry put his elbows on the table and cradled his face with his hands. "What if Kate's here?"

"I didn't think of that. You are smart." I joined Larry at the table.

Larry squinted. "But we will look for her, anyway, won't we?"

"In a way. Let's visit Gary."

"You lost me."

"That's what Kate sent me here to do. Find Gary."

Palace Guard raised an eyebrow.

"Fine. Kate said Gary would find me. Is that better?" I glared at Palace Guard. "It's practically the same."

Palace Guard narrowed his eyes.

I growled and crossed my arms. "It is too."

"You're arguing with Palace Guard?" Larry asked. "You know, I agree with him."

Spike raised his hand and stuck out his tongue at me.

"Stay out of this, Spike. Nobody asked you." I marched to my bedroom and slammed the door.

I gazed at the sky as a brown pelican soared to the beach. *That's it. Pelicans.*

I rushed out of my bedroom and beamed. "I've got it. We need to soar, skim, and swoop."

Larry cleared his throat. "Sounds. Different. What does that mean? How do I help?"

"I haven't figured out the details yet. Let's walk to the Gulf."

After I changed my boots for running shoes and Larry grabbed his new cap, we headed to the beach. Larry walked alongside of me, Spike was in front, and Palace Guard brought up the rear.

When we reached the sand, I breathed in the salty air. "Pelicans fish together by flying in a formation and beating their wings on the surface of the water to drive the fish to the shore. That's what we need to do. Larry, can Rosa return?"

"I can check with Heather. But she left because her ex was on her trail."

"Right. Can Moe or Heather get him off the trail?"

We headed into the wind and strolled along as the rising tide below the surface forced the air up and left bubbles in the sand. Sand crabs skittered along the wet sand, and the sanderlings ran back and forth along the water as the waves ebbed and flowed.

The wind lifted the bill of Larry's ball cap, and he turned his cap backward. "I can ask. This is right up Moe's alley. What else?"

"Detective Ewing was digging into Reynolds' death. I'm thinking the techie Maggie could work that from Georgia."

"I could give her a copy of my notes, and there's a Galveston officer on the case now too."

"So, if we have you, me, the imaginary men, Rosa, Moe, Detective Ewing, also known as techie Maggie, and the Galveston officer, then we've got a good pod to go fishing, right?"

"Pod?" Larry frowned. "Oh. A group of pelicans is a pod; am I right? What do I do?"

"You've got the cruise ship. I'm convinced that's the key."

Larry beamed. "I'm the pivot man."

We headed to the apartment. When we reached the road, I stopped. "I wonder if Ellen and Jay would be interested in stirring up the water to get the fish moving?"

"What did you have in mind?"

"Suppose you tell Jay that Ewing is close to solving the cold case?"

"That's easy. We've stayed in touch. I'll call him. What about Ellen?"

"I need the scoop on Mona and Irene. I can't get a handle on the truth between those two fibbers."

Larry nodded. "That's a real tangled mess there. If anybody can sort through the nonsense, my money's on Ellen."

CHAPTER EIGHT

When we reached the apartment, Larry stopped at the bottom of the stairs. "What about Kate?"

"I'll leave that up to Jennifer. She can keep the search for Kate in the news."

After we were in the apartment, Larry opened the refrigerator and pulled out two beers. He handed me one. "What else?"

I sat on the sofa and called Ellen. "Ellen, it's Maggie. I need a few favors."

"We'll be here longer, and I need a house with a yard. Glenn can bring Lucy here."

Larry took a long drink of his beer and opened the cupboard. "Let's have some chips and salsa. What's Lucy going to do?"

I opened a new jar of salsa and divided it into two bowls. "Keep Spike out of trouble."

"That won't happen." Larry wiggled his eyebrows and dipped a chip into his salsa bowl.

Palace Guard and I laughed, and Spike danced his wacky jig.

"Well done, Larry. Spike did his wacky dance."

"Glad to oblige." He headed to the back door. "I'll step outside and give Jay a call."

"Oh good," Ellen said. "I hoped I could help."

"Do you know Irene at Diane's Diner and her friend Mona?"

"You mean the two warring best friends? I sure do. What do you need?"

"I've got notes with conflicting stories from the two of them..."

"Neither of them knows how to tell the truth. Shall I sift through your notes for you? Unless you'd rather I just beat it out of them. That would be fun too." Ellen chuckled. "I might be kidding, you know."

Larry joined me at the table and dug into the chips and his salsa.

I snickered. "I might save that for later, but there is one more thing. We'll be here longer than we planned and may need to find another place."

"I can handle that too. I'll get back to you. Are you emailing me your notes tonight?"

"I need to merge them first. It might be early tomorrow before you see them and thank you for everything."

"This is exciting. Talk to you later."

"Saving what for later?" Larry asked after I hung up.

"Ellen offered to beat the truth out of Irene and Mona."

He nodded. "Whatever works."

When I raised my eyebrows, he said, "I work at the docks. No cops here."

"Good to know. Time to call Glenn."

When Glenn answered, I said, "Nothing's wrong."

"I've got you on speakerphone," he said. "Jennifer's hovering."

"I'll put you on speakerphone too. Larry's here. I've got a request for each of you. Glenn, if I take off work on Wednesday, would you mind meeting me in Biloxi with Lucy? We'll be here longer than we expected."

"She misses you too," Jennifer said.

"Would it be easier if I bring her to Galveston?" Glenn asked.

"It's a long drive. If we split it up, it will be easier for both of us. Could we meet at noon?"

"I'll pack a lunch," Jennifer said. "We can all have lunch together."

"You're going too?" Glenn asked.

Jennifer cleared her throat.

"Of course, you are. My intonation was off," Glenn said.

"Jennifer, I have a plan, and I need your help."

"Consider it done," she said. "Whatever it is."

"We need the media to focus on Kate as a distraction, but don't initiate any real searches."

"You need a tie-in with Galveston?"

"It has to be subtle, but yes."

"Subtle is my middle name. Don't you say a thing, Glenn."

I chuckled. "See you on Wednesday."

After we hung up, Larry said, "I'll take the day off."

"You're too valuable on the cruise ship. We can't lose that advantage. You need to become a fixture and blend in."

Larry frowned. "Okay if the guys go too."

I filled two glasses with iced tea. "I've got an idea about that. Let's sit."

I sat on the sofa, and Spike sat next to me. Larry pulled a dining chair around and sat across from me. Palace Guard stood next to Larry.

I stared at Palace Guard, and Larry followed my gaze.

"Palace Guard is next to me? Not on the sofa?" Larry asked.

I kept my gaze on Palace Guard and cocked my head. "You know what I'm thinking, don't you?"

Palace Guard grinned.

"Well, I don't." Larry crossed his arms.

"Spike goes to work with me tomorrow and to Biloxi on Wednesday, and Palace Guard stays with you. You're tuned to Palace Guard. He can watch your back."

Palace Guard nodded.

Larry stared at the floor next to him where Palace Guard stood. "Okay. We'll try it." Larry held out his fist, and Palace Guard gave it a bump. Larry grinned. "We can do this."

"I need to get my notes organized and off to Ellen. It's late. Maybe we can go over my ship questions first thing tomorrow."

Larry grabbed a book and kicked off his shoes. He leaned back to read, and I pulled out my notes. After two hours, my notes were complete and coherent. I whirled around in my chair to tell Larry. *Oops. He's sleeping.*

I sent my notes to Ellen then rose and checked the door locks.

"Larry. Time for bed."

He rubbed his face, yawned, and pulled himself to a sitting position. "I was resting my eyes."

"Good night. See you in the morning." I padded to my bedroom.

I woke at five-thirty. *Lucy tomorrow*. I jumped up and dressed. I hurried to the kitchen and started coffee. Before the coffee finished perking, Larry sauntered into the kitchen. He wore jeans and a black T-shirt "How about breakfast tacos? They open at six. Where's your sling?"

"I donated it to Stuart. Let's go. We can wait for them to open if we're too early. What time do you leave for work?"

"Eight. But I get a better parking spot if I get there at seven-thirty. When are you leaving for Biloxi in the morning?"

"I thought I'd leave at five-thirty. Gives me time to stop for breaks. I'll pick up a car after I get off work today."

We ate our tacos in the parking lot overlooking the water before we headed back to the apartment.

Larry and I sat together at the computer while Palace Guard peered over my shoulder. I pointed to the blueprint. "This is the cargo area. I can't tell what the accessibility is and whether there are areas to store smuggled items out of sight."

"Not drugs, right?" Larry asked. "Drug-sniffing dogs are part of the daily routine."

"Right. Not drugs because they have the highest risk of law enforcement detection. The smugglers' product is out of the ordinary and has a high-dollar profit and low risk of discovery."

"It would be too easy if we had answers, right?" Larry smiled.

"Of course. We don't do easy." I returned his smile. "I'll bet the smuggling involves hepatitis somehow."

"Well, that narrows it down." Larry cleared his throat. "Sarcasm. You need another sling. You keep rubbing your arm. I'll make you one. I've got a triangular bandage in my backpack."

After Larry applied my new sling, he and Palace Guard left. I looked up the number for the car rental place. *Too early to call.*

I searched the history of smuggling on cruise ships with Spike by my side and scanned article after article. I turned off my computer and rose.

"Almost all those articles talked about mules: people who carry cocaine and other drugs hidden on their person or in their luggage. Except they are the smugglers in jail."

Spike nodded.

"The rest of the articles explained tricks for passengers to smuggle alcohol on board, but most of them were ads for a product. None of them sounded practical to me. My favorite was the binoculars with a tiny flask inside. Wouldn't a suitcase full of binoculars arouse suspicion?"

Spike mimed looking through binoculars and tipping the binoculars for a nip.

I chuckled. "Exactly."

At nine, Diane texted she was on the way. I put on my sling, locked the apartment, and Spike and I waited for Diane on the stairs. When Diane pulled into the parking lot, Spike and I climbed into her car.

"I need tomorrow off to pick up my dog. I know it's short notice, but can you spare me?"

"We'll manage. Mona will have to work instead of complaining. The real question is, are you okay with listening to her litany on Wednesday?" Diane chuckled.

"I am sorry about the inconvenience for you."

After we reached the diner, I stopped outside the door to the kitchen. "I need to call the car rental place. Won't be long."

A woman answered, and I asked, "Is Albert there today?"

"Who? I don't know any Albert. You want to rent a car?"

"I need a car for two days. I'll leave town before six tomorrow morning."

"We don't open until nine. Rent it for three days and pick it up this afternoon. We close at five. We don't have after hours pick up or drop off."

"A four-day rental then. I don't expect to be back until after five."

"It's extra if you go out of state. You don't have a dog, do you? That's an extra three hundred dollars a day."

"Yes, I have a dog. Thanks anyway."

When I went into the kitchen, Diane asked, "You all set?"

"No. I'll call another company that allows dogs in the car."

"That's awful." Diane put her hands on her hips. "I'll rent a car, and you can take mine."

I brushed away a tear. "Thank you, Diane. You really don't need…"

She waved her hand. "Forget it. Let's get busy. What's the menu today, Chip?"

"Meatloaf, mashed potatoes, and green beans. Ms. Irene isn't here. Will you make the pies today?"

"Didn't plan to but guess I will." Diane grabbed an apron. "Wish Mama had let me know. What about Mona? Is she in the dining area?"

"No Mona either, Ms. Diane."

I checked. "Chip's right. No Mona. I'll get busy too."

I measured coffee and water for the first pot and scurried to place salt and pepper shakers on the tables.

"You want some help there, Gray Lady?"

I hid my smile with my left hand and turned to face the kitchen door. "About time you showed up, Rosa."

"Bus a table or two for me today, and I'll split the tips with you." Rosa winked and slipped to the kitchen. "Diane, step away from the flour. I'm the pie girl."

Diane carried the register drawer into the dining area and perched on a counter stool. "Sure am glad Rosa's back. It was a fluke I even got her. She called me last night and asked if she'd left her black sweater here. We chatted, and I asked her to return."

"Perfect timing." I tugged at my shirt neck where the sling pulled.

"Nice to have her back." Diane narrowed her eyes. "Your sling bothering you?"

"Rubs my neck." I checked the silverware. "Need more forks."

"Good catch." Diane pushed the cash drawer into place. "When word gets out Rosa's back, we'll have her fans here for coffee and pie. Check on the small plates too."

"Ms. Rosa's here." Chip beamed when I returned from the storeroom with more dessert plates. "We have a happy kitchen again."

"I hadn't thought about that. You're right," I said.

My phone rang. *Jennifer.*

I stepped out and answered.

"Everything okay?" I asked. Spike hovered.

"We have to change our plans. Glenn was carrying in groceries last night when he stepped wrong and twisted his knee. We elevated his knee and put ice on it, but he had a rough night. We're at the doctor's office now, and they just took Glenn to an examination room. It doesn't look like we can make the trip tomorrow. I'm so sorry."

"I'll see Lucy soon. Don't worry about it. I'm sorry Glenn fell."

"Not near as sorry as I am. He's an old bear. Can Lucy and I bring you Glenn? Just kidding."

I chuckled. "He'll feel better when he gets home and has some pie and ice cream."

"Love it. Might sweeten his disposition," Jennifer said. "I'll let you know what the doctor says."

I paced the parking lot, and Spike trailed me. "We're not picking up Lucy tomorrow. Glenn injured his knee and is at the doctor's office." Tears slid down my cheek. "I looked forward to seeing Lucy, and I feel awful for Glenn. He's not a sit-around kind of guy."

Spike's face reflected my disappointment, and he patted my shoulder.

I brushed away the dampness that had rolled to my chin. "We'll just have to push and find Gary."

I texted Larry. "Glenn fell & hurt his knee. No Lucy trip."

"Sorry. Take the day off anyway."

I showed Spike my phone and shoved it into my back pocket. "Larry doesn't understand anything." I stormed to the door. "Let's get back to work, Spike."

When I opened the door to the kitchen, the sweet aroma of baking apple pies swept away my irritation with Larry.

"Pie fixes everything. Remember Ella's shirt?"

Spike grinned.

"Not really. Who's Ella?" Diane asked.

"A good friend who introduced me to how tasty pie is at a diner. I met her when I was job hunting right after college. You'd like her."

Spike narrowed his eyes, and I cleared my throat. "I won't be picking up Lucy tomorrow. Glenn twisted his knee and can't get around for a while."

"I'm sorry, Gray Lady. Take the day off, anyway? We've got everything covered. Maybe you could do some tourist things."

Spike nodded.

"Thank you. I can catch up on household chores.""After work we can pick up a car for you. My friend recommended a rental company nearby."

Irene burst in from the back door. "What's everybody standing around jawing? We've got work to do. I need to..."

"Rosa's back, Mama," Diane said.

"Of course, she is. I can see her right there. Now that you pointed her out. That's good. I've got things to do."

"Mama, do you know where..."

Irene rushed to the office and slammed the door.

"...Mona is?" Diane shook her head. "Sometimes I don't understand Mama. What about the car, Gray Lady?"

"If you could drop me off, it would be convenient for me to have a car since Larry needs his own transportation."

Irene stepped out of the office. "I caught Mona snooping."

She hoisted her canvas barber pole bag stuffed with papers onto her shoulder. "The office door needs a lock." She dashed out as Diane entered the kitchen.

"I thought I heard Mama."

"She was in a rush," I said.

"Always is these days," Diane mumbled.

At ten-thirty, the sky grew dark, and Diane flipped on the lights. By eleven, the showers had turned to heavy rain, and customers dashed into the diner and stomped their feet on the mat at the entrance.

"Gully-washer, for sure." A man stood at the door and shook his jacket.

When I returned to the kitchen for more coffee, I asked, "Will the rain keep away customers?"

"Not really. Everybody still has to eat. The diner will smell like wet dogs, though." Diane snickered.

"Order up," Rosa said. "Diane, you aren't kidding. This place is ripe. Good thing I love dogs."

"I love dogs too," Chip said.

"Do you have a dog, Chip?" I asked.

"Yes. My dad and I met our dog at the shelter two years ago. Sally's a Saint Bernard. She's a good girl. Maybe you can meet her sometime."

"I'd like that."

"Ride along when I take Chip home. Sally is a sweetheart," Rosa said.

"Maybe tomorrow?" I asked. "I planned to pick up a rental car today."

"We could pick up your car after we visit Sally," Rosa said.

"Yes. Decided," Chip said.

"Diane, I think my plans have changed," I said.

"I hear that." She chuckled. "We'd better get busy before Mama comes back and has a fit."

After our last customer left for the day, Rosa and I sanitized the tables then Rosa swept, and Chip mopped the diner.

"Do I mop again?" Chip asked when he was past the front door. "I can still smell the doggy odor."

"No. It'll be fine when it dries," Rosa said.

I loaded and ran the dishwasher while Diane scrubbed pots and pans. Chip mopped his way to the kitchen then Rosa and Chip put away the cleaning supplies.

"No need to watch the floor dry," Diane said. "Y'all go on. I've got paperwork to do."

"Thank you, Ms. Diane. See you tomorrow," Chip said.

Chip bounced ahead of us to Rosa's car.

"I may be just as excited as Chip," I said.

When Rosa unlocked her car, Chip held the passenger's door open for me then opened the back door and climbed in. Spike jumped in with him.

"I always ride in the back seat. My dad says that's best." He stared out the side window.

On our way, Rosa said, "It's six miles to your house, Chip. Did you know that?"

"Yes. I'm a good walker. Why did Ms. Mona wait for us to leave the diner?"

"Where did she wait?" I asked.

"She parked her car at the dry cleaners, but after we left, she pulled into Ms. Rosa's spot in the employee parking lot."

"Maybe she wanted to talk to Ms. Irene in private," Rosa said.

The tires crunched as Rosa pulled into a driveway of a modest adobe house with a driveway and a front yard of crushed seashells. Three papaya trees grew in the side yard. Pots of petunias, snapdragons, and hens and chicks lined the short walkway to the house entrance of blue tiles.

"Your house is beautiful," I said as Chip bounded to the front door. I closed the car door Chip had left opened and glanced at the road. A black SUV with dark-tinted windows crept by the house and turned right at the next corner.

"Chip and his dad are also southwest gardening fanatics," Rosa said.

When Chip opened the door, a curly-haired brown and white St. Bernard padded out and dropped to the patio, and Chip wrapped his arms around her and snuggled her massive head.

"This is Sally," he said.

When I reached Sally, I held out my hand for her to sniff. She rose and slobber-licked my hand. Her drool drizzled onto my boots as I scratched her ears. Rosa rubbed her back, and Sally flopped down with a thud next to Chip. The three of us stroked and patted. Spike sat on the ground with Sally, and she rolled over for a belly rub.

"Time for us to go, Sally. Sorry," Rosa said.

"Thank you for introducing me to Sally. She's a sweetheart," I said.

"I'll give Sally her afternoon snack, so she won't be sad," Chip said. Sally followed Chip into the house, and Rosa and I headed to Rosa's car.

Rosa pulled out of the driveway, and when we passed the side street, I glanced out my window. The black SUV idled in the driveway nearest the corner. I gazed at my side mirror, and the car backed out and maintained a short distance behind us.

"There's a black SUV following us," I said.

"Yep."

"Good guys or bad guys?" I asked.

"Doesn't matter. They've been with me since I came back. Either good guys who have my back or bad guys who need surveillance training."

I raised my eyebrows and pointed to my ear. Rosa winked and nodded.

"How's your arm doing?" she asked.

"Healing. My sling is exhausting." I removed it and rubbed my neck.

When we reached the car rental, Rosa said, "I'll go in with you to be sure there are no problems."

Before she opened the door, she said in a soft voice, "I'll rent the car."

Rosa stepped up to the counter. "My boss called about a renting a car."

The young man beamed. "Diane your boss? I've got the paperwork right here. Got your driver's license?"

He entered the license number then handed Rosa her license and a receipt. "Thanks, Irene. You can pick any car in row four. The keys are in the car."

Rosa handed me her car keys. "Thanks for the ride, Sis. I'll pick up our dry cleaning and stop at the grocery store for a few things. See you at home."

Spike raised his eyebrows, and I nodded.

After I left the car rental, I checked my rearview mirror. The black SUV was four car lengths behind me. Our two-car parade headed to my apartment. When I reached the parking lot, Larry had parked the rental car in my slot, and I diverted to the vacant apartment spot. I sneaked a peek at the entrance as I climbed the stairs, and the black SUV crawled past my apartment and circled Rosa's car.

Looking for a vacant slot?

Spike shrugged when the black car pulled into apartment Five-B's assigned spot.

"You're right," I unlocked my door and went inside. "They will get keyed."

"Who will get keyed?" Larry asked.

"My stalker. Well, Rosa's stalker."

I grabbed Larry before he rushed out of the door. "Wait. They might be good guys."

Larry jerked his arm out of my grasp. "Don't care."

He reached the bottom of the stairs, and I yelled after him. "The toilet's overflowing."

He shook his head, turned back, and stomped up the stairs. "Did you turn off the water?"

He slammed the door when he came inside then leaned against it. "Toilet?"

"I panicked."

I snickered when Spike did his dance. "Dang it, Spike. I'm supposed to be contrite."

Larry crossed his arms. "What about the stalkers?"

"They've been following Rosa, but we switched cars. She picked up my rental, and I drove hers. They followed me here. You can't be around when she comes to exchange cars because Rosa knows you are Officer Ewing and Larry. Officer Ewing is in Georgia, which means Larry is too. You can't stay."

"I'm not leaving. I'll wait in the bedroom." Larry bit his lip. "Or in the bathroom with the toilet."

"Does that mean you aren't mad?"

"Maybe." Larry reached under the sink and pulled the half-full trash sack out of the trash can. "Dumpster around back?"

He strolled out the front door. Spike hurried to the window and raised his eyebrows.

"He's smart. He'll be fine. I hope."

A few minutes later, Larry returned. "I don't know who they are. They didn't pay any attention to me.

You're right: their attention is on Rosa's car. Can you contact Rosa? Tell her to stay away."

"I'm going for a run." I changed to running shoes, shorts, and a sweatshirt to cover the bulge in my waistband.

"Are you crazy?" Larry asked.

"You always call me the crazy lady, so that must be a rhetorical question." I headed to the front door, but Larry blocked the handle. When I tried to reach around him, he shifted.

I narrowed my eyes. *When he shifts again, I'll toss him over my hip.*

Palace Guard shook his head, held his arm across the door, and joined Larry in blocking my exit.

"What are you doing? I want to catch Rosa before she turns at the apartment driveway. Palace Guard's going with me."

"Is that so? Then why is he standing next to me?" Larry held out his fist, and Palace Guard bumped it with his.

"He is not." I feinted to the right, but Spike appeared at Larry's other side.

"Your upper lip glistens when you lie," Larry said.

My phone rang, and I answered. "Pete's Auto Repair."

Rosa said, "This is Irene. Just letting y'all know my car's running fine, and I won't bring it in after all. Gotta go. My friends are waiting." She hung up.

"Rosa's not coming. She knows the stalkers are here."

"Why did you answer..."

"I don't know. Just popped into my head." I glanced at Spike who side-glanced at Palace Guard. "Thanks, Palace Guard. It gave Rosa a good opening."

Palace Guard saluted with two fingers.

I strode to the refrigerator and grabbed two beers. I offered one to Larry. "Truce?"

Larry frowned. "You won't toss me and dash out?"

I set his beer on the table and backed to my computer desk. "I called truce."

Larry picked up his beer and scooted a chair next to me. "Want to hear about my day? I don't think our contraband is being transported in the cargo area. Companies track containers with a standard label that identifies the owner, country, and physical description of the container."

I pulled up a ship's blueprint and pointed. "What about there?"

Larry scooted closer to my computer screen and leaned against me. Spike pinched Larry's shoulder, and Larry smacked at his shoulder. "Cut it out, Spike. I'm just trying to see."

Palace Guard patted Larry on the back, and Larry smiled. "That's the ballast. Perfect if you want to smuggle air or water. That's sarcasm."

"Makes no sense. A gallon of water weighs 8.34 pounds. The amount of water needed to improve the stability of a ship depends on the weight of the cargo, right? In theory, the heavier the cargo, the less water needed."

"What's this about ballast water and invasive species?" Larry pointed at a link on the screen.

"Ballast water taken on board in one body of water and discharged in another transports a variety of aquatic plants, animals, and bacteria. It's interesting but frightening reading. I don't think it relates to our smuggling investigation."

Larry leaned back. "A repeated accidental introduction of an aquatic species that carried hepatitis to people of a specific level of income seems remote in terms of probability."

"Yes." I cocked my head and stared at Larry. "However, smuggling a nonaquatic species that carried hepatitis suggests expensive exotic animals or parts of animals."

Larry jumped up and drained his beer. "So what are potential sources of hepatitis not included in the usual studies?"

"A little more complicated, but you've just defined my next search."

Palace Guard beamed.

"You're right," I said. "He is smart."

"Palace Guard thinks I'm smart?"

I turned back to my computer keyboard. "He does, and so do I."

Larry swaggered to the trash can and tossed in his bottle.

"Cop-walk," I said.

"You don't know. You didn't even look."

"Heard it."

When my phone buzzed an hour later, Larry rolled to face the back of the sofa and snorted in his sleep. Palace Guard and I read the text from the unknown number: "Demise complex. Reassigned. Maggie T."

I stared at the phone. "Oh, I get it. Techie Maggie. Paul's death was complex. But why was Maggie T. reassigned?"

Palace Guard frowned and shook his head.

My phone rang, and I jumped.

"Hello Maggie. It's Ellen. I have some answers about these notes you sent me. Hope it's not too late to call."

"I've been on the computer. Good time for a break." I poured a glass of sweet tea and returned to the computer desk.

Ellen cleared her throat. "I've known Irene and Mona for years and always thought Irene's exaggerations had an element of truth in them, but Irene has a problem with making things up on the spur of the moment. Mona has never been on my list of trusted people. Your observations peeled away the facades, and I had a fresh view of the two of them. Overall, Irene's reports are okay, although, like I said, she sometimes slips and embellishes with a lie here and there to paint herself in a better light. Makes her feel superior, I think. Mona, however, wouldn't know the truth if it slapped her in the face. I wouldn't trust her to take out my trash without stealing it." Ellen snickered. "I know. Tell you how I really feel, right? I've jotted down details and added other tidbits. Do you want me to give you a few highlights or send you my notes?"

"Both."

Ellen laughed. "I knew that. An interesting point about Irene's barber story and her daddy is she neglected to mention her brother was jealous, maybe rightly so, because their father never asked him to become a barber. Paul and Mona always teamed up against Irene even though Mona was Irene's friend."

"Wow." I rose from my computer desk and stepped outside to the balcony so I wouldn't disturb Larry. Palace Guard and Spike crowded next to me to listen.

"The run-in with Irene and Veronica? Paul and Veronica were sweethearts while she was still in high school; Irene never liked Veronica. I think Irene based her judgment on gossip because Mona spread terrible stories about Veronica. Paul and Veronica broke up before she graduated, and I suspect Mona was behind it. I always thought Paul should have stood up to his sister and defended Veronica. My opinion."

"Veronica and Paul? What about Paul and Mona being married?"

"That was a Mona lie. If Veronica heard it, I'd put my money on finding Mona in a ditch. When I was digging, I found a marriage license. Ready? Paul and Veronica married three years after she graduated from high school."

"Whoa." I dropped to the chair.

"They divorced five years later, and she left town. I didn't realize she was back. Mona's company fired her, but the details are fuzzy. Veronica's claim of embezzlement might be right. Jay's looking deeper into that too. He has unofficial resources I don't have access to. Anyway, I'll send you my full report, at least what I have so far. Mona's disappearance puzzles me. This has been fun. I didn't know how much I loved digging for answers."

"Thank you."

"Thank you. Don't tell Jay, but I understand now why he was so reluctant to retire and why he volunteers to mentor the young detectives. I'm enjoying the thrill of the hunt myself."

After we hung up, I said, "This is a shift. I'm still not sure how Gary fits in though. Wonder if Rosa would be Veronica's friend?"

Chapter Nine

Larry joined us on the balcony and handed me a glass of iced tea. "I have another idea."

Spike rolled his eyes, and I punched his arm.

"Did you just punch Spike?" Larry asked. "We need an expert on ship construction and ballast, right? Let's go to the Houston Maritime Museum after we get off work tomorrow. If we're lucky, we'll find a volunteer who is an expert, and you can get all your questions answered. For your college paper."

"That's brilliant." I toasted Larry with my glass.

"I know." He clinked my glass. "Let's get tacos for supper."

"Taco Tuesday. Let's go."

"No stalkers. They must have gotten bored," I said as we headed to Larry's car. "Where are we going?"

"We could eat at a restaurant. Sit and relax. Watch people and eavesdrop."

"Tempting. Or order takeout and eat here. Your choice."

"The usual."

I called our taqueria and ordered. Larry pulled into the line at the takeout window.

While we waited, I said, "Ellen called me. She said Irene exaggerates, but Mona lies. That's the short version. She'll send a detailed report, and you can read it when we get it."

"Anything interesting?"

"Oh yes. Paul married his high school girlfriend, not Mona, for starters. Mona is probably an embezzler. I think I need to push Irene harder for information about Gary."

Larry paid for our order. "Wow. That's a lot. I should nap more often. A joke."

"Okay." I fake-laughed.

"Well done, Mags. That was almost a sarcastic laugh."

"Really? Thank you."

After we ate, I received the email from Ellen. I printed it for Larry to read, updated my database with her information, and read my screen.

"Maggie." A large hand rested on my shoulder. "Time for bed."

"Time for bed," I mumbled as I checked the door locks. Larry was asleep on the sofa.

"Go to bed, Larry." I hobbled off to my room.

While Larry showered for work early the next morning, I cooked breakfast. When he bounded into the kitchen, I poured his coffee and set a plate of food at his seat.

Larry's eyes widened. "This is amazing. Eggs, biscuits, gravy, and grits beat my cereal and toast." He dug in. "How can you pull together a breakfast so quick?"

I sat down with my plate of food like Larry's but with smaller portions. "I'm a short-order cook. A two-top is easy compared to a table of six."

"What's a two-top?"

"Two-person table."

After he finished eating, Larry loaded his dishes into the dishwasher. Before I ate my last bite, he washed and rinsed the pans and set them in the drainer to dry.

"Thanks again for a great breakfast. See you this afternoon."

"Thanks for scrubbing the pans."

Larry saluted. "My pleasure, ma'am." As Larry approached the door, Spike followed him.

"You're coming to work with me today?" Larry asked.

Spike shoved him and grinned. Larry shrugged, and the two of them headed out.

I headed to my computer and paused. *Wait, a minute. Did Larry see Spike?*

I reviewed my nautical blueprint and jotted down a list of questions for my college paper, as Larry called it, before I left for work.

When I reached the diner, Irene had parked her car next to the diner's back door. Rosa and Chip rolled into the employee lot, and Rosa parked at her usual spot near the road. Irene unlocked the diner and rushed inside. As I locked my car, I cocked my head and sniffed at a pungent odor. *Rotten eggs? Gas?*

"Do you smell..."

The roar and heat of the fireball rolled out the diner's back door. The blast of an explosion tossed me away from my car. I crawled to Rosa and Chip. Tears rolled down my face. *Not again.*

Rosa was on top of Chip with her arms around him. I gasped in horror and collapsed into the sand. I willed myself to push up onto my elbows then crawled closer. Debris had crushed the back of Rosa's skull. I cradled her head and eased her body off Chip. Chip was face down in the dirt and sand, and his sobs tore at my heart. I choked back a scream as I gazed at Rosa's lifeless eyes and closed them.

Chip rolled to his side, clutched Rosa's body, and shouted. "No, Ms. Rosa. Wake up. You can't leave us."

A torrent of tears blinded me, and I couldn't breathe. Chip's cries intensified to a guttural roar that tore into my soul.

Irene!

Palace Guard helped me to my feet, and we sprinted to the diner. The fierce flames pushed me back, and I dashed to the front where the extreme intensity of the heat forced me to retreat to the other side of the road. The thick black smoke billowed inside the diner, and flames rolled and danced on the ceiling. A red pickup truck screeched to a stop, and Smitty, one of our regulars, jumped out.

"No!" I screamed. Palace Guard and I raced to cut him off. We dived at him before he rounded his truck and knocked him to the road.

"What the hell's wrong with you?" he asked. Blood trickled from a laceration on his cheek. He struggled to get up, but Palace Guard and I held him down.

"Flashover." I shouted as the fire exploded and the windows blew out from the overheated gases. Flames engulfed the entire diner. I struggled to my feet, but when I reached for the truck door on the side away from the diner, I burned my hand and jerked it away. Palace Guard caught me when I lost my balance and put his arm around me. I limped away from the fury of the fire.

Smitty caught up with us and engulfed me in a hug. "You are one strong tiny thing, and you saved my life. Thank you, Gray Lady." He lifted me and planted a big kiss square on my mouth and set me down.

My head swirled from the shock and from the cacophony of sirens and shouts. Palace Guard braced me as we made our way to Chip and Rosa. Chip sat on the ground with Rosa cradled in his arms. He rocked her and moaned.

Tears tricked down my face, and I wiped my nose on the back of my hand. "It's my fault she was here. If I hadn't asked for her, she'd still be..."

Palace Guard stepped in front of me and held my gaze.

Chip.

"You're right. If Chip hadn't ridden with Rosa, he would have waited at the back for Irene to open." I sobbed. "And Rosa threw her body between the explosion and Chip. She saved Chip."

I couldn't stop sobbing. "But it's my fault she was here and died."

My knees weakened, and I reached for Palace Guard.

A police officer approached us. "Everybody okay?"

"No," I said. "We need medical here. For him." I inclined my head toward Chip.

"Is she..."

"Yes." I straightened my back. "Rosa's dead."

"Was anyone in the diner?"

"Yes. Irene, the owner, was inside before the explosion."

The police officer rushed away as he spoke into his radio. I choked on the acrid smoke, and Chip coughed and wheezed.

"Let's move out of the smoke, Chip."

Chip wheezed. "Can't leave Ms. Rosa."

I coughed and had trouble getting my breath. I grabbed Chip under his arms to pull him away, but he was too heavy for me. Palace Guard joined me, and we dragged Chip away from Rosa and the smoke.

"Can't leave Ms. Rosa." Chip sobbed.

I sat on the ground and hugged him. "We can watch her from here. She'd like that."

Chip gazed at Rosa's body. "She'd like that," he echoed.

Chip covered his ears as the engine roar of fire trucks and engines, radio traffic over loudspeakers, and shouts intensified. Two ambulance crews with stretchers rushed across the parking lot. One crew headed to us; the other crew rushed to Rosa.

"Will they make Ms. Rosa better?" Chip asked.

"No. They can't."

Chip nodded.

I rose and pointed to Chip. "I don't know what his injuries are. Give him time to process questions before he answers."

The lead paramedic nodded, and her team back boarded Chip and loaded him onto the stretcher. As they rolled away, Chip blew a kiss to Rosa, and my tears renewed.

The paramedic stared at my shirt.

I glanced down. "Not mine. I'm fine."

A man put his arm around me. "I'm a paramedic. I've got her."

My knees buckled at the sheer relief of the sound of Larry's voice, and he caught me.

"Is she hurt?" he asked.

Palace Guard shook his head.

"Maggie, I'm parked one street over."

"Let's go," I said.

Larry and Palace Guard supported me as we headed to Larry's car. Spike had his hand on my back.

"Your split lip is bleeding, and you have an abrasion on your cheek." Larry maintained a tight grip on my arm.

I winced as I stepped. "I think I skinned my knee when we knocked down Smitty."

"What? I'll hear more later, right? Hospital or a clinic?" Larry asked.

"Taqueria," I said.

Spike patted my back.

"Don't encourage her, Spike." Larry growled.

As we drove away, the silence washed over me, and I leaned back in my seat. "How did you get there so fast?" I asked.

"Spike punched me in the stomach, and I doubled over. I told my supervisor I was sick, and we left."

I glanced at the back seat, and Spike beamed. I leaned back in my seat and closed my eyes. "You see Spike and Palace Guard, don't you?"

Larry pulled into a clinic parking lot. "Yes. We'll get you checked here; if they don't send you to a hospital, we'll get tacos."

"And if they send me to a hospital, you'll smuggle them in."

"Of course. Not a joke."

After three hours, we left the clinic. "Told you," I said as I climbed into the car.

"Yes, you did. Your injuries are minor. Taco time, and I'm ready for the story about the man you knocked down."

"I went around front to see if..." I sobbed. "Rosa died. It's my fault."

Larry parked at the beach and opened my door. "Let's sit."

The four of us sat on the soft sand near the water's edge of high tide. The waves lapped at the shore, and the seagulls called out.

I leaned against Larry and sobbed. "Rosa died, and Parker died."

"I know." Larry wrapped his arm around my shoulders.

When I ran out of tears, my eyes burned, and my chest ached. We returned to the car in silence, and Larry drove to our taco stand.

"Our usual," I said.

"Always."

After we returned to the apartment and finished our tacos, Larry said, "You know you can go home if you like. Just say the word."

"I'll lie down for a bit. I'm too exhausted to think." After I kicked off my boots and swung my feet up on the bed, I lay back with my head on my pillow. My neck and shoulders relaxed, and I stared at the ceiling. *I can't go home yet.* I rose and tiptoed to the living room in case Larry was asleep.

Larry had spread out the papers I'd given him on the kitchen room table. His elbows were on the table, and his hands propped his chin. "The fire and explosion dominate the news. I texted Glenn and told him you're fine so he can let Sergeant Arrington and your mother know. You're not going home yet, are you?"

I joined him at the table. "I'm torn about finding Gary. Why do you suppose you can see the imaginary men?"

"You won't get mad? After my car crash, I saw shadowy forms then I made out Spike when we left for the ship. I saw Palace Guard with you at the diner. I'm guessing the crash knocked some sense into me."

"You should have told me." I crossed my arms and glared.

Larry stared at the papers. "What do rich people do after they've bought everything they wanted ten times over and travel bores them?"

"Fine. We'll talk about something else. Spend time with their friends?"

"Their friends are just as rich and bored as they are, or they did drugs and are post-rehab, brain-fried, or dead."

"Doesn't sound like they're having much fun." I rose. "Want some tea? I'm parched." I poured our tea. "Irene was very elusive, but she said some people weren't what they seemed, and other people wouldn't accept her help. Not much there."

"Does that apply to rich people?" Larry ran his finger around the top of his glass and made it ring.

"That's cool. How did you do that?" I tried, but my glass squeaked. "Maybe the rich people help others?"

"I'm not sure they'd know how to do that except through money, and they'd have staff to do that."

"Sounds sad to me."

"I think you're onto something. What makes people not sad?"

"Having someone to love and love them. Like Lucy and me, except they'd still be rich, so wouldn't they want something nobody else had? Like an exotic pet?"

"Might be worth looking into."

I stared into my glass.

"Are you okay, Maggie?" Larry put his hand on my arm.

"No need to find Gary," I said.

"What?"

"Kate said Gary would find me. The explosion was on the news; he'll find me if he wants to. Let's check on Chip. He'll want to see me."

"So Gary's following you? Do I need to make myself scarce?"

"No. He would already know you're around and who you are. If Chip's still in the hospital, I wonder if there's any way we could sneak Sally in."

"Who?"

"Sally. Chip's St. Bernard."

Larry spewed his tea and choked. "Warn me next time."

I hid my grin as I jumped up and flipped a towel to Larry. "Here you are. Want to change your shirt before we leave?"

I relaxed when Larry turned to avoid the diner on our way to the hospital. The emergency department parking lot was full, but Larry pulled into a spot in front of the emergency entrance as a car pulled out.

I raised my eyebrows, and he grinned. "Told you."

When we were inside the hospital, the paramedic from the diner headed to the exit. The driver with a graying mustache and tic in his right eye followed her with the stretcher. He was the rig driver from the shooting; he saluted me.

The paramedic's eyes widened when she saw Larry. "Take the cot to the unit. I'll be there in a minute."

"How's the girl? Your patient from the diner?" she asked as she approached Larry. I turned my back and examined the hospital map.

"Fine. Superficial injuries. What about your patient?"

"The same. They'll release him." The radio on her hip crackled. "Wouldn't you know? Gotta go. Maybe we can get together sometime. I'm at station fifteen." She hurried to the exit.

"Nope," I said in a quiet voice.

"What?" Larry asked.

I cleared my throat. "Do you think we should wait here or go to Chip's house?"

Larry pointed to a seat near the exit. "Why don't you wait there, and I'll see if I can find him." Larry strode to the information desk.

A hospital orderly in green scrubs pushed a wheelchair down the hallway toward the exit. *Chip.* A tall, muscular man with a brown beard and a ruddy complexion accompanied them with his hand on Chip's shoulder.

Chip's frown and down-turned mouth shifted to a bright smile. "Ms. Gray Lady! You're okay."

"Yes, and happy to see you."

His frown returned. "Ms. Rosa's not okay."

"You're right. Her injuries were too bad."

"She was my friend," he said as I walked alongside him.

"Yes, she was. She would be happy to know you are okay."

He nodded.

"I'm Walt, Chip's father." The bearded man held out his hand, and we shook.

"I'm Maggie, but everybody calls me the Gray Lady," I said.

"Chip said you were there too."

"I was. Rosa saved Chip."

"Yes," Chip said. "Ms. Rosa was my friend."

"Chip has been asking for you. Thank you for coming," Walt said.

Larry met us at the exit and put his arm around my shoulder. Chip reached for my hand, and we waited while Walt strode off to his car. When Walt returned, the orderly helped Chip into the passenger's seat. Walt and Larry shook hands.

"Thanks for bringing the Gray Lady, Larry," Walt said. "Chip's been asking for her."

Walt fastened Chip's seatbelt, and Chip rolled down his window. As the car drove away, Chip waved.

"How do you know Walt?" I asked.

"We work together." He gazed at me. "You okay?"

"I need to see Diane." We strolled to the car.

"Thought you would. I have her address."

On the way to Diane's, Larry said, "According to the news reports, the preliminary findings suggest a gas leak. No sign of Irene yet."

I stared out the side window. "I don't think it was an equipment failure. Irene told me her stove has been reliable for years, and there weren't any problems since I've been there. I smelled the gas from the parking lot." I rubbed my forehead. "Someone extinguished the pilot light last night, and the gas accumulated. The fire marshal will investigate, but it takes time."

"If it wasn't accidental, who was the target?"

"Could have been me; could have been Rosa; but I think Irene was the target."

"Related to the attacks on you and me?"

"I think so. All related. I've got questions, and I think Gary has answers. Or maybe somebody else does."

"There's Diane's house," Larry pointed. "I'll park a half-block away. Wait while I see how she's doing."

I rolled my shoulders and nodded. Spike patted my back. Larry trotted down the street with Palace Guard behind him.

The surrounding houses were sandy-brown or off-white adobe. The lots were small, and the houses were close together. Some had small grass lawns; most had front yards of gravel, boulders, and cactus; a few homes had flowering shrubs near the windows, and others had small trees. All the yards were well-groomed. I stepped out of the car, and the light breeze relaxed me with the mingled fragrance of citrus and flowers. The traffic from the highway that was two miles away was a soft purr of white noise. *Lucy and I need more space, but this is a pleasant neighborhood.*

Larry strode down the sidewalk. "Diane would like to see you, but she said she preferred a more private talk in her backyard. Her small house is noisy."

Diane sat under a pergola on a cedar bench. She rushed to greet me and held my hand as we walked to the bench. Larry, Spike, and Palace Guard waited at the edge of the yard.

"Thank you so much for coming to see me, Maggie. Were you there? Can you tell me what happened?"

I nodded. "Rosa, Chip, and I arrived about the same time. We had parked, and when I got out of my car, I thought I smelled gas. Irene went into the diner." I bit my lip, but the tears escaped. "The explosion threw Rosa, Chip, and me across the parking lot. After I checked Chip and Rosa, I ran to the diner, but the flames..." I cleared my throat. "The flames were too hot. I ran to the front, but I saw billowing smoke and rolling flames on the ceiling. The fire flashed over, and the entire diner was on fire."

"Mama was in the diner." Diane spoke more to herself than to me.

"Yes."

"Thank you, Maggie. Not knowing was tearing me apart."

Diane rose and went inside her house. Larry offered me his hand, and he helped me up. Palace Guard put his arm around my shoulder. Spike had his hand on my back, and Larry linked my arm through his.

When we reached the sidewalk, I exhaled. "I didn't realize I was holding my breath, and y'all are crowding me."

Nobody budged, and I rolled my eyes. *Protective men.*

On our way to the car, I said, "I'd like to go to the museum, but I'm not sure I'm up to it."

"We wouldn't have much time before closing anyway," Larry said. "Let's see how you feel tomorrow when I get off work."

"I can review my notes from Ellen this evening and dive into new research; I'm curious about the medical condition outliers of the rich and the open question of fulfillment for the wealthy. Maybe it's a status thing, but more than status. Thrill, maybe?"

"You may have something there. Not just status. Status plus."

"If it's status, it needs to be something kind of disposable or maybe easy to store, so the rich person can chase the next big thing. I also need to update my database. I have a stack of notes to record."

"Maggie, you need a break." Larry scowled. "I'll take you back to Georgia anytime you're ready."

"No. I won't rest until..." I gazed at the sandy beach and undulating gulf. "We find Rosa's killer."

I spent the afternoon researching growth in reported diseases in the US. I changed my search from hospital admissions to health department data then refined the data by level of income.

"Sun's going down." Larry waved his hand in front of the computer screen. "I walked to the diner and picked up your car. No damage. Want a walk on the beach?"

I set a pace fast enough to stretch my legs. When we reached the sand, we slowed to a stroll and headed west. The cool wind off the Gulf brought a mist with the taste of salt. The brilliant orange and pinks of the sun's remnants lit up the sky between the dark clouds and the horizon, and the cricket frogs and the crickets chirped their nightly duel.

"Thanks for the break from the computer. Want to hear what I've found so far? A strain of the hepatitis B virus with confirmed infections. The macaque monkey, which the US banned from import in 1975, is the source of the hepatitis simiae strain. While the records report only a few cases in the US, all the infected people fall into a higher income level."

"Will you print the hepatitis B information for me?"

"Done. I found several detailed articles for you to read, and I can show you online ads offering pet monkeys for sale."

"How could anyone smuggle monkeys without drawing attention to the noise, and I'm guessing, smell?"

"Good question for our expert at the shipbuilding museum."

"I'm hungry," Larry said. "What if we break away from our usual tacos and get something different?"

"Like tamales?" I asked.

Larry laughed. "I like how you think, Crazy Lady. Let's do it."

We headed to our favorite taqueria. Larry ordered a sack of tamales and tacos, and I raised my eyebrows.

"In case we need a snack later," he said. "Let's sit on the back patio. We can eat alfresco."

"That's fancy," I said. "Does beer go with fine dining?"

When we approached the turn for the apartment parking lot, I said, "I thought what we needed to know died with Irene, but that's not true. I need to organize my notes."

"Food first, though."

Larry carried the sacks to the balcony, and I grabbed our beer.

Larry dashed inside and returned with a towel. He tossed it over the tiny patio table. "Fine dining, my lady."

As the sun sank on the horizon, we devoured tacos, tamales, and guacamole salad with tortilla chips and drank our beer.

"Should I have grabbed glasses for our beer? Since we're being all fancy and all." I drained the last of my beer.

"Fine dining, not extra dishes," Larry said. "Another? And a brownie?"

"Sounds perfect." I leaned forward to rise.

"Don't move. I got it." Larry jumped up and returned with beer and brownies.

"Dessert," he said.

"Thanks." I yawned.

When I woke the next morning, the apartment was quiet. I tiptoed to the kitchen and found a note on the table. "Hope you slept in. L"

I dressed and sipped coffee while I reviewed my notes. Spike sat at the kitchen table with me.

"This might be a stretch," I said. "Irene said she had a lead on her brother's murder then later she whispered to Maynard, Gus's brother. I never saw Irene whisper to anyone else. She was always full volume. I wonder if she shared her information with Maynard."

My new phone buzzed a text. *Glenn.* "Call? Nothing urgent. Bored."

I refilled my cup and called.

"I'm not supposed to bother you. If I hang up, Jennifer returned early from the store." He chuckled. "Just kidding. We're on speakerphone, and Jennifer and Lucy are right here with me."

"He's a mess," Jennifer said. "We wanted to check on you. We heard about the diner. Thank goodness you're okay. The news about P.J. devastated Thomas. I don't know if you knew P.J. was his daughter, and she worked for Kate."

"I knew that. We were friends." Spike patted my arm.

"I'm so sorry," Jennifer said. "Her service will be private. Family only. Are you okay?"

"I'm okay. Maybe a little shell-shocked. P.J. saved a young man. She protected him when the blast hit."

"That's what we heard." Glenn cleared his throat. "We have something else. Tell your cousin we heard from his mother, and she's doing fine."

I plopped down on the sofa and spilled coffee on my jeans. *Aunt Katherine.* "Oh, really?"

"Yes," Jennifer said. "It was great to hear from her. It's been a while. We'd lost touch."

"I know." Tears slipped down my face. "I'll tell him."

After we disconnected, I jumped up. "They heard from Kate. She's fine."

Spike and I danced.

"I don't know why they had to talk in code, but that's the best news I've heard in a long time. Now I want details."

Spike pointed to my phone.

"No, I won't bother Larry at work. Maybe we'll find more good news." I refilled my cup then returned to my computer and doodled while I read.

After an hour, I rose to change my jeans and glanced at my scribbles with *Irene* in the middle of the paper and *Diane, Gary, Maynard, Gus, Veronica, and Mona* around her. I rubbed my forehead as I read the names.

Palace Guard sat next to me at the computer. "No Chip." I scrolled back through my records. "Why don't I have any notes about Chip? He even told me people don't see him." I tapped my pen on the table. "Walt worked with Paul, and Paul was a porter. Does Walt ever mention Paul? I'll ask Larry."

My old phone rang. When I answered, Ellen asked, "How are you? Would you care to go somewhere quiet for lunch? I can pick you up."

"I'm fine..." I cleared my throat. "Lunch sounds good. Why don't we meet? I could pick up the groceries I need afterward."

"There's a small sandwich shop near the port. Why don't we meet there at eleven-thirty?"

After Ellen gave me the address, I jumped into the shower. I dressed in my jeans and a gray short-sleeved cotton shirt Mother would call a "blouse."

A light fog gave the day a gray cast. The seagull calls reminded me of the diner noise and Irene barking out orders. After Spike and I pulled in front of the sandwich shop, I turned off the engine. "Looks like they don't open until eleven-thirty. Let's window shop." When I opened the car door, I inhaled the heady aroma of smoking applewood.

"We may have found an alternate to tacos."

The sandwich shop was in a strip mall with a nail store, a hardware store, and a store on the end that Mother used to call a five and dime. I pushed open the door. "Maybe I can find a red scarf like Rosa's here."

Spike and I strolled the aisles. I didn't find a scarf that suited me despite our careful search. Spike tapped my arm and pointed to the front window. A slight man with a full gray beard rounded the corner of the building. *Maynard?* We rushed to the door, but he had disappeared. Spike dashed around the corner, but when he returned, he shook his head.

As we sauntered to the restaurant, Ellen parked next to my car. When we stepped inside the shop, the fragrance of baked bread welcomed us.

Ellen beelined to a table in the middle row near the back. "This is my favorite table. Close to the exit, and we can watch the front and the back of the shop."

The server brought us tea and small bowls of chunky pickle chips.

"Smoked turkey half sandwich on sourdough with a cup of tortilla soup." Ellen pointed to the menu.

"That sounds good. I'll have the same."

"Are the pickles an appetizer?" I asked after the server left.

"Sure are. Supposed to be good for the digestion. They pickle their own, make their sourdough bread on site, and have a smoker in the back."

"I've got to bring Larry here. He'd love it."

Ellen chuckled. "If I'd told Jay where we were having lunch, he'd be right here with us. I rarely get invited to help Jay with an assignment. You're my favorite."

I bit into a pickle. "Spicy." My eyes watered. "Yummy. Favorite assignment?"

"Jay needed to meet up with Larry. He said having dinner with y'all would be the best way. That host was an obnoxious flirt, wasn't she? So, what do you have for me? I thought you might need help." Ellen crunched into a pickle.

I sprinkled my napkin with salt to keep the sweating glass from sticking. "I have some questions, but you first."

"Jay said I can't tell anyone I overheard him say that Paul was undercover, so I won't talk about the Rangers. I'm not that into baseball, anyway." She snickered.

"Baseball is interesting." I smiled as I reached into my backpack for my Irene scribble, but kept it in my lap. "Irene told me she had a lead on her brother's murder. Who would Irene have confided in?"

"Diane is the obvious answer. The next person might be Maynard. Do you know him? Gus is his brother, and I'm sure he is, or was, a regular at the diner. Maynard was an old high school friend of her husband's and always had a soft spot for Irene."

"That explains why she whispered to him."

"Irene whispered? That's hard to believe."

"True." I unfolded the paper and smoothed it on the table. "I doodled last night while I read through my notes on the computer."

Ellen pulled the paper close and read while our server refilled our tea. "Let's go around your circle, and I'll tell you what I know. You want to take notes?"

I pulled out my notebook.

"Let's start with Diane," she said. "Diane had a cranky teenage stage, but not as long as her friends. They still haven't outgrown the drama. I could tell you stories, but that's not what we're doing today, is it?" She leaned on the table and lowered her voice. "Another time. Anyway, Diane and her mother were always close. Irene didn't much care for Diane's husband, but I'm not sure any man was good enough for her daughter in Irene's eyes. He was a hard-working mechanic and a good one too, but he died in a car wreck a month before the baby was born. Tragic."

A young man in a suit and tie rushed into the shop to pick up an order. Ellen switched the conversation to her white camellias.

After he left, Ellen continued. "Told you about Maynard, except he was law enforcement before he retired. U.S. Marshals. People said he was one of those flight marshals, but I suspect he worked with the witness protection program."

Our lunch came, and Ellen folded the sheet and handed it to me. "Let's eat."

I stuck the sheet in my notebook, and we dug in. I took a bite of sandwich then a bite of pickle. "Mmm. The spicy pickles taste even better with the smoked turkey."

Ellen sipped her soup. "Still too hot. My brother's in the import business, and he may have known Paul, now that I think about it. My brother Kenny and I were never very close, and Jay didn't like him at all. It's been ages since I've seen him, but maybe I could get hold of Kenny to see if he knows anything that might help."

"Sure..."

Spike frowned and waved his arms.

"On second thought, no, I don't think it's worth digging. Now if you want to dig up any dirt on Mona..." I wiggled my eyebrows.

"I'd need a wheelbarrow. No, a backhoe for that one."

We laughed, and Spike winked.

"Funny about Gus. He's been around forever, but all I know about him is he's the fish man." Ellen blew on her soup.

Original gray man. Hidden in plain sight. I sipped my soup. "This is great."

Ellen talked about getting a cat and complained about the bugs that attacked her rose bushes. After we finished eating, our server cleared our dishes and handed us a dessert menu.

Ellen gazed at her menu. "I always do this. I never have room for dessert."

"Cookies-and-cream pie to go?" our server asked.

"Of course." Ellen grinned.

"I'll make that three."

"Better make it four." Ellen patted my hand. "Lunch is my treat."

On our way to the apartment, I pointed to the sack on the seat next to me. "Dessert is melting. I haven't needed an ice chest until now."

Spike dashed up the apartment stairs, and I chased him. After I unlocked the door, Spike pushed me inside.

"I thought we were racing."

Spike crouched, and I copied him. I peeked out the front window as a black SUV with darkened windows crawled through the parking lot then stopped at Rosa's car. A large man climbed out of the SUV and approached her car. He glanced around and tried to open the driver's side door.

"That's Stuart," I said. "Butch. That's what the men at the diner called him."

He stared at the apartment building that was closest to Rosa's car and headed to the rear of the vehicle. A white panel van with a local electrician's logo on the side pulled into the drive and turned to the right where Butch's car blocked the roadway. Butch rushed back to his SUV, and his tires screeched as he left the parking lot.

"Not very stealthy. Is he that klutzy or a distraction? I need to know more about Butch."

Chapter Ten

I put the dessert into the refrigerator and called Walt. I left a message then scanned through my notes. "Why did I not do this earlier?"

I called the motel where Mona said Gary Sloan stayed. While the phone rang, I wondered if I should ask for Gary Sloan or Ernie Parker. I was about to hang up when the clerk answered.

"Gary Sloan, please," I said.

"Not here." The clerk hung up.

"What does that mean?" I slammed my fist on the table. "Gone down the street? Never there? Checked out?"

Spike shrugged. The front door opened, and Larry and Palace Guard sauntered in. Larry and Palace Guard dressed alike in blue jeans, LSU T-shirts, and work boots.

"Who checked out? I had a great day. The guys asked me to join them in the weekly pool game this weekend.

I'm an excellent pool player. It's okay if I go, isn't it?" He chuckled. "I said I'd check with you, and one guy said he never asks if he can go out. The rest of them laughed, and a guy said that's because he doesn't have a woman at home. They don't call me the new guy anymore. A few of them even remembered my name."

He ambled to the refrigerator and pulled out the pitcher of tea. "Want some?" He reached for glasses in the cabinet. After he dropped in ice cubes and filled the glasses with tea, he sat at the table. "The supe said I'm doing fine, but I'm too particular. I need to step up the pace."

"Soup?" I scratched my head.

"Supervisor. But all of us guys call him *Supe.*"

Palace Guard nodded and winked. I coughed into my elbow to hide my giggle.

"I need a quick shower before we go to the museum. My Texas coworker on the Reynolds case arranged for an experienced volunteer to meet us. I let him know we'd be there this afternoon. Have you had lunch? I ate with the guys. Guess I should have let you know. I need to carry my lunch to work. Do we have lunch sacks or a cooler and something to carry coffee in?" Larry ambled to his bedroom then headed to the bathroom with a change of clothes.

"Good job, Spike. Your trainee has the undercover thing down pat. You too, Palace Guard."

Palace Guard ambled to the front door and back, and Spike and I cracked up.

"Yep, just like that. Sounds like we need to do some shopping to pick up lunch supplies and sandwich stuff and snacks. Guess I'll make a list. We'll call it *Larry's Lunch List*."

"What would you like for lunch tomorrow? We can pick up groceries on our way back."

"Pimento cheese? Do you think we could make tortilla soup? The guys have soup and a sandwich. Okay if we stop by a sporting goods shop for my lunch box? I know the best place to get one."

"Kate said you'd be a natural at hostage negotiations, but I think you're a natural at undercover."

Larry beamed and held up his hand. Palace Guard smacked a high-five.

"Thanks, PG," Larry said.

I glanced at Spike, and he shrugged.

Larry pulled into a parking lot with an oversized sign that claimed a fifteen-minute walk to the museum. I carried my sweatshirt along for later.

"It's supposed to cool down. I should have brought mine too," Larry said.

We made our way along the narrow walkway in the same direction as the traffic flow. I flinched at the squeal of brakes behind us and glanced over my shoulder. A sports car sped up as it roared past us, and I cringed. A truck's air brakes hissed, and I tensed my shoulders. My ragged breathing quickened.

After we'd walked a block, Larry asked, "Are you okay?"

"Fine," I said in a terse voice.

Palace Guard stepped in front of me. When I stopped, he held my gaze and breathed in through his nose, held his breath then breathed out through his pursed lips. I copied him.

"Is it the traffic?" Larry asked after I'd settled down.

"I can't keep track of the cars or the occupants."

Larry frowned. "What would help?"

"It helps that you understand." I leaned with my hand against the nearest building and focused on my breathing.

"Let's cross the street and walk against traffic," he said. "It will be easier to see the cars as they approach."

"You're right."

The four of us turned back to the nearest traffic light and crossed the street.

When we neared the museum, we returned to the other side and left the major street behind us.

"Much different. Thanks," I said. Palace Guard and Spike applauded.

When we approached a nondescript house in the middle of the block of the warehouse district, Larry reached for the door and stopped with his hand midair. "You ready?"

"As long as there's no traffic."

Larry laughed and hugged me. "I never know what you'll say. Am I right, PG?"

Palace Guard nodded, and Spike and I stared. Larry held the door for me, and when I went inside, I scanned the room in awe at the anchors and models of ships. Larry strode to the Information Desk and leaned down to speak to the woman behind the desk. She smiled and picked up her phone. I wandered into the museum gift shop. Spike pointed to the display case with pirate paraphernalia for sale and grinned.

"Good find. Just like Rosa's."

I bought the red paisley scarf and tied it around my neck. When we stepped out of the shop, my eyes widened as a man with a full gray beard strolled down a hallway toward Larry. *Maynard?*

Maynard and Larry shook hands. Spike pushed me, and as I approached, I caught the end of their conversation.

"Oh, the hat?" Larry laughed. "No, SMU. First two years then I transferred to LSU."

Maynard smiled and turned to greet me. "You're a beautiful sight, Gray Lady. I heard you and Chip survived the fire, but it's nice to have living proof. And you're wearing a scarf just like Rosa's. What a nice tribute. You have any trouble finding a place to park?"

"Not at all. We parked at the lot south of the museum." Larry said.

"Nice day for a walk. What can I do to help you?"

We parked north of the museum. Why did Larry say south? Palace Guard shrugged.

"I'm interested in the options of smuggling in a cruise ship," I said. "I'm working on a paper for a class. Not drugs. Too obvious. Everybody does reports on drugs. Needs to be more generic. I want to keep my options open on what is being smuggled, for example, even live animals. I have cruise ship blueprints and some ideas, but I need to see a model to scale."

"Criminology class?" he asked. "Interesting class for a librarian to take."

"It's a sociology class I need for my doctorate. My project for the semester is sociological deviancy of subculture groups as impacted by conformity to regional norms."

Spike raised his eyebrows.

Maynard chuckled. "That's a mouthful. How does that relate to cruise ships and smuggling?"

I smiled. "The class assignment was smuggling. I chose cruise ships, and the professor approved my topic. That was only hurdle number one."

Maynard offered his arm, and we strolled down the corridor. Larry and the imaginary men followed us. Maynard recapped while we waited for the elevator. "Not drugs, because drug-sniffing dogs are everywhere. Maybe go with live animals as an example because that covers everything else except for frozen items. We'll need breathable air and sufficient space that isn't accessible to the passengers or usual crew. The smugglers may need access to provide water and food while at sea. We'll see what we can come up with and test our theories with a cut -away model."

When we were in the elevator, I said, "It was a surprise to see you. How did you get interested in shipbuilding?"

"I always wanted to be a pirate. Ships were my passion. I gave up being a buccaneer, but I never outgrew my love of sea-worthy vessels. At nineteen, I joined the Navy and spent eight years with submarines before I turned to my career of foiling bad guys, but I've always been close to the sea."

Spike saluted Maynard. I glared, and Larry coughed.

After we exited the elevator, Maynard said, "Down this way. Your smuggling scheme had a better chance on an old pirate ship. Unless forced, nobody would go below deck where the cows, horses, goats, and chickens were. The stench was suffocating, and the trapped methane gas caused more than one vessel to blow up."

My eyes widened when we entered a library with hand-hewn wooden floors. My heart quickened at the sight of the shelves from floor to ceiling that were crammed with books and rolls of blueprints and maps. *Wonder if they need a librarian?*

"Let's look at blueprints first then we'll inspect models. Sit here. I'll be right back." Maynard pointed to a massive teak table. He returned with an oversized roll of blueprints. He rolled the scroll open to a blueprint and smoothed the drawing in front of us.

"You tell me," he said. "Where will you place your animal cages?"

Larry and I rose to get a better view as we leaned over the detailed page.

"I don't see any unused space," Larry said.

"The ship's not hollow. A solid structure compartmentalizes the ship for protection against sinking, and the wooden interior construction keeps the ship afloat longer."

"The ballasts are large," I said. "Do they always contain water?"

"They aren't all filled with water, but they aren't as large as you might think," Maynard said. "We'll look at the model."

"Depends on the weight of the cargo," I said.

"Right, but that's easy to calculate. Which brings us to the next point, you'll need the right crew."

"How many people would it take?" Larry asked.

"On the ship, two oilers and a porter could handle everything. That's onboard. You'd still need an organized group on the land at both ends to coordinate the logistics and provide the care requirements and resources for the smuggled goods." Maynard cleared his throat. "I could go on for hours. Why don't I let you ask questions?"

"Oiler? Is that the same as an engineer?" I asked.

"Sure is. Without getting too much into details, the two oilers can manage all the onboard tasks besides their regular duties while underway, and the porter can move the illicit cargo to the ship long before departure time then after everything else is off the ship."

"What about the likelihood of getting caught?" Larry asked.

"The better question is whether it's worthwhile. Have you heard of any smugglers using cruise ships?"

Larry shook his head. "Good point."

"Aye, matey," Maynard said in a pirate voice. "So either no one is smuggling with cruise ships because it's not profitable or else the risk of being caught is low. The best pirates know the trick is to keep it simple and never work with anyone who's greedier than you are."

"Good advice for anyone." Larry chuckled. I frowned, and Larry whispered, "I'll explain later."

"Let's examine a model and test our theories," Maynard said.

We inspected the model Maynard had selected for over an hour.

"The ballasts are too small for any cargo." Maynard handed me a card. "Here's my museum business card with my cell number. What was that class again?"

"*Sociological deviancy of subculture groups as impacted by conformity to regional norms*," I said.

"That's it." He shook his head. "You'll think of more questions later, I'm sure. Call me. And come back to see the pirate ships."

Before we left the museum, Larry said, "Why don't you wait in here while I get the car? I can walk faster alone."

Larry jammed on his LSU cap, and Spike left with him. Palace Guard and I sat on a bench near the door. A man and woman stood near us and discussed dinner plans while their two preteen boys examined an old whaling ship model. The boys disappeared around a corner, and the man dashed after them. The woman pointed to the bench. "Mind if I sit?"

Palace Guard jumped up, and I scooted to make room. "Not at all."

"Appreciate it." She eased herself onto the bench and rested her hands on her swollen belly. "The boys wear me out sometimes."

"Would you care for a drink?" I waved at the water and coffee station the museum had set up for their customers.

"Thank you. Water sounds good, if you don't mind."

I made my way through the departing crowd. Palace Guard pointed to the hallway to my right. Maynard had his back to me with his hands on his hips while he faced two men. As I approached the drink station, the shorter, overweight man clutched his fists as he spoke. The thin, younger man picked at his face and shook his head. I gulped. *The men from the beach. The stalkers who shot at me.* Maynard pointed to the exit and crossed his arms.

I threw on my sweatshirt and pulled up the hood. As I filled the cup with water, the two men rushed toward the front door. I turned and mingled with a group of women on their way to the door. The group stopped to assign drivers and passengers. I gave the pregnant woman her drink then the group, and I left. The women crossed the street to the nearest parking lot, and I turned to head back the way we had come, but Palace Guard shook his head. I followed him in the opposite direction. When we came to a bus stop half a block from the museum, I stood at the far end of the bench where an older woman sat with two shopping bags next to her. Palace Guard pointed to my scarf, and I removed it and stuck it into my pocket.

A bus approached the stop.

"Your bus?" the woman asked.

"No, ma'am."

She waved the bus on and lifted her bags to her lap. "Why don't you sit? Next bus doesn't come for fifteen more minutes."

I sat next to her and mimicked her with my backpack on my lap and clutched to my chest.

"You remind me of my granddaughter." She patted my hand. "My baby's in college and very smart. I know she'll be an outstanding teacher."

A black SUV drove past us. I glanced at the driver. *It's the overweight stalker.*

"When does she graduate?" I asked.

"Next spring." She beamed and told me about how much her granddaughter loved to read when she was little. I chuckled at her delightful stories of a mischievous girl who sneaked books to read at the dining table and even under her pumpkin costume onstage to read during a Thanksgiving pageant.

A bus came into view, and she rose. "You remind me of her. Same sweet laugh."

"Thank you." I helped her onto the bus and waved as it drove away.

"Where's Larry? He should be here." I rubbed my arms.

Palace Guard pointed to the museum as Larry's car pulled into the loading zone. I sent a text. "Down the street. Bus stop."

Larry backed out, and Palace Guard and I dashed across the road. Larry pulled to the curb, and I jumped in. I glanced at the back seat, and Palace Guard grinned.

"Just once, I'd like to beat you." I turned to Larry. "What took you so long?"

"I was being followed. I ducked into a store on the way to the parking lot." He grinned. "A pawn shop. Wasn't hard to spend a little time browsing. I bought a mag pouch. What about you? What were you doing at the bus stop?"

"Maynard and the stalkers who shot me had a little hallway meeting."

Larry slammed the steering wheel, and I jumped. "I knew something was off."

"Is that why you told him we parked south of the museum?"

"You caught that? Yep. He asked me how I knew the Galveston detective. I told him I went to school with his son. The detective had told me his son graduated from SMU. What about your class?"

"It was logical and fit."

When Larry stopped at a light, he stared at me. "How did you remember the class name? He was checking you, wasn't he?"

"Of course he was. I expected him to. It was a reasonable name for a sociology class and easy to remember."

"Easy for you," he mumbled as he accelerated onto the highway ramp.

Larry focused on the evening rush hour traffic, and I leaned back to rest my eyes. My phone startled me when it rang.

"Gray Lady? This is Walt. Chip's dad. Chip had a rough day, but he's been asking for you. Could you drop by this evening? I think he'll relax after he's seen you."

"What time?" I asked.

"Maybe seven-thirty?"

"I'll call you back in a minute."

"What?" Larry asked.

"Chip wants to see me. His dad wanted to know if I could come to their place at seven-thirty this evening."

Larry drummed his fingers on the steering wheel. "What do the guys say?"

Palace Guard blew on his finger, and Spike nodded.

"As long as you're there, it's okay."

"Really? They said that?" Larry glanced in the rearview mirror at the back seat. When he held up his right hand, Palace Guard and Spike smacked it.

"Okay, then." Larry straightened his back and pulled back his shoulders.

"Never saw anybody swagger while driving." I returned Walt's call. "Tell Chip my cousin and I will be there at seven-thirty."

"Will do. Thank you, Gray Lady."

After I hung up, I said, "We have time to do our shopping then we can drop off the groceries before we go see Chip."

When we reached the recommended sporting goods store, Larry drove past the rows of cars and parked near the front entrance. The four of us trooped inside the store, and I soaked in the country pine fragrance and eye-candy displays of red and gray plaid flannel shirts and throw blankets. Palace Guard and I headed to the back of the store to check out the guns, and Larry and Spike veered off to the camping gear.

The two clerks in the gun section were busy with customers, and other customers, mostly men, peered into the glass counters. Palace Guard stood behind me as I joined the lookers. When I moved to a new section, Palace Guard was the unseen buffer between me and anyone who might come up behind me.

Larry joined us as I examined the revolvers in the display case.

"I found what I need. What about you?" he asked.

I tilted my head and gazed at him. "What would you look for here?"

"Depends," he said. "Weight would be my primary criteria."

"When I looked at the displays, it surprised me how many I'd cleaned. The ones that interested me were the ones I hadn't cleaned and taken apart yet."

Larry chuckled. "Buck was your trainer, wasn't he? He'd be proud of you. It's a wonder you didn't become a gunsmith after all the time you spent at the range cleaning the rentals. I heard you had the talent."

"Really?" My face grew warm, and I frowned. "Blushing used to be a problem for me. I thought I was over it." Palace Guard nodded, and Spike winked.

"Grocery store next?" Larry asked.

"I've got my list." I waved the old envelope I'd used to write on.

Larry put away groceries while I dropped the chicken into the slow cooker with chicken broth and water. I added carrots, onion, garlic, tomatoes, green chile, a dash of lime juice, spices, and cilantro and set it to four hours.

"We'll have tortilla soup for supper and enough leftovers for your lunch tomorrow and two more meals," I said.

"That's it?" Larry asked.

"Pretty much. You ready?" I grabbed my go-bag and sweatshirt.

"Add talented cook to the list." Larry locked the apartment.

Spike pretended to pull a pencil from behind his ear, lick the tip, and write on a pad.

I pursed my lips and climbed into the passenger's seat.

When I stepped out of the car at Chip's house, Sally bounded out of the door and down the walkway, and Chip raced out behind her. Sally stopped short of knocking me down and flopped onto the sidewalk. "This is Sally, Larry. She's a sweet girl."

Larry held out his hand for Sally to sniff, and she rewarded him with a slobbery kiss. Spike kneeled next to her, and she rolled to her back for a belly rub.

"She likes belly rubs. Your friend is nice," Chip said.

Larry raised his eyebrows, and I said, "That's Spike."

"I know. I like Mr. Spike. He's quiet." When Spike held up his hand, Chip smacked a high five.

"I'm on your team, right?" Chip asked.

"Yes, you're still on my team."

Walt stood in the doorway. "Let's invite your friends inside, Chip."

Chip offered me his arm. "Would you like to go inside, Ms. Gray Lady? I made appetizers after you told my dad you could come. Are you hungry?"

"An appetizer sounds wonderful. Thank you."

Larry, Palace Guard, Spike, and Sally followed us into the house. Chip had loaded the dining table from one end to the other: spinach cream cheese squares, baked crab dip in a bread bowl, guacamole, homemade flour and corn tortilla chips, coconut shrimp, empanadas, and cheesecake bars.

"Chip, you're an amazing chef."

"Yes, ma'am." He handed me a plate, and I stacked my appetizers with the skill of an expert master builder of a house of cards.

Larry's eyes widened at my plate, and I tossed my hair. "I need to keep up my energy."

Larry selected a larger plate. "I need extra energy too, just to keep up with you."

Spike patted Larry on the back, and Chip said, "Mr. Spike likes you, Mr. Paramedic."

Larry's face reddened, and he cleared his throat. "Thank you, Chip. You made all this after Ms. Gray Lady said we'd come to your house? You have remarkable skills."

Chip beamed.

"My son is a talented chef. He likes to cook for his friends." Walt picked up the same sized plate as Larry. "We have a nice patio out back where we can relax, if you don't mind the cooler weather."

"I'll grab our sweatshirts, Maggie." Larry dashed out the front. When he returned, Larry leaned close and whispered, "No extra visitors."

Chip poured drinks for everyone and sat at the table next to me. "Ms. Rosa died. She was my friend."

I pulled the red scarf out of my pocket and placed it on the table. "I bought this because it reminded me of Ms. Rosa. Can I give it to you?"

"Yes." Chip patted the scarf then smoothed and folded it. "Thank you."

"You're welcome." I blinked back a tear, and Larry, who sat on my other side, wrapped his arm around my shoulder.

"Is Mr. Paramedic on our team?" Chip asked.

"Yes, he is." I bit into the empanada.

"Good." Chip sipped his tea.

"Did you have something to tell Ms. Gray Lady?" Larry asked.

"Yes."

Larry popped a cheese square into his mouth.

Walt rose. "I have paperwork that needs my attention. Come get me if you need anything."

"Ms. Rosa and I talked when we rode together in her car. She told me it was okay to talk to you because we were on your team." Chip scooted his chair to face Larry and me.

"Ms. Irene told Mr. Maynard that Ms. Mona had her brother killed because he could prove Ms. Mona embezzled money from work. Ms. Irene had evidence and wanted Mr. Maynard to go with her to the police. Mr. Maynard said he would schedule it. Then later, Ms. Mona asked Mr. Maynard what he wanted her to do about Ms. Irene, and he told her to let him handle it."

"Did Ms. Irene say where she had the evidence?" Larry asked.

"She told me she kept all her important papers in her office until she caught a looky-loo busybody. She said nothing's better than a blood letter and an old sale, but I didn't always understand her words."

I picked up a cheesecake bar. "What did Mona say when Maynard told her he'd handle it?"

"She was mad and yelled lots of bad words. She said he was interfering."

I nodded and bit into the sweet dessert. "Where were they? Did anybody else hear Mona yell? Did they see you?"

"They were behind the diner. I was inside near the stove where Ms. Irene stood to listen to people talk. The old stove pipe carried sound from outside. She said she heard good information from the old stove."

I gazed at my plate. *One coconut shrimp left.*

"Did Ms. Rosa say anything she'd want you to tell me?" I stabbed the shrimp with my fork, dragged it through the crab dip, and popped it into my mouth.

"We talked about the weather, and I talked about birds. Except she talked about her family on the morning when..." Chip wrung his hands.

"Take your time," Larry said.

Spike sat next to Chip and put his hand on his shoulder. "Thank you, Mr. Spike. Ms. Rosa told me she needed to get a message to her aunt. Her aunt needed to watch out for crested birds. Ms. Rosa knew I keep a log of birds and could help because I talk about birds all the time. I have a good pair of binoculars."

"What did she say?"

"She said to tell Ms. Gray Lady about the birds and my binoculars. I just remembered. Do you need binoculars?"

"I have some that my mother gave me, but if I need better ones, I know who to ask. Thank you."

"Does your mother miss you?"

"She does. If I go visit her, I'll write to you."

"I like to get mail."

Larry rose and stretched. "If it's okay, I'll go inside to tell Walt we're ready to leave."

After Larry left, Chip said, "Some of me died with Ms. Rosa. I have a hole in my heart."

"I understand. Someone I loved died last year. I'll always have a special place in my heart for Parker, but the hole is healing."

"It takes a long time," Chip said.

"Yes." I put my hand out, and Chip's hand dwarfed mine. I gazed at the clear night sky. The bright lights from the nearby chemical plants and warehouses washed out most of the stars, but the North Star twinkled.

"Ms. Rosa was special," Chip sobbed and went inside the house.

Tears slipped down my cheeks. "Yes, she was."

On our way to the apartment, Larry asked, "Did you understand what Chip was talking about? I didn't at all. And what about Maynard? And your stalkers? Should we leave Texas?"

"Bloodletter and sail. That's barber pole and canvas; it's Irene's favorite tote bag. Let's drop by the hotel where Mona said Gary was. Maybe the clerk won't be too busy to talk."

CHAPTER ELEVEN

Larry parked in front of the hotel entrance. "Do you want me to wait here?"

I glanced at the back seat. Spike shook his head, and Palace Guard frowned. I snickered. "We need you to go in. You're better at talking. I'm great at listening."

I led the way to the desk. The clerk sat on a stool at the far end of the counter. She glanced at me and yawned. When she lifted her head and looked past me, she jumped up, smiled, and flapped her eyelashes.

I'm officially invisible. Spike poked my arm and grinned.

"How can I help you?" She leaned against the desk and her eyelashes twitched again.

Wonder if she's seen a doctor about that tic?

Larry strode to the desk. "Gary Sloan?" he asked.

"Mr. Sloan said he was expecting..." She squinted at me. "...the gray lady. I thought he was joking. I'll give him a ring."

"What's his room number? I'll save you the trouble." Larry leaned against the counter, and the clerk's inhale and exhale was wheezy. "My sister can run tell him we're here."

"He's in two-two-eight."

"I'll be along in a minute, Sis."

When the imaginary men and I reached the two hundred hallway, Larry joined us. His right fist was closed.

"What have you got in your hand?"

"The key. In case he's not there, we can leave a note."

"And the paper?" I tilted my head to read it.

"Nothing. Just a phone number." He stuffed it into his pocket, and Spike's eyes widened.

Larry pouted. "I'll throw it away later. I didn't plan to call her. You know that, Spike."

"Sure didn't take you long to get it," I said, and Spike nodded.

"I won't argue with the two of you. Where's the room?" Larry strode down the right hallway.

"This way." I turned left.

"Dang, Maggie," Larry said when he caught up to me. "Do you always have to be right?"

"Why not?" I stopped. "Here's two-two-eight. We should knock first." I tapped on the door. "Ernie?"

I knocked again. Larry unlocked the door and opened it part way.

I spoke louder. "Ernie?"

I pulled my knife out of my boot. Larry stood to the side and counted to three on his fingers. When I threw open the door, Larry stepped in front of me with his pistol drawn. I peered around him. The clean room had no visible signs of use or personal items. He pointed to the closet and waited while I checked it then headed to the bathroom.

"Clear," he said.

"No clothes in the closet. There's a note by the phone." I read aloud. "Honey, got a job. Tell your dad I'll be in touch."

I stuck the note into my sweatshirt pocket, and we headed back to the car. When we reached the front desk, the clerk's eye tic went into high gear. As I continued to the door, Larry stopped. "Be there in just a minute, Sis."

As I stood next to the car, I crossed my arms and tucked my hands into my armpits. "Good thing I have my sweatshirt. It's chilly."

Palace Guard stood close to me. Spike waved from the backseat.

"Sometimes you're a real stinker."

"I needed to return the key. I told her we missed him and would come back tomorrow. She's off the next two days. She wanted to be sure I still had her phone number." Larry unlocked the car.

I slid into the passenger's seat. "I was talking to Spike. He sat in the car while I froze. But then, you're the one who had the key."

Larry hung his head. "I'm so sorry."

He side-glanced at me, and I giggled. "You're incorrigible. Both of you."

Spike poked Larry.

"It means we can't be improved," Larry said.

I rolled my eyes.

"So, what did the note mean, Maggie? Sounds like code to me. Gary's your father, right?"

"Kate is the code guru; not me. Gary may be my biological father, but he knows Glenn is *Dad*."

"So, do we go back to Georgia?"

"After I find Rosa's killer."

"This is my text to Glenn." I handed my new phone to Larry.

"Izzy's ex has a job. Plans to visit u."

Larry frowned at my phone. "Are you sure you don't do code? What does this mean?"

"Mother's name is Isolde, but Sergeant Arrington calls her Izzy." I unplugged the slow cooker and turned on the stove to heat the teakettle.

"Did her friends call her Isolde?"

I stared at him. "Don't know. Never thought about it."

"I'll take some tea too. It's cold..."

Palace Guard placed his hand on Larry's shoulder and shook his head. Larry bit his lip.

"Too late," I said. "Fix your own tea."

After I poured the steaming water into my cup, I flounced to the computer.

"I found cake in the refrigerator." Larry slid a small plate onto my computer desk and set a folded paper towel and a fork next to it.

"Thank you."

"I'll put the soup in the refrigerator after it cools. What are you doing?" he asked.

"Verifying ship construction." I pointed at the screen. "Why do you suppose Maynard gave me bogus information?"

Larry scooted a chair next to me. "Whoa. Have you searched Maynard?"

"Not yet." I took a bite of my cake and leaned back. "All my background information about Maynard came from Ellen."

"I trust Chip, but I'm paranoid about everyone else," Larry said. "I need to go to bed. You do too."

"One more thing, then I will."

At three in the morning, I woke to a nudge in my ribs. Spike stood next to me with his arms crossed. I plodded off to bed.

The smell of coffee woke me the next morning. I threw on my gray robe and warm red socks before I hustled to the kitchen.

Larry sat at the dining table with a bowl of cereal. He wore jeans and a Houston Oilers blue T-shirt under his open red flannel shirt. "Were you up late last night?"

"Not really." I poured a cup for myself and refilled his. I dished up tortilla soup into a pot and turned on the burner. While the soup warmed up, I made a pimento cheese sandwich and cut it into two triangles. I popped the sandwich and chips into Larry's new lunchbox.

After I poured coffee into one container and soup into another, I joined Larry at the table.

"What's your plan for today?" he asked.

"Research and see Diane. I expect to hear from Glenn this morning."

"I need to check shipbuilding details. Maybe Maynard's just out of date. Thanks for lunch." Larry rushed out the front door.

I picked up the notebook next to my computer and tried to read my handwritten scrawls from last night. Palace Guard squinted at my notes and shrugged.

"I don't understand them either. I should have gone to bed when Larry did, but don't tell him that."

Palace Guard wiggled his eyebrows and feigned a zip across his lips.

My new phone rang. *Glenn.*

"Hope it's not too early for you. Loved the code. Took Jennifer a minute to decipher."

"Did not," Jennifer said. "You asked me who Izzy was."

"Busted," Glenn said. "Jennifer doesn't know why we'll have a visitor though."

Jennifer cleared her throat. "And you do?"

I refilled my coffee. *I could spend all morning listening to Glenn and Jennifer banter.*

"You okay?" Jennifer asked in her mom voice, and my eyes welled.

"I'm officially homesick," I said.

"Come home," Glenn said.

"You're staying to find Rosa's killer, aren't you?" Jennifer asked.

"Rosa had a message for my aunt. Rosa said my aunt needs to watch for crested birds. I don't know what that means."

"We'll get the message to her for you. Might take a day or two," Glenn said.

"I appreciate whatever you can do."

"Anything else?" Jennifer asked. "We miss you."

"That's it for now."

I stared at my phone. *Jennifer understands.*

After two hours of computer time, I rubbed my eyes and leaned back in my chair. "What I've found unusual about Maynard is that he is squeaky clean. Minimal online presence. No previous addresses. No social media."

Palace Guard raised his eyebrows.

"I agree. Sounds scrubbed, doesn't it? Ellen said she thought he'd worked in witness protection. He'd have the resources, wouldn't he?" I logged off and shut down my computer. "I need a shower before we go to Diane's."

After my shower, I filled a container with tortilla soup for Diane's and set aside a second, smaller container for Larry's lunch on Saturday. When the three of us arrived at Diane's, cars packed the driveway, side yard, and both sides of the street. The imaginary men and I parked a block from her house. A mockingbird serenaded us on our way until a troop of blue jays cleared the neighborhood with their warnings. As we approached Diane's house, Spike pointed to a yellow cat that stalked a squirrel. The squirrel dashed up a tree and scolded the feline from the highest branch.

Smitty met me at the door. "Nice of you to come, Gray Lady. Diane will be glad to see you." He reached for the soup. "I'll take that. We've got all kinds of pies and cakes. Diane will enjoy soup for lunch. Come on in."

I followed him to the kitchen.

"Honey," he said, "Gray Lady's here."

"Good. I want to go over to Mama's house and pick up a few things."

Diane met me in the doorway and hugged me. "Will you go with me?" she asked.

"Of course."

"Smitty, can you hold down the fort while we're gone?"

He nodded as he rearranged the contents in the refrigerator to make room for the soup.

"My car's out back."

As Diane pulled out of the driveway, she said, "Everyone's here to show their respect, but it's hard to think with all the noise. Mama keeps all the tax records at her house."

When Diane parked at Irene's one-bedroom yellow adobe house, she said, "Thanks for coming with me. It's my excuse to get away from some of Mama's more dramatic friends. Smitty told Mona to go home. He's a keeper."

I raised my eyebrows.

Diane smiled. "We've been together for almost ten years. I guess I assumed everyone knew that. We must be old news if we've dropped off the gossip radar."

Diane unlocked the door and took in a sharp breath before she entered the home. "Might be too soon for me. I need to step outside a minute. Can you check Mama's room for papers and bank statements?"

"Should we come back later?" I asked.

Diane shook her head and sobbed. "Mama's not..." She stepped off the porch and stared at the sky.

I searched the bedroom, beginning with Irene's dresser where I found bank statements and invoices in the bottom drawer and keys in an envelope taped to the back of the dresser. After I tipped the mattress and found envelopes stuffed with cash, I stacked the papers and envelopes on the dresser. Next, I stripped the bed and folded the linens and blankets. When I stooped to peer under the bed, I found two of Irene's barber pole tote bags. The front door creaked then Diane leaned against the bedroom door frame.

"When I walked in, I expected Mama to yell at me for not knocking. Let me get you a bag to put everything in, and I'll check Mama's desk and the kitchen while you're in here."

After I moved to the closet and checked the pockets on shirts, pants, and jackets, I found more cash.

Diane stood in the doorway. "I have three large bags for you. Let me know if you need more. Mama was a packrat."

She helped me fill one bag with money and put papers in the other two. "We might need more bags," she said.

She returned with two more bags. "I'm glad we separated the cash and the papers. Mama stashed money in the kitchen too."

When I finished in the bedroom, I had two large grocery sacks of cash and three of papers. Diane and I carried four large sacks of money and five sacks of papers to her car.

"Where are you parked?" Diane asked on our way back.

"About a block up the street."

"I'd like for you to take the papers with you. There's too many people coming and going at my house right now. I hate to ask, but I'd appreciate it if you could sort through the papers for me. Smitty will take the cash and deposit it into our account."

We moved the documents to my car then continued to Diane's house.

"I couldn't have managed all this without your help. Please let me know if there's anything I can do for you." Tears slid down Diane's face. After she parked in her carport, she said, "Do you mind asking Smitty to come to the car?"

"Not at all." I slipped through the crowd in the kitchen. Smitty was in the living room. He chatted with two women that were Irene's age. I motioned to him, and he bent down so I could give him the message.

"Carport," I said.

"Excuse me." He strode to the kitchen.

A woman tapped my arm. "Aren't you the Gray Lady? Irene talked about you all the time. She said you are a fabulous cook."

"Not as good as Chip," the second woman said.

"Well, I wouldn't say that to her face. Who could beat Chip's fried chicken?"

"His chicken fried steak. That's his signature dish. He could be a chef in New York City."

I wandered away as they competed in their praises of Chip.

"Not too surprised to see you here." Maynard came up behind me. "You doing okay?"

"I'm fine. Irene had more friends than I realized."

Gus clapped Maynard on the shoulder. "How ya doing, brother? I think the entire island's here. Irene was a treasure."

We nodded in unison. Spike joined in, and Palace Guard rubbed his forehead.

Another diner regular joined us and shifted the conversation to stories about Irene and her temper. I slipped away to the kitchen and moved close to the corner near the back door.

"Nice of you to come, Gray Lady."

I shifted around and looked up at the speaker. *Veronica.*

"Irene and I had our moments, but Diane is one of my best friends. My heart broke when I heard about Rosa, though. She and I go 'way back. Did you know her very well?"

"She was a great coworker at the diner," I said.

Veronica cocked her head and squinted. "Could we have coffee sometime?"

"I'd like that. When?"

Veronica chuckled. "I heard you were literal. How about tomorrow? Do you know where the taco stand at the beach near the diner is? Meet at eight?"

"Sounds good. Their breakfast taco is my new favorite."

"This is my cell number." Veronica handed me her business card. "Were you here when Smitty tossed out Mona?"

I shook my head.

"Sorry you missed it. Smitty is a force when it comes to Diane. He was awesome."

Someone in the living room called out. "Hey there, Veronica, where's KB?"

"See you in the morning," she said as she left the kitchen.

More people congregated at my spot, and I moved away.

I stood near a table loaded with food, and a woman with a cane reached for a deviled egg. "You're the Gray Lady, aren't you? Irene talked about you all the time."

The woman waved her hand as more people arrived. "Nice to see everyone here to support Diane."

"Sure is." I craned my neck toward the living room. "Have you seen Mona?"

"Oh, have I. You must not have been here when she threw her tantrum."

"Tantrum?"

"She'd been drinking..."

I raised my eyebrows.

"Yes. This early in the morning. Anyhow, she claimed Irene faked her own death. She said Irene stole money from her to pay some spy. Smitty took her arm and walked her out. It was beautiful. She screamed he was breaking her arm. I heard him mumble, 'Not yet, princess.' Priceless."

"I'm sorry I missed it. Must have been quite the spectacle. What do you think about what Mona said?"

"Poppycock. Irene was a wily woman, but no way would she have hurt Diane by faking her own death."

"I agree."

The woman peered at the table. "There are oysters on the half shell. I'll bet Gus brought those. He's a generous man. Nice talking to you." She cleared her path with her cane as she made a beeline for the other side of the table.

She's awesome. Spike and Palace Guard applauded her.

When she reached the oysters, she bowed her head in the style of a queen and toasted me with the half shell. I giggled.

Smitty stood at the back door and motioned to me, and I scooted to join him. "Diane said you'd be ready to leave and sent me to walk you to your car. I don't mind escaping this crush, either."

"Thank you."

Smitty accompanied me around the house to the sidewalk. "Thanks again for saving my life. I still don't know how you held me down." He put his hand on my shoulder. "You're not a lightweight at all when you put your mind to it, are you?"

He hugged me with the fierceness of a Glenn hug. When he let go, he gazed at my face. "Anything you need. You tell me."

I strolled to my car with Palace Guard who stayed in front of me and Spike who walked backwards behind me. I stopped to gaze at the clear blue sky as pelicans glided overhead. The warm sun, light breeze, and a warbler that sang in a bottlebrush tree erased my tension from the crowded, noisy house. Along the way, I dawdled to admire the trimmed bushes and blossoms that surrounded the modest homes in the quiet neighborhood.

After we reached the apartment, I said, "Our walk from Diane's to the car cleared my head. Veronica is on a fishing expedition. Hope I'm not the bait."

I hauled the tote bags and sacks of papers up the stairs in three trips and poured a glass of sweet tea. While I sipped my tea, I rough-sorted through the sacks and organized the papers in piles: financial, personal, business, and miscellaneous.

"This reminds me of Olivia except on a much smaller scale. Irene's an amateur compared to a head librarian on hoarding papers. I could use a little help."

I called Glenn. "Are you busy?" I asked.

"I'm bored out of my mind. Jennifer is at the store. She said I'm driving her crazy. Do you have something for me?"

"Diane asked me to go through her mother's papers. I'll review the financial statements, contracts, and miscellaneous papers."

"Can you scan them and send them to me, or are there too many?"

"I can scan them in less than an hour. You don't mind?"

"Not at all. And Jennifer will appreciate it too. This is her second trip to the store today. Is Larry still there?"

"Yes."

"Good. I know the men are there too. I breathe easy knowing you're protected."

After we hung up, I scanned in all the documents from the sacks. I slid the sacks with the papers under my bed.

Catalog was the title of the first packet in the lighter tote bag. After I read the next five pages from the bag, I pushed away from the table. "I need to scan all these before I go any farther."

I scanned the documents from the first tote bag then stretched and made a pimento cheese sandwich. While I ate, I scrolled through an article about the diner fire that talked about the old equipment and the dangers of not keeping up with maintenance. *So far, sounds like the preliminary findings point to equipment failure. Not sure Irene would agree.*

After I scanned the contents of the second tote bag, I saved all the documents to Mother's cloud and sent Sergeant Arrington a text. "System update."

His reply: "Got it."

Catalog had three sections: *Transport, Products,* and *Destinations*. The description for *Transport* included the capacity of different sizes of transport boxes, handler protective gear requirements, recommended temperature ranges, and short- and long-term warehousing. *Products* were order sheets in two major categories. The first was primate research models, and the second was biological specimens. *Destinations* listed the customer's physical and email addresses for invoices.

I spread all the papers out on the table, and the three of us raced to organize them into one of the three sections. Spike raised his hands in victory.

"Stand up," I said.

Spike shook his head then Palace Guard pulled the chair out from under him. Spike lunged toward Palace Guard, but I growled, "What's this?" and pointed to the papers on his chair.

Palace Guard and I laughed when Spike pouted.

"You're just mad because you got caught." When I picked up Spike's documents, a yellow slip of paper fluttered to the floor. I snatched it up and read. "Accurate and dangerous. Take care. G."

Palace Guard and Spike's faces reflected my shock. After we sorted the rest of Spike's documents, I moved the electronic documents into one of the three folders and uploaded the computer folders and contents to the online storage.

"What was it Chip said?" I brought up my notes. "Here it is. The conversation between Irene and Mona that Chip couldn't hear very well. *Man's keys.* Monkeys. *Ex-Scots.* Exotics. That means Mona knew about the monkeys, and someone wanted her to change her distribution reports."

I shuddered. "These notes make me nervous. Where would be the best place to keep them?"

Palace Guard pointed to the front door, and Larry came in.

"What's wrong?" Larry asked.

"We've got a problem. Let's sit." The four of us sat on the sofa. I squeezed in between Spike and Palace Guard. Larry smashed against Palace Guard and the sofa's arm. I described the canvas bags that Irene had removed from her office right before the fire.

"Why do you suppose she did that?" Larry asked.

"I don't know. I don't think anyone besides me saw her take the totes out, but even if they did, they were her shopping bags. She always used the totes when she went to the grocery store."

"G. is Gary, right? What do we do now?"

I rose and paced to the back then to the front door.

"You're not usually so agitated. What are you thinking?" Larry rose and put his hand on my shoulder.

"I'm thinking it's time to catch a snake."

"I'm in. Can we have tacos and beer first?"

I picked up the two totes. "I like your priorities. Where do we put these bags?"

"Let me think." While Larry washed his lunch dishes, I arranged the papers on the table.

"You scanned the digital copies of the invoices and detailed customer data to the cloud," he said. "Let's mail the papers to Moe."

"Moe. Okay with you guys?" I asked. Spike nodded. Palace Guard stared at Larry.

"I think there's a leak, but I don't think it's Moe," Larry said.

Palace Guard nodded.

"Wish we could check with Kate," I said.

"Try Glenn. Do you have any innocuous papers we can put into the totes?"

"Under my bed." I sent a text to Glenn: "Urgent family meeting. Include Moe?"

Glenn: "Taking poll."

Larry emptied two of the paper sacks from under my bed, filled the totes with the worthless documents then slipped the invoices and other critical papers from the diner into the two sacks.

"Let's go. We can get a box and mail them this afternoon."

After Palace Guard clarified the parking lot was clear, we took our sacks with the sensitive evidence to Larry's car.

On our way to the post office, Glenn texted: "Moe is family."

I crowded Larry while he addressed the plain box that he bought from the post office. I snickered when he addressed it to Detective Ross.

"Yep. Immature," he said under his breath.

When we got to the car, Larry opened the passenger's door. "I'll give Moe a quick call."

Larry headed to the driver's side, but stopped before he opened the door. Several minutes later, he climbed into the car.

"Moe's set. I sent the box to his house, not to the department. He said the department had a leak, but he didn't know who. He said before you and Kate left for Galveston, a rumor circulated that the FBI had a young woman undercover to investigate the Reynolds case. Do you think that was Rosa? The assumption in the department, which means the entire world, is it was you. He said he'd help find the leak. *Tell Maggie I'm in with her plan, whatever it is.* His exact words."

"Moe said he was *in*? That sure puts pressure on a plan, doesn't it?"

Larry chuckled. "Your plans are famous. Not a joke."

"Turn around. Go back to the grocery store."

Larry pulled into the parking lot. "This part of a plan?"

"Impromptu. I saw Mona pull into the parking lot. Drop me off."

On my way into the store, I grabbed a grocery cart. My final destination was the ice cream freezer. I cruised each aisle at the clip of an experienced shopper, picked up a can of black beans, added two boxes of rice, and grabbed a can of sliced olives. As I neared the last aisle, I spotted Mona in the wine section. I parked my cart near Mona, picked up a bottle of red wine, and examined the label.

Mona clutched my arm and hissed. "What are you doing here?"

"Hi Mona. My turn to cook." I wiggled my arm loose.

A bead of sweat broke out on her upper lip. "Everybody knows you're a cop. You don't have to pretend with me."

"I'm a librarian." I squinted my eyes in my best librarian glare.

She snorted. "That's what Maynard said when I told him you were a cop. You sure don't look like a librarian."

"I hear that a lot. I've had a question for you: why was Irene so interested in monkeys?"

Her eyes widened. "Monkeys? She talked to you about monkeys? Why did she do that?"

"I'm a librarian. She asked me to do some research."

"Oh, did she now?" Mona's face reddened, and she grabbed a bottle of wine.

"Yep. Irene said she needed to fix some records and needed accurate information about macaque monkeys in particular."

"Irene said she needed to fix records? She's such a liar. I'm the one who had to change the records from exotic to stuffed. I only did one delivery and asked her to go with me. She wasn't supposed to handle..." Mona grabbed my arm again. "You really are a cop, aren't you? I just did what I was told. Irene never had the good sense to keep her nose out of other people's business. She and Paul were just the same. All self-righteous and holier than thou. Believe me. I didn't mean to hurt anybody."

She glanced at the front of the store, snatched back her hand, and paled. "Get away from me. Nobody should see me with you."

She set her bottle of wine in my cart and rushed to the women's restroom.

CHAPTER TWELVE

I turned toward the checkout lines. Butch stood near the exit door with his arms crossed as he scanned each aisle. I took advantage of being short and stepped behind a display of crackers. Palace Guard faced Butch. He tapped my shoulder and pointed to the front. As I peeked around the crackers, Butch hurried out.

I abandoned my groceries, sauntered to the exit, and sent a text to Larry: "Ready."

Palace Guard tapped my bracelet.

"You're right. I need to talk to Larry."

Larry parked in front of the exit. When I climbed into the car he said, "You wouldn't believe who went inside. Butch. Then he hurried out and left. Mona must still be in the store. Did you find her?"

"Yep. I asked her about monkeys and records. She said she changed the records from exotic to stuffed. She claimed she did what she was told. I'll document the details and you can read it."

I pointed to the bracelet. "How did you locate me?"

"My phone." He bit his lip. "Which I no longer have."

"Who tracks it now?"

"I don't know. Maybe Heather." Larry glanced at the review mirror. "Your idea?"

Palace Guard nodded.

"Another question. Is the GPS always active?" I asked.

"Yes, it would be."

"Is it an asset or a liability? We need tacos."

We splurged and ordered guacamole with our to-go tacos. While we ate at the kitchen table, my phone buzzed a text. I grabbed a tortilla chip before I checked my phone.

"Glenn said *call*." I shook my finger at Larry. "Don't eat my last taco."

"Can I have half?" Larry asked.

I picked up my plate to guard my taco and called Glenn.

"I reviewed medical records," Glenn said. "Did you know about chronic Hep B?"

My eyes widened. "That's interesting."

"We thought so too. We love you."

After we hung up, I stared at my phone.

"Maggie? Mags?" Larry put his hand on my shoulder.

"Irene had chronic hepatitis B. She must have had direct contact with the monkeys. She disappeared during the day." I rubbed my forehead. "To take care of the monkeys? What are the symptoms of hepatitis B? Mona disappeared for several days. What do you think? A rush delivery? Was Mona sick too?"

I handed Larry my plate and hurried to my computer.

After a quick search, I leaned back and stared as Larry cleared our dishes. "You already ate mine?"

"Sure. What did you find?"

"Symptoms are nonspecific. Abdominal pain, fatigue, loss of appetite. We don't know if she suffered an exposure."

"Do you want any ice cream?" Larry dished up two bowls.

"Thanks. I'll be right back. I need my old phone to send a text to Maggie T."

When I returned, Larry had the two bowls in front of him. "Your ice cream's melting."

"Leave it." I growled and pulled away my chocolate ice cream. I showed Larry the text: "Know a horse expert? GL"

"What do we do now?" Larry scraped his bowl for the last drop of melted ice cream.

"I need to get the tote bags back to Irene's house." I called Diane, and the phone went to voice mail. "Hey Diane. It's Maggie. I've been through the tote bags. It's invoices over ten years old. Just letting you know. If you'd like for me to return the totes or the invoices, I will."

I finished my ice cream, and Larry put the dishes into the dishwasher. "I do my best thinking when I'm doing dishes. Let's scroll back through your Ellen notes. Did she mention her brother's name is Ken?"

"Yes. She said Kenny is her brother, but she hasn't seen him in a while, and Jay doesn't like him."

I shifted to my computer and searched for my Ellen notes.

"I work with a man named Ken. He's quiet; keeps to himself. The guys say Walt's the only one who could calm Ken down when he used to go into a rage."

"Wonder why?" I pulled up my notes. "Ellen said he's a porter."

"The Ken I know is an oiler. Ken Bushman." He scooted a chair next to me and raised his eyebrows. "You're checking marriage licenses?"

"Yep. Ellen Bushman. Thirty-seven years ago. At least, that's what Jay said, and Ellen didn't correct him."

"You are amazing. You know that, right?"

I scrolled and read my screen. Palace Guard poked my back.

"What?"

Palace Guard raised an eyebrow.

"Oh. Thanks, Larry."

"I'll just go read," Larry said.

After an hour, I rose. "Here we go. Application for marriage license: Ellen Bushman and Joshua Davidson. Thirty-seven years ago."

"I'll ask Moe to check for a criminal record." Larry marked his place in the book with the yellow note.

I shook my head. "We can't afford an official inquiry until we know where the leak is."

"The deeper we dig, the deeper it gets." Larry frowned. "What does that mean? Now I'm agitated. Let's take a beach break."

I switched from my red cowgirl boots to my running shoes. Larry glanced at my feet and changed his boots.

"You're on, Crazy Lady." Larry dashed out the front door.

I trotted behind him for a few blocks, then Palace Guard and I sprinted past him. Palace Guard ran next to me then left me. I didn't check for Larry; I chased Palace Guard.

After three miles of a hard run, I slowed. Palace Guard doubled back and joined my cool-down pace toward the apartment. Larry ran full speed toward us, tumbled into a dune, and landed face down.

I knelt next to him and bent with my face next to his ear. "Are you okay?"

He kept his head down and spoke in a voice muffled by sand. "No. I officially died of embarrassment." He rolled to a seated position, brushed sand off his face, and sputtered and spit grit out of his mouth. "Why can't I keep up with you?"

Palace Guard and I sat on either side of him. "You run like a cop. You need to run like a thief. I trained by running away from a Palace Guard."

"Oh." He draped a sandy arm around me. "You and the guys would be great trainers for a class of rookie cops."

Palace Guard and I laughed.

"I'd pay money to see the tiny librarian and her two imaginary men kick some arrogant rookie backsides." Larry chuckled, and Palace Guard grinned.

Palace Guard offered Larry a hand and pulled him up while I jumped to my feet.

Larry hobbled back.

"It'll be worse tomorrow. Stretch tonight and again in the morning, but it still will be bad," I said. "And brush off the sand before you go inside to take a shower, or you'll clog the drain."

The next morning, I dressed and made coffee before Larry stirred. He shuffled out of his bedroom and leaned against the wall. "I'll take a shower and some medicine for my pain. Unless you want me to pack right away because we're leaving for Georgia."

I handed him a cup of coffee. "Here ya go. Not this morning. I'll get your breakfast ready and pack your lunch."

Larry stopped at the door. "Anybody going with me today?" Spike shook his head, and Palace Guard pointed to me.

"Good. Extra protection for Maggie."

After Larry left, Spike pointed to my laptop.

"Good idea. I can work if Veronica's late."

We trooped to my car and headed to the taco stand to meet her for breakfast. When I parked, I checked my phone. A text from Maggie T.: "Ditch it. Barn door wide open."

I showed my phone to Palace Guard and Spike. "We'll take care of that after breakfast."

I put my window down to inhale the salty air and powered up my computer and read my notes for the past two weeks.

After twenty minutes, I sent Veronica a text: "R we still meeting? Maggie"

A car pulled into the parking lot and a young woman honked three quick times. I spied the tops of two heads with wispy blond hair in the two baby seats. The slender middle-aged cook sprinted outside with a white sack and handed it to the driver. She blew kisses to the backseat passengers.

After the car pulled away, the cook strolled to my car. "We provide a special curbside service for mamas with babies." She cocked her head. "You waiting for somebody?"

"We planned to meet at eight."

"Come inside for a breakfast burrito and coffee to keep up your strength while you wait."

I followed her into the shop. I perched on one of the three stools at the counter. After I ate my burrito, I carried my coffee refill to my car.

Veronica cruised into the parking lot and sauntered to my car. "I thought I was early, but you beat me. Smart to get a cup of coffee. Let's take our breakfast over to the beach. I love looking at the water."

I ordered another cup of coffee, and Veronica ordered coffee and a breakfast burrito. After we paid for our orders, we walked across the road to the park that overlooked the Gulf.

"No wonder you're so skinny. You don't eat," Veronica said.

Spike and Palace Guard bent with laughter, and I glared.

"It's hard to believe Irene and Rosa are gone," Veronica said. "How long have you known Rosa?"

"Only the few weeks I've been at the diner. She had a kind heart. I miss her." The light breeze off the water blew my hair in my face, and I smoothed the stray strands behind my ear. "Were you and Rosa good friends?"

"Oh yes. We were in school together. I was a grade ahead of her in high school, but we were in the band together." She brushed her cheek. "We were always close."

Spike sneered. I bit my lip to keep from sneering too.

She crinkled her empty burrito paper. "What brought you here?"

"Diane and I have a mutual friend. When Diane asked if anyone could help Irene at the diner while she visited her daughter, I volunteered to fill in for a few weeks."

"Makes sense." She shaded her eyes and peered at the ocean. "Who do you think killed Irene and my dear Rosa?"

"What? You're saying it wasn't an accident?" I widened my eyes but refrained from a dramatic pose with my hand on my cheek.

"Of course," she snorted. "Everybody knows that."

Her phone buzzed, and she glanced at it. "Nice to see you. I need to dash."

Spike waved as she drove away.

"Not very subtle, was she?"

After we climbed into the car, I tapped the steering wheel in thought. "I've got it. Let's send the horse to Albuquerque. Or Denver. I'll pick up some glue then let's go to the bus station."

While I was in line at the drugstore, I inspected a display of charms. I picked out a dog charm that reminded me of Lucy.

"Where's the closest bus station?" I asked as I paid for my items.

"East of Houston," the clerk said. Palace Guard frowned and tapped the back of his wrist.

After we were in the car, I said, "Two hours to travel plus a half hour at the station, and we'll return before Larry gets off work unless the traffic's bad. Was that your worry?"

Palace Guard shrugged.

"Do you have a better idea?" I pulled out the map of the Galveston area.

Spike leaned over the seat and pointed to the port. Palace Guard and I stared at him.

"You're brilliant," I said.

He blew on his fingernails and polished them on his shirt.

"I'll regret I said that, won't I?"

Palace Guard nodded.

"Maybe we can pick up a shuttle schedule or even talk to somebody."

When we reached the port, I cruised the lot for a parking space. "Let's channel our inner Larry and drive up close."

To my surprise, a slot was vacant. I pulled in, and we strolled to the shuttle kiosk.

"You here to pick somebody up?" The overweight clerk didn't look up from his phone.

My eyes widened. *Albert from the car rental place.*

"Hi Albert. What level are you on now?" I asked.

His head jerked, and he peered at my face. "I remember you. You were nice. Peggy, right?"

I smiled. "How did you remember?"

He set down his phone and grinned. "I remember everybody."

"An underrated talent or the burden of a curse?" I raised my eyebrows.

"Right? Pretty much both." He peeked at his phone. "Waiting for an attack."

"How did you know I wasn't taking the shuttle?" The babble of the disembarking passengers floated our way.

"No luggage, Peggy. That was an easy one."

"Which shuttle leaves the port next? I know, strange question."

Albert pointed. "The second one on the right leaves in two hours. Why?"

"I'm in a live-action game and need this charm to go to the airport." I pulled the horse off the bracelet and handed it to Albert.

"What did you have in mind? What if I slide it on the floor under a seat?"

"That would be amazing. I brought glue because I thought I'd glue it to the bumper, but I like your idea better."

"Be right back." Albert locked the kiosk and sauntered to the shuttle with a clipboard under his arm. He boarded the van and checked off items listed on his clipboard.

Albert grinned when he returned. "If we're lucky, somebody will pick it up and take it on a plane, right? Let me know if there's anything else I can do to help you. If I'm not here, I got fired again. Not everybody understands how important winning is. But I'll be working somewhere."

I held out my fist, and we fist-bumped. "Thanks again, Albert."

When we were back at the car, I put the dog charm on my bracelet held my arm up, and the charms jingled. "Much better."

After I parked at the apartment, I admired my charms one more time before I reached for the door handle, but my door didn't open. I pushed with my shoulder and realized Palace Guard leaned against the door.

"What are you doing? I can't open the door." I tapped on the window.

Spike ran upstairs and disappeared. I scooted to the passenger seat, but Palace Guard waited at the door. Spike appeared outside the apartment and nodded. Palace Guard stepped away from the car with his hands in the air.

I stormed out of my car, slammed the door, and stomped up the stairs to the apartment. When I unlocked the front door, I choked on the sharp odor of bleach. Intruders had splintered the jamb, knocked the back door off its hinges, overturned my desk, scattered papers, and left the refrigerator door ajar.

The floor around the refrigerator was a mess of broken glass and spilled food. They had opened the kitchen cabinets, smashed most of the glass dishes, and knocked everything else to the floor.

I slumped against the doorjamb. "This is what they call tossed, isn't it?"

Spike nodded.

"Veronica's involved. I'm sure of it. First, she was late, and second, could you believe her questions? Is everybody involved with the criminal activity? Why are we even here? Why don't we step back and let them harass each other for a change?"

Spike shrugged, and Palace Guard shook his head.

"You're right. Whine over. I want to see what they took. How did they reach the second story?"

We rushed to the balcony, and I leaned over the railing. A ladder lay across the dumpster below.

"There's the how. Let's see what they took. Why such a big mess? Could one person have done this alone? I'll check my bedroom first. Isn't that where everyone keeps cash, jewels, and important papers? I don't have any, but we can see whether they took the papers under my bed."

We passed the compact washer and dryer on our way. A bleach container lay open on its side in a small pool of bleach.

When I stepped into my bedroom doorway, I grimaced. The intruder had dumped out the drawers and tossed them into a corner. I checked under my bed and pulled out Irene's tote bags. "Empty. Everybody would recognize her tote bags, but they took the papers."

I opened my closet door. "Big mess. All my clothes are on the floor and wet."

I picked up a shirt and coughed at the suffocating odor of bleach. "Jerks poured straight bleach on my clothes. Hateful creeps. Everything's ruined."

Spike patted my arm.

"I'm fine. No, I'm angry. This was without a doubt personal."

We checked Larry's room. The intruder opened the drawers and left them open, but the clothes remained intact. His closet was as neat as Larry had left it.

"Personal," I growled.

I pulled out three trash sacks and headed to my bedroom; I leaned against the doorjamb and rubbed my forehead. "I have a headache from the fumes."

Spike snatched the sacks from me, and Palace Guard led me outside. I grabbed my phone on the way out. We strolled across the parking lot to the lone wooden bench with missing boards that the apartment manager called "The Park." We sat on the bench, and Palace Guard motioned for me to breathe in to clear my lungs.

A gray squirrel scampered toward us but diverted to the closest tree. He scolded us for occupying his bench. Larry pulled in and parked near the apartment.

I frowned. "What's he doing coming home so early?"

Palace Guard rose and waved to Larry.

"What are you doing sitting out here?" he asked. "I unloaded the last ship. A storm is brewing in the Gulf, and the port is diverting shipping traffic. We may end up leaving after all. The guys expect an evacuation order for the island sometime tomorrow."

Larry pushed on the bench. "This bench wobbles. I talked to Walt. Why don't we go inside?"

"Sit," I said, and Palace Guard nodded.

Larry sat next to me and put his arm on the back of the bench.

"Someone broke into the apartment while I was at the taco stand."

Larry jumped up, tore up the stairs, and rushed into the apartment.

"Maggie, this is awful." Larry shouted.

"Guess our break is over." Palace Guard and I vacated the squirrel's bench.

"This place reeks of bleach," Larry said when we stepped into the apartment.

I sniffed. "Not as bad as it did, thanks to Spike. He took my clothes out to the dumpster."

Larry rubbed his hand through his hair and paced from the living room to my bedroom and back. "Your clothes?"

"Please sit."

Larry glowered but flopped onto the sofa. "Tell."

"Someone broke in and searched the apartment. Their intent was to find something..." I held up my hand before Larry could speak. "Either they didn't find what they expected, or they tried to intimidate me. They poured straight bleach on my clothes in the closet."

Larry stared at me. "There's more."

Spike elbowed Palace Guard, and Palace Guard nodded.

"I got a text from Maggie T. She said to ditch the horse. It's on its way to Hobby Airport."

"How did you do that? How does trouble find you so fast?"

"I went to the port, and a friend put the horse on an airport shuttle. I don't know. Special talent?"

"What friend? Never mind. Let me tell you what I learned from Walt. Then I'll clean up the glass."

I sat next to Larry, and he put his arm on the back of the sofa behind me. Spike eased toward the sofa but stopped when Larry glared at him.

"Ken Bushman had serious anger management issues besides a criminal history, but he always had a soft spot for Chip. When Chip was in high school, he was a frequent target for bullies, and Ken heard about it. He taught Chip to fight and spoke to the other boys. Ken told the boys he'd trained Chip to break every bone in their bodies if they stepped out of line. Walt said the boys believed Ken and never bothered Chip again. Walt said Chip's confidence showed a vast improvement. Guess Walt and Ken have a special bond. Mutual respect."

"Have I ever seen him?"

"Don't think so. He's not as tall as I am, overweight, and has black curly hair. Something's wrong with his back. He's kind of hunched-back."

"I think I've seen him somewhere." I frowned.

"Probably at the port."

"Maybe. I'll get the broom and dustpan, and you can sweep. I'll pick up papers."

My new phone buzzed a text.

Glenn: "Call. Your convenience."

I showed the text to Larry, Palace Guard, and Spike then called Glenn.

"I have a message for you. You okay to talk?" he asked.

"Yes. No, wait. Let me go outside." I trotted outside to the road. "Okay. It would be difficult for anyone to listen in over the traffic noise."

"Kate said the Gray Lady needs to disappear. I gave her your new phone number. She said you'd have a plan. Do you have a plan?"

"Not quite, but I will."

Glenn chuckled. "I have every confidence in you. Let me know what I'm supposed to do."

"Thanks, Glenn."

After I hung up, Larry and the two imaginary men strode toward me.

"Gray Lady has to disappear. That shouldn't be too hard. Just need a plan."

"Let's get this place cleaned up then turn in your car," Larry said. "You can tell them your cousin came to pick you up if they ask."

After we finished cleaning, I said, "I'm starved. Let's get lunch. I need clothes different from what I wear."

"I know where we can go: the farm store where I got my shirts. They have women's shirts too. Your hair needs a change. The gray is too obvious."

"Cut it ultra-short?"

"No, you need a color change. We like your long hair. You can cut it too if you want though."

Spike nodded.

No pressure, right?

Palace Guard smiled.

On our way to the taco stand, I called for a hair appointment.

"She'll squeeze me in this afternoon at three," I said.

"Where are we disappearing to?" Larry asked.

My phone rang. *Diane.*

"I got your message. I'm sorry to be slow getting back to you. As far as the totes, I don't care to have them around. You can have them. Do what you like."

After we hung up, I said, "Diane doesn't want the totes. Maybe Chip would like to have them."

"I'll call Walt after we eat. We need our brain food."

We ate in the car. Larry finished before I did.

When he picked up his phone, I said, "Don't call Walt. Kate said disappear. People don't announce a disappearance."

"Hadn't thought of that."

"You can keep your job and get a place. Kate said disappear, not go away."

"You're being literal, but I like it. Where will you stay?"

"With you."

"I need to find a place. I'll make some calls. We have time to drop off your car and shop for clothes before your hair appointment."

"I need to stretch my legs. I feel like I've forgotten something."

I stepped out of the car and strolled to the beach. The strong breeze off the water smelled tropical: salty and sweet with hints of palm trees. The waves churned and the dense towering clouds on the horizon warned of an impending storm.

Larry joined me at the water's edge. "I found a place. She said she'd hold it for us. She said we should get a head start and evacuate. You okay with that?"

"Sounds like a good way to disappear."

"I agree." Larry stared at the horizon. "That's impressive, isn't it? Ready?"

We stopped at the apartment for my car, emptied my trunk, and moved my camping gear, go-bag, and travel bag to Larry's car. Larry and Palace Guard followed Spike and me to the car rental center. When I opened the door, the line of angry people turned in unison to glare at me.

"Anyone turning in a car?" the clerk called out. "Step outside to lane three."

I headed outside, and a middle-aged staff member just an inch taller than me took my arm and led me away from lane three.

"They would have mobbed you. We're out of cars. The airlines canceled flights, and people want to evacuate today." She cocked her head. "Why are you turning in your car?"

"My cousin was in Houston, and mama told him he had to come get me. You know how cousins are."

"Is he ornery? All my boy cousins are. I've got the paperwork ready in the service area."

I followed her into the bay.

"Got it right here, Irene. If you'll give me your keys, I'll give you a receipt."

I handed her the keys. "You have a great system for taking in cars."

"Thanks. Like they say, not our first rodeo." She chuckled and pointed to the emergency exit. "You go out that way. I'll tell your cousin where to pick you up. What does he look like?"

"Tall red-headed guy."

"Is he smarter than he looks?" she snickered.

Larry's smart, but how smart does he look?

Palace Guard shrugged as she left to find Larry. Larry pulled up, and when I opened the passenger's door, he and Spike glowered.

"Get in."

We traveled to the farm store in silence. When he parked, Larry asked, "Why did the manager say I looked smart enough?"

Palace Guard closed his eyes.

"Because you're my cousin."

Larry snorted. "You're lying. Let's get you some non-Maggie shirts."

Larry and Spike dropped every color of plaid snap-front shirts in my size into the cart.

I counted. "Six shirts. I'm set."

I headed to the front counter, but Larry picked up a T-shirt with the farm store logo on it. "On sale. Sixty percent off. Perfect."

I looked at my feet. "I need new boots. Brown."

I tried on a brown pair with a rounded toe and red trim. "I like these. I'm ready to check out."

I pushed my cart to the front and checked out. Larry carried the sacks to the trunk of his car. "We set a shopping record, didn't we?"

"We were outstanding. Do we have time to stop by the apartment to wash the sizing out of my shirts?"

"We do." Larry merged with the traffic. "Pack while I remove the tags and wash your new clothes. I want to pick you up and leave town from the shop. Which reminds me, we need to pick a shirt for you to wear after your stylist finishes. Do you own any shirts that aren't gray?"

"No. I'll wear a new shirt."

"Perfect. The T-shirts are the softest."

Larry pulled into the apartment. "Have you thought about what color you want your hair?"

"I don't care. Whatever she does is fine as long as it's fast."

Larry and Spike nodded. Palace Guard raised his eyebrows.

I stacked my unbleached jeans and underthings on my bed and rolled them for packing while Larry loaded laundry into the washer. We discovered bleach in my suitcase, and Larry carried my ruined luggage to the dumpster. I stuffed my clothes into Irene's tote bags. "If you get me red and green permanent markers, I can draw a hook and holly to transform the barber pole to a candy cane."

"Will do. Let's stack all your things on the sofa. I don't want to forget anything."

"If the grocery stores aren't too crazy, I'll pick up some drinks, fresh fruit, and crackers."

On our way to the stylist shop, I asked, "Where are we going when we leave town?"

"We'll head to Georgia. If the storm doesn't hit or dissipates, we can turn around. If the storm threatens Galveston or gets any bigger, we'll be in Georgia."

"That's brilliant."

After we parked, Larry said, "I wrote a note and included money in the envelope. If she finishes your hair in less than an hour, I'll double what I put in the envelope."

"Incentive. Good idea. Can I give you some names to send to Moe to check? I have theories, but I need data."

"Sure. Can you put them on paper for me?"

I handed him my note I'd written earlier. "Here you go."

Larry stuffed the paper into his shirt pocket.

"Wait. What's your name? Em? Emmy?"

"No, not Emmy. Peggy. That's what Albert calls me."

"Who is Albert?"

"The car rental and shuttle guy."

"Okay, Peggy. Let's do this."

When we entered the shop, the woman at the desk didn't look up as she waved to the corner where six ladies waited. "Have a seat. We'll get with you as soon as we can."

Larry approached the desk and spoke in a low voice to the receptionist. She scurried to the backroom and returned with another woman. Larry spoke to her. He had the complete attention of the seven of us who sat in the waiting area, but I couldn't hear what he said. He gave the woman the envelope.

"Mrs. Ewing?" she asked.

When Palace Guard pulled me to my feet, I caught on.

"Come with me. I'll take your application myself."

I followed her to a room, and she pointed to a chair. "My name is Lisa, but I'll skip my usual chit chat. I'll get you out of the shop in less than an hour. Your husband explained your condition."

What condition? Is Larry getting even?

Palace Guard shrugged and stood at attention in front of the door.

Lisa combed and quick-snipped my hair. She pointed to the chair at the sink. Lisa ran the water until it warmed then shampooed my hair with a relaxing scalp massage. She rinsed and added a conditioner. After a second rinse, she wrapped a towel around my head and waved for me to return to the first chair.

She rubbed my hair with the towel and combed out the tangles. "Don't move. I'll be right back."

She returned with two white bowls with dark goo in them. *We're going dark.*

Lisa's fingers flitted from one section of my hair to another. I was dizzy from watching her. She piled my hair on top of my head and stretched a shower cap over my hair.

"Come sit under the dryer. Let me know if it gets too hot."

The hair dryer was warm, and I closed my eyes to listen to the drone. The dryer stopped, and Lisa tapped my arm.

"Let's get you rinsed."

I moved to the chair at the sink, and we rinsed. She towel-dried, combed, and blow-dried my hair.

"Done. Fifty minutes. Let's go out the back door. Almost forgot, Mr. Ewing said you'd need to change your shirt. I'll turn my back and you can change."

I changed. She went out the door with me. Larry waited in a white four-door pickup truck with a topper over the truck bed. I climbed into the passenger's seat.

"Excellent, Lisa. We appreciate it." Larry handed her a second envelope.

Lisa peeked inside the envelope and grinned. "Thank you. Any time. You take care, Mrs. Ewing."

As we headed to the interstate, Larry said, "I got your markers, but the grocery stores were busy. I'll stop at a small store down the road for some drinks and food."

Larry pulled into the parking lot of a variety store. "I gave Moe your list. He had a message for you from Sergeant Arrington. Sarge said to call your mother. I won't be long."

I picked up my old phone. I crossed my fingers while it rang, hoping I wouldn't have to leave a message.

"Hello, Margaret? I worry about you. Did you know there's a big storm in the Gulf? Are you okay? Big D and I can come get you if you're afraid to drive. Can I send you anything? Do you need a raincoat? Big D and I had dinner at the Coyles' last night. Franklin went along. Did you know Lucy likes cats? She is a sweet dog. Lucy and Franklin snuggled on the Coyles' sofa after dinner. It was cute. Glenn is not a man to sit around, is he? Jennifer said he'd heal faster if he'd stay off his feet."

Mother took a breath, and I jumped in. "I'm fine, and I'm sure Glenn enjoyed having friends over. I've been wondering. What did my father call you when I was little?"

Mother chuckled. "Gary used to call me Red. It was while my hair was still red. Naturally, I mean. He always called you Maggie, even though I told him that your name was Margaret. When I was a girl, everyone in school including the teachers, called me Irish because of my green eyes and red hair."

Larry came outside and lifted the three sacks of items in triumph.

"Franklin goes to the pet spa today. Time for us to dash. Big D. said you were fine, and if my Duane says he has no worries, then I know you are okay. I still like to hear for myself. Now Franklin and I can rest easy." Mother hung up.

I shook my head. "She never says goodbye."

Larry climbed into the truck. "Success."

"Mother worried about the storm. When I asked, Mother said Gary used to call her Red. I never knew that. When she was a girl, they called her Irish. It's curious that she's always called me Margaret. I wonder if that's because no one ever called her by her name. I thought I'd made up Maggie, but that's what my father called me."

Larry accelerated on the ramp to enter the interstate and slipped the truck into the middle travel lane. "I turned off my phone, and you need to turn off your old phone too. I gave Moe your new number as our contact information. Glenn has your number, right? Kate too?"

"Yes. What happened to your car?"

"I found a tracker on it two weeks ago. A guy from work sold me his truck, and I left it at his house until the right time to change to a different vehicle. The rental car will be halfway to Dallas by tomorrow along with everyone else."

"You bought a truck?"

"I needed one. All the guys have a truck."

Larry's a star at blending. "Brilliant plan."

"Your hair looks nice."

"Is it too dark? I didn't see any mirrors."

"So you haven't seen it? No, it's not too dark." Larry bit his lip, and I frowned.

"What's wrong with my hair?" I pursed my lips and glared. I turned to the back. "Is my hair okay?"

Chapter Thirteen

Spike grinned and raised both thumbs. Palace Guard's mouth twitched into a half-smile, and he nodded.

"Where is a mirror?" I growled.

Larry pointed to my visor and kept his attention on the traffic.

I flipped open the mirror.

"Red?" I squinted and turned my head to different angles in case it was just the lighting. "It's red!"

"I like it," Larry said. "What was it you told me? Red is the new gray?"

"But it's red, and I don't look like me."

"That was the whole idea, right?"

I narrowed my eyes. "Your idea or Kate's? Never mind. It was yours."

I crossed my arms and stared out my side window. *I will never speak to Larry again. Ever.*

Watching traffic is boring. I glanced at the truck clock. *Ten minutes since I quit speaking to Larry.*

I leaned back and listened to the rhythmic hum of the tires. My eyelids grew heavy, and I relented and closed my eyes.

My head jerked and my eyes snapped open. "I remember what I forgot."

"What was it?"

"Kate said disappear. Going to Harperville isn't disappearing."

"That's true, but Kate knows you're literal. What did she expect?"

"I need to call Glenn."

He picked up after one ring. "You okay? You on the road?"

"I'm okay and on the road. I called about Jennifer's house up north."

"You can get there and get in?"

"Yes, sir."

"Be safe. We love you." Glenn hung up.

"We're going to the Coyles' cabin. It's north of Harperville. We'll disappear." I pulled up the map on my phone. "When we get to Mobile, take sixty-five north to Montgomery."

I checked the distance from Galveston Island to Mobile. "If we snack on the road, I know a great truck stop in Mobile for a break and a good meal. We'll be there around one in the morning. We can even catch a nap in the parking lot before we move on."

"Sounds like a plan."

We arrived at the truck stop west of Mobile at one-thirty in the morning. The light fog from an hour ago had thickened as we traveled. The parking lot was full, but Larry pulled into a space in front of the diner. I shook my head. *Typical Larry.*

When I opened the truck door, the humidity was an invisible spider's web that clung to my skin. I shuddered and rubbed my arms, but when I breathed in the delicious aroma of frying grease from the diner, my stomach growled in anticipation.

Larry met me at the front of the truck, put his arm around my shoulders, and squeezed. "I'm starving. Awesome choice."

When we entered the diner, I didn't see any vacant stools at the counter or any empty tables, but Larry led us to an empty booth he'd spotted. *Travelling with tall people has advantages.*

The overweight waitress with short blue-black hair delivered plates of food to the booth behind us. The sweet fragrance of mashed potatoes and gravy swirled in her wake.

"What can I get y'all to drink? We have no more menus left. What would you like?"

"What do you suggest?" I asked.

"Chicken-fried steak with mashed potatoes and gravy."

"Sounds good, and tea for me," I said.

Larry said, "The same except I'd like coffee."

She waddled to the order window. "And buttermilk pie."

While we waited for our drinks, Larry said, "Maggie, I'm having a hard time with Peggy. Mags or Little Red?"

Larry held out his hand, and Spike and Palace Guard smacked it.

"What?" I narrowed my eyes and lowered my voice. "Don't you dare."

Spike crossed his arms and pouted.

"I don't care if you do like it, Spike. No."

Larry snickered, and Palace Guard turned his head away.

Our waitress dropped off our drinks and returned to the pickup window for an order. A shouting match erupted outside the diner.

"Not my business." Larry shrugged, but he didn't turn his gaze away from the parking lot until the two men parted in opposite directions.

"Those two are always fussing," the busboy said while he refilled Larry's coffee. "More tea, ma'am?"

He raised the pitcher in his other hand, and I smiled. "Thank you."

The waitress set our plates in front of us and rushed to pick up her next order.

"Hard workers here." Larry unwrapped his napkin, and his silverware rolled out.

Spike stuck his finger in my gravy, and I smacked at his hand with my fork. When I splatted gravy on my shirt instead, Spike laughed, and Larry and Palace Guard grinned.

"Not funny, Spike. Stay away from my food."

After I cleaned most of the gravy off my shirt, I tasted my chicken fried steak. "Mmm. Fried to perfection. The gravy is delicious."

We dug in and didn't speak until we'd eaten our fill. Larry's plate was clean; I'd eaten all my mashed potatoes and gravy and half of my steak.

"Keep your forks." Our waitress carried two plates. "Here's your buttermilk pie."

She picked up Larry's plate and smiled at mine. "Shall I clear your plate, honey?"

"Yes, please." I broke off a piece of pie crust with my fingers and ate it like a cookie.

"We don't get many natural redheads in this old diner," the waitress said. "It's refreshing to have you two here. Y'all brought a little class to the joint. Pie's on us."

Palace Guard poked Larry. "Gosh," Larry said. "Thank you for the pie and the kind words."

Palace Guard nodded.

She beamed and walked away.

"Thanks. I was tongue-tied for a minute there," Larry said.

We polished off our pie then Larry drove to the gas pumps to fill the truck's tank.

While Larry washed the windshield, I stared at the eighteen-wheeler trucks that eased into the lot for food and fuel and the others that rolled out to the highway to their next destination.

"Would my life be different if Parker hadn't died?" Spike put his hand on my shoulder and tears welled up in my eyes. Spike patted my back with an awkward touch that was a mixture of tender and rough.

"Thank you, Spike." I pulled up the neck of my shirt and dried my eyes. When I glanced at Palace Guard, he blew on his finger, and I chuckled.

"We do like Larry, don't we? If he calls me Little Red one more time, I'll call him Big Red."

The three of us high-fived as Larry climbed into the truck.

"What's going on?" he narrowed his eyes.

"We like pie."

"I don't know why I bother to ask."

After we turned to the northeast on highway sixty-five, the fog lifted in patches.

I pulled up the map. "Let's plan on a rest break when we get to Montgomery. It's about three hours away."

Larry checked his side mirror and moved to the left lane to pass a slow-moving car. "How much farther after Montgomery?"

I checked the map. "About two hours."

"Breakfast in Montgomery, then continue on?"

I frowned. "We could take a power nap in Montgomery."

"Let's push on with the option to stop for a break if I get drowsy. Speaking of naps, why don't you see if you can catch one?"

"I'm fine." I yawned and rolled my jacket into a pillow to place against the door then leaned against my improvised pillow and closed my eyes.

"Maggie? Maggie, honey."

Parker called me honey. We like Larry. I opened my eyes.

"We're about five miles outside of Montgomery. Ready for breakfast?"

"I must have fallen asleep."

When I straightened up, my jacket fell to the floor. I picked it up, stretched it across my knees, and pulled my phone out of my pocket. "Take interstate eighty-five east out of Montgomery. We can watch for a place for breakfast, and I'll check the Galveston weather."

I raised my legs and stretched my ankles. "Tropical storm warning. Voluntary evacuation for Galveston Island expected to be mandatory later in the morning. Storm surge."

"What's our plan?" Larry asked.

"Lay low, wait for Moe, and I've got a few loose ends to check. You can run with Palace Guard."

"We'll need groceries too, right?" Larry pointed to a billboard with eggs and biscuits. "What do you think? Go there?"

"Sounds good. We need coffee."

When we exited the highway, Larry said, "Truck stop on the right. Good price." He filled up the truck.

When we pulled into the restaurant parking lot, Larry said, "This is a good sign. Pickup and work trucks. They must have the same regulars as Diane's Diner."

When Larry opened the door, the aroma of pancakes, bacon, and sausage pulled us in. A waitress breezed by with four plates heaped with stacks of pancake. "Sit wherever y'all like."

Larry guided us to an empty booth toward the back of the diner. A fifteen-year-old carried cups and a pot of coffee to our table. "Coffee?" she said as she poured.

I raised my eyebrows, and she laughed. "You had that desperate coffee look, ma'am. My mama says I have an eye for observation. I don't mean to say what I see, but sometimes it spills out."

I snickered. "I do too."

Before we'd gulped half of our coffee, the waitress came to our table. "What do you like? We don't have menus."

"I'd like eggs over medium, grits, bacon, and a cinnamon roll," I said.

"You'll get biscuits and gravy." She chuckled. "You, sir?"

"Eggs over easy, sausage, and a short stack."

"Blueberry, pecan, or plain?"

Larry furrowed his brow.

"Blueberry, got it." She cackled and rushed to put in our order.

Larry chuckled. "She reminds me of a young version of Irene. Order whatever you like, and you'll get the special."

I smiled. "You're right."

The teen refilled our coffee and kept moving.

Larry said, "Did you notice the customers are two-deep at the counter? Wonder if they eat in shifts?" He sipped his hot coffee and yawned.

Our waitress served our breakfast, and the teen was on her heels with the coffeepot. She refilled our cups.

"Put a napkin over your cup when you're finished," she said in a low voice and winked.

"She's right," Larry whispered as he glanced around the diner. "We'll look like locals."

My eyes widened at the size of the portions when she served our plates. I ate less than half of the food on my plate and put a napkin over my cup one cupful before Larry.

Larry left half a pancake on his plate and yawned.

"Your turn to nap," I said.

Larry, Palace Guard, and Spike nodded.

"Do you know where you're going?" Larry asked.

"Pretty much. Help me watch for a grocery store."

"You have a list? Never mind, of course you do."

We found a grocery store close to the diner. We split the list and filled our two baskets full.

"This is a lot of food," Larry said when we rolled our carts to the truck.

"I don't know what we'll find at the cabin. Most of what we bought will keep. The rest we'll eat in the next two days."

"Sensible."

After we loaded groceries into the truck bed, we were on the road.

"When I get close, I may have to park and walk the road to find the driveway. That's how it's done, but I have the advantage of Palace Guard and Spike. You'll see."

"I'll just close my eyes for a minute." Larry scrunched down in his seat.

"My jacket's behind you."

Larry rolled it into a pillow and put it against the door. His soft, rhythmic snore reminded me of Lucy's.

When I turned off the paved two-lane road onto the dirt road with narrow shoulders, Larry jerked up his head. "I fell asleep." He yawned. "Are we there?"

"We're close."

After a few miles, I turned right onto a dirt road with no shoulders. "So far, so good."

The ruts in the road were deeper than I remembered. I slowed to watch for the driveway. Palace Guard tapped on my shoulder, and I stopped. He went into the brush and came back out five minutes later. He motioned for me to follow him a few yards then pointed to the brush. I turned in, dropped the truck into four-wheel drive, and drove through the overgrown path.

"Are you sure about this?" Larry clutched the dashboard and the armrest.

"Of course," I said.

Palace Guard held up his hand when the truck was deep enough in the woods and pointed.

"There's my tree. It fell on the path during a storm. Doesn't it look like a dead end to you?" I asked.

"Does that mean it isn't?" Larry asked.

I made a sharp right turn and backed the truck into the brush as Palace Guard and Spike guided me.

"I should have gotten out," Larry said. "Or maybe not. Are there snakes here?"

When Palace Guard held up his hand, I stopped and turned off the engine.

"We're here," I said.

"Where?" Larry squinted at the surrounding area.

"We'll carry our things to the cabin, but it's not far. Palace Guard and Spike will make sure everything's okay."

When Spike returned and gave us the *all clear*, I said, "Might make sense to make two trips. It'll be easier to push through the second time."

On our way to the cabin, Palace Guard blocked our way. He crossed his arms and glowered at Spike.

Spike shrugged and pulled a fierce face.

"Here?" I whispered, "Kate is here?"

"What..." Larry spoke in a normal tone, and the three of us shushed him.

"Kate's here. Spike was leading us into an ambush."

Spike hung his head.

"Here's what we'll do. Larry, go to the front door. Kind of block the door so she doesn't go out front. Palace Guard, I'll need you to run with me if she gets up after I ambush her."

Larry and Palace Guard nodded.

"Spike, we'll go to the back. After Larry goes in the front door, you go in the back door. Tell Kate that I'm on the same side as the clothesline. I'll be on the other side and ambush her. Everybody got it?" I held up my hand, and my three men smacked it.

Larry and Palace Guard tromped to the cabin while Spike and I slipped around to the back.

"Yo, the cabin," Larry called out.

Well done.

Spike nodded.

Larry knocked on the cabin's front door hard enough for me to hear in the back.

The front door creaked open. "Just you, Larry?" Kate asked.

"Maggie's behind me."

I nodded for Spike to go inside the cabin from the back. I headed to the same side as the clothesline. After Spike went in, I hid. When Kate dashed out to go around the cabin, the door slammed against the cabin. I raced into the cabin to the front door where Palace Guard and Larry waited.

When Kate sprinted past the front door, I said, "Hi Kate."

She halted and dropped her head in defeat. "You did it. I'm ambushed."

"Truce?" I asked.

"Of course. How did you do that?"

"Spike always cheats. I knew he'd tell you where I said I'd be."

Spike raised his eyebrows, and we laughed.

"You need to work on your innocent look, Spike," Larry said.

"No way." Kate flopped onto the porch. "You see Spike?"

"Doesn't everybody?" Larry grinned and headed to the truck.

"Wait up. We'll help carry," I said.

"I brought beer. What did you bring?" Kate asked.

"Groceries and beer," I said.

"My beer's colder," Kate said. "And I need one while I hear the story of two redheads."

Larry and Kate's strides left me behind.

I hugged myself; I was excited to see Kate. Palace Guard strolled alongside me. He held up his hand, and I jumped to smack it. By the time Palace Guard and I reached the truck, Kate and Larry had everything except my travel suitcase and my jacket.

Larry asked, "Is that a makeup case? You don't wear makeup."

Kate and I snickered.

"Glenn always said to ignore them," he mumbled.

Palace Guard nodded.

"It holds my ammo," I said.

Larry shook his head. "My fault: I asked."

When we reached the cabin, Kate asked, "What's for supper and who's cooking?"

"We have two steaks. You and I can split one and still have leftovers because Larry picked them out."

I'll make German potato salad," Kate said.

"After we put away the groceries, I'm ready for a nap after the all-night drive." I yawned.

Kate set her sacks on the kitchen counter. "I'll fix a snack while y'all put things away. Larry, the hunting cabin has only one bedroom with two twin beds. Mom picked the sofa for the tall Coyle men. According to Dad, it's comfortable."

Larry opened the refrigerator and put away the cold items. "I'm exhausted. If the sofa's Glenn-approved, then it's perfect for me."

I carried my things into the bedroom. "You made a mistake, Kate. You put your suitcase on my bed."

"No mistake," she called from the kitchen. "That bed is more comfortable. It's mine."

Is not.

When I returned to the kitchen, Kate said, "Sit. I'll have crackers and cheese on the table in a second." She poured three glasses of tea and set mine on the table. "Larry, want cheese and crackers before you collapse?"

"We had a big breakfast." I made a cracker and cheese sandwich. "This is perfect. Thanks, Kate."

Larry nodded and munched on a double-decker cracker sandwich.

I drained my glass of tea. "I'll set my alarm for a two-hour power nap."

Larry pushed away from the table. "Good idea. Wake me when you get up, would you?"

As Kate cleared the dishes, she said, "I left my car at the Smith farm. I'll bring it here."

"How far is that?" Larry fluffed the sofa pillow.

"About three miles. I won't be long."

Kate put on her running shoes, and after she left, I moved her suitcase and slipped under the sheets. My feet touched something cold. I pulled out the rubber snake and tossed it onto Kate's pillow.

My alarm sounded. The mingled aromas of cooling blackberry cobbler and potatoes in the oven wafted into my room. *Sure hope I'm not dreaming.* After I slipped on my socks and boots, I tiptoed into the kitchen in case Larry still slept.

When I eased out the back door, the cardinals flashed crimson in the underbrush. I inhaled the earthy aroma of acorns, decaying leaves, and pine straw. *Love the woods.*

"Have some tea." Kate stopped rocking and handed me a glass. "I heard you stir and knew you'd find me."

"Why did your plane crash?" I gulped my tea.

"I had to be in places that had nothing to do with you."

"Why did you tell me to disappear?"

She smiled. "I needed to talk to you and knew where you'd go."

Larry stepped out of the cabin with a glass in his hand. "I figured the pitcher of tea was out here."

He held out his glass, and Kate filled it and refilled mine.

"We were on our way to Harperville until I realized going to my hometown wouldn't be disappearing," I said. "Only one place that would work."

Larry sat on the porch steps.

"You two were about to step on a Texas snake." Kate poured the remaining tea into her glass. "I diverted the results from Moe. Now's your chance to walk away."

Larry leaned against the porch post and cocked his head. "You ready to walk away, Mags? Either way, I'm with you."

Kate narrowed her eyes. "Even if it means you're fired?"

"Kevin Ewing would be fired, not me." Larry grinned and winked at me.

I cleared my throat to hide my smile. "What are the results from Moe?"

Kate shook her head. "I need to work on my intimidation skills. You two are impossible."

Spike crossed his arms and glared at Larry.

"Thanks for the support, Spike," Kate said. "Maggie, you not only stirred up the bad guys, but you also stomped on the sensitive toes in the classified information department."

I drained my glass of tea and gazed at the clear sky. The call of a Bob White broke the silence.

Kate set her empty glass on the porch. "You're just stubborn. Fine. Here's what I can tell you. Ken Bushman has a criminal record."

"Thanks, but we already knew that. And nothing you can say about Gus, Maynard, or Jay. So why did Gary go to Harperville?"

"Classified."

"He went to Harperville to investigate the leak, didn't he?" I glanced at Palace Guard. *Heather? Maggie T?*

"Is Heather clean? Techie Maggie?" I asked.

Palace Guard's back stiffened, Larry sat up straight, and Spike frowned and covered his ears.

"Nothing classified about either of them," Kate said.

Larry and the imaginary men relaxed.

"I can find the leak, if you need any help," I said.

Kate raised her eyebrows. "Really?"

Larry held out his fist, and Palace Guard bumped it with his fist.

"Remember the bracelet Heather gave me? The horse rode a shuttle to the Houston airport. If we're lucky, someone picked it up, and it had an enjoyable flight. The other option is the horse will hunker down in the shuttle garage."

"What? Flight to where?"

I shrugged. "That's what Maggie T. can tell us. Our leak will know where it went."

"I'll check with Maggie T. What else?"

"We need Lucy." Larry smacked at his arm.

We stared at Larry.

"Let's go inside. The mosquitos are on attack." Larry rose and went inside the cabin.

"You need Lucy?" Kate asked.

"Guess so."

Kate went inside. I removed the grate and poured charcoal into the bottom of the grill. After I soaked the briquets and tossed in a match to light the fire, the flames flared and danced.

I staggered back as memories overwhelmed me, and my eyes welled up. *Parker loved it here.* After I replaced the grate and closed the lid, I gazed at the dark sky. *No stars tonight.* I shook off the melancholy, brushed the tears off my cheek, and hurried into the cabin.

"Larry makes sense." I pulled the two steaks out of the refrigerator.

"How?" Kate raised her eyebrows as she relaxed at the table with her beer.

"When we go back to Galveston, we'll be Larry, his red-headed sister, and their dog. Right, Larry?"

He grinned. "That's it: we're going for a different demographic profile. The Gray Lady went home to family, but not Harperville. I'll go back to work, but my sister will have to lay low. Ellen and Diane, for example, would recognize you."

"I'll make a list of people to notify that I'll be at my aunt's house in Tennessee. I'll use my old phone."

"Later? Let's eat before I starve. You grill the steaks, and I'll make the salad," Kate said.

"I'll set the table," Larry said.

The steaks sizzled when I dropped them onto the hot grill, and the wisp of smoke and whiff of seared beef reminded me of Glenn.

Larry joined me. "It's customary to bring the grill master a refreshment."

He handed me a beer and gazed at me. "Are you sure? About Galveston?"

"Thanks." I tipped my beer in a toast. "Why wouldn't we?"

Larry snorted. "It's not safe."

I gazed at him. "Would you rather not go?"

"I'd rather you were safe, but I'm with you."

"After we eat, I need a little computer time to check a few things on my database. As soon as we get Lucy, we can go to Galveston. We need a place that allows dogs."

Larry chuckled. "Ahead of you on that. I'll just bask in my light of brilliance."

"You thought about Lucy when you arranged for the new apartment?" I applied light finger pressure to the steaks to check for doneness like Glenn taught me.

Larry swaggered to the porch. "Except it's a house, not an apartment, and it has a fenced yard. A guy at work asked his sister to help me out, and she found it."

I tilted my head. "Are you obligated to take her to dinner?" I poked the steaks and turned them over with my tongs. "We'll take her somewhere nice."

Larry spewed his beer and coughed. Palace Guard grinned and patted him on the back, and I frowned.

Kate opened the back door. "You okay, Larry?"

She joined me at the grill and handed me a clean plate. "I texted Mom. I'll leave in the morning and pick up Lucy. If I leave early enough, I'll be back in time for a late lunch." She peered over my shoulder. "Steaks about ready?"

"I'll pull them off the heat to rest a bit."

Larry carried the steaks to the kitchen. Before I served them, I divided the second steak into two portions. Mine was smaller than Kate's. After we finished eating, we all had leftovers. "I'll wrap these for tomorrow for breakfast steaks."

"I'll make cinnamon rolls tonight," Kate said. "Steak and eggs and cinnamon rolls."

"Perfect. I've missed cinnamon rolls," I said.

"You cooked," Larry said. "I'll take care of the dishes."

After I wrapped and marked the leftovers, I sat on the sofa with my laptop.

"No internet," Kate said.

"I have a copy of my database on my computer," I said. "I have a few things to check. Kate, was Paul Reynolds undercover?"

"Why did you think of Reynolds?" Larry asked.

"Verification of hear-say," I said.

"Is it important? It must be." Kate bit her lip. "I can't say."

"Thanks." I focused on my database.

After he cleaned the kitchen, Larry sat next to me on the sofa with his new book.

At eleven, he patted my knee. "Bedtime. We've got a busy day tomorrow."

I closed my laptop and stumbled off to bed. I snorted when I reached the doorway. Kate slept in my favorite bed, and she'd put a second rubber snake on my pillow. After I put a snake into her backpack, I hid the second one under my mattress and smiled as I climbed into bed. *I've missed you, Kate.*

The sweet fragrance of hot cinnamon rolls mingled with the sharpness of fresh coffee woke me. I rushed to dress and hurried to the kitchen.

"About time." Kate handed me a cup of hot coffee and smirked. "How'd you sleep?"

I took the coffee with two hands and stuck out my tongue.

Larry smiled and pointed to my seat with his cup. "Better sit, Mags. I'm on my second cinnamon roll."

Kate set my plate on the table, and I dug in. "What time is it?" I asked between bites.

"Sure you want to know?" Kate chuckled. "It's four."

After I'd eaten my steak, egg, and half of my cinnamon roll, I pushed away my plate.

"I'll wrap it up for your morning snack, Maggie," Kate said.

When Larry raised his eyebrows, Kate chuckled. "And the rest for you."

Kate grabbed her backpack. "Turn on your old phone. I'll ask Dad to pick up a pay-as-you-go phone for me. You aren't the only one who is nervous about a leak."

After Kate left, I made another pot of coffee and turned on my laptop. I frowned at the screen as Larry refilled our cups. Larry paced then sat on the sofa.

"Mags, what have you got?" Larry asked. "You've been brooding in front of your computer since we got here."

"How much is conjecture?" I frowned.

Larry shrugged and patted the sofa next to him. I rose with my coffee and notes and joined him. He scooted closer and peered at my notes. "To quote Kate, *tell.*"

Chapter Fourteen

I flipped my notebook to a page I'd dog-eared. "Two men met in the alley behind my apartment my first night in Galveston. Remember I said Ken Bushman looked familiar? He went into an apartment at the building across the alley after the first man gave him an envelope and said, *This month's bonus plus instructions.*"

Larry narrowed his eyes. "I know you. There's more."

Palace Guard and Spike nodded and moved closer.

"The man who gave him the envelope looked like Jay."

Larry raised his eyebrows. "Wow. Looked like?"

I rolled my shoulders and rose. "They were in the shadows, but Ken Bushman's stance is distinctive. Jay has an average-type build, and it was his voice."

Larry furrowed his brow. "I need to review my notes on what Jay told me. Maybe if I read them to you, we'll find any false trails. What else?"

"I asked Kate about Paul Reynolds because Ellen told me he was undercover. I'm guessing she heard or overheard it from Jay. Ellen told me Jay arranged our encounter with them because he wanted to meet you."

Palace Guard stood at the back door. He wore his running shoes and shorts and pointed to Larry.

"Save me some coffee," Larry said. "Time for my training."

Larry changed to running clothes, and the two of them dashed out the back door. Spike waved then came inside with me. Spike pointed to my notes.

"Hadn't thought of the card Ellen gave me. It's in my backpack."

When I opened my backpack, I laughed at the rubber snake coiled in my running shoe. I pulled out the business card and turned it over. *Pesckey's Fish Market.* I flopped down on the bed and stared at the card. Spike joined me and pointed to my old phone.

"Call Ellen? I'll wait until the storm moves on then we can run to the hill near the Smith farm."

I replaced the business card, and we headed to the kitchen. "Larry asked for coffee. Let's make some sweet tea too. I suspect he'll enjoy it when he gets back. Do you suppose Palace Guard ran him to the Smith farm?"

Spike shook his head.

"You're right. I would, and you would, but Palace Guard has a kind heart."

Palace Guard trotted in the back door, and Larry stumbled in behind him. Spike raised his eyebrows, and my mouth quivered as I suppressed a smirk. *So much for a kind heart.*

Larry groaned. "Need medical."

"Sweet tea?" I bit my lip to keep any snickers at bay.

"That's medical." Larry flopped onto the sofa.

I handed him a tall glass with ice and tea. He gulped it down, and I refilled his glass.

"Ready for a snack?" I placed a plate with two cinnamon rolls on the kitchen table.

"Help me up."

I raised my eyebrows, and Spike and I crossed our arms.

"Fine." Larry pushed himself up and limped to the table.

I high-fived Palace Guard. My old phone rang, and I peered at it.

"It's Ellen, do I pick up?" I asked.

Larry nodded. "Keep it short."

"Maggie? Jay wanted me to call to see if y'all are okay."

I moved close to Larry so he could hear both sides of the conversation. "We're fine. How about you?"

"We came in a little farther inland."

Jay spoke in the background, but his voice was unintelligible.

"Jay wants to know if you're on the road."

I raised my eyebrows at Larry. "No, we evacuated early. Bad cell reception."

"Good to hear you're safe. Bye."

"Isn't it interesting Ellen told me Jay wanted her to call?" I asked. I picked up my notes. "Jay has all the guilty earmarks, but what about Maynard? When Irene denied she knew Gary Sloan, his face showed he knew she was lying. Chip heard Irene tell Maynard she had evidence that Mona embezzled money, and Maynard said he'd go with her to the police."

"So how does Maynard know Gary Sloan?" Larry frowned. "Why did Maynard give us bogus information about cruise ships when we were at the museum?"

"I don't know. And why did the two thugs who attacked me meet with Maynard at the museum? One more thing: when Ellen and I went to lunch, I spotted Maynard. He must have followed us."

Larry rubbed his forehead. "This is confusing. Are there any ties between Maynard and Jay?"

"Now you see why I think everybody is guilty. Back to Jay. Chip said Rosa planned to tell Kate to watch for crested birds. Isn't a blue jay a crested bird?"

"Larry rubbed his forehead. "Too much to process."

"My turn to run," I said.

"I'd like to look through Irene's papers to see if I can find the evidence she planned to take to the police."

I turned on the laptop and handed it to Larry. "Enjoy."

After I'd changed, Palace Guard waited at the back door. He grinned and bounced on his toes. I dashed past him with my head down and heard him behind me. I stayed on the path because I couldn't swerve to avoid a tree at my break-neck pace. When I reached the fork that led deeper into the forest and to the Smith farm on the left, I turned toward the Smith farm.

When I was a half-mile from the Smith farm, Palace Guard appeared on the path. He lowered his hands palms down, and I slowed my pace. The two of us jogged to the hill that overlooked the farm.

Palace Guard crouched, and I copied him. We eased through the brush, and he pointed. I peered through the trees. On the other side of the fence at the edge of the trees, a cow cleaned her newborn calf. Each lick was more vigorous than the one before, and the baby wobbled to his feet.

The faint sound of an engine grew louder. Palace Guard pointed to a far field where a farm utility vehicle headed toward the cow and her calf. We backed away in silence and trotted to the cabin.

When we were a mile from the cabin, I sped up. When I didn't hear any footsteps behind me, I pushed myself harder. *He's taken a shortcut through the brush.*

I burst through the clearing, and Palace Guard stood in the front of the steps. He grinned, and I dashed past him and slammed into the door.

"Winner!" I raised my arms and danced in victory. "I beat you to the door."

Larry opened the door. "You need inside?"

"Thanks." I strutted into the cabin, but Palace Guard was inside.

"Too late. I already won." I grinned. "Best run ever. Thanks."

"I found some documents you'll be interested in." Larry motioned to the computer, and I followed him.

"I have two identical documents included in different groups." Larry pointed to the screen. "The first is a detailed annual sales record for Exotic Research N.H.P. Prices range from five to ten thousand dollars for each unit, and the codes begin with M, F, X then the number one, two, or three. My interpretation is that NHP stands for NonHuman Primate."

I scooted a chair closer and squinted at the screen.

"The second document is a duplicate except it is for Stuffed Reserved NHP T.O.Y. and its first page has the word updated written by hand and Ramona Braun's signature. It's dated three months before Paul Reynolds died."

"So this was Irene's proof against Mona," I said. "Items, dates, costs, and customer names and addresses. Do you think this implicates Mona in Irene's death?"

"At the very least, it begs for further investigation."

Larry closed the two documents. "I found a handwritten note on a page from a cookbook between the third and fourth pages of newspaper ads for apples, crackers, and pawn shops. The recipe is Mock Apple Pie."

Larry flipped to the pawnshop ad. An arrow on the page pointed to a name brand knock-off watch.

I squinted. "The arrow's pointing to a phony watch."

While Larry flipped back to the cookbook page, I said, "I've never heard of Mock Apple Pie."

"It's an old recipe from the times when apples weren't available because they were out of season or too expensive. It's made with pie spices and crackers instead of apples."

I raised my eyebrows. "Phony Apple Pie?"

"Yep." Larry read the note on the recipe page. "*Sis, I've always loved your amazing pies. This page is from Mom's cookbook. It reminds me of the son of Nun. I found Mom's Bible. Will send it to you. Love, Paul*"

"Who is a nun's son?"

Larry chuckled. "I cheated. I texted Glenn. The son of Nun in the Bible is Joshua."

I grabbed Larry's arm. "Ellen Bushman married Joshua Davidson. That's Jay. If I'm right, Paul told his sister that Jay is a phony."

Larry put his hand on top of mine. "The evidence against Mona is clear, but Jay? All conjecture."

"I need something to drink. Ready for more conjecture?" I asked.

"Always." Larry grinned and squeezed my hand as I rose to pour two glasses of tea.

I handed Larry his glass, and he followed me to the sofa. "Strictly theory, but I think Maynard tried to keep us safe. Maybe Irene told him about Paul's message, and that's why he followed me when I met Ellen for lunch. Maybe his intent at the museum was to divert us away from investigating cruise ships because he saw Mona's original version of the sales records."

Larry frowned. "And the two assailants at the museum?"

"Maybe they followed us, and Maynard saw them lurking and threw them out?"

"A stretch, but possible. Are you thinking Maynard is undercover?"

"Not so much that as protective. He knows Gary and knows Gary is my father. Ellen said he had a soft spot for Irene."

"What about Jay? Does he know Gary? Did he plan to keep track of us?"

My eyes widened. "I just remembered something. Ellen told me she didn't know much about Gus except he was the fish man. So why did she give me his card with her cell phone number on the back? Am I reading too much into it?"

"I hate this," Larry said. "We get everything figured out then one more detail turns everything upside down."

"I just remembered another...Did you hear a whine?" I dashed to the front door, and Spike was kneeling next to Lucy and rubbing her belly.

"Lucy." I squealed, and she scrambled to right herself to get to me. I wrapped my arms around her neck and murmured. "Pretty girl. I missed you, sweet Lucy girl." My tears dampened her collar.

"I'm here too." Kate carried two large grocery sacks and had her backpack slung over her shoulder.

"Good timing." Larry took the sacks from Kate. "We have some evidence for you."

Larry and Kate went inside the cabin, and I stayed on the porch. Lucy rolled onto her back, and I sprawled on the floor next to her. We cooed to each other while Palace Guard rubbed her belly, and Spike scratched her ears.

Kate called from inside the cabin. "Better get in here, Maggie. Mom packed sandwiches and thumbprint cookies, and I can't keep Larry away from the food much longer."

I rushed inside, and Lucy scrambled along with me. When I joined Kate and Larry at the table, Lucy flopped on my feet.

Kate pointed to our glasses. "I made your raspberry tea at home while Mom pulled together our lunch."

I reached for a half of a sandwich but paused. "Don't take another bite yet, Larry. Before I forget again, when I was at Diane's, I ran into Veronica. As I was leaving, someone asked her where KB was."

Larry narrowed his eyes. "Oh really? I understand why you say that everybody's involved. And thanks for the warning." Larry finished his last bite of sandwich and reached for another one.

"I met with Gary, Maggie. He wanted me to talk you out of returning to Galveston," Kate said.

Larry frowned. "And?"

Kate laughed. "I told him it was above my pay level."

Kate held up her hand, and we all smacked it. After Larry finished the last sandwich, we dove into the cookies.

"How long can you stay, Kate?" Larry asked.

"I need to leave soon because I hope to get back to Mom and Dad's before dark, if possible. When I sent Moe a text about Mona's sales documents, he replied with *what else?* He knows the Gray Lady, doesn't he? Moe and I will meet in the morning, and I'll walk him through your Jay theory. He may see a way to trace the leak from Jay to the source in Harperville, and Maggie T's itching to find the scum. Her words. You'll be interested to know Heather's throwing a fit to join you in Galveston. Chief says he can't send everybody."

Larry snorted. "Chief doesn't have a chance, does he?"

Kate snickered. "By next week, Chief will say it was his idea."

Spike did a happy dance, and Larry raised his eyebrows.

"He's a big Heather fan," I said.

"The man has good taste," Larry said.

I glared as Larry carried the dishes to the sink.

"Oblivious." Kate mouthed. She motioned for me to follow her outside, and Lucy trotted along with us.

"Mom said to tell you she knows you miss Parker, and I'm supposed to give you a big hug. I told her I couldn't because you'd toss me to the ground." Kate sat on the steps, and Lucy leaned against her. "It's the first time I've been to the cabin since..."

Kate cleared her throat, and my eyes welled up. "Parker died. I realized during lunch I expected Lucy to jump up any time, and we'd hear *Halloo, the cabin.*"

I sat on the other side of Lucy, and she put her paw on my arm.

"Thanks for bringing Lucy." I buried my face in Lucy's neck. "How's Glenn?"

"Mom agreed to take him to their office tomorrow, so he won't be lonesome."

"Taking every advantage?"

We giggled.

Larry joined us. "What's funny?"

"My dad," Kate said. "I'll grab my backpack and head out. Find Rosa's killer and the leak and come home safe, you two."

After Kate left, I said, "The cell signal close to the Smith farm is decent. Want to take a quick run to check the Galveston forecast?"

Larry snorted. "A quick run with you and Palace Guard? You're on. You carry the cell phone."

Palace Guard and I waited for Larry in the back. He barreled out and dashed down the path. Spike stood on the porch with Lucy and waved. I ran like I chased a thief and was being chased by a Palace Guard. I couldn't see Larry, and I realized Palace Guard wasn't behind me.

Palace Guard took a shortcut to meet up with Larry. They'll take a shortcut to the farm. Stinkers.

I sprinted left into the woods and raced to the cleared brush around the fence line. I crossed under the fence at the point where it shifted to the right and continued my fastest pace across the field. *Hope the ticks can't catch me.* The thought of ticks spurred me to speed up. The farm fence and I met at an angle, and I crossed back to run into the woods. I gave my legs every ounce of power I had until I spied the clearing ahead. I shifted to a quiet pace. When the sound of a runner behind me became louder, I sped to the clearing and raced to where Palace Guard stood. He grinned and saluted me.

When I heard footsteps, I stepped behind Palace Guard. *Is it possible to hide behind an imaginary man?*

Palace Guard shrugged and signed his Maggie two-gun, but Larry was focused on the ground as he ran. He stumbled to a stop in front of Palace Guard.

"I did it. I beat her." Larry puffed up his chest.

Palace Guard shook his head.

"What do you mean, no?" Larry asked.

Palace Guard stepped to the side.

"How did you cheat? I know you did." Larry growled and stomped past me to the fence.

I pursed my lips and followed him. *No gloating.*

I turned on my new cell phone. Larry peered over my shoulder.

"Good signal," he said.

I handed the phone to him. "Want to check the weather?"

He tapped and scrolled. I wandered to the fence and scanned the field for a cow with a tiny calf. Palace Guard pointed to the right toward a barn. I squinted but didn't see a calf.

"I need Chip's binoculars," I said.

"Bring them next time. Maybe they will slow you down," Larry said. "In fact, bring a flashlight too. And your backpack. Not sarcasm. I want to win. We should check again early in the morning. The weather might be okay enough to return to Galveston. Can we walk back?"

Palace Guard nodded.

"Thanks," Larry said.

On the way back, Larry walked beside me on the path. "What do we do in Galveston?" he asked.

"You go to work."

"Are you sure? Aren't we done with the cruise ship?"

Larry stopped, put his hand on my shoulder, and pointed to the left. A doe stood between the trees thirty feet from us. She remained still and watched us. We were motionless. She flicked an ear and sauntered away. Two fawns frolicked after her.

"Beautiful," I said.

We resumed our walk. "When Palace Guard and I ran this morning, we saw a cow with her newborn baby calf in the neighbor's field. I love it here."

When the path narrowed, Larry led the way.

"Want a stick to knock down spider webs?" I asked.

"Great idea."

I stooped to pick up a three-foot long broken branch with three smaller branches on one end.

"Custom-made for spider webs." Larry waved his arms and his stick with the skill of a seasoned orchestra conductor.

"You look musical," I said.

"Thank you. I was the drum major for my high school marching band. It's refreshing that you're literal. I don't have to worry about any double-meaning or sarcasm in what you say."

I frowned. *What double meaning would musical have?*

"As far as the cruise ship, look at the contacts you have," I said. "For example, can you imagine Walt's response if Detective Kevin Ewing had asked about Ken Bushman? We still have open questions about Ken Bushman and Jay, Ken and Veronica, Butch, and Maynard. Not to mention we have theories about the monkeys but nothing concrete except Mona's paperwork. You're still the point man."

"You're right."

I tilted my head. "Of course I am."

When we returned to the cabin, Spike and I coaxed Lucy outside for a walk. I stared at the sky. A bank of dark clouds from the west had replaced the morning's high, wispy clouds.

Lucy took a few steps and sniffed the air then the ground. She meandered to a patch of grass and munched on the waving blades. "I used to think dogs ate grass when they had an upset stomach, but Lucy loves her wild salad at the cabin, doesn't she?"

Spike grinned. He stayed between her and the woods as she prowled in a malformed circle then squatted to pee.

When she peeked to be sure I had her back, I said, "Good girl."

She scraped at the grass with her hind legs and trotted to the back porch where she nosed the door.

"Is our walk over? Time for a nap, girl?" I asked.

I opened the door, and she leaped to the sofa and stretched out. Spike joined her and scratched her ears until she fell asleep. The sound of her light snore and the darkening sky gave a sense of coziness to the cabin.

"Too bad it's too warm for a fire. Do we have any hot chocolate?" Larry opened the front door and inhaled. "Smells like Galveston. Tropical air."

"I'll look." I searched the cabinets. "Nope. How about some cold sweet tea?"

"Let's take it on the back porch and watch the storm roll in."

After we settled on the steps, I said, "I've thought about our plan for our return to Galveston Island."

"Will I hate this? Because I feel I will." Larry narrowed his eyes.

"No, you won't," I said. "I can't think of any reason we need to send the Gray Lady away or keep her around, either. There's no diner. Why can't you go back with your cousin Maggie and her red hair? People who know the Gray Lady well would recognize me: Chip, Diane, Maynard, Ellen, and Jay."

Larry gazed at the darkening clouds and ticked off pros and cons on his fingers. "Keeps me from slipping up and calling you *Maggie*. Big plus. You can move around without the fear of being recognized. Incognito is not your style. Another plus. You'll go from the Gray Lady target to the Maggie target. Big double minus. I don't like it."

"Good. You don't hate it. It's settled then."

"Why do I bother?" Larry threw up his hands, and Palace Guard shrugged.

Larry stomped to the back door.

"You getting more tea?" I asked.

"No." He slammed the door behind him.

A squirrel high in a tree chattered its complaint at the noise. The treetops swayed in the wind, and a rolling rumble of thunder provided the bass for the tree frogs' song of impending rain. A light sprinkle turned to large drops then to heavy rain. The wind blew the downpour onto the porch.

"Sometimes I think raindrops are teardrops from the sky." Palace Guard put his hand on my shoulder as the torrential rain washed my face and tears.

Larry rushed outside. "Maggie? Is something wrong? You're soaked."

We like Larry. I glanced at Palace Guard, and he smiled as we headed to the door.

"Let me grab you a towel. Take off your boots, and I'll dry them for you."

I leaned against the door and struggled with my boots. *Dang hard to take off boots with wet socks.* I sat on the floor and pulled off my boots then my socks.

Larry returned with two towels. "Are you okay, Maggie?" He lifted me off the floor and wrapped one towel around my shoulders and draped the other over my damp hair.

"Go change. You're soaked." He hugged me. "Are you all right? Is it too hard being at the Coyles' cabin? You need dry clothes."

"Okay." His chest muffled my voice. *I'm okay.*

Larry walked me to the bedroom, and I waved him away and closed the door. I dried and dressed in my new farm clothes then towel-dried and brushed my hair. When I stepped out of my bedroom, I bumped into Larry. "Are you hovering?"

He smiled. "I heated water for hot tea."

Lucy trotted to me and sniffed my legs then click-clicked back to the sofa and jumped up with Spike.

"I feel guilty about Rosa and still grieve for Parker. Sometimes I spiral. Sorry." I bit my lip. *And I was a little afraid you'd stay mad.*

Larry pulled me into an embrace that was both gentle and fierce. "No need to apologize."

My mouth quivered. "Thank you. You are the kindest person I know."

He released me and met my gaze. "Even when I slam the door?"

I smiled. "Especially. It's not too hard being here. I love the cabin."

Larry returned my smile. "I understand why. It's a special place away from crowds and traffic and close to trees, birds, and animals."

Larry shifted to the stove and poured hot water for my tea while I sat at the table.

"I'll bet it's something when it's cold and there's a roaring fire in the fireplace."

"It is." I reached for my computer, and Larry jumped up. "Can I get you anything?"

I turned on the laptop. "I may have holes in my data to investigate after we have internet access again."

"You don't mind if I settle down with a book? Kate has some outstanding books here."

I frowned at the screen. Palace Guard kicked my shin. "Not at all. Sit in the old recliner. It doesn't look like much with the cracked leather, but it's comfortable."

"Thanks," Larry said. "I was afraid it might, you know, have memories."

When I rose, my chair scraped and almost tipped; I put my hands on my hips. "Kevin Ewing, you don't have to worry about anything. You are my best friend and can sit wherever you like."

His eyes widened. "Best friend?" He swaggered to the bookcase.

I took my seat, and Palace Guard raised an eyebrow. I sighed. *He'll be hard to live with now, won't he?* Palace Guard grinned.

Two hours later, Larry said, "Maggie. Maggie?"

"Did you say something? Sorry."

"It's stopped raining."

I rose from my chair. "Ugh. I'm stiff." I stretched and peered outside. "Sun's going down. Too late to go to the farm."

"Let's go watch the sunset." Larry handed me a beer.

Lucy led the way outside. She eased down the steps but pulled back her paw when it touched the grass. She backed up the steps and nosed the door.

"Change your mind?" I opened the door, and she scrambled inside.

I sipped my beer. "My theory is the leak in Harperville is one person. It takes only one person with the right access. The most obvious type of person would be a Maggie T. I suspect everyone's focused on finding a techie."

Larry raised his eyebrows. "But you don't agree."

Hidden cicadas buzzed and camouflaged tree frogs chirped.

"I've never seen a cicada. Have you?" I asked.

"Never thought about it. I guess I haven't." Larry tipped his bottle and swallowed. "What are you thinking?"

"The standard investigations aren't working. I'm convinced our leak hides in plain sight. Tree frogs blend in; cicadas stop buzzing and change location when someone gets near. We need someone in Harperville who blends into the environment too."

"Heather, right?"

I saluted Larry with my bottle. "Correct. Heather is a wizard at blending into an environment. She's worked in every department. Everyone's seen her so often in her disguises that she's invisible. Just Heather."

"Brilliant," Larry said. "The idea is she hangs around different departments in one of her outfits, just like every other day. Moe can swing this, and I think Heather will jump at the idea. I'll send Moe a text from your phone to call in the morning. We'll go to the Smith farm."

"We might not need to do that." I dashed inside and checked the bedroom closet for the box I'd left. After I carried the box outside and opened it, I pulled out the booster Sergeant Arrington bought for me to use at the cabin.

"Cell phone signal booster. We don't have to go to the Smith farm for a phone call."

"Why didn't we use this to check the weather?"

I frowned. "Because I didn't think of it."

"Hallelujah, my Maggie's not perfect." Larry danced his version of Spike's wacky dance, and Palace Guard and Spike applauded.

I ignored them and plugged the phone into the booster, and Larry sent Moe the text: "Call GL. K."

"I could have attached it myself," Larry grumbled.

I put on my poker face, and Palace Guard nodded his head.

My phone buzzed with a text: "30 min."

"While we're waiting, I'll put Jennifer's casserole in the oven and bribe Lucy to come outside and onto the grass. If it gets much darker, she can't see and will claim she opted to wait until morning."

After I preheated the oven and popped in the casserole, I grabbed a handful of treats and waved one under Lucy's nose. She opened her eyes and eased off the sofa in slow motion.

"Let's go for a walk, Lucy." Spike bounded to the door, and I held her treat low as I followed him. Lucy tracked behind me with her nose near the treat.

When we reached the porch, I closed the door, and she sat for her treat.

"Good girl." I held the treat in front of her and lowered it to the porch while she watched.

"Why put her treat on the porch?" Larry asked, while Lucy munched.

"We think one eye has lost most of its sight, and she has no depth perception. She'd snap at the treat, and I'm not sure I'm fast enough to move away my fingers."

She sniffed the porch then flopped down. Spike kneeled next to her, and she rolled for her belly rub. When he stopped and headed to the grass, she flipped over and cocked her head.

I waved another treat in front of her and let her sniff it. I eased back with the treat in front of her. She rose to her feet and took one deliberate step toward me.

"Slow process, isn't it?" Larry asked, and I nodded as I eased back into the grass.

I held two fists in front of me. "Which one, Lucy?"

She trotted to me and nosed my left hand. "This is the tricky part." I stared at Lucy and tossed the dog cookie in an arc. She snapped the air and snagged her cookie.

"Good aim," Larry said.

I chuckled. "We don't miss often."

"Why can't she catch inside the house? Never mind. The floor's too slick."

My cell rang.

"Thirty minutes goes by fast." Larry dashed into the cabin.

Spike tossed a small limb three feet from Lucy.

"Get it, girl!" I called out.

Lucy sniffed in a sweep toward the branch. She leaped on it and trotted around the yard with her head and stick high. Spike pretended to chase her, and she dodged and darted to the edge of the grass near the woods. Lucy squatted and relieved herself then pranced across the yard to the porch with her stick. After she flopped onto the porch, she cradled her stick with both paws and gnawed.

Larry opened the door. "Success?"

"Yes. Your call was quick. Good news?" I asked.

"Maybe. I can't growl as well as Moe, but I'll try."

Chapter Fifteen

Larry cleared his throat for his Moe impression then lowered his voice to add Moe's gravelly touch. "Maggie's idea? Of course. Need to check resources and bounce it off the team and the chief. Get back to you in the morning."

Larry grinned. "Then he hung up. Your aunt Katherine has rubbed off on him."

"Yep, she never says goodbye. I think it's her way of knocking on wood."

I smacked my thighs with two quick pats. "Ready to go inside, Lucy?"

Larry opened the door. Lucy dropped her stick and danced inside.

Larry raised his eyebrows.

"No sticks inside. Might be her rule. She knows it's time for her evening repast," I said. "She hasn't caught onto that phrase yet; otherwise, I'd be stumbling across the cabin to her you-know."

I dished up Lucy's food then she posed with her most regal stance. When I set her dish in front of her, she remained motionless until I said, "Okay."

She dived in.

"She's amazing," Larry said. "Who trained her to wait?"

"Jennifer." I grinned. "Lucy loves Jennifer and food, in that order."

"Speaking of food, how much longer until we eat?" Larry's stomach rumbled. "We're hungry too." He wiggled his eyebrows, and I chuckled.

"I'll pull together a salad," I said.

"I've got the rest."

By the time I had the salad ready, Larry had set the table, poured our tea, and pulled out the casserole to cool a bit.

After we ate, I yawned. "Lucy needs to go outside one more time before bed."

"I want to check the weather in Galveston and between here and there," Larry said. "But cleanup first."

Larry carried our dishes to the sink then picked up the casserole dish. "Almost too much to throw away. What about the leftovers?"

I peered into the dish. "Breakfast."

Larry covered the dish and placed it in the refrigerator.

"What's next?" he asked.

"You want to clean the kitchen or the bathroom?"

"Kitchen. That includes the sink, stovetop, oven, inside the refrigerator, and the countertops, right?" Larry asked.

"That covers it. Want to race?"

I dashed to the bathroom with cleaning supplies then called out, "Go."

When I finished the bathroom, I raced to the living room where Larry relaxed on the sofa with a book. He glanced up and draped his arm across the back. "Oh. You finished."

"What do you mean? You cheated and skipped something." I stomped to the kitchen. *Refrigerator and Freezer? Clean. Stovetop and oven? Clean. Countertops? Spotless. Sink? Gleaming. Floor? Swept.*

"How did you do it?" I glared.

"Show me your shortcut to the farm, and I'll tell you."

I laughed. "Fair enough. The shortcut isn't far. Grab a flashlight and I'll show you."

As we headed down the path, I said, "We'll watch for the point where the path curves to the right. That's where we cut into the field."

We jogged along together. When it curved, Larry asked "Here?"

"That's it. Easy, once you know about it."

We crossed the fence into the field. "Now we go straight, which means we ignore the woods."

Larry pointed to the next hill. "If we go straight, we'll go into the woods."

"That's right. And then we'll see the Smith farm. The bypass takes at least five minutes off my time. I spotted it this morning when Palace Guard showed me the newborn calf."

On our stroll back I asked, "So how did you clean the entire kitchen so fast?"

"You won't be mad, right?" he asked.

I shrugged. "I don't know."

"Kate told me the custom is to leave the cabin clean for the next visitors. She said you'd give me a choice, and the easiest to clean is the kitchen if I do the dishes every meal and clean as I go along."

I punched his arm.

"Ow." He grinned.

"If I had a gauntlet, I'd smack you and challenge you to a duel."

"Cleaning rags at dawn?" Larry snickered.

"Ha. Ha." I pursed my lips to hide my grin.

"Are you mad?" Larry's brow furrowed, and he glanced at me.

"Darn right. Mad I didn't think of it first." I snickered.

"Kate set me up, didn't she? We'll get her back, won't we?"

"Of course." I stepped on a log and grabbed for Larry when it rolled under my feet. "Thanks. But we'll wait awhile. She expects immediate retaliation."

When we reached the cabin, Larry asked, "Ready to check the weather? Does Lucy need to go out?"

"If you'll pull up the weather, Spike and I will coax Lucy outside. Spike's good with her. She'll follow him for a belly rub."

Spike and I lured Lucy outside with minor difficulty, and I hurried inside. Larry had connected the cell to the booster.

"The storm stalled for a while according to the news but is moving to the northeast faster than the earlier forecast expected. Remnants of rain bands and tropical winds in the morning."

"Sounds like we can head back." I covered my mouth and yawned. "Can you check on the house?"

"Good idea. I'll do that now."

While Larry was on the phone, I stepped outside to join Spike and Lucy while they relaxed porch.

"Did she take her stroll? Any success?"

Spike nodded and scratched Lucy's ear. Lucy rose and nosed the door. When we went inside, Larry was still on the phone. I flopped onto Kate's chair and flipped up the footrest.

When his call finished, he moved to the sofa. "She's a talker. She called a friend who lives near the house. The house is fine, and the neighborhood has its electricity back. I have the key, so we can go straight there. It's furnished, but she called it bare bones, so I asked her what it has."

"Let me guess. A refrigerator, stove, and a few pots and pans, and beds. Anything else?"

"Sounds like the kitchen is the best-furnished room of the house. It has a refrigerator, stove, dishwasher, dishes, silverware, and plenty of pots and pans. She said the sofa is comfortable, and the kitchen table is adequate, whatever that means." Larry chuckled.

"We can stop in Montgomery for cleaning supplies," I said.

"We need to pick up a cooler, ice, and food."

"I'll make a list."

Larry nodded. "Always."

I struggled with the footrest. "This is a Kate trap. I should have known."

Larry slammed it shut for me.

"Thanks, I didn't realize I was so tired."

After I completed my list, I left it on the table. "Goodnight."

I opened my eyes when a whiff of coffee tickled my nose. I dressed in the dark and hurried to the kitchen. Larry's backpack was at the front door, a pot of coffee sat on the stove, but no one was inside the cabin. I slipped the leftover casserole into the oven, poured myself a cup of coffee, and hurried outside. Larry and Palace Guard grinned, and Spike waved from the grass where he followed Lucy.

"Y'all are up early." I sipped my coffee.

Larry snorted. "Lucy's idea. We've been out here for a half hour, and she's still on the prowl for the right spot."

"I'll go pack my things and get breakfast on the table."

"Did you hear that, Lucy?" Larry said. "We can all go in for breakfast as soon as you pee."

Lucy squatted, and I laughed. "Guess she needed motivation."

When we went inside, I stripped the sheets and carried all my things to the front door.

"Lucy's fed, and I've set the table," Larry said.

After we ate, Larry loaded the truck while I washed dishes, and Spike took Lucy outside for one last walk. Lucy trotted outside then hurried to the front.

As he turned onto the paved road, Larry said, "I checked the weather in Galveston. I don't think we'll see any rain when we get there. We may run into showers around Montgomery."

I glanced in the back seat, and Lucy had curled up on Spike's lap. Spike cradled her, and she slept with her head snuggled into the crook of his arm.

My phone rang. *Moe.*

"Answer it. I'll pull over," Larry said.

"We're on the road. We'll pull over."

After Larry stopped the truck, he took the phone. "Good news?" he asked.

He listened then frowned. "We're missing a great opportunity."

His eyes narrowed, and his face turned red. "Got it."

He hung up and slammed the steering wheel, and I jumped.

"What?" I asked.

"Moe said Heather's on another assignment, and no other resources are available. Not up for discussion."

He exhaled. "Okay. I can drive now." He eased back onto the road, and we continued in silence.

When we reached the outskirts of Montgomery, the sun had risen, and cows had gathered in groups in their fields. "That doesn't sound like Moe. Something's up," I said.

Larry took the next exit and pulled into a super store parking lot. He parked a few rows away from any other vehicles. "I don't want a kind-hearted soul to see Lucy and think her owner left her alone in the truck. We don't need a smashed window."

"Groceries or camping gear?" I asked on our way in.

"I get to choose? Camping gear."

Larry rushed to the left when we were in the store, and Palace Guard and I headed to housewares then grocery. After we found all the items from my list, I pushed my full cart to the camping department.

"This was harder than I thought." Larry stood in an aisle with coolers and had placed a small one in his cart. "I'm glad you're here."

I scanned the shelves. "We need one large enough to hold food and ice. And we should pick up reusable ice packs." I pointed. "This one has rollers."

"That one it is then." Larry lifted it off the shelf and set it on the floor. "All the others are smaller. The cooler's too big for a grocery cart."

"We can check out then come back."

"I'll grab a cart." Larry dashed to the front.

"Or you can run get a cart." I snickered, and Palace Guard grinned.

My efforts to push my cart and pull the cooler reminded me of the work to rise from Kate's chair. *I'll just wait here.*

Larry returned with a rolling flat and lifted the cooler onto the flat. "Ice is up front."

Larry pulled the flat and led the way to the front of the store with a swagger.

Not a cop swagger. More like a hunter swagger. I lifted my fist, and Palace Guard bumped it with his.

When we reached the truck, I loaded the ice and groceries into the cooler while Larry loaded the large items. He had reserved space for the cooler and lifted it into the truck.

After he merged with the interstate traffic, Larry said, "You might be right."

"Of course. About what?"

"Moe. He's hiding something."

I nodded. "Heather's on it."

Larry held up his hand, and we all high-fived. Spike put the back of his hand on his forehead and brushed back his hair in his Heather impression.

"You're right, Spike," Larry said. "Nobody could do it but Heather, and Moe would do whatever it takes to keep Heather safe."

I pulled out my notebook and added more points. After I redrew the circle I'd shown Ellen, I drew a graph with the title *Motive vs. Opportunity* and assigned the people from the circle to data locations using my best judgment.

"Traffic's lighter than I expected," Larry said.

I nodded and added more people who hadn't been on the original circle.

"It's all subjective," I said.

"What? Larry asked.

"I plotted motive and opportunity for everyone I could think of."

Larry glanced at my graph. "The data points cluster in the middle. Why don't you drill down into motive?"

I glared at him. *Because it's too hard.*

Palace Guard poked my back.

I had listed reasons for murder then classified them. Most of the motives were money, revenge, or the fear of exposure. I tapped my pencil on my pad. *Maybe a motive is money plus the fear of being exposed?*

"Still subjective?" Larry asked.

"Yes, but with a different view." I rubbed my forehead and stared at the words *fear of exposure.*

"It's not the fear of exposure, it's the consequences of the exposure."

"Did you say something?" Larry asked.

"Processing," I said. I stared outside. The landscape had changed from farmland to coastal. "Where are we?"

"West of Mobile."

"Is there a rest stop ahead?" I asked.

"About ten miles. Be good to stretch our legs. Do we have anything to snack on?"

"Cheese and crackers. I stuck the crackers in the cooler, so they'd be easy to find."

I slid my notebook into my backpack and leaned back. The light traffic moved as a unit. When we came to a slow car, the unit passed the vehicle in line order. When the car two vehicles behind us passed the car in front of it then zoomed past us, I frowned. *Now you're out of order.*

"Two miles," I said. "I'm ready to stretch out the stiffness."

"Here we are." Larry flipped his right turn signal and slowed for the ramp. Three cars from our line followed us. Larry backed into a spot across from the building, and the other three parked in line order.

Larry, Lucy, and the men headed to the pet walk area. As I headed to the restroom, a woman stepped out of the passenger seat of the SUV next to us and opened the back door. Three little girls ranging from three to seven scrambled out. The girls held hands as they crossed the road, and their mother held out her arms to keep them together. I waited for the four of them and held the door open. The girls were tiny versions of their mother. All of them had black ringlets and brown eyes except for the smallest one who had green eyes.

"Are you sure?" the mother asked.

"Of course."

The mother and the two oldest ones trooped into the restroom.

"Thank you, Red Lady. My name is Charlotte." The smallest one giggled then caught up with her sisters.

Charlotte's mother marshalled her brood into one stall. The ceramic floors and walls amplified the squeals and shrieks. While I washed my hands with cold water, a woman came into the restroom and smiled. "Best part?" She said in a quiet voice. "Not mine." We giggled, and I fluttered my hands and dried them on my jeans.

When I reached the truck, Lucy and her men were inside. I reached for the handle, and Palace Guard pushed the button to unlock.

"That was impressive, Palace Guard, thank you."

I noticed a tattooed, muscular man in a leather vest with patches as he strode across the road to the car next to us. He pounded on the car's hood, and I jumped out of the truck and rushed to the front. The SUV driver, an overweight man with gray hair, heaved himself out of the vehicle then the men embraced and laughed.

Charlotte and her sisters rushed out of the restroom and squealed. Their mother turned to thank the woman who held the door for them, and Charlotte dashed into the road. A car barreled from the exit into the rest area, but Charlotte's focus was on the man in the leather vest. Palace Guard and I dived toward her, and he grabbed her and me. As the car tires screeched, the three of us sailed across the road and rolled onto the grass. I cradled

Charlotte in my arms. Her eyes opened wide, and she stared at Palace Guard. "He's amazing, isn't he?"

I smiled. "Yes, he is."

Larry raced to us and helped us up. The driver of the speeding car stepped out of the car. Her face was pale, and her knees buckled. She collapsed, and people ran to help her. Charlotte's mother and the man in the leather vest dashed to us, and the older man collected the two older girls.

"Charlotte. Are you okay?" Tears flowed down her mother's face.

"The Guard saved me. He's 'mazing."

The man with the tattoos reached for her, and she wrapped her arms around his neck. He hugged her and cooed. He held her tight as he carried her across the road. Charlotte looked over his shoulder and saluted Palace Guard.

Charlotte's mother wiped her cheek and stared at Larry and me.

"Did you save her, sir?" she asked. "She has invisible friends."

Larry shook his head.

"She's right. The Guard saved her." I bit my lip, but I couldn't stop my tears.

"Thank you, Guard." The mother nodded in the direction Charlotte had saluted then rushed to join her family.

Palace Guard's face was a light pink. I sobbed while Larry and Palace Guard walked me to the truck and while I clicked my seatbelt.

"I'm glad they stayed in line," I said.

Larry hugged me not with a *poor you* hug but with a *I got you* hug, and I relaxed.

"You'll explain later, right?" he asked.

I brushed away the last tear. "Maybe." My mouth quivered into a smile.

"That's my crazy lady." Larry chuckled.

We drove away from the rest stop without our troop of cars.

A few miles down the road, I said, "We forgot our snack."

"We were busy. We'll stop at the next rest stop."

I'm literal. Larry's practical. I leaned back and closed my eyes.

The truck slowed, and I opened my eyes. "Where are we?"

"Louisiana." Larry followed the exit to a Rest Area and Visitor's Center.

Well-kept landscaping with native grasses and brick walkways surrounded the main building. Larry parked in front of a covered picnic table near the pet walk. I snapped the leash on Lucy, and she grinned.

"You're right, girl." I chuckled. "We know it's for show."

Spike, Lucy, and I wandered the pet area while Larry dug in the cooler for drinks and snacks. Palace Guard covered Larry's back.

When we returned, Lucy ambled to her bowl of water. I sat on a bench, and Larry beat Spike to the seat next to me. Palace Guard sat across from us, and Spike pouted.

I gulped down half of my drink. "Didn't realize how thirsty I was."

"Breeze feels good." Larry reached for crackers and cheese. "Tell me about the line."

"It started with our informal travel group. Everyone noticed when someone got out of order in the line. Then when we parked at the rest area, we all parked in order. Charlotte and her sisters held hands when they crossed the road to the restroom. When they came out, she broke from her line, and Palace Guard and I noticed." I frowned at the crackers. "You're getting ahead of me."

I picked up a handful of crackers and more cheese. "As long as the bad guy stays in order, no one notices, but when he murdered Paul Reynolds, he stepped out of line. Same with Irene and Rosa, and the attacks on you, me, and Detective Ewing. The stakes are so high that he's willing to risk the exposure. As long as he stays in line the risk of being exposed is low, but when the level of threat escalates, he jumps out."

Larry stared at me. "He's no longer motivated by staying in line. You have an idea, don't you?"

"Just a working theory right now."

"I'm smart enough to wait until you tell me more." Larry and Palace Guard smiled, and Spike lost his pout.

We finished our crackers and cheese and piled into the truck.

When it was close to four, Larry said, "Let's stop for gas. We can have another snack or stop somewhere on the road around Lake Charles. It's about two hours away."

"Is there a GPS in your head?" I asked.

He chuckled. "I should say *yes*, but I memorized the route from Galveston to Georgia and back. If we ran into any problems, I wanted to be ready with a detour. You threw me with the route change to Montgomery at first, but I adjusted."

"Let's check around Lake Charles. If we see nothing interesting, we can snack. Irene mentioned she had an old friend in Louisiana, but, typical Irene, she didn't say where."

"If we don't get tacos tonight, we'll find some in the morning."

"I have a taco obsession." I pulled my notebook out of my backpack and examined my notes. "What's a cop's biggest fear?"

"Not counting death or injury of family? Going to prison."

"But if the risk is low because the cop is clean, that particular motivator has little impact."

I flipped my notebook to the first page and read. After an hour of reading and taking notes, I asked, "Do you suppose Louisiana has tacos?"

"I'm sure they do, but we should have Louisiana food like a po' boy or shrimp étouffé."

"What's that? Not that it matters. I'll eat anything. It comes from years of not knowing how to cook. I either ate what was in front of me or starved."

"Never thought about it, but I've never seen you turn down anything to eat."

Larry slammed on his brakes when a car swerved around us and cut him off as it sped to the exit ramp.

"Drive much?" Larry mumbled then siren-whistled between his teeth. "A po' boy is like a sub except the bread is New Orleans French bread with a crispy crust and a fluffy center. It has roast beef or something fried like shrimp, oysters, crawfish, or crab. The dressing for a fried po' boy is melted butter and pickles. I take it back. It's nothing like a sub."

Larry rolled his shoulders. "Shrimp étouffé is shrimp in a thick gravy with rice on top. I think tomatoes, celery, onions, and green pepper are in the sauce. And hot sauce. It's spicy like we like our food. I'm making me hungry. We need to find you some good creole cookbooks. You'd be a remarkable Cajun cook."

I added Cajun cookbook to my shopping list.

I flipped back to my graph. "What if Maynard and Jay are both undercover and trying to keep us from being killed?"

"I doubt it, but where are you going with that?"

"I need to give some other people the same scrutiny I've given those two."

Larry raised his eyebrows. "Like?"

"Veronica and Gus."

Larry rubbed his chin. "No argument here."

I pointed to a billboard. "Po' boys ahead. Three miles."

"We're stopping, right?"

"Yes. But if their kitchen has a microwave, we leave."

Larry shuddered. "You'll check the kitchen?"

"Sure. Haven't you ever heard of professional courtesy?"

"I'll be close by." Larry growled.

"Okay, but Lucy needs a walk. I'll just pop in."

Palace Guard tapped Larry's shoulder.

"Palace Guard goes with you; otherwise I'm not stopping."

"You can't make rules for me." I meant to growl, but my voice squeaked.

Larry snickered, and I tossed my hair. "I choose Palace Guard to go in with me."

"If you insist," Larry said.

I examined his face. "Sarcasm?"

"Not at all. Just trying to be accommodating."

"Okay then."

Larry exhaled and turned at the exit. He parked in front of the packed restaurant and waited in the truck until Palace Guard and I went inside. I waved, and he opened the door for Lucy.

I scanned the restaurant. *Clean.* Palace Guard nodded.

The hostess approached me. "Table for one?"

"Not yet. I'm here to visit the kitchen."

"An inspector? Yes, ma'am. Right this way. We'll let Chef Daryl know you're here."

She signaled a waitress who scurried ahead of us and dashed into the kitchen.

A voice boomed from the kitchen. "Another one? What happened to that sorry slug Antonio? Send her in. We got nuttin' to hide."

When I strutted into the kitchen, a tall, overweight man guffawed. "What's dis? You ain't no inspector, Missy." He narrowed his eyes and growled. "Git outta my kitchen."

I stepped toward him. "You're Chef Daryl? Irene's friend? I'm the Gray Lady."

"You? The Gray Lady? No." He narrowed his eyes as he circled me. "Irene's friend, you say? What's her signature?"

"Barber pole." I smiled.

He chuckled. "Nobody but Irene, right, red-headed Gray Lady? So whatcha doin' in my kitchen?"

"I need to learn how to cook real food. You know, Cajun."

"Come sit, little miss red-headed gray lady. You came to the right place. You need work? I hire you on da spot. I hated what happened to my sha Irene. Big loss. Left a hole in my heart." He pounded his fist on his chest.

I sat on a stool at a prep table, and Chef Daryl pulled up a stool across from me.

"Irene was a real force. She told me you were an old friend." I shook my head. "Just passing through."

"Dat be true. You here by yerself?"

"No, my cousin's with me. He's taking my dog for her walk."

"Hey, Christy." He bellowed, and the hostess dashed into the kitchen. "Go find dis red-headed gray lady's cousin and get him in here."

She scooted out, and he turned to me. "I have no manners. My name is Daryl." He held out his hand, and we shook.

"I'm Maggie."

"Well, Miss Maggie, the best way I can teach you is for you to watch me cook for you. We need to show your taste buds real food." He threw back his head in a hearty laugh as Larry came into the kitchen.

"The cousin," Daryl said. He rose and held out his hand. As they shook, I said, "Daryl, this is my cousin Larry."

"I woulda known dat. You two favor, except you sure are short, Miss Maggie. No offense."

Larry chuckled.

"None taken." I smiled at Chef Daryl and stuck out my tongue at Larry when Daryl hurried to his walk-in cooler.

Larry and I sat at the prep table while Daryl cooked, commented on the process and ingredients, and told hilarious, gossipy stories about other chefs.

He set four dishes in front of us and two plates. He pointed with his chef's knife. "Here you have your shrimp po' boy. Dis bowl's crawfish étouffé. Dat's gumbo with a side of rice and a side of potato salad. And dis last one's alligator tail. Bon appétit."

I cut the po' boy in half with precision, and Daryl grinned. I put a small serving of the rest of the dishes on my plate. Larry picked up his half of the po' boy and bit in. "Mmm."

I took a bite of mine. "Shrimp is light and crunchy. Do you bake your own bread?"

"Ha. I do, Sha."

"Touch of garlic and lemon in the butter."

Daryl grinned.

By the end of our meal, I had a good idea of the ingredients and how to cook each dish, including dipping the alligator tail in a hot sauce and buttermilk mixture before dredging.

"I soak ever-ting in da buttermilk with hot sauce. I have a surprise for you, Miss Red-headed Gray Lady Maggie. I been working on my cookbook for years. Be right back."

He rushed to his office and returned with a shoe box overflowing with papers. "Here ya go, Sha. I don't need no recipes, and no one wants dem."

"They are fools," Larry said.

"You right der." Daryl raised his eyebrows. "You treat my Maggie good or..."

He planted his knife into the cutting board and grinned.

"Thank you so much for everything, Daryl," I said.

He hugged me. "You drop in anytime you in da neighborhood. And you tell Miz Diane I'll help her anyway I can."

As we drove away, Larry said, "I am stuffed. Daryl is an amazing chef."

"What do I do with the recipes?" I asked.

"Pick out the ones you want and scan them then give the box to Jennifer."

I stared at him. "Now that is brilliant."

"Of course. Our visit with Daryl set us back two hours, but it was worth it, right?"

I shuffled through the papers. "I'll translate for Jennifer. The recipes are in English, French, and Cajun."

"What does sha mean?" Larry asked.

"It's Cajun for the French *chère*, dear."

"How do you know that?" he asked.

"I studied US regional dialects for a year when I was thirteen."

Larry gaped and shook his head. "Of course."

I opened my notebook. "Why was Paul Reynolds murdered? I need to talk to Gary."

Chapter Sixteen

We rolled into Galveston Island a little before midnight. I gazed at the houses as the truck crept down the residential streets.

"A few houses with lights on."

"Not that much debris on the road. The locals already picked up or moved it to the side," Larry said as he pulled into a driveway. "Here we are. Let's see if we have electricity then unload the truck."

Larry unlocked the door and flipped the light switch. "This isn't bad," he said. Lucy pushed past him to investigate.

"Not at all." I inspected the kitchen. When Larry brought in the cooler, I said, "Refrigerator's clean and cold. I'll bet this is a vacation rental because the kitchen's well furnished. There's a stacked, apartment-sized washer and dryer combo by the back door." I emptied the cooler.

Larry sat on the sofa. "I shouldn't have done this. It's comfortable." Lucy trotted to the sofa and jumped next to him. She put her head on his lap, and he scratched her ears.

"Come on, Lucy. I'll unload the truck, and you can check the yard."

Lucy followed Larry outside, and I used my flashlight to check for bed bugs. Larry brought our things inside and carried his backpack to the front bedroom.

"That's my bedroom," I said.

Larry stopped in the hallway. "The other bedroom is larger, and I'll be less likely to wake you up when I leave for work. Can we fight over this tomorrow?" Larry dropped his things in the front bedroom and stomped out to the truck.

I checked the back bedroom again with Palace Guard. "It has a good view of the alley. Better defensive position than the kitchen. Not bad. But I'll wait until tomorrow to tell him." Palace Guard grinned. I made up the beds with the sheets and blankets we'd bought.I found Lucy's water bowl and filled it. When Lucy and Spike came inside, she trotted to the kitchen for a drink then took her place on the sofa. Larry locked the truck and brought in his last load.

"Made the beds and plugged in the phones to charge." I yawned and pulled off my boots. "Time to collapse. Good night."

The next morning Larry and I took our coffee outside while Lucy explored the sandy back yard. Dead flower stems dangled from two hanging pots, and the southwestern planter on the small patio contained brown sticks that were small bushes at one time.

"Put plants on our list. This is pitiful," Larry said.

A phone rang, and Larry dashed inside to answer it. When he returned, he brought the coffeepot and refilled our coffee.

"That was work. I'm glad you plugged in the phones last night. Supe wants me to come in for a few hours. What do you think?"

"Up to you. I can make breakfast before you leave. I've got plenty to do with laundry and unpacking. If you're okay with where I put things." I sported my best wicked smile.

Palace Guard furrowed his brow, and Larry snickered.

I stomped inside, and Larry brought Lucy in. While Larry prepared for work, I fed Lucy and made him an egg sandwich.

Larry rushed out of his bedroom. "Do you suppose..."

I had his sandwich wrapped in a paper towel in one hand, and his thermos in the other. "Egg sandwich for the road? And your coffee?"

"You're the best." Larry rushed out the door.

"Of course."

After he left, I gathered dirty clothes for rounds of laundry. I started the washer and emptied the sacks and boxes of food onto the table so I could plan where to put things.

My old phone rang. *Ellen.*

"Maggie, where are you?"

"Back in Galveston Island. We took advantage of evacuating and picked up my dog."

"That's great. We came back to the house yesterday. We picked up the yard, but the house had no damage. Jay's out helping one of our older neighbors clean up his yard. Ninety-three years old and thinks he's seventy." She chuckled. "I guess seventy sounds old to you. Are you in your apartment?"

"No, Larry found a small house that allows dogs. I think it's a vacation rental. He's gone to work, and I'm working on laundry."

"I'm doing laundry today too. I need to shop for groceries later this morning. Would you like me to pick you up? If the grocery stores are too crazy, we can grab a few things and leave."

"That would be great. We have nonperishables, but I could use something to cook tonight and to make Larry's lunch tomorrow." I gave her the new address.

"You're close to us. I'll text you before I leave."

After we hung up, I flipped through Daryl's papers. *Gumbo sounds interesting.* Spike peered over my shoulder and smacked his lips. "The recipe says to serve sides of rice and potato salad with gumbo and includes

Daryl's potato salad recipe. I'd never heard of potato salad with gumbo, but it was good."

I sat with the recipes and listed the ingredients I'd need then drew a sketch of the cabinets and planned where items would go. After I put all the items on shelves in the cabinets, I inventoried to see what else I might need. Flour and sugar were at the top of my list.

I opened the refrigerator. "More eggs, milk, and butter."

I emptied the tiny washer and tossed the clothes into the dryer. After I started the next load, I called Diane.

She answered immediately. "Maggie, are you okay?"

"We are. We took advantage of evacuating and picked up my dog. What about you?"

"We didn't evacuate because I didn't want to. Smitty reminded me of that when I complained about how scary the wind noise was." She chuckled. "We had a window break from debris, but Smitty fixed it as soon as the winds died down. He's picking up the yard now."

"On our way back to Galveston Island, we ran into an old friend of your mother's outside Lake Charles. Chef Daryl. Do you know him?"

"Do I ever. When I was a girl, Mama and I used to visit him. He told the funniest stories, and some of them were naughty. Mama would snap a towel at him and tell him to clean up what he said in front of me. He'd wait until Mama was busy then tell me another story. Chef Daryl would sit me up on a table, and I'd swing my feet while he said *taste this*. He said it was a taste bud challenge, but now I think he was educating my palate. It was our game. How is he?"

"Hasn't changed. He told gossipy stories and checked my palate. He gave me some recipes if you'd like copies of them."

"I learned most of his recipes in his kitchen, but you've given me an idea. A Texas Cajun diner. I can teach Chip the recipes in two or three days. He's amazing."

"He is."

"I need to see Chef Daryl. Smitty and I can go tomorrow. I'll talk to him about opening another diner here. He'll tell me what he thinks; I have no doubt about that. Thank you so much for letting me know where he is."

After we hung up, I resumed my laundry drill. Spike and Lucy stood at the back door, and I opened the door for Lucy. "I'll be out in a minute."

I texted Glenn with my new phone: "Back in TX. Need 2 talk 2 ur visitor."

I poured a glass of water and headed to the back yard. Lucy was still with her neck extended and one foot raised. When I scanned the direction she pointed, I saw it. A lean jackrabbit with black tips on its ears. *Its ears are as long as its back legs.*

"Good girl," I said.

The rabbit twitched an ear and bounded out of our sight. Lucy trotted to me for her reward, and I scratched her ears until she flopped over for a Spike belly rub.

"I don't think I've ever seen a jackrabbit before. I'm surprised at how big it is."

After her belly rub, Lucy patrolled the yard until I brought her inside for a drink and a rest.

As I folded clothes, Ellen texted: "On the way."

I grabbed my list. "I'm going shopping with Ellen. Who's going?"

Spike raised his hand, and Palace Guard nodded.

Ellen tooted her horn, and we hurried to her car.

"Oh, my gosh. Love your hair," Ellen said when I opened the passenger's door.

I touched the side of my head and frowned. *Brushed it same as always.*

"The color is great. Is red your natural hair color?"

I chuckled. "I'd forgotten all about it. Seems natural to me. Larry's hair is red now too. I think red suits him better than it does me."

"That can't be true." Ellen backed out of the driveway. "Your hair is beautiful."

On our way to the store, Ellen said, "Most of these houses are seasonal rentals. Good find."

"We got in around midnight, so I haven't seen the neighborhood yet. We didn't know what we'd find. It's not so bad."

"The brunt of the storm hit Houston. That's where we were, wouldn't you know? But it wasn't a major hurricane, and it moved fast. Sometimes we evacuate, and sometimes we don't. Every time we evacuate, Jay says never again."

She pulled into the grocery parking lot. "It's not as busy as I feared. I have a long list. We ate or threw away the perishable items we couldn't take with us in case the electricity was out for an extended time or we couldn't get back. Is that okay with you?"

"I've got a long list too."

I had organized my list by aisle. Ellen peered at my list, "I should do that too, but I'm lucky to get everything on my list to start. You might finish before I do."

"If I do, I'll help you finish up."

Ellen skipped the produce section because it was sparse, but I found carrots, celery, a green bell pepper, potatoes, and onions but no okra.

Seafood case was empty. I put chicken in my cart and stared at the sausage.

"Can I help you, miss?" asked the butcher. His smile, white hair, and ruddy face and round stomach under his white, stained apron reminded me of a beardless Santa Claus.

"I need andouille sausage for gumbo."

"None out here. Be right back."

He returned with a sausage. "People pick up andouille sausage then complain because it's too spicy. You just let me know when you want andouille, and we'll have it for you."

Spike wiggled his eyebrows, and I cleared my throat. "Thanks. This is great. Chef Daryl would have a fit if I made gumbo with ordinary sausage."

"You know Chef Daryl? You're right about that. He'd have my head for not getting you the right sausage." The butcher chuckled.

On a whim, I diverted to the frozen vegetable case. The overall inventory was very low. No broccoli, peas, or corn. Spike danced in front of a glass freezer door. *Okra.*

"Thanks. Let's work backward since I switched our order."

When I rolled into a checkout line, Ellen pushed her cart in behind me. "They didn't have half of what I had on my list. Looks like you did well. Frozen okra? Are you making something southern?"

I unloaded items to the conveyer belt. "Gumbo."

"I'll bet you make good gumbo. I've never tackled it. I'm not the best cook."

"It's a chef's recipe. Chef Daryl from Lake Charles."

"You have Chef Daryl's recipe? You know he's a famous Cajun cook."

I raised my eyebrows, and she chuckled. "I don't cook, but I'm a foodie. How do I get an invitation to dinner?"

I don't know. Ask? Spike punched me.

"Would you and Jay like to come to dinner tonight? No guarantees I'll make it as good as Chef Daryl does, but you can tell me if there's a difference."

"I don't want to put you to any bother."

"Okay." Spike punched me again, and I glared at him.

"It's okay. No bother," I said.

"What time?" she asked.

"How does six sound?"

"Perfect. I'll bring wine and beer."

On our way to the new house, Ellen chattered about gumbo, Chef Daryl, and other chefs she'd met. Spike smiled and nodded, and I copied him. He held up two thumbs, and my smile was genuine.

I cocked my head. *I'm forgetting something.*

Spike shrugged.

Ellen pulled into our driveway. "Listen to me go on. Do you need help with the groceries?"

"I can manage them in two trips if you want to wait in the car."

"If you're sure."

"I'll be okay. I'll zip in and out. Won't take me long." *No need to come inside.*

Spike glared.

After I put the groceries away, I made hot tea, and Spike sat with me while I sipped my tea. "Ellen was excited, and I was a dud. Am I tired or cranky?"

Spike held up two fingers, and I laughed. "Cranky. You might be right. I'll feel better when I'm cooking. Do I have an apron from Diane's Diner? I need to look. I remembered what I forgot. I meant to ask Ellen if she'd mind if we stopped off for plants. Dang. I was too busy being cranky."

I rooted through the dirty laundry and found my barber pole apron. I tossed a new load into the washer with my apron.

I made our beds with the clean sheets, cleaned the bathroom and kitchen countertops, and swept.

"Much better. Cleaning is the best antidote for cranky."

I made a fresh cup of tea and read my notes. Palace Guard joined me at the kitchen table. "I have this

Veronica, Ken Bushman, and Jay connection. If I ignore Jay and focus on Veronica and Ken, Veronica is more likely to be in charge with Ken being the muscle. Ken could be a killer following Veronica's orders. If we throw in Jay, he's the general pulling the strings; Veronica's the sergeant barking the orders; and Ken is the foot soldier. No, he's the thug."

Palace Guard nodded.

"Wonder if there's a connection between Jay and Veronica? I can't ask Ellen. Maybe I could ask Diane. In fact, I have some questions for Diane. I'll jot them down so I don't forget, and maybe we can go by her house tomorrow. I can tell her about the gumbo."

I rose to empty the dryer then I shifted the wet clothes from the washer to the dryer. "One more thing. Mona is unpredictable. If Mona set up the explosion, it's unrelated to all the other attacks. Maybe she meant to burn down the diner, not kill anyone. Mona might be in danger."

Spike shrugged.

"I know. Doesn't matter if she only meant to destroy the diner; she still killed Irene and Rosa."

I read the potato salad and gumbo recipes and set nonperishable ingredients on the counter. I chopped celery, onion, and bell pepper then peeled and cubed the potatoes and dropped them into a pot of salted water. "Reminds me of Irene. What a fierce spirit of competition."

Larry burst into the front door. "Supe says he put me in for an award."

"That's exciting."

"I know." He swaggered like a cowboy to the refrigerator. "How'd you get groceries? Oh, wait."

He dashed out the door and returned with a flat of plants. My mouth dropped open and tears rolled down my cheeks. He set the plants on the floor, and he rushed to hug me.

He wrapped his arms around me. "Maggie, I'm so sorry. What did I do wrong? I thought you'd like flowers. Did I stir up old memories? I'm sorry. This was a bad idea. I should have checked with you first. I'll take them to the curb. Maybe someone else can use them. Are you mad?"

"No, you big goof. You're wonderful."

Larry led me to the sofa, and we sat. He put his arm around my shoulders. "What's wrong?"

More tears escaped down my cheeks. "I've been cranky all day. Even Spike said so. Then you do something so nice." I sobbed.

"Can I get you a glass of tea?"

"No," More tears fell. "I haven't made any."

"Want to show me where you want the flowers and herbs?"

"I'd like that."

Larry picked up the flat, and I opened the back door. "I wasn't sure if we'd need it, but I got potting soil too." Larry pulled up the dead plants. "Yep, we do. Be right back."

I read the tags: Hibiscus, Butterfly plant, Salvias, Pentas, Jalapeno, Big Jim pepper, Tomato, Rosemary, and Basil.

"What do you think?" Larry carried three sacks of potting soil.

"Magnificent choices. The flowers will draw pollinators. Will we have space for them all?"

"I thought we could put the flowers in the house pot and planter and the peppers, tomatoes and herbs in pots we take back to Georgia. I got five pots, potting soil, and garden soil. You won't cry again, will you?"

"I might." I fake-snuffled, and Larry snickered.

"I need to work on supper. Almost forgot to tell you. Ellen invited me to invite them to supper because I'm making Chef Daryl's gumbo."

"What? Gumbo? That's outstanding." Larry frowned and hung his head. "Do we have enough? Do I need to cut back?"

I hugged him. "Never. There will always be plenty for you."

He wrapped his arms around me. "So tell me, Miss Red-headed Gray Lady, do we bring Jay out back to beat a confession out of him, or do we let Ellen do that?"

He guffawed, and I laughed.

"Time to start the gumbo." Before I closed the door, I said, "Ellen."

I pulled my apron out of the dryer and reread the recipe. *Daryl said I'd do my own tweaks after I made it a few times.*

I held my wooden spoon high. "First, we make da roux." I giggled, and Palace Guard smiled.

When Larry came inside, he said, "All done. Like your apron."

"This can simmer a minute. I'll come see."

"I got a sprinkler and hose, but I didn't get a timer. I can get one next time I go to the hardware store." Larry frowned.

"It's so pretty. Thank you." I kissed him on the cheek and dashed into the house. Palace Guard and Spike's mouths were open. "I know. Me too. I hope he's not mad. I loved the flowers and his thoughtfulness. Should I go apologize?"

Palace Guard smiled and shook his head. Spike frowned and nodded. Palace Guard pushed him, and Spike stormed away.

"I'm taking longer to make this than it took Chef Daryl. Should have known."

Larry came into the house. His cheeks had spots of red. "Shall I make lunch, or do you want me to go on a taco run?"

"Make it a snack because they'll be here at six." I frowned and waved my wooden spoon. "You still standing dere lookin' at me?"

"Maggie made a joke." Larry and Palace Guard high-fived. "On my way. Be back in a few."

After he left, I said, "I'm afraid every time he leaves. Do I have an anxiety disorder?"

Palace Guard shrugged then brought his right fist to his chest.

"You're right. He is strong, but I still worry. Back to gumbo."

When I had the gumbo at a slow simmer, I read the potato salad recipe. "It doesn't tell me how long it takes. Here's a note at the bottom. *Serve warm or cold*. I can hear him. *Suhve dat wahm or code, Sha*."

I rinsed the potatoes and filled the pot with fresh salted water. I set the potatoes on the second burner of two and turned on the heat. "Not sure if we're having warm potato salad or cold. Probably warm. It will take longer to cook potatoes on this tiny electric stove. That's what I get for being spoiled by gas."

Palace Guard nodded.

"Watched potatoes won't boil." I made tea then set it on the counter to cool.

After I removed my apron, I pulled out my notebook and turned on the computer to read all the notes I had on Jay. As I read, I compiled questions. Palace Guard scooted a chair next to me. "These are the questions I need answered. This is to help me focus on what I listen for."

As I put the tea in the refrigerator, Larry and Spike came into the house. I raised my eyebrows at Spike, and he shrugged.

"You and Spike have a fight? No, that's silly. The house smells amazing. Garlic, onion, peppers. Like I'm back in Chef Daryl's kitchen."

He set a large box on the table. "They had a special on tacos. Hurricane Special or something. Two dozen were cheaper than two. I couldn't turn it down. We can eat them for breakfast and lunch tomorrow. I could surprise the guys with tacos at lunch."

"Brilliant on their part. They'd rather their customers ate the tacos than throw them away. And you're right. Those won't go to waste." I closed my laptop and put away my notes.

While we ate, Larry asked, "What are you working on?"

"Questions about Jay that I can't ask. I'll listen to see if he drops any hints. According to my training, bad guys like to flaunt their superiority. We'll see."

"I can't get over how smart you are. Why didn't Kate hire you for her FBI team?"

"Glenn said not everybody thinks it's possible to see imaginary men and not be unbalanced. I'm okay with being unbalanced, if that's the definition."

"Will I be fired?"

"Nope."

"That's too bad. I like my job here, but only if you and Lucy stay. And the imaginary men because it's too dangerous to be around you without backup."

Spike and Palace Guard nodded.

Larry cleared the table when we finished eating and shoved the tacos into the refrigerator. After he loaded the dishes into the dishwasher, Larry sat next to me. "What are some of your questions?"

"You already know one. What is the tie between Veronica and Jay? Here's another one. Why did Jay give money to Ken Bushman? I have other questions like did Jay know Rosa? Did he know about Irene's evidence?

There's more, but you understand what I'm listening for."

"Let me look at your list a bit. He may say something when the two of us are alone."

"Excellent. And Ellen has been a wealth of information so far, but she's careful around Jay."

I set the table while Larry read my questions. He slipped my loose notes into my notebook. "What if after dinner Jay and I go to the hardware store to look at what? Sprinklers or irrigation systems? No. It needs to be something he's an expert in. Maybe generators. I'll figure it out."

I took the notebook, papers, and laptop to my room and slipped them into my backpack. When I returned, I glanced at the stove. "The potatoes are boiling. Good. I just need them to be fork-tender. I'll throw the meal together about the time they get here."

"Let's sit with a beer and enjoy the flowers."

"Best idea of the day. No, the flowers were."

We sat on the patio steps.

"I can't wait for the butterflies and bees to find our flowers," I said.

We clinked our bottles, and I leaned back. "This is nice. Peaceful neighborhood."

The screech of tires rounded our corner, and the four of us dashed inside to our positions. Spike lifted Lucy and carried her inside. After he set her down, she grinned and followed me to my room.

Shots rang out, and Spike disappeared. The crunch and boom of a crash rattled the windows. *Sounded close. In front of the house?*

I grabbed my small mirror from my backpack and checked outside my side window. *Can't see anything.* I draped my red scarf over my pillow and held it up at the window. I cringed, but my pillow didn't explode in my hands. I peeked out the window. *Nothing.* I returned to my position at the back window, and Lucy flopped to the floor next to me and fell asleep.

I used my pillow again at the back window. *Nothing.* I peeked with my mirror and saw a car drift by in the alley.

"Car. Alley," I said. The car continued its slow crawl away from me. Mud obliterated the rear license plate.

"Car tag covered."

Spike chased the car and brushed the mud off. He kneeled in the dirt and wrote the license number.

"Spike got it."

When the car reached the end of the alley, it turned toward the interstate.

"Car's gone." I kept my position near the window and waited.

"Crashed car in front. Bullet holes in driver's door." Larry said. "Palace Guard checking. I'm calling medical."

"I'm clear. I can see Spike. He's guarding the tag number. Appears clear."

"I'm clear, and Palace Guard's clear," Larry said. "Medical on the way. Going out front to check."

"I'll go out back to copy the tag number." I grabbed a marker off my desk.

I eased out back with my weapon drawn. I continued with caution to Spike and the license number in the dirt. I copied it on my arm, confirmed it with Spike before I obliterated it in the sand, and headed to the house under Spike's supervision.

Palace Guard waved for me to come to the front of the house, and I followed him. The sound of sirens surrounded me. When I rounded the corner, I recognized Jay's car. The driver's car door was open, and Larry leaned into the car. I gasped and rushed to the passenger's side. When I saw Ellen, I exhaled. *No blood.*

"They shot him." Ellen's voice cracked. "Will he be okay, Larry?"

"He's breathing. That's a good sign." Larry peered at me. "I'm holding pressure on his chest wound. Need a towel."

"Be right back, Ellen." I squeezed her hand and dashed to the house. I handed Larry two towels and returned to the passenger's side.

I inspected Ellen for injuries. "Ellen, are you hurt?"

She tugged at her seatbelt. "The seatbelt grabbed me when we crashed, and the airbag smashed me in the face, but I'm fine. I wasn't shot."

"You've got an abrasion on your chin."

"Stupid airbag." She managed a weak smile and struggled to unfasten her seat belt. "Can you undo my seatbelt?"

I reached over and released the belt. "Do you want the ambulance crew to examine you?"

"I'm fine. I want the ambulance crew to focus on Jay. Is he still breathing, Larry?"

"So far, so good." Larry's calm, reassuring voice contradicted his grim face and Jay's gray skin tone and ragged breaths.

The ambulance pulled behind us, and the paramedic jumped out of the passenger's side. My eyes narrowed. *It's the paramedic I don't like. Do they only have one paramedic in Galveston?* When she reached Larry, she asked, "Were you involved too, sir? Oh. It's you. What've you got?"

"Gun shot. Breathing. Not conscious. Open chest wound. I haven't done a survey, so there may be other wounds. I've been holding pressure. Low speed impact collision with the tree."

"What about the passenger?" she asked.

"No injuries. Seat belted. Likely to refuse treatment and transport. Could she ride with you and your patient?"

"No. The second ambulance will be here shortly. They will take her to the hospital."

The paramedic and driver were all business as they loaded Jay onto the gurney. The paramedic replaced the towel with a trauma dressing, and the driver placed an oxygen mask on Jay. As the driver wheeled Jay to the ambulance, the paramedic touched Larry's arm. "We've got to get together sometime. You live around here?" She glanced around.

He shook his head.

"Well," she twirled her hair. "I've got to go. I'll give you my number. Call me."

She pulled a small notebook out of her pocket, scribbled on a page, and tore it out. She stuffed it into his shirt pocket and patted his chest.

"Want me to beat her up for you?" Ellen whispered.

I snorted. "Not a very good poker face?"

"Not hardly. Larry isn't your cousin, is he? Does he know how you feel?"

I glared, and she held up her hands. "Fine."

"Like the hair-twirler said, you can go to the hospital in the second ambulance," I said.

"It would take me the rest of the day to get out of their clutches and see Jay. No ambulance."

I nodded. "We can take you to the hospital, but Larry may have to talk to the police for a bit. You want to come inside the house until we can leave?"

"You'll stay with me?"

"Yes." I helped her out of the car, and Ellen leaned on me. I matched her hesitant pace as we headed to the house. When we were inside, Ellen paused at the doorway. "Smells heavenly."

Palace Guard raised his eyebrows.

"Did you have lunch? Would you like a bowl?"

Thank you.

Palace Guard smiled.

"I didn't have time for lunch, but I don't think I could eat a bite. Maybe a small bowl." She sat at the kitchen table while I fixed her bowl of gumbo with a side of rice and a side of potato salad.

"Cold or hot tea?" I asked.

"Cold with gumbo. What about you?"

"Good idea."

I served her tea and pulled together two more servings of gumbo, rice, and potato salad. I left Larry's plate near the stove.

After I joined her at the table, I asked, "Did you see the shooter?"

"Not really. It happened so fast, but the driver didn't shoot. It was the passenger."

"Two men?"

"I'm not sure. I think the shooter was a man. I got the impression he was a big man." Ellen scooped up a dab of rice, a bite of gumbo, and a dab of potato salad on her spoon.

"Mmm," she said. "Chef Daryl sneaked in here and cooked this. Wonderful, Sha."

Larry came into the house. "Police need to talk to you, Maggie."

I rose from the table. "Ellen didn't have lunch. I said we'd take her to the hospital."

"Sure. Gumbo smells good," Larry said.

As I headed out, Ellen said, "Yours is on the counter, Larry."

When I went outside, I told the waiting police officer with the nametag, *Lopez*, about the slow-moving car and that I had the tag number. He copied it off my arm.

"Pretty smart. Say, aren't you the Gray Lady? I used to eat at Diane's Diner at least once a week. You're a local celebrity. Don't tell me. Red is the new gray, right?" He chuckled.

I smiled. "Exactly. Did you know Jay?"

"Not really. He retired before I joined the force. But he had a reputation for following the law. There are stories he beat up a rogue cop that outranked him when he was a rookie."

"Wow."

"Yeah, right? Most rookies are afraid to even talk to a lieutenant. Rumor has it he wasn't disciplined, though. The rogue cop tried to pass it off as a misunderstanding, but the chief fired him."

"Who was the rogue cop?"

"Don't think anybody ever said. Good question." He glanced at his notebook and closed it. "Thanks for the tag number. Guess I better go. Let us know where you work next. You've got an entire police force who are your fans." He grinned and waved as he walked away.

I hurried inside. Larry had put away the food and loaded his and Ellen's dishes into the dishwasher.

Larry glowered, and Spike crossed his arms. "About time. Ellen needs transportation to the hospital. Guess that didn't occur to you. I'll get the truck." Larry stormed out of the house.

I finished my last two bites of gumbo and put my dishes into the dishwasher. "What does he mean? The truck is out front. What's he so mad about?"

"Let me guess," Ellen said. "The police officer was young, right? Attractive?"

"I suppose."

"Thought so. Larry dumped his potato salad and rice on top of his gumbo and stood at the front window where he ate and fumed. Y'all are very entertaining."

She rose from the table, and after I locked the front door, we climbed into the truck.

Larry dropped us off at the emergency entrance and left to park. We stood in line at the information desk. When we were next, Ellen stepped up to the desk, and I sat where there were four seats together to wait. The paramedic-I-hate and her driver rolled the cot to the exit and left. *Hope she doesn't see Larry. I'll send Ellen out to check.* I chuckled.

Chapter Seventeen

A few minutes later, Larry and Palace Guard came into the waiting room. Larry sat next to me. "You want any coffee?"

I thought we weren't speaking.

Palace Guard shrugged.

"No, thank you."

"The gumbo was amazing."

"Thank you." Palace Guard frowned.

"I'm glad you liked it." *Thanks. I'll learn.*

Palace Guard nodded.

Ellen joined us. "I'm glad we took time to eat. They won't let me go back. They say they are still evaluating him."

After an hour, a nurse came to talk to Ellen. "They're taking your husband to surgery. The doctor will update you later." The nurse patted Ellen's hand and left.

"The waiting is awful." Ellen said. "Thank you for being here with me."

"Do you want anything, Ellen? Coffee? Something cold?" Larry asked. "I'd ask if you want anything to eat, but what could match that gumbo?"

"Isn't that the truth? Best I've ever had. You're a talented cook, Maggie."

I just follow recipes.

"Thank you, Ellen."

"You must have been cooking since you were a child. You're such a natural. Larry, if it's no bother, coffee sounds good."

"No bother at all. Mags, change your mind?"

"Coffee sounds wonderful."

Larry beamed and hurried away in search of coffee.

"They do like to be helpful, don't they?"

I nodded.

"So how have you been, Maggie?"

"Perplexed," I said.

"Tell me the details. I wouldn't mind thinking about something besides stressing over Jay when there's nothing I can do."

"Remember when we talked about Veronica?"

Ellen nodded. I told her about the strange Veronica meeting, my apartment broken into, and my clothes bleached.

After I finished, Ellen said, "I'm with you. Veronica kept you away from your apartment."

"Do you know if she remarried or is involved with anyone?"

"I heard rumors she dated my brother for a while, but he broke it off. Jay would know about that. He's been in contact with Kenny off and on. I think he helped Kenny find work once or twice. Funny. Jay never liked my brother, but he'll help anyone who wants to make better choices. I've tried to tell Jay that Kenny is a lost cause, but he says I'm just grumpy."

"I hope you don't mind, if I ask..."

"No, go ahead."

"Larry told me Jay beat up a rogue officer when he was a rookie. Is that true?"

"Lord, that was so long ago. It's true. Jay told the guy to resign, or he'd turn him in. The guy threatened to harm Jay's wife if he did."

I raised my eyebrows.

"Right. Jay is a protective man. Kind of like Larry is with you. The man's threat crossed the line. Jay's goal was to give the cop as much pain as possible. One thing about Jay, when he takes on a project, he gives it his all." She chuckled, and I smiled.

"What happened next?"

"The chief already had proof the cop collected protection money from businesses. He arrested the cop and gave Jay a small bonus. That money was a godsend because we lived paycheck to paycheck. We had a three-year-old looking forward to Christmas, and I was pregnant with baby number two."

"Who was the cop? Did he go to prison?" I asked.

"I never knew who he was. Jay said it was better if I didn't, and I was busy with the babies. The papers didn't report any charges, and Jay told me he never wanted to see a cop go to prison. I think the ex-cop paid restitution and moved out west where he started up his own business."

"No record of it?"

Ellen pursed her lips. "There would have been a record of the charges and conviction, but courts sometime bury records."

Maggie T will find it. "Sometimes I think Mona turned on the gas at Diane's Diner and maybe meant to burn it down."

"I'm not a Mona fan, but I don't think she would have burned down Diane's Diner. She and Irene fought, but Mona loved Diane. Mona couldn't have children and took care of Diane while Irene worked. In some ways, I think Irene resented Mona because of Diane's attachment to Mona when she was little. Now if you told me Irene set fire to Mona's house, I'd believe it."

I chuckled. "When I was at Diane's house right after the explosion, a woman told me Smitty threw Mona out of their house. Mona had been drinking..."

Ellen shook her head. "Mona drinking? That's not good. Mona was a heavy drinker until Diane was born, then she quit cold turkey so Irene would trust her to take care of the baby. Mona must have been a mess. She was always a mean drunk."

"Makes sense now. The lady said Mona screamed Irene staged her own death because Irene stole money from her to pay off a spy."

"That's like the crazy stuff Mona claimed when she drank. Irene would never have paid off anybody. Remember the rogue cop? Rumor has it he tried to threaten Irene, and she pulled out a shotgun. He skipped Diane's Diner after that. It's a wonder she didn't just shoot him on the spot. She must have been in a good mood for once."

I snort-laughed. When the people around me moved, Ellen snort-laughed too.

Larry brought the coffee. "What's going on here?"

"Ellen is full of stories."

"Good. So, here's coffee."

He sat next to me and whispered. "I'll hear later, right?"

"Oh, yeah."

We finished our coffee, and I collected cups to throw into the trash.

"I'll walk with you," Ellen said.

After I threw away the cups, Ellen stopped me.

"I need to visit the powder room."

Palace Guard nudged me.

"Shall I go along?"

"Is that old-fashioned of me? When I was a girl, we visited the restroom in pairs to avoid being accosted."

"Backup is good."

"I like the way you think, Gray Lady."

"The police officer at the house recognized me as the Gray Lady. I thought that was interesting."

"Your natural red hair just looks like you, and you are the Gray Lady. Does that make sense?"

"No."

Ellen chuckled as we reached the restroom.

"I won't be long," she said.

I had a good view of the emergency entrance. A tall, overweight man with a hunched posture walked into the emergency room and scanned the room. *What is Ken Bushman doing here?*

I went into the women's restroom, and Ellen was drying her hands.

"Your brother is here."

"What? At the hospital? May be hope for my worthless brother yet. Thanks for the warning. Maybe I can keep my grumpy self under control."

When we came out of the restroom, Ken Bushman was at the Information Desk.

"Here I go." Ellen headed to the Information Desk.

"I'm backup."

I strolled to Larry and sat next to him. "The man Ellen is talking to is her brother."

Larry leaned forward and whispered. "Is she in danger?"

"I don't think so, but she knows I'm her backup which by default includes you."

Spots of red appeared on Larry's cheeks. "Really?"

My brow furrowed. *What does really mean?*

Palace Guard and Spike nodded at Larry, and I copied them.

Larry stared at the imaginary men then at me. He chuckled. "You're copying them, aren't you? Your literal self is trying to figure out what 'really' means. Am I right?"

"Yes." I beamed.

He hugged me and whispered, "You are so special."

Ellen headed toward us with her brother in tow.

"These are my friends, Maggie and Larry. This is my brother, Ken."

We shook hands, and Ellen smiled.

"Ken will stay with me until Jay is out of surgery and will take me home when I get tired. I know I can call you if I need you."

"Any time," Larry said. I nodded.

Ellen and I hugged. Larry patted her shoulder, but she hugged him.

When the automatic doors wheezed open, I inhaled the fresh air. Larry pointed to the first row. "We're right here."

We climbed into the truck.

"Suppose I could have more gumbo when we get home?" he asked.

"Sure can. I need to send a text to Maggie T."

My text: "Jay Davidson, Galveston Rookie, beat up Rogue Cop who was fired & chged extortion, 38 yrs ago Need name of Rogue Cop."

Text: "On it."

When we were home, Larry and Spike took Lucy out for a walk while I heated the gumbo and steamed the rice. When Lucy finished her stroll, Larry fed her and pulled two beers out of the refrigerator. I sipped my beer and stirred the gumbo.

"Did you know the only spoon allowed in gumbo is a wooden spoon?"

"Yes. Chef Daryl said that."

"Right. Did you know the only way to stir gumbo is counter-clockwise?"

"No. Did you make that up?"

"Of course not. It's a tradition to keep hurricanes away. I read that when I was eight."

My old phone rang. *Diane.*

"Maggie, it's Smitty. We just heard Mona was found in a canal, and Diane's devastated: first her mother then Mona. There's speculation of suicide, but that's not Mona. Diane asked me to call you because she said the Gray Lady would find the killer. We appreciate whatever you can do."

Larry stirred the gumbo while I was on the phone.

After I hung up, I said, "That was Smitty. Somebody murdered Mona, and Diane wants me to find the killer."

Larry frowned. "What are you thinking?"

"We must be getting close."

I took over the stirring, and when the food was hot, I dished up two servings of gumbo, rice, and potato salad: a generous serving for Larry and my version of a normal serving for me.

"Let's eat," I said.

Larry leaned over his bowl and inhaled. "Ahh. This is great."

"We'll see if we prefer the potato salad warm or cold."

"Interesting. The taste of cold potato salad isn't the same as the warm potato salad. I like it warm, because that's when it's fresh, and cold, because that means we had enough for leftovers."

"Makes sense to me."

After we ate, Larry cleared the table and ran the dishwasher. I jotted down notes from my conversations with Ellen and handed them to Larry.

"It'll be easier if you ask questions as you read."

Larry relaxed on the sofa to read. I turned on my laptop and sat on the sofa to review my database.

"So Jay's been in contact with Ken Bushman for a while."

"Yes."

"Your text to Maggie T. was for the name of the rogue cop?"

"Right."

"I almost missed this. Irene and the rogue cop. Are you thinking the rogue cop is the bad guy?"

"Could be."

"Sad about Mona. Complex relationship there: Irene and Mona."

After Larry finished reading, he said, "Let's go back through our previous thoughts."

"One of the biggest stumbling blocks we have is the son of Nun in the message from Paul to Irene."

"Right. Joshua. And Jay's given name is Joshua," Larry said.

"We need to dig deeper."

"Second stumbling block is Rosa's message to Kate: watch for the crested bird."

"The blue jay is a crested bird," I said. "We didn't consider any other possibilities."

"Because we thought we had the answer. Obvious again."

I fetched two more beers from the fridge. "The meeting between Ken and Jay is less ominous now that we know their relationship and history."

"Sounds like Jay and Ken might be okay but not Veronica, at least so far. Is that right?"

We clinked bottles.

My phone buzzed a text from Ellen: "Jay out of surgery. Removed bullet. No vital organs hit. Ribs broken. Doc says prognosis good and okay for me to go home tonight. Ken will give me a ride. TY."

Three men read my phone. "Good news," Larry said. "Ellen must be relieved."

"Yes. I'm glad her brother was with her."

I sipped my beer. "Back to my line and order. Someone moves without being noticed."

"A true gray man that has mastered blending in." Larry reread the notes. "We need to leave this alone. Find something we can do for fun. Something recreational."

"I can play poker," I said.

"I would never play cards with you. You would cheat."

"I wouldn't cheat. I'd show you my magic tricks."

"We could take a walk. No. Bad idea."

"Do you know how to dance?" I asked.

"Of course. Do you?"

"No. I've never danced. I heard people at the diner talk about the cotton eyed joe. You ever heard of it?"

"I've never danced the cotton eyed joe, but let's find a video, and I'll teach you. I'm a quick study."

My eyes widened at the video's rapid heel and toe taps in front and behind, foot sweeps, turns, and bounces. I laughed. "I could never do that."

"Sure you can. Just takes practice. Let's prop the phone against a book, and I'll see if I can keep up. Then I'll teach you the slower version."

Palace Guard crowded in to see the video then danced alongside Larry. Spike did his wacky dance, and I stumbled over my feet.

Larry said, "Stop looking at your feet. Pretend you're running with Palace Guard."

A half hour later, I said, "You're brilliant. This works."

After two hours of dancing and laughing, Larry and I collapsed on the sofa.

"Our best dancer award goes to Palace Guard," Larry said.

We applauded, and Palace Guard bowed.

"Outside, Lucy girl." Spike and I accompanied her on her yard roam.

After I dressed the next morning, I put on a pot of coffee. Spike and I took Lucy outside. The morning's light fog hung low, and the birds chirped and sang their song of no rain today.

When we went inside, I fed Lucy and cooked breakfast. Larry hurried to the coffeepot, and I set his breakfast on the kitchen table.

"I'd rather pack your lunch cold. Can you heat the gumbo at work?"

"One guy has a hot plate, and there's a toaster oven we can use at the office."

Spike put his palms together and tilted his head on his hands.

"What's wrong with you, Spike?" I asked.

Larry laughed. "I think he said we sounded domestic."

Spike grinned, and I said, "It is nice to get back on a routine without interference from killers."

"Now that's a topic you don't hear at every breakfast table." Larry saluted Spike with his cup.

When we finished breakfast, Larry cleared the dishes and loaded the dishwasher while I packaged his lunch and the lunch for the guys. He filled his thermos, grabbed the gumbo and tacos, and hurried out the door.

"My plan for the day is to clean then call Ellen. Don't worry, Spike. You'll help by entertaining Lucy."

Lucy and Spike went outside, and I started my cleaning frenzy with the back bedroom.

I zipped through the rest of the rooms, and as I wiped down the stovetop, my phone buzzed a text.

Maggie T: "Record closed. Trying back door."

I stared at the phone and texted back. "Not worth getting into trouble."

Maggie T: "Pshaw. Spelled right? Trouble is my middle name, just like GL. GTL."

I snickered. Me: "Spelling good. Can't dispute T."

Lucy and Spike came in. Lucy flopped onto the sofa, and Spike scanned the living room and kitchen. "You're safe, Spike. Cleaning's done."

When I called Ellen, her phone rang around to voicemail. I texted: "Checking in."

I reached for my laptop, but paced instead. "How can I ask Gary questions? The lack of response from him sure reinforces my opinion. Shows up at his own convenience. I'm cranky. Anybody want to knife-fight?"

Palace Guard rushed to the back door, and I followed him. I approached him with caution, and he reached out and flipped me to the ground. Spike and Lucy sat on the patio. Spike signaled *again*.

"No kidding," I mumbled and walked away from Palace Guard then whirled to dive at him feet first. I kicked his legs out from under him. Before I could roll away, he pinned me.

Spike signaled *again*.

After an hour, I was dirty, bruised, achy, but not as rusty. "Good session. I need cold tea and a warm shower."

When Larry came home, he washed and rinsed the lunch containers. "The guys at work loved the gumbo and the tacos. They said if you wanted to start up your own food truck, they'd pitch in to help pay for one. Supe asked if you catered. His wife has a big shindig planned in two months and needs a caterer."

Larry stared. "What happened?"

"What?"

"You have a bruise on your cheek, and your forearm has an abrasion."

"Training. I was out of practice."

"With Spike and Palace Guard?"

"Mostly Palace Guard. Spike and Lucy supervise."

"I need training too."

"I need groceries."

"Take the truck. We'll train. What did you train on this morning?"

"Knife-fight. Train with Palace Guard. Spike cheats." I grabbed my backpack and the truck keys. "Have a good session."

When I got home, Larry had an ice pack on his shoulder. "It was an accident. I accidentally thought I could beat Palace Guard."

I snickered. My phone rang. *Ellen.*

"Sorry I missed you, Maggie. Jay's sister called, and she can talk. My brother can't take me to the hospital until later. Would you mind giving me a ride?"

"I don't mind at all. After we put away groceries, we'll be there."

"Was that Ellen?" Larry asked.

"She needs a ride to the hospital. Are you up to going?"

"Sounds good. Can we visit with Jay?"

"I didn't ask. We can see when we get there."

Larry rose and brushed his jeans pants legs.

"You're all dirty. Grab a quick shower while I put groceries away."

Larry trudged to his room for clean clothes then off to his shower.

Ellen called again. "Maggie, I hope you don't mind. I don't need a ride because Gus called and asked if he could visit Jay. He'll pick me up. Sorry I'm so flighty."

"Not at all. Larry asked if we could visit Jay too. Let us know."

"Will do."

Larry came out of the bathroom in fresh clothes and his wet hair combed flat except for his cowlick. I stared. *Do I fix it?*

Palace Guard nodded.

"Let me have your comb and sit at the table. I want to tame your cowlick."

"Do I have to sit?"

"You sit, or I climb on a chair. Your choice."

Larry sat. I inhaled his fresh soap and shampoo aroma mixed with his man-scent. "You smell good."

"Thanks. Glad you're literal."

My phone buzzed a text, but I re-combed Larry's hair before he could bolt.

The text was from Maggie T. "Giosuè Ulysses Stornelli." I gaped at my phone.

"What's wrong, Maggie?" Larry asked.

"Gus was the rogue cop that Jay beat up. Let's go." I grabbed my backpack and laptop, and Larry grabbed his backpack.

On the way to the hospital, I called Ellen.

"Hi, Ellen. Larry wanted to visit Jay. Do you mind waiting for us? We're not that far behind you."

"Sure, Maggie. Gus just now pulled up, so you might even beat us."

After we hung up, I said, "We may get there ahead of them."

"What's our plan of attack?"

"I think Gus plans to kill Jay, but why does he need Ellen along? Why don't you stick with Gus, and I'll stick with Ellen? What do you think, Palace Guard?"

He nodded.

"If Gus backs off because we're around, I'd like to hang out with Jay. Can you clear that with Ellen?"

"I'll ask Ellen to tell the staff you're a nephew. She'll understand why."

"How will you do that without alerting Gus?"

"Powder room."

Larry grinned.

Larry dropped me off then parked. I stepped into the lobby. *No Ellen.*

I waited inside near the entrance, and Larry joined me. Gus drove up, and Ellen climbed out of his car. He drove away to park.

Larry leaned to speak near my ear. "Man's a born killer. Didn't help the lady out of his car."

I giggled.

"Hi, Ellen." I waved as she entered.

"You're here on a mission, aren't you?" She grinned. "I didn't mention to Gus that you'd be here. Was that right?"

"Perfect. Let's go to the powder room."

We walked arm in arm to the women's restroom.

"What's up?" she asked when we were inside the empty restroom.

"Larry wants to stay with Jay. He's convinced that Jay needs protection. Is there any way you can introduce him as Jay's nephew?"

"Let's make it grandson. Consider it done. Give me a second. I'll call his nurse. She gave me her direct number. I just have to tap in his patient number."

Ellen pulled out her phone and tapped in numbers. "Hello, this is Mrs. Davidson. My grandson just came into town. His name is Larry Ewing. He wants to stay with his granddad. They are very close. Is that okay?"

Ellen listened and nodded. "That's great. Thanks. He'll be right up. My granddaughter and I will be in the gift shop. We'll be up a few minutes later. Thank you so much."

When we stepped out of the ladies' room, I waved at Larry to join us.

"You're Jay's grandson, Larry Ewing. Ellen cleared the way. You can go right now."

Ellen handed Larry a card. "Here's the room number, his nurse's name, and her direct line. Go." She grinned.

Larry rushed to the elevator, and Ellen and I waited for Gus.

"This is an excellent idea," Ellen said. "You think the shooter might try to return?"

"Larry's not taking any chances."

"Now that we're related, I can tell you what to do. You need to put your brand on that young man."

"I don't have a brand."

Ellen chuckled. "Yes, you do. Tell Larry what I said. See what he says."

I narrowed my eyes. *Is Ellen setting me up?*

Palace Guard nodded.

Gus entered the lobby and strolled toward Ellen, but he paused when he saw me. His eyes narrowed and his lips tightened, then he rushed toward us with a smile that didn't reach his eyes.

"Maggie, what a pleasant surprise. Here for moral support for Ellen? I came inside to ask Ellen what time I should come back to pick her up, but if you're here, she can ride home with you. Give Jay my best, Ellen. Talk to you later."

"You sure ruined his day, Maggie. Let's go see Jay."

When we walked into Jay's room, he was sleeping, and Larry sat in the corner. Ellen slipped to Jay's side, kissed his forehead, and stroked his hair. He opened his eyes. "Hello, cutie."

She smiled. "You rest. I want you home soon. Larry will stay with you."

"Good." Jay closed his eyes. Ellen tiptoed out the door.

I headed to Larry. "What can I do?"

"I need supper and a book. Come back in the morning around five-thirty to replace me. I'll dash by the house and take a shower for work. After work, I'll take over. Don't worry about breakfast or lunch for me."

"Want Palace Guard to stay with you?"

"Oh, yes."

I hugged Larry. "Be safe."

When I opened the door, Ellen stood at the doorjamb.

"Were you snooping?"

"Maybe," she said. "What's our plan?"

"Larry and I will cover Jay in shifts so Larry can go to work. I'm the granddaughter, Maggie Sloan, like you said. Can you let Jay's nurse know we'll be with Jay around the clock?"

"Like it. I'll call on our way home."

On our way to the parking lot, I said, "I'm making chicken fried steak tonight and will bring Larry a plate. Can I bring one by your house?"

Ellen stared at me, pulled a tissue out of her purse, and blew her nose. "You are so kind. I have no words. Thank you, that would be wonderful. Text me when you're on your way, so I won't slow you down on your way to feed Larry."

"It's always easy to find the truck when Larry drives because he has the knack of finding the closest spot. See?" I pointed to the truck.

"Everyone has talent." Ellen chuckled.

I helped Ellen into the vehicle, and she called Jay's nurse on the way to her house.

"What else can I do to help?" she asked as we walked to her door.

"Don't discuss Larry and me with anyone. Don't ride anywhere with Gus. In fact, don't answer your phone if Gus calls. Tell the nurse no visitors you haven't approved. Remind her otherwise she may have a bunch of rowdy cops in her unit. Might want to ask Ken to help you rent a car."

"Got it," she said. "Will you be safe without Larry?"

"Oh yes, I've got a great watchdog."

"I'll sleep tonight knowing you and Jay are safe. Did I tell you a second bullet was stopped by Jay's ID and old badge in his jacket pocket?" She shook her head. "He'll turn that into a story."

When I got home, I filled Spike in on everything.

"See any holes?" I asked.

He nodded.

"You do? Thought I was thorough."

Chapter Eighteen

I rubbed Lucy's ears and cooed until she fell asleep then I went back over my notes.

"Rule One." I slammed my notebook on the table. "I can't believe I forgot Rule One. That's it, isn't it? *Never overlook the obvious. And never let the obvious cause you to overlook your enemy.* It's the first lesson in *Detecting Your Enemy*." I knocked over my chair as I rose in irritation. Lucy opened her eyes then went back to sleep.

Spike danced his happy dance.

"Remember son of Nun?" I asked.

Spike shrugged.

"Paul Reynolds wrote a note to his sister on a recipe for Mock Apple Pie made with crackers, not apples. Phony apple pie. He said the recipe reminded him of the son of Nun in the Bible. That's Joshua. Irene knew who Paul meant. Jay's given name is Joshua, but Paul didn't mean Jay. He meant Joshua which in Italian is Giosuè. Gus's given name."

Spike narrowed his eyes, and I paced.

"The second strong hint that we missed was Rosa's message to Kate: watch for the crested bird. We are forest dwellers, a crested bird in the trees is the blue jay. Jay again, and wrong again. We aren't in the forest; we're at the Gulf. Rosa meant a local bird: the kingfisher, a deadly bird that hunts from above. That's Gus. He's the king of fish around here. So far, he's stayed out of the messy business of killing, but I think he's ready to dive."

Spike applauded, and I curtsied, at least I did the best I could in jeans. I updated the notes in my notebook then put my notebook away. "We've got three orders of chicken-fried steak to cook and plate up before Larry starves."

I pounded the cube steaks then let them rest while I scrubbed red potatoes and rinsed fresh collard greens. Spike grinned.

"I never knew how energizing it is to cook."

An hour-and-a-half later, I dished up three plates of chicken-fried steak, mashed potatoes, gravy, and collard greens and covered the plates with aluminum foil.

I placed a small towel over a cookie sheet then after I put the plates on the towel, I flipped another towel over them.

"Ready to go. You staying?"

Spike nodded.

"Thanks for staying with Lucy. I'd worry about bad guys hurting her."

I selected a book for Larry and carried my laptop and backpack out to the truck. After I returned for my make-shift serving tray, I placed it on the truck floor and texted Ellen.

When I reached Ellen's house, she stood in the front yard in her relay position to be ready to receive the baton of a dinner plate of chicken-fried steak. I jumped out of the truck and rushed to the passenger's side. When I opened the door, she readied her hands in anticipation. She snatched the plate with two hands and sashayed with deliberate steps to her door. *Impressive.*

When I reached the hospital, an SUV backed out of a prime space, and I pulled into the spot. *Does Larry find parking spots remotely or was it the magic of chicken-fried steak?*

I snickered and wrapped my two plates in a towel. I slung my backpack and laptop over my shoulders and rushed into the hospital. A pharmacist entered the elevator with me. He inhaled, deep and slow, and peered over his glasses at me with his ice-blue eyes. "Ahh. Another invasion by the rebel smuggling forces."

When he exited at the floor before mine, he stopped the group that waited to go up. "Hospital emergency. Sorry." He pushed the button to close the door and winked.

I hurried to Jay's room. Jay was sitting up with his eyes closed, and Larry rose to help me. "That smells delicious."

Jay opened his eyes. "I need some too."

His food tray was next to his bed. It was a full meal of fried chicken, roasted potatoes, green beans, applesauce, a roll, and something in a small container for dessert.

Larry scooted Jay's food onto a paper towel then rinsed and dried his plate. I added a portion of my chicken fried steak, mashed potatoes, gravy, and collard greens to his plate. I cut the chicken-fried steak into small bite-sized pieces.

Larry moved the food tray in front of Jay and raised the head of the bed to an upright position. "Can you manage?" he asked.

"Oh, yes." Jay stabbed a piece of steak. "Mmm."

"We'll join you." Larry pulled our chairs together, threw the towel over a tray table, and lowered the table.

As we sat, the door cracked open, and the pharmacist walked in. "Just one bite and I'll keep my mouth shut."

I laughed as I cut him a portion of chicken-fried steak. He handed me a small paper plate.

"Do you stalk the elevator at suppertime?"

He straightened his shoulders. "I'm the advance guard for the rebel smuggling forces."

I added steak, mashed potatoes and gravy, and collard greens to his plate. My plate reached my preferred serving portion.

He took his plate and bowed. "I'll retreat to my sentry tower. Thank you."

After he left, Larry said, "What a great way to get a home-cooked meal."

"He stopped by several times to check on me before Larry stayed," Jay said.

My eyes widened.

"What are you thinking, Maggie?" Larry asked.

"He carries a pocket-sized light saber."

Jay nodded, and Larry chuckled.

"Is your plate magic?" Larry asked. "Your plate looks like what you would have served yourself at home."

"Mange. Eat," I said.

After we'd eaten, Jay leaned back. "Wonderful, Maggie. Healing food."

Larry lowered Jay's head to a reclining position and moved away the tray table. "Do I put the food back on his plate?"

"Yes. We'll let Ellen decide how to handle the hospital."

Jay smiled. "Poor hospital." He closed his eyes and drifted into a soft snore.

I showed Larry my notes about mock apple pie, the son of Nun, and the crested bird.

"Wow. Our logic was wrong, but our instincts saved us. I like that. I've never heard that." He pointed to rule one.

"Rookie spy rule and I'm embarrassed."

Larry hugged me. "Don't be."

My phone buzzed a text from Ellen. "Heavenly. Thank you!"

I responded: "We gave Jay a small plate & he ate it all. He hadn't touched his hospital meal. Can you let the nurse know he's eating well without busting us?"

"On it."

The door cracked open, and a small woman with silver hair and bifocals entered. She wore a volunteer vest. "My husband, the pharmacist, sent this. He said you needed reinforcements. It's homemade."

She handed me a small box and slipped out of the room.

I opened the lid, "Cheesecake with cherries."

Larry asked, "Jay, you awake? Want any cheesecake?"

"I'll get mine later," he mumbled.

"I believe him," I said.

"Who knew about this whole underground smuggling support society in a hospital?" Larry asked as he ate his creamy cheesecake.

I nodded. "We'll get fat."

Palace Guard nodded, and Larry snickered. "Don't care. Nobody trusts a skinny smuggler. I made that up."

Larry and I chatted and giggled until eight. I rose to leave, and he accompanied me to the door.

"What's our next action?" he asked.

"Waiting makes little sense if we don't have a trap. I've got some ideas. I need to talk to Maynard."

"You're sure Maynard isn't working with Gus?"

Jay nodded, and I said "Yes."

Palace Guard raised his eyebrows at Jay and nodded.

Larry whispered. "The unconscious man and the invisible man agree with you. Can't get any endorsement better than that."

Palace Guard and Larry fist-bumped.

"What can I do?" Larry asked.

"Stir things up at work. Tell the guys you heard somebody was smuggling monkeys. Expect them to laugh because you're the new guy, but you'll have planted the seed."

"What if Gus hears and thinks you're the source?"

"He will. He's focused on the obvious. You can fuel that if you like."

Larry pointed to the couch. "That makes into a bed. The nurse brought me sheets, a blanket, and pillows."

"Good. Rest well."

Larry hugged me and gazed at my face. "Stay safe, Maggie."

"Stay safe, Maggie." Jay repeated.

"Will do."

When I exited the elevator, an elderly man dozed in the lobby in a corner seat near a window but away from the entrance. *Homeless. Invisibility at its best.* I took the seat next to him and touched his arm.

Maynard's eyes opened, and he smiled. "Hello, Maggie. I was just resting. Waiting for a friend."

"Am I that friend?"

"I'm getting rusty."

"No, you're not. I was watching for you. We need to talk."

He stretched. "Not here. You free tomorrow?"

"After three."

He nodded. "You and Larry are taking shifts. I'll be around."

I rose and returned with the cup of coffee I'd bought and gave Maynard a dollar. "Thanks for everything."

He raised the cup in a salute and smiled.

A woman who sat nearby clutched her purse and moved two seats away from him. She glowered at me, and I raised one eyebrow and peered at her in my best disapproving glare. Her face broke into splotchy red, and she stared at the floor.

"Be nice." I strode to the truck.

When I reached the house, Spike and I took Lucy outside then I showered and fixed a cup of tea.

I set the alarm for four-forty-five, slipped into the bed, and punched my pillow. *I'll never sleep.*

My alarm woke me. I scrambled to the kitchen and made coffee. I filled the thermos and a cup for myself and made two egg-and-cheese sandwiches.

When Spike and Lucy came in from outside, I gulped down my coffee. "Would you like to ride with me to the hospital? You and Lucy can ride back with Larry."

I grabbed all my usual gear, and the three of us headed to the hospital.

Spike and Lucy waited in the truck, and I rushed to Jay's room. Larry had folded his sheets and blankets and set them on the back of the bench.

"Hi, Sweetie," Larry said.

Jay opened his eyes and grinned. "Hi, Sweetie."

"You two are a matched set."

Larry beamed.

"You've got a dog, a companion, and an egg sandwich in the truck and a thermos of coffee at home. No lunch. Sorry."

"I didn't expect breakfast. Thanks!" Larry kissed me on the cheek and dashed out.

I touched my cheek. It was warm where he kissed me. I touched my other cheek. *Warm too.*

"Yep. You're blushing," Jay said. "Is what you're feeling a surprise to you?"

I set up my laptop on the spare tray table. "Yes."

I ate my cheese sandwich.

A hospital worker brought in Jay's breakfast tray. "Would you like some coffee, Miss?"

"Thank you."

I pushed the bed buttons to raise Jay's knees and raised the head to a vertical position. After I raised the tray table, I asked, "Are you comfortable? Ready for breakfast?"

Jay raised his eyebrows. "Did you cook it?"

"Let's see what they've got for you."

Jay pouted at his tray, and I narrowed my eyes. "I spent months in a hospital after being injured in an explosion. I'm not a big eater, but I'm a foodie. Hospital food does not cater to the foodie palate, but my priority was to get out which required eating bland, uninteresting food."

"You forgot to say unappetizing."

"Unappetizing. Take one for the team. Bon appétit."

Jay lifted his orange juice. "To the team."

The hospital worker slipped in and handed me a cup of coffee.

"The team." I raised my cup.

I sipped my coffee. "Ahh. Brings back memories. I forgot to say tepid."

"To tepid." Jay raised his glass then gulped the rest of his orange juice. He emptied two sugar packets on top of his oatmeal and ate half of it. He lifted the top of the English muffin and poked at the microwave-scrambled egg with his fork. "If I eat all my oatmeal and my fruit every day, will you bring me an egg sandwich tomorrow?"

"I toughed it out." I glowered.

"Yes, but you're fierce."

"Oh, really? What was it you did before you retired? Police department detective? What was your specialty? Interrogations? Negotiations?"

"I'm injured. You cheat."

"Yes, I do." I jumped up and did my version of Spike's wacky dance. "Eat the rest of your oatmeal or the egg sandwich as fierce as you can."

Jay glared and ate his oatmeal and the canned fruit. I pushed back his tray table.

"Can I trust Maynard?" I asked.

"With your life."

I lowered the head of the bed to a reclining position.

"Mr. Davidson." A large woman with an infectious smile and the reddest hair I've ever seen came into the room. Her booming voice matched her appearance. "Let's go for a walk. The ladies are waiting."

She hustled to his bedside. "Are you the granddaughter? You remind me of your grandmother. Your eyes see everything, don't they?"

"You're Granddad's physical therapist?"

"Sure am. Come on, Mr. Davidson. I add five extra minutes to the end of your therapy for every minute you dawdle."

I stepped outside the room. Jay opened the door with the physical therapist on one side of him. He had a belt around his waist, and she held onto a strap attached to his belt.

Jay growled. "My leash. My master. Going for a walk."

"I told you, I've been there. Overachieve. Make the therapists cry."

He stopped and met my gaze. "That's the trick?"

I nodded.

He shook off the therapist's hand. "Let's go, Girly." He took off at a slow pace.

His therapist raised her eyebrows.

"Wait up, Speedy." She whispered, "Thank you, Honey."

"Catch up, old woman. My granddaughter wants me to watch some blood-curdling crime movie with her. Her mother raised her right."

When Jay and his physical therapist returned, he glistened with sweat, and his therapist beamed. "You did great, Mr. Davidson."

I accompanied his therapist to the hallway. She whispered, "You are a breath of fresh air for that old man. Keep it up. He challenged another patient to a race and won. The race of the turtles."

She chuckled and hurried down the hall with her belt and straps.

When I returned to Jay's room, he was asleep. I relaxed with my laptop.

A thin young man slipped into the room and strode to Jay's bedside. "Mr. Davidson, time for your medicine."

He jostled Jay's shoulder. "Hey. Take your medicine."

"What's in the cup?" I stepped closer to Jay's bed. The man jerked his head, picked at his face, and rushed toward me.

Palace Guard and I knocked him down, and I put my gun to his head. "What's the medicine?" I asked. "You ready to face an attempted murder charge? Or are you more interested in cooperating?"

Palace Guard put his knee into the attacker's back.

The attacker's hand clenched, and I said, "Don't move."

Jay pushed his call button. "Need security in here immediately. Man tried to attack my granddaughter. She's a detective and has him subdued."

Two large security guards rushed in, and I holstered my gun. "She tried to kill me," the man sobbed.

When Palace Guard rose, the man attempted to get up. The two security guards snatched him to his feet, and one twisted the attacker's arm behind him while the other one called for police.

"Unclench your hands," I said.

The second guard pulled out handcuffs. "You heard her. Do it."

When the attacker unclenched his hands, the medicine cup fell. The security guard clicked the handcuffs and asked, "What's the medicine?"

"I don't know. I swear. They said give it to the old man."

The security guard picked up the crushed cup. "Something in there. We'll all stand right here until the police arrive."

The attacker whimpered. "She hurt me. I'm gonna sue."

"Don't blame you, man. She's the meanest five-foot, hundred-pound girl I've ever seen."

"We'll be your witnesses, man," the other guard said. The two men chuckled.

I glanced at Jay, and he winked.

"Who sent you?" I asked.

"Nobody," he said.

I stepped toward him, and the attacker cringed. "Keep her away from me."

"So tell her. Who sent you?"

Two police officers rushed in. One of them was Officer Lopez.

"What ya got?" the older officer asked.

The young officer stared at me.

Jay answered, "The attacker came into my room. When my granddaughter asked him what the medicine was, he rushed her, and she subdued him."

"She hurt me. I'm gonna sue."

"He had a pill in a cup. He dropped it from his hand in our presence. Here's the cup with the pill still intact," a security guard said.

"That you, Captain Davidson?" the older police officer asked with awe in his voice.

"Sure is, son. How've you been?"

"Working hard like always. Your granddaughter? Apple doesn't fall far from the tree, does it?"

Officer Lopez stopped writing in his notebook and shook his head.

The first police officer turned to the security guards. "Back up is on the way. Stick around until we tag the evidence."

Four more police officers rushed in. After the police officers took the attacker away, the security guards shook my hand and Jay's hand. "Any time you need a job, sweet lady, you look us up," the first security guard said, and the second one nodded.

Our two original officers stayed to take our statements.

The older officer left and Officer Lopez stopped. "I heard the Gray Lady was multi-talented, but you are amazing. Are you Jay's granddaughter to guard him in the hospital? Excellent cover."

He removed a business card from his pocket and scrawled a number on it. "My cell. In case you need a friend."

After they left, Jay said, "This is the most excitement I've had in ages. You are remarkable, Maggie, and thanks for being here. Where did you get your training?"

"I'm FBI-trained but not FBI material."

"Really? What's wrong with them?"

"I see things other people don't." Palace Guard nodded, and I snickered.

"That's obvious. Their loss for letting your talent slip away, but thanks for being here."

An orderly burst into the room. "Now that we've cleared our hallways of those nasty bad guys and brave police officers, it's time for our shower. All that commotion got us off schedule."

Palace Guard stayed, but I left the room. I strolled to the visitor's room where I contemplated the coffee pot. I poured a small amount and sipped. *Ugh.* I poured out the scorched brew, walked the hallway, then returned to Jay's room. The door was still closed, so I waited outside.

The orderly opened the door. "There you are, sweetheart. He's all spiffy."

The aroma of sage leaf shampoo and laundry soap wafted from the room. The orderly had replaced Jay's crumpled bed linens with crisp, hospital-corner sheets. Jay sat straight up in bed with his face scrubbed, hair combed, and head high.

"You look wonderful," I said.

"I know. Feel good too. Doc came by. He said I may go home in two days. Yesterday he said I might be here a week. Thank you, Maggie. Grab that notebook of yours. Don't you have more questions?"

I sat in the visitor's chair next to his bed. "I saw you outside our apartment one night. You and Ken Bushman were in the alley, and you gave him some money. Why did you do that?"

"Does Ellen know?"

"No reason for me to mention it."

"I paid Ken to repair homes for people who couldn't afford to hire anyone while he looked for permanent work. He's a very skilled carpenter and has good electrical skills. I think the work bolstered his ego because his customers appreciated his quality work. Funny. Only once did I feel watched. Must have been you. I'd appreciate it if you wouldn't mention it to Ellen."

"You'll tell her yourself." I grinned.

"You're right." Jay smiled. "It'll make a good story."

"Do you think Mona embezzled money?" I refilled Jay's glass of water.

"Yes, but I don't have any evidence. I'm not a Mona fan, but I don't think Mona committed suicide or turned on the gas at Diane's Diner. She loved Diane and wouldn't hurt her or the diner."

"What about Veronica?"

"Wish I wasn't retired. I think she arranged the gas leak at the diner. I'd find a way to charge her for Irene and Rosa's deaths. She's a snake."

I nodded as I flipped through my notebook. "Those were my burning questions."

The door opened, and Jay raised his eyebrows.

"Hello, Maggie," a familiar voice behind me said.

"Hello, Gary." I faced him and glared.

He shook his head. "You weren't supposed to be a target, but someone leaked there was an undercover agent and implied it was you."

Jay's eyes narrowed. "Is that what triggered the original attack on her?"

Gary stepped closer to the end of the bed and faced the door. "Bad news, yes; good news, it was our first confirmation we had a leak in the organization."

Jay glowered. "You used your daughter as bait? Isn't that beneath you, Gary?"

Gary's brow furrowed. "That was not the intention. I expected her presence to agitate the criminals into making mistakes, but I misjudged her impact."

Jay's expression softened. "She is a force."

I snorted. "She's right here. What's your next move, Gary?"

"The international crowd is nervous. I need to strike there."

Jay narrowed his eyes. "As long as you leave Maggie out of it, good luck."

Gary stepped toward me but stepped back when I glared.

"See you, Maggie. You are amazing." Gary left.

"You okay, Maggie?" Jay asked.

"I'm fine, but I have strange parents." I flopped onto the chair next to Jay. "I understand him, though. He is obsessed with finding bad guys."

"Right, but he missed out on being around an exceptional young woman." Jay sipped his water. "My turn? How do you feel about Larry?"

"He's a good cop, and my best friend."

"That doesn't tell me how you feel." Jay raised an eyebrow.

"I haven't thought about it." My shoulders slumped, and a wave of sadness rose in my chest.

Jay took my hand and met my gaze, and I pursed my lips.

"I don't want Larry to die." The tears flowed down my cheeks, and I put my head on Jay's chest and sobbed. When I regained my composure, I told Jay about Parker: my police detective, my first love, who was murdered.

"Ellen can tell you that the biggest fear of every cop's wife is that she kissed him for the last time as he left for work. Besides grieving the loss, there's survivor's guilt. Sometime when you are brave and fierce, tell Larry you don't want him to die."

The door opened. "Lunch, Mr. Davidson, and I brought you sweet tea, Miss." She set the tray down and dashed out.

"You're a skilled negotiator, Captain Davidson. Brave and fierce? I give you..." I removed the tray cover. "Lunch."

He swallowed as he peered at the plate. "This doesn't look half bad. Chicken salad sandwich with limp lettuce and a slimy pickle. Chips with sodium and chemicals, and a something in an aluminum covered plastic cup."

He picked up his sandwich and asked, "What's for supper?"

"Whatever I pick up at the store."

While Jay ate, I opened my laptop to update my database with information about Jay and about the attacker. My phone buzzed a text from Larry.

"Lots of discussion. It'll get out fast, and everyone will look for monkeys. *Lagniappe*. Bonus."

I pulled out my new cell and sent a text to Glenn. "Tell her bad guy close. Not unknown."

Jay fell asleep, and I curled up on the soft bench with Larry's pillow to take a nap. Palace Guard tapped my shoulder an hour later. After I stretched, Ellen and Ken came into Jay's room. Jay peeked then closed his eyes.

Ellen tiptoed to his bed and kissed him on the cheek. He grabbed her face with both hands and gave her a full-on mouth kiss.

Ellen giggled and swatted him. "You old goof. What's wrong with you?"

Jay chuckled. "Doc says he might release me in two days if I keep up the improvement."

"Oh, really?" Ellen stared at me.

"True."

"I walked to physical therapy without help and challenged an old coot to a race. I won."

Ellen said, "I'm proud of you, Jay. Where are my manners? Maggie, this is my brother. Ken, this is Maggie, my friend I told you about."

"Welcome to the family, Maggie." His smile was shy, and he held out his hand. I strode across the room to shake his hand. His handshake was firm but not intimidating.

"It's nice to meet you, Ken. Thank you."

Jay told the story of the attacker that burst into his room. According to Jay, I swung the bad guy over my head and tossed him across the room. We laughed throughout his story.

When he finished with the bad guy begging to go to jail, Ellen wiped her eyes and asked, "Is that what happened, Maggie?"

"Beyond belief, isn't it?" I smiled.

"Well said, Maggie." Ken grinned.

"Is it over?" Ellen asked. "Say it's over."

"No," Jay said. "He was following orders."

Larry came into the room. "Hello, Ellen. Good to see you, Ken." The two men shook hands.

"Hi honey, I'm home." He winked. "How you doing, Jay?"

"Doing great. Do you know about our excitement?"

Larry glanced at me. "He doesn't," I said, and Larry cringed.

Jay went through his story with more embellishments, and we laughed even harder than we did at the first story.

Larry put his arm around me. "Who was it?"

"The skinny guy who carried the rifle that shot me."

"Want me to make a call?" Jay asked.

"I'll take care of it. The rest of the story?" Larry asked.

"Edited for the TV screen, and I need to scoot," I said. "More later."

"Don't plan on me for supper." Ellen smiled. "I know how kind you are. Ken and I are going out. We need to catch up."

I stopped for groceries on my way home. When I turned onto the street that intersected with our street, Spike and Lucy were on the sidewalk. I stopped, and they jumped into the truck.

"What is it, Spike?"

He put his two hands together and waved them like a fish.

"Gus? At the house?"

He nodded and held up two hands and shot with an imaginary rifle.

"Alone?"

He nodded again.

"If the police arrive with lights and sirens, he'll make a dash for it. Where's his car parked?"

Spike pointed to the alley behind us. I backed up and pulled into the alley behind a Pesckey van parked near a vacant house. I called Officer Lopez.

"It's Maggie. There's a man in my house with a rifle. I'm a block away."

"On my way. Call nine-one-one. They'll send a SWAT team."

"Be loud. I need lots of sirens."

I called nine-one-one. "There's a man with a rifle in my house. I was just attacked at the hospital in Captain Jay Davidson's room."

The dispatcher took down my address. "We have two officers en route with others to follow. Don't approach the house."

I backed out of the alley and parked the truck on the street away from the van's line of sight. Spike and I walked to the van.

"I think my best cover is the van itself. Let me know which way he approaches. I better let Larry know or he won't speak to me ever again."

I texted Larry. "Gus at the house with a rifle. Lucy, Spike, and I are a block away. Police maybe SWAT on the way."

My phone rang. "I'll be there. Ken can bring me."

"I thought about that. Gus may have a second attack planned for Jay after he shoots me."

"Hate it, but you could be right."

After we hung up, my phone rang again.

"Maggie, I'm looking for you at the hospital."

I forgot about Maynard.

"Could you go to Jay's room to relieve Larry? He's guarding Jay."

"Sure could. I'll be in Jay's room in two shakes."

The distant sound of sirens grew louder.

I texted Larry. "Maynard is coming to guard Jay. I'm at the alley a block away from the house. Sirens close."

The din of sirens surrounded the neighborhood. Spike appeared and pointed. Gus rushed from the opposite end of the alley toward us. His rifle was slung over his shoulder. When he was six feet from his van, I said, "Drop it, Gus."

He unslung his rifle and raised it to fire, and I shot twice. He screamed and collapsed to the ground. Spike ran to him and kicked the rifle away from him then kicked a kidney. Gus writhed and screamed on the ground. Spike stood over him.

I called Officer Lopez. "He raised his rifle at me in an alley. I shot him."

"Be right there."

I returned my gun to its holster and walked to the end of the alley.

Officer Lopez turned at the alley and parked. "You still armed?" he asked as he opened his car door.

"Yes. It's holstered at my waistband."

"Let's put in on the hood of my car."

I pulled out my pistol and placed it on the hood of the patrol car. Gus continued to scream.

"I guess he's hurt. How many times did you shoot him?"

"Twice. Once in each kneecap. Didn't want him to go anywhere but didn't want to kill him either. I suspect he and his friends will fall all over each other to incriminate each other."

"I'll get medical."

Spike rushed to me and threw his arms out in a wide arc.

Explosives?

He nodded.

"He may have rigged my house with explosives."

Officer Lopez spoke into his radio.

I sent Larry a text. "Don't go home. Find truck and Lucy on next street and come to the alley."

Larry, Palace Guard, and Spike dashed to me. Larry wrapped his arms around me in a crushing hug.

Crushing is good.

Palace Guard nodded.

An ambulance arrived for Gus. I didn't recognize the paramedic. *Good. Wasn't in the mood for hair-twirling.*

After the police officer took my statement, we waited for the bomb team to disarm the explosives. Officer Lopez strode our way. "Are you doing okay?"

I nodded.

"Your would-be sniper told my supervisor how to disarm the explosive. He's starting early with negotiating."

"Remember the rogue cop?" I asked.

Officer Lopez's eyes widened. "That's him?"

I nodded, and Officer Lopez whistled as he sauntered toward his cruiser.

The two imaginary men, Larry, and I climbed into the truck with Lucy and headed home. Larry carried in the groceries, and I put them away.

My phone rang. *Ellen.*

"Maggie, you were right. Another attacker that was short and over-weight came to Jay's room. The attacker rushed in, and I was next to Jay's bed. He pushed me out of the way, but Maynard punched his throat with a chop, and the man dropped. I was off balance, and I stepped on his hand as he fell. Jay claimed I stomped on his hand until I heard all the bones break. That's not true, but I'm telling you before Jay does; I'll call you if I need bail."

I chuckled. "When you and Ken go out to dinner, get a plate for Jay. He's not a fan of the hospital fare. And you'll need a second plate for the advance guard for the rebel smuggling forces. He's been guarding Jay too."

"Will do. Rebel smuggling forces. Got it. What's next for you and Larry? Will you stay around?"

"I don't think so. I agreed to two weeks, and I've been here over a month."

"Safe travels."

"Everything okay?" Larry asked.

I sat on the sofa and leaned back. "Ellen said a man attempted an attack on Jay, but Maynard stopped him. Ellen broke the man's hand when she stepped on it. Won't it be an epic story when Jay tells it? The attacker is in police custody. With Gus in custody, his thugs will scurry into the woodwork or scramble to be the first to tell all. It's in official hands now."

"What's your plan?"

"Tacos. We need tacos."

"Wasn't what I meant, but that's great. I need a shower."

After Larry's shower, I said, "Ellen asked if we plan to stay here."

My new phone rang. *Moe?* I handed it to Larry.

"Ewing here."

Larry listened then said, "Thanks."

"Heather uncovered the leak, and Moe has the evidence to press charges. It was someone high up in the department administrative office; no one you know. Anyway, word about the arrest in Texas got out, and his lawyer asked for a meeting."

Larry pulled two beers out of the refrigerator. "Let's go out to the patio."

Lucy and the imaginary men followed us. Spike strolled to the middle of the yard, and Lucy followed him. Butterflies fluttered around the flowers, and a lone pelican soared overhead to the water. I sat on the stoop and gazed at the clear sky. Larry joined me on the stoop.

Condensation rolled down my bottle and dripped onto the patio. I dried the bottom of the bottle on my jeans and cleared my throat. "Larry, I need to tell you something."

"What's that?"

"I don't want you to die." I bit my lip, but a few tears escaped.

Larry scooted closer and wrapped his arm around my shoulder. "Is that what's been between us? I thought..."

"It was Parker? No." I gazed at Larry. "The idea of something happening to you terrorizes me. I don't know whether to pull you close or push you away."

"How do you think I feel about you? Sometimes I'm reluctant to go to work because I'm afraid something might happen if I'm not around."

"Really?" A tear escaped, and I brushed it away.

I leaned on Larry's shoulder, and he held me with his gentle fierceness. Lucy nudged my hand, and I scratched her ear. "Your police work here is done, right?"

Larry nodded. "I expect to get a call to report to work on Monday."

Lucy trotted to Spike and flopped on the sand for a belly rub. *We like it here, but it's time to go home.*

"Another reason to have tacos," I said.

He nodded. "It'll be different in Harperville. We were on assignment here. You'll be at your house, and I'll be at my apartment."

"You're right. Different." My mouth quivered as I stifled a smile. "You plan to sleep in the horse pasture to keep an eye on me?"

Larry grinned. "I might."

We clinked bottles.

Ready for more Maggie?
HIDDEN BY FIRE
MAGGIE SLOAN THRILLER, BOOK 3
The sudden attacks on our Gray Lady, Maggie, escalate. Someone wants her dead.
Maggie, Larry, and the men investigate the puzzling clues that point to a long ago unsolved heist of famous works of art. As the attacks on Maggie intensify, she

intends to discover the truth hidden behind the art theft and the series of fires and why the killer is so obsessed for her to die.

Visit BARRETT BOOK SHOP for Exclusive Bargains and Deals!

Browse, shop, read, enjoy!

BarrettBookShop.com

ABOUT THE AUTHOR

Judith A. Barrett lives in rural Georgia with her husband, two dogs, and a dozen sassy chickens. She writes stories for her readers: thriller, mystery, cozy mystery, clean romantic mystery, and post-apocalyptic sci-fi. Stories with a twist: Not your typical stories from not your typical author!

You keep reading; I'll keep writing!

Website judithabarrett.com
Subscribe to the eNewsletter via her website
judithabarrett.com/newsletter